THE LAST EXILE

After acting on false intelligence, officer Paul Tallis shoots a suspected terrorist in a Birmingham shopping centre. Suspended from his job, his career is over. A year later, Tallis is approached by a shadowy figure working for MI5. The offer is simple – unearth four illegal immigrants accidentally released from prison and hand them over to the authorities. The plan runs like clockwork, until Tallis makes an ugly discovery. He's become a pawn in a complicated game and now it's down to him to make sure he reaches the last exile before anyone else...

THE LAST EXILE

THE LAST EXILE

by

E. V. Seymour

Magna Large Print Books
Long Preston, North Yorkshire,
BD23 4ND, England.

MAGNA (handwritten)

British Library Cataloguing in Publication Data.

Seymour, E. V.
   The last exile.

   A catalogue record of this book is
   available from the British Library

   ISBN   978-0-7505-3138-2

First published in Great Britain in 2008 by
Harlequin Mills & Boon Ltd.

Copyright © Eve Seymour 2008

Cover illustration © Valentino Sani by arrangement with
Arcangel Images

The moral right of the author has been asserted

Published in Large Print 2009 by arrangement with
Harlequin Enterprises II B.V./S.à.r.l.,

Magna Large Print is an imprint of Library Magna Books Ltd.

Printed and bound in Great Britain by
T.J. (International) Ltd., Cornwall, PL28 8RW

ACKNOWLEDGEMENTS

This book would not have come into being had it not been for a small number of serving firearms officers. Because of reasons of security and protocol, I am neither allowed to mention them by name nor state the place where we met. They know who they are, however, and I thank them for their time, generosity and good humour. I should also add that my take on a firearms officer's job is just that, with dramatic licence. Moreover, the views expressed in the book are not those necessarily shared by those I talked to.

Major thanks go to my agent, Broo Doherty, for having the perspicacity to encourage me to write something completely different and, most importantly, giving me the confidence to do it. Thanks also to Catherine Burke, my editor at MIRA, for spotting the book's potential and putting it through its paces, and indeed the whole of the MIRA team for their warmth and infectious enthusiasm. Most notably, Guy Hallowes, Sarah, Oliver on the marketing side, and Ian on Sales – not the Ian to whom the book is dedicated; we got on well but not *that* well! Those I've failed to mention in person, apologies! Thanks, too, to Jana Holden for turning my schoolgirl Croatian into colloquial Croatian, and for sharing a little of her family history with me.

Lastly, thanks to an unlikely individual, to Tim, the inspiration for Jimmy. But that's not an excuse for further turning up the volume!

For Ian
With a song in my heart...

PROLOGUE

The woman was running. Running for her life. Small and sinewy, she moved at speed, twisting like a desperate vixen. But there was no escape. Not for anyone. She knew it. Tallis knew it. From the instant he and Stu barrelled through the automatic doors, he understood how it was going down, how it was going to be. All of them were ensnared in a dance of death.

Tallis didn't register the glossy-looking, brightly lit stores, or the homely sweet aroma drifting from a biscuit stand nearby. He failed to admire the display of brand new Minis parked at the mall's entrance. He didn't detect Paul Young crooning hoarsely through the centre's speakers. Sound, taste, smell, touch all disappeared. His focus was on the woman. Only the woman. The woman with the rucksack on her back.

Fuck, she was going down the escalator the wrong way. Tallis sharply elbowed a middle-aged man aside, and leapt on, feet skimming the moving parts, shoppers cursing his jostling form. Stu, close behind, snarled an order to get out of the frigging way. An acne-faced youth spat at them then, seeing the guns, recoiled and cowered, his bottle gone. Men with weapons in full tactical firearms kit represented the visible arm of the law. Guys in plain-clothes, whatever their rank and standing, were scary, unknown quantities.

Women and children started to scream. Tallis, fearing it would force the woman to detonate her lethal load, bounded clear of the moving staircase, feet landing square, the fleeing figure still ahead, ducking and weaving. For the second time, Tallis shouted a warning. Again he used her native tongue, yet there was no break in step, no change in pace, no backward glance. Relentless, Tallis thought, but not nearly as relentless as me. Whatever the cost. Whatever the personal sacrifice.

People were fleeing now. Those who'd ordered morning lattes were dropping them where they stood, the contents spooling over a floor the colour of rancid butter. Boisterous school-kids already bored by the prospect of long summer holidays dived for cover. A security man too old and fat for the job looked clueless then slack-jawed then barked a *What the hell?* into a mobile phone.

Area should be cleared by now, Tallis chafed as a woman pushing a baby buggy almost cannoned into him. What the fuck was going on? Where was back-up? Two foreign-looking men selling cosmetics from a stand extolling the virtues of Dead Sea salt turned and gazed, the laconic expression in their eyes suggesting that they'd seen it all before.

Tallis's earpiece crackled. A designated senior officer had already confirmed the identity of the target, an Algerian woman with links to the recent failed bombing in Birmingham. Now he was upping the game, issuing instructions to prepare to eliminate the threat – code for execute or shoot

14

to kill. Tallis tightened his grip on the Glock but judged the scene too chaotic and unstable to take aim and fire should the final code word be given. Public safety, threats of criminal proceedings, phrases that tripped off the tongue in the aftermath but made no sense in the context buzzed round his brain like a swarm of demented hornets. Strained faces were everywhere, there seemed more shoppers than ever. And that was dangerous.

Tallis was subliminally aware of Stu drawing abreast of him, feet pounding the floor. They were gaining now but another escalator loomed ahead, ascending. Glancing up, Tallis saw two colleagues openly brandishing weapons, sealing off the exit. The woman's head lifted minutely in mid-pace. She saw it, too. Tallis caught his breath. His gut tourniqueted. This was when she'd do it. This was when she'd blow them all to kingdom come. He raised his weapon but a group of gormless-looking lads oblivious to the action wandered across his line of vision. Stu let out a yell, making them scatter.

Tallis picked up the pursuit again, speeding around a corner flanked with banks and building societies, the financial heart of the mall. The woman was only metres ahead, losing pace, through stitch or fear, the fight abruptly abandoning her. *Nothing left to lose,* Tallis thought, raising his weapon a second time, imagining the blinding flash, broken bodies, twisted wreckage, crippled lives. This time he took aim, homing in for a head shot. 'I can take the shot,' he radioed back to Control.

'Take it,' was the response.

Then something happened, something more terrible than he could imagine. In that heart-charged split second, she turned, small hands spread in a defensive gesture. Young, her dark face was arresting rather than beautiful. She had a wide, noble brow and brown eyes wet with tears and terror. Not that it mattered, Tallis thought coldly. An order was an order. Question the method, the timing, but never the command. Even so, Tallis experienced an ugly sensation, felt something he wasn't paid to feel. His earpiece crackled. Maybe they were going to be asked to stand down, he thought wildly hopeful. It crackled some more: the gold commander was giving the code word authorising the use of lethal force.

Before Tallis could act, two shots rang out from Stu's Glock, one winging wide, missing by inches a startled bank clerk taking a break, and ricocheting harmlessly off a pillar. The other felled the target. Tallis ran forward, saw the stain from a wound in the young woman's shoulder spread and dye her T-shirt a darker hue. In shock, she made no sound. Just fluttered a hand towards her body, a movement that, whatever instinct was stirring inside him, was to cost her her life. With the colour still draining from her skin, Tallis emptied five bullets into her head and neck, witnessing her final second of life, hearing her last breath, watching as her life-blood flowed freely on the floor.

An eerie stillness descended. People stood silent, in dread and awe and shame, all of them

16

witnesses to something they neither understood nor desired. One woman was weeping. The bank clerk, white with horror, eyes drilling into Tallis, murmured, 'Murderer.'

'Job done,' Stu said, the relief in his voice drowned out by the gathering clamour of local police and forensics in full cry.

Tallis nodded, feeling hollow.

CHAPTER ONE

One year later

Red silk tie or navy? Paul Tallis held both of them against the white shirt and dark blue jacket hanging from the top of the doorframe. Maybe red would come across as a bit aggressive, a bit over the top. Then again, he wanted to look as if he knew how to do the business. But he was supposed to be protecting a school-kid, not some foreign head of state, he reminded himself. Navy, then. Gave the impression of responsibility, reliability, confidence. Yeah, navy was definitely a safer bet.

He turned away, satisfied with his choice though not quite so thrilled with the out-of-shape figure reflected back from the long mirror propped against the wall. At six feet two inches, he was able to carry several extra pounds and get away with it, but lately his trousers had started to feel a little tight around the waistband. Sure, he

17

knew that to the untrained eye he still cut it. It was more a case of not being as super-fit as he used to be. Always happened when you reined back on a fairly demanding exercise regime. Fact was, in twelve months he hadn't run much, been to the gym or cycled. Hadn't seen the point. The best he could muster was a quick thrash up and down Max's swimming pool and that was only because he wanted to impress the au pair. Pathetic, he knew. Felka was considerably younger than himself, bright and fresh-faced, and with an innate sweetness and innocence that he had no intention of despoiling in spite of the fact that, on a number of occasions, she'd made it quite plain that she wouldn't have minded.

He let out a sigh, smoothing his not-so-taut six-pack. No matter, he thought. His future employers weren't going to interview him in the buff, and with his clothes on he still presented a commanding figure. He clowned a face in the mirror, thrust his chin out, the way he did when he shaved. Still had all his own hair and teeth, which at thirty-three he bloody well ought to have. The faint scar across his forehead made him look interesting rather than dangerous, he thought, and he still had the *up-for-it* look in his eyes. He grinned and winked. Once he got the job, could see a way forward again, he'd get back to his old exercise routine, get back to his old self. He'd done it before after he'd spent a stint undercover early on in his police career – nothing more guaranteed to screw up your brain and pile on the pounds than hanging out with people whose lives revolved around pubs, clubs and fast food. He'd had to drink so much alcohol to fit in that his weight had ballooned to Sumo proportions.

Not like Stu, Tallis thought grimly. The more the guy drank, the thinner he seemed to get. Last time they met he'd been wasted before Tallis had sunk his first pint. Tallis had ended up piling him into his car, a shit-heap in Stu's opinion, and taking him back home or *hame* – the more drunk, the stronger Stu's Glaswegian accent. Stu's *hame* had turned out to be a room in a house full of dead beats. Oh, how the mighty had fallen. Yet Tallis recognised that he, too, was one of them. It still astonished him how quickly one's fortunes could change. In one single minute he'd ripped up the ground from beneath his feet. One false decision and the world, as he'd once known it, had changed for ever. To say he regretted the shooting didn't even come close. An innocent woman had died, for Chrissakes, but there were other regrets: the collapse of the team and loss of personal identity.

It took him twenty minutes to shower, shave and clean his teeth, five minutes to dress and splash on the last dregs of aftershave. He'd shined his shoes the night before. Half an hour to kill, he thought, glancing at his watch, flicking on the radio. 'The men were arrested in South London last night. The raid followed a long period of surveillance by police and M15. It's thought...' Tallis switched off and picked up the TV guide, idly flicking through the pages. He usually worked in the evening so TV was a bit of a luxury. Maybe he'd take in one of those home make-over shows, he thought, closest you could get to property porn. Might give him

19

some ideas about how to transform his less than glorious surroundings. He suddenly became acutely aware of the horrible floral design of the wallpaper, the decrepit-looking gas fire in the tiled fireplace, the campaign table which was really a fold-down from Ikea and for which he'd paid six quid, the smell of old lady and lavender. In the thirty years his grandmother had lived there, she hadn't changed a thing.

The phone rang. Tallis eyed it warily. After the shooting, and in spite of strict orders not to talk, his phone had never stopped. Since his fall from grace, it had never rung at all. He'd become a social and professional pariah: no status, no self-esteem. Someone once said that you could judge a man's standing in the world by the number of calls he received. Applying that criterion, his was on the same level as an amoeba's.

'Paul, it's Max. You OK?'

Tallis smiled in relief. 'Bit nervous.'

'Yes, well ... erm, there's been a change of plan.'

'Yeah? No problem,' Tallis said cheerfully. Flexible was his middle name, especially if it meant the prospect of landing a decent job that paid well. Since his decision to leave the force, finding work had proved a soul-destroying task. There weren't too many orthodox lines of business for an out-of-work killer, as he'd been famously dubbed. To keep body and soul together, he'd taken a rubbish job as a security man at a warehouse. The work was tedious in the extreme, the pay lousy, with the result that he was seriously into his overdraft. That his grandmother had left him her crumbling wreck of a bungalow should have saved him from penury, but he'd spent so much time and money attempting to sort out the faulty plumbing and dodgy wiring, it was haemorrhaging his already limited resources.

'Thing is,' Max said, strain in his voice, 'they've changed their minds, Paul.'

'Changed their minds about having a bodyguard or changed their minds about me?'

Sweaty silence. Tallis imagined Max rubbing his face with a paw of a hand. In looks, they were quite similar – tall, dark-haired, dark-eyed, 'fucking good-looking' according to Max in one of his more expansive moments. 'It's all my fault,' Max said. 'I should have come clean, told them the truth from the start.'

Tallis almost laughed. The truth that we were given duff intelligence, he asked himself, or the truth that we were obeying orders? 'Don't worry, mate. Notoriety does strange things to people. To be honest, I'm not sure babysitting an over-pampered public schoolboy is really my thing anyway.' Tallis felt his neck flush. Pride was a terrible thing. Another month playing security guards and he'd go mental and be no good to anyone.

'I feel really bad about this,' Max said, deeply apologetic. 'It was me who put you up to it, for Christ's sake. Look, if there's anything I can do...'

'You can. Have a nice holiday.' Tallis loosened the tie from his collar. 'When do you fly?'

'Leave Heathrow tonight. Kids are so excited they're already driving Penny nuts. Think she's beginning to regret not taking Felka with us.' Paul smiled. He liked Penny enormously but she didn't strike him as a natural at motherhood.

21

How would she cope for six whole weeks without her au pair?

Max was talking again, hell-bent on trying to make amends. 'Why not take a trip out to the sticks, check on the house, give it a once-over?'

'Doesn't need a once-over. It was me who advised you on security, remember?'

'Well, go and see if Felka's all right. She doesn't leave until tomorrow. You could have a swim, make sure she's not throwing a party or entertaining unsuitable young men.'

'You asking me?' Paul laughed.

'Keep an eye on her, I said, not get your leg over.'

'The thought had never crossed my mind.' It had, and often, but he wasn't going to admit that to Max. For reasons that baffled him, he'd acquired an unfair reputation for being a womaniser. In his book, there was a huge difference between having erotic thoughts about a woman and having base designs on one. It was all right to look and admire, but not to act on every instinct, which was why he was careful to keep his thoughts and emotions about the female of the species to himself. Somewhere lurking at the back of his mind, he suspected his brother had started the rumour. From the time they had been in their teens, Dan had always been jealous of the fact that women were more attracted to his younger brother than to him. So much easier for Dan to accuse him of being a letch rather than recognising the simple, uncomplicated truth that women preferred men who were nice to them.

'And if you need a decent set of wheels...'

'What's wrong with my car?'

'Where to start?' This time Max laughed.

Tallis had to admit that his car was neither cool nor sexy. It wasn't even very practical. Price alone had guided his decision to buy a Rover. After the demise of Longbridge, they had been practically giving them away.

'I'd look on it as a personal favour if you took the BMW out for a good run,' Max said persuasively. 'No point the lovely beast sitting in the garage for all that time.'

Tallis almost punched the air. Things were looking up. This wasn't just any BMW. This was a Z8, the dog's bollocks. 'Deal.'

'Good man,' Max said, voice warm with absolution as he cut the call.

It was too early for a beer but Tallis decided to have one anyway. Screw the fitness and weight-loss regime.

CHAPTER TWO

Several beers later, Tallis was in danger of feeling maudlin. He'd changed back into jeans and T-shirt, feet up on the coffee-table because there was nobody there to tell him not to, and was considering his lowly domain. The road in which he lived, a mile out of Birmingham city centre, was the type where people regularly dumped litter and the remains of last night's tikka Marsala in the privet. Dog shit regularly anointed the pavement. Compliments of the next-door neighbour's fourteen-year-old son, rock guitar blasted out at all times of the night loud enough to shatter the windows.

Tallis could cope with all that – just. But not the bungalow. Bungalows were for others – disabled, retired and those who cared not a jot about image. In short: for old people. For a bloke with all his life ahead of him, living in one was a travesty. Because of his less than cool surroundings, he'd actually bottled out of bringing a woman back. Once. The thought made him feel ashamed and disloyal. His gran had been exceptionally generous in leaving the place to him but, aside from the obvious lack of refurbishment, Tallis felt she'd handed him a poisoned chalice. Certainly his older brother, Dan, already as bitter as cyanide, viewed it that way, citing his younger brother's devious ability to deceive and wheedle his way into an old woman's affections as clear evidence. His mum had been restrained in any form of criticism, (difficult as it was her mother who'd played fairy godmother). Dad, utterly predictable, had taken Dan's side.

Tallis wondered what his grandmother would have made of the ensuing family fallout. He'd loved her to bits. A Croatian by birth, she'd never fully got the hang of English even though she'd lived most of her life in Britain after marrying his grandfather. It had been Gran who'd given him a love of foreign language, Gran who listened when nobody else had, who'd never judged, never taken sides, and though he was glad that she wasn't around to witness his current circum-

24

stances, he badly missed her. Not that he'd been short of takers desperate to hear his tale of woe. Plenty of people had listened at first, the I-jackers, as he thought of them, the people who'd hijack a conversation with the express determination to talk only of themselves. Fortunately, Tallis had Max, the closest he'd come to finding a confessor. They'd met several years before in a pub and had hit it off from the start, probably because both of them had been three-quarters of the way down a bottle of Bourbon at the time. Max, Tallis often thought, was the most elegant drunk he knew. Beyond this, and their joint lust for life, theirs was an unlikely pairing. Max came from a wealthy background where nannies and public school, university and a job in the City were normal. Tallis was a guy who came from humble and uncomplicated origins – left school at sixteen to join the army, eight years on joining the police. Then much, much later, had made the screw-up of all screw-ups.

Her name was Rinelle Van Sleigh, a Liberian who'd overstayed her visa. The explanation for her frantic flight from the police that mid-July morning a year before was explained by the stolen pair of trainers she had been concealing in her rucksack. Perhaps her over-reaction to the law had been connected to growing up in a country where coups and civil war had been commonplace. Aside from his brief stint in the army, Tallis had heard enough from his grandmother about the breakdown of law and order that could befall a nation, the hatred and suspicion it generated, and the madness that ensued. Maybe the Liberian girl had recognised something horribly familiar in the eyes of the plain-clothes police officers, and in her fear, a fear not misplaced, had turned tail and run. Tallis revisited that day often, playing the events through in his mind, frame by frame stopping, rewinding. To kill the wrong person was a firearms officer's worst nightmare. That it had happened to others before provided no solace. But to kill someone you instinctively believed to be innocent was like a fast track to eternal damnation.

Tallis rubbed his temple, replacing the image of the dying woman with the memory of the second-by-second news coverage, the graphic headlines. Only the better quality press had emphasised the importance of correct intelligence, the chain of command, the fact it had been a dynamic or fast entry rather than an operation of containment based on accumulated information. As usual everyone had blamed everyone else. Overnight he'd shot to fame but one not of his choosing. He'd heard himself and Stu described as gun-slingers and woman-haters, of being institutionally racist.

Tallis grimaced at the irony. Throughout his life he'd constantly defended the rights of the black man, mainly against his own father, a man who harboured a rabid and irrational dislike of people whose skin colour was different from his own. To be accused of holding those same views was a terrible insult to Tallis. For a time he and Stu had been the talking point of every radio phone-in and television show. While experts had opined and members of the public heaped insults, Tallis had received death threats. All this while he'd been on suspension, another force engaged in finding out if rules had been broken, and the Independent Police Complaints Commission investigating the case with the certainty of an internal inquiry and the possibility of criminal proceedings.

He recalled the debrief afterwards. Stu had already chewed his ear off on the journey back to base.

'You entered that shopping centre with the absolute conviction that you were doing the right thing, ridding the world of a bomber, saving people's lives.'

'Yes, but–'

'No *but*,' Stu snarled, sharp eyes glinting.

So Tallis told the great and the good what they wanted to hear: yes, he'd believed that lives were in danger; yes, he'd believed the woman had been a suicide bomber; yes, he'd been convinced beyond the shadow of a doubt.

He'd been returned to a desk job and normal duties, the standard procedure following suspension, and usual after the discharge of a firearm. He didn't remember much of his time spent in the close company of a computer. He'd been too much in a state of frozen shock. Everything had seemed amplified. People, noise, as if all his senses had been in revolt. He'd become almost agoraphobic.

And then there'd been Belle. Immediately his mind tumbled with memories. His heart began to race. He thought about that very first time they'd gone out for dinner. He'd wanted to take her to an Italian restaurant but, because they were meeting out of town, they'd settled for a tiny French place serving *international cuisine*. The food hadn't been bad but neither of them had eaten very much, as he recalled. Time had seemed too short for something so functional. But there had been something else. With each precious second that had passed, both of them had known that they were closer to saying good-bye, both of them, even then, had sensed how it would end between them. As it turned out, and for everyone's sake, they'd agreed to go their separate ways, a hard decision made painful by the simple truth that they loved each other. After the shooting, he'd wanted to call her but had known it wouldn't have been fair on either of them. He didn't have the right to open old wounds.

Eventually, he was cleared through the formal channels of any wrongdoing, though absolution in his own eyes was harder to come by. Legal proceedings against the force were still pending, the inquest adjourned. Offered his old job back, he didn't feel up to it. Hesitation could get him killed. Fear might kill someone else.

Staring at walls dingy with age and neglect, he thought the bungalow reeked of defeat. He really ought to get off his rear and go to the super-market, if only because the beer had run out.

He'd taken to frequenting the cheap end of the food market. Sunglasses protecting his identity, he could lurk behind aisles piled high with boxes of cut-price goods without being noticed. The products all seemed to have strange-sounding

28

names that reminded him of supermarkets in the far reaches of the Czech Republic. The clientele were interesting, too, in a lurid sort of a way. In summer they sported tattoos and nipple rings, in winter cheap, shiny imitation leather jackets – and that was just the women. The blokes had necks like tree-trunks, shaved heads and *what's your problem* expressions.

Making a brief detour to the newsagent's to pick up a copy of *Loaded* magazine, he dropped the shopping off at home – stashing the beer in the fridge, frozen stuff in the freezer – and grabbed some swimming gear, then headed the car south-west. Traffic was dense, with a succession of roundabouts, traffic lights and speed restrictions to further impede the motorist. The more ground he put between him and the city, the leafier the landscape. Clent Hills stretched out on one side, a whisper of Kinver Edge on the other, nothing like the place where he'd grown up in rural Herefordshire, home and county to the Special Air Service. Once upon a time, Tallis had nursed hopes of joining the SAS but hadn't been considered good enough. It had been the first time he'd seriously encountered disappointment. Up until then he'd seemed to have led a charmed life, which was probably why he'd dealt with the rejection in his laid-back, don't-give-a-fuck fashion. For the rest of his brief, if eventful, army career, he'd stuck with the First Battallion, the Staffordshire Regiment.

Belbroughton, the highly desirable village in which Max Elliott and his family lived, was the kind of place where the size of houses was only

29

rivalled by the size of lawnmowers. Even the council homes were gabled. So-called down and outs could generally be found sitting on one of the many wooden benches donated by some worthy, consuming strong cider while speaking into expensive mobile phones. Cars louchely parked on block-paved driveways fell into the BMW, Mercedes, Porsche category. Aside from the village's upmarket credentials, the place was steeped in history, a subject dear to Tallis's heart. It was a regret to him that he'd not taken the subject more seriously at school, though he'd done his best in later years to make up for it and educate himself. When walking through the village on previous visits he'd studied a plaque on the main wall that told the story of a young woman convicted of theft and packed off to Australia. He'd also discovered various references to scythemaking, indicating that it had once been the mainstay of Belbroughton, the industry having petered out somewhere around the late 1960s. As Tallis drove past yet another multi-million-pound house, he couldn't get past the feeling that had assailed him when he'd first discovered the village, that he'd entered a little oasis of glamour. God knew what the neighbours thought of him driving up to Max's not inconsiderable pile in his lowly Rover.

Keying in the code to the security pad, the electronic wrought-iron gates swung open allowing Tallis a tantalising glimpse of the house, which was Italianate in style with arches and domes to rival the Duomo. On his first visit there, Tallis had harboured serious suspicions about what exactly Max Elliott did for a living, fearing either he was a drug dealer or bent lawyer rather than the City financier he proved to be.

A paved drive led to a gravelled area and what Tallis called the tradesman's entrance but was really the indoor pool and sauna. Spotting him through the glass, Felka beamed, threw aside the magazine she was reading, and swivelled her neat, deliciously put-together body off the sun-lounger to greet him. Tallis got out of the car, glanced up and smiled for the camera, part of the state-of-the-art security system. He'd personally advised Max on it free of charge after discovering that his mate had been royally ripped off by a cowboy security firm that didn't know the first thing about protection and was only interested in taking a sizeable wedge of the client's money each month on a bogus maintenance contract.

'Paul,' Felka said, 'I didn't expect you.' Felka had trouble with x's and s's, so it sounded like 'eshshpect', one of the many quirky things Tallis found deeply sexy about her. She had flame-red hair, pale features and the greenest eyes imaginable. Slight in build, she was wearing a bikini displaying perfectly rounded breasts and an enviably flat stomach. He suddenly felt old.

She tipped up on her toes and planted two impossibly chaste kisses, one on either side of his cheek. Tallis inhaled her perfume of musk and roses. 'Max said you had an interview.'

'Change of plan.' He shrugged.

She studied his face for a moment, her expression suddenly serious. 'You are sad,' she said. 'I can tell.'

That obvious, he thought. He hoped she wasn't too much of a mind reader – she'd be appalled by what else he was thinking. 'Not for long.' He broke into a grin.

'Come,' she said, grabbing his hand. 'We swim.'

'No splashing,' he teased.

The pool was thirteen and a half metres by six and a half, and over two metres deep at the far end. The floor, painted turquoise, gave the impression of clear Caribbean. Tallis let her push him in but not before he'd scooped her up off her feet, making her squeal, and threatened to dump her unceremoniously into the water.

'Promise we talk in Polish,' he said laughing, dangling her squiggling body over the edge.

'I promise. I promise,' she shrieked.

'Rude words, too?'

'Yes, yes.' Yesh, yesh.

Afterwards they sprawled out and watched the warm early July sunshine pour through the smoke-tinted windows. Several statues graced the outer perimeter of the pool. They looked like snooty guests, Tallis thought, sipping the coffee Felka had made.

As far as he understood, Felka was leaving to go home for a holiday the following morning, home being Krakow – a city on the river Vistula. According to Felka, and if he'd grasped it right, Krakow had been the capital during the fifteenth century, existing now as an industrial centre producing tobacco and railway equipment. Who needs work? he thought. This way I get history, geography and a foreign language all in the space of an afternoon.

'Can you tell me how to get from Euston station to Heathrow?' She was speaking in Polish again.

Tallis took a stab at it, pretty sure he had the right vocabulary but, worried he might send Felka off in the wrong direction, lapsed back into English. 'Don't want you ending up in Scotland.' He grinned. 'I'll draw you a map.'

'Good idea' she said, jumping to her feet. That was the thing he loved about her. She was so full of zing. As she scurried off, he took a long look at her luscious, retreating form. There was something unbeatable about a semi-clothed woman with wet hair.

Felka returned with a notepad and pen and dropped them playfully on his chest. He picked them up and lightly swiped her bottom, making her break into peals of laughter. Sketching the route, he advised her to take a cab rather than tube because she had a very poor sense of geography. She'd once managed to get lost with the kids in the city centre. Penny had spent nearly an hour walking up and down trying to locate her, and that had been with the aid of mobile phones.

Felka frowned. 'Much expensive.'

'Too expensive,' he corrected her.

She stuck the tip of her tongue out, half playful, half come-on. Tallis ignored the gesture. 'Believe me, it would be safest.'

'No, no, I take the tube. I like the tube,' she insisted.

'But–'

'I'll be fine.'

'All right,' Tallis sighed, advising her to take the

33

Victoria line Euston to Green Park and change onto the Piccadilly line for Heathrow. He wrote it all down, sketched a map and handed her the notepad. 'You must be looking forward to seeing your family.' He could manage that bit in Polish.

'Especially my little brother,' Felka said. 'He changes so quickly. I hope he'll still remember me.'

'Course he will.' How could he forget? Tallis thought.

'And you, Paul. You have a brother, too?'

Tallis flinched, wondering what was coming next. 'Yes.'

'His name?'

'Dan. We don't see so much of each other,' he added quickly, heading her off. 'You know how it is.' Except she didn't, of course. A sudden memory of Dan piling into the bedroom they'd shared, years before, flashed through his mind. Dan had had an infuriating habit of getting up in the middle of the night and switching the lights full on, often to locate his copy of *Penthouse* magazine. It hadn't mattered that Tallis had been fast asleep. Usually it had ended in violence. And that had meant their dad had got stuck in. On Dan's side.

Felka frowned. 'That's sad. Brothers should be close. Is he older or younger than you?'

'Older, but not by much – eighteen months or so.' Not that it felt like it. For as far back as he could remember, Dan had been like their father's emissary, taking every opportunity to push him around, spy on his activities, report back to base. Because of Dan, he'd been continually in trouble

– caught smoking red-handed, out after dark, consuming his first illicit pint, you name it. Because of Dan, he thought darkly, he'd often been humiliated in front of his mates. She nodded thoughtfully then spontaneously took his hand, squeezed it. 'I will miss you.'

'No, you won't. Think of all those lovely Polish lads.'

Felka pulled a face.

'You don't like Polish boys?'

She let her viper-green eyes rest on his then slipped her arms around his neck, drawing him close. 'I think I prefer English,' she whispered softly, nibbling his ear.

Tallis felt quite the gentleman as he drove home. It had been a long time since he'd so firmly rejected the charms of a lovely young woman. It wasn't that he didn't fancy her. He'd have to be deaf, dumb and blind not to, but he knew in his heart of hearts that Felka neither wanted nor needed him. She only thought she did. And she really was very young. There were too many sad bastards flaunting their younger and more malleable girlfriends to shore up their own in-adequacies, and Tallis didn't intend to join their club. Fortunately, his gentle put-down hadn't offended Felka. He'd told her how gorgeous she was, sensitive and intuitive beyond her years, but that an affair was out of the question because of Max and Penny – they were his friends and she was their employee. It wouldn't look good. She'd nodded solemnly then broken into a radiant smile. 'Another time,' she said.

'Another place,' he agreed in a worldly way, believing he'd spotted something like relief in her young eyes.

'We're still mates, then,' she said, slapping his arm.

'Best mates.' He laughed.

He got home shortly after six, intending to take something out of the freezer and bung it in the microwave. He'd bought some cheap Italian wine from the petrol station on the way back in honour of his considerable self-restraint and a mark of his confirmed celibate status. If it was good enough for Catholic priests, it was good enough for him.

He parked the car in the lean-to, loosely described by estate agents as a carport, and walked up the short path to the front door, expecting to encounter the same old silence. Except he didn't. There wasn't sound exactly, nothing you could readily identify. It was more a recognition of some disturbance, something different, the kind of feeling he'd sometimes experienced as a soldier.

Tallis put the bottle of wine down on the low wall that edged the garden, and moved forward cautiously. Since receiving death threats, he was more attuned to detail, to things not being quite right. A quick visual told him that the porch door was locked, the front door closed. All just as he'd left them. Skirting down the side of the building, he checked the back – again, door firmly locked, no telltale footprints in the overgrown borders, no sign of broken glass or break-in. Peering in through the windows, he saw no signs of disturbance in the kitchen, nobody lurking in the bedroom. Bathroom window was shut tight. At least bungalows had some advantage, he thought as he continued his tour of duty. They might be easy to break into but they were also a doddle to check and clear. Feeling the pressure ease, he glanced in through the side window at the doll-sized sitting room, and tensed. The image seemed to dance before his eyes so that he had to blink twice to take it in: an immaculately dressed blonde, classy looking, hair swept back in a ponytail, long tanned legs, sitting on his sofa, as cool as you like. To add insult to injury, she was flicking through his brand-new copy of *Loaded*.

CHAPTER THREE

'Who the bloody hell are you?'

The woman glanced up as if he were an unreasonable husband demanding to know why his dinner wasn't on the table. 'You normally greet people like this?'

'Only when they break into my house.'

She arched an imperious eyebrow and transferred her gaze to the walls. Tallis felt his jaw tighten. 'How *did* you get in?'

'Does it matter?'

'Yes.'

She smiled – nice set of white teeth – and leant towards him. 'Aren't you a tiny bit intrigued to know why I'm here?'

She sat back again, uncrossed her legs, re-crossed them. She was wearing a dark brown linen dress with a plain square neck and three-quarter-length sleeves. Her arms were slender, fingers long. Apart from a thin gold necklace, she wore no other jewellery. He estimated her as being the same age as him, possibly a little older. She was actually very beautiful, he thought, and she knew it. She had soft brown eyes displaying vulnerability she didn't possess, small breasts, about which he had a theory. Women with small breasts were dangerous. You only had to look at Lucrezia Borgia, the illegitimate daughter of a Spanish pope with whom it was rumoured she'd had an incestuous relationship. Even by sixteenth-century standards, Lucrezia was judged to have been cruel and avaricious.

'Who are you?'

'My name's Sonia Cavall.' She extended a hand. He didn't take it. She let it drop. 'Aren't you going to sit down?'

'You still haven't told me what you're doing.' Tallis said, ignoring the invitation.

'I'd have thought that was obvious.' She put the magazine away, slowly, carefully, met and held his gaze.

He blinked. This was barmy. She was so composed, so in control. Was he going mad? Or was he missing something? Horrible questions hurtled through his brain. Had they met before? Had he been drunk? Had they slept together? Christ on a crutch, was she pregnant with his child? No. He gave himself a mental shake. He was always very, very careful about stuff like that and he hadn't slept with a woman for God knew how long. 'Explain or I'll call the police.'

Again the astringent smile. 'Oh, I don't think so.' Confident. Authoritative. He immediately thought *spook*. 'Consider me your fairy godmother.'

Playing games, are we? Tallis thought. All right, baby, let's play. He donned a smile. 'I never read the Brothers Grimm.'

'Should have. They're quite instructive. Full of moral fervour.'

'Can we cut the crap now?' He was still smiling but he felt fury. Whoever this woman was, she was too smart for her own good.

'What if I said you've been selected for a job?'

'What job?' Suspicion etched his voice.

'Finding people.'

He burst out laughing. 'Come to the wrong house. It's not what I do.'

'What *do* you do?' There was a scathing intonation in her voice.

He should have thrown her out on the spot yet he badly wanted to know what this was all about. 'What sort of people?'

'Illegals.'

'A job for Immigration, I'd have thought.'

Cavall said nothing. Tallis tried to fill the gap. Immigration remained in rather a pickle, which was why the latest Home Secretary, like all the rest, had pledged to take a robust approach to failed asylum-seekers and illegal immigrants.

'We're talking about people released from prison after serving their sentences,' she told him, 'and mistakenly released into the community.'

'Mistakenly?' Tallis suspected some inter-agency cock-up.

'They should have been deported,' Cavall said, ice in her voice.

'Not exactly original.' Tallis shrugged. 'It's happened before.'

'But these individuals are highly dangerous. It's feared they may reoffend.'

'Ditto.' And everyone knew the recidivist rate was high. The only difference was that released British lifers were monitored. One slip, even for a relatively minor offence like drunk and disorderly, could land them back in prison. The people Cavall was alluding to had presumably dropped off the radar.

'A decision has been taken at the highest level to have them located.'

Tallis shrugged. So what? he thought. Bung them on a website or something.

Cavall's face flashed with irritation. 'You don't seem to understand the seriousness of the threat.'

'Oh, I understand. It would be a source of great political embarrassment should it come to the attention of the public, particularly if one of them should reoffend.'

'We don't want to spread panic and fear,' she said evenly.

'So put your finest police officers onto it.'

'We already have.'

'We?'

'I represent the Home Office.'

This time Tallis's smile was genuine. Which bit? he wondered. 'So this is an arse-covering exercise.'

'Damage limitation,' she corrected him.

To protect reputations and ease some politi-

40

cian's way up the greasy ladder of success, he thought. 'Britain's finest failed, that right?'

'I'm sure you're aware of the pressure on police resources.'

Code for they'd got nowhere. Doesn't quite square, he thought. The British live in a surveillance society. With over four million cameras tracking our every move, each time we log on, use our mobile phone or sat nav in our car, fill in a form, make a banking transaction, someone is logging it. Except, of course, the information is fragmented. It takes a measure of expertise to draw the right inferences, match the electronic footprints and plot the trail back to an identity. While the ordinary citizen might feel threatened and guilty until proven innocent by the power of technology, a determined criminal could still manipulate it and evade detection. Either he stole someone else's identity or had no identity at all. 'Why not wheel out the spooks?'

'Snowed under with the terrorist threat.'

Tallis flinched. The security service had foiled many plots since 9/11 and 7/7. They were mostly doing a fine job in difficult circumstances, but the death of Rinelle Van Sleigh was a stain on their history. Somehow, somewhere, there'd been a chronic lapse of intelligence, and for that an innocent woman had paid with her life. To a far lesser degree, so had he: life as he'd once known it was over. 'So these individuals aren't on control orders?'

'They pose no terrorist threat,' Cavall confirmed.

'What happens if and when they're found?' He

suspected a form of extraordinary rendition.

'They're handed over and deported, like I said.'

'Handed over to whom?'

'I think you're forgetting that these are extremely dangerous individuals.'

'They still have rights.'

'So did their victims.' Her look was so uncompromising, he wondered fleetingly whether she'd been one of them. 'Rest assured, they'll be handed over to the authorities responsible for deportation.' She smiled as if to put his mind at rest.

'How do you know these people haven't already left the country?'

'They don't have passports.'

Tallis blinked. Was she for real? 'Heard the word "forgery"?'

'No evidence to suggest that's the case.'

Tallis stroked his chin. That had not been a good answer. There was something fishy about all this. Too much cloak and dagger, smoke and mirrors. What authorities, what agencies? 'You say a decision was taken at the highest level.'

'From the very top.'

'And it's legal?'

'Yes.'

He studied her face – impassive, confident, certain, the type of woman who once would have appealed to him. He idly wondered, in a blokish way, whether she was beddable. 'Why me?'

'Because you have the right qualities. We need someone who'll follow orders, but also kick down doors. We need someone with a maverick streak, Paul.'

Tallis frowned. He didn't recognise the man

42

she was describing.

'At eighteen years of age, during the first Gulf War, you were part of a reconnaissance troop that came under friendly fire by the Americans. You rescued a colleague showered with shrapnel and pulled several others to safety then, still under fire, retrieved an Iraqi flag, waving it in surrender until the firing ceased. For that you received the Queen's Gallantry Medal for Heroism. The citation ran "outstanding courage, decisiveness under fire". On joining the police, you became a firearms officer, during which time you fell out with a sergeant who tagged you as a chancer.'

A stupid, dangerous bastard, Tallis remembered. So concerned with procedure, the man daily risked the lives of his men. 'I was put back on the beat.'

'And swiftly caught the attention of CID, where you became rather a good undercover operative until you got your old job back and then graduated to the elite undercover team. You also speak a number of foreign languages. Your credentials are impeccable.'

'Aren't you forgetting something?'

A killer smile snaked across Cavall's face. 'Trust me, Paul. I forget nothing.' She glanced at her watch, an expensive Cartier. 'Goes without saying there'll be generous terms and conditions.'

'Well, thank you but, no, thank you.'

'You don't have to decide straight away.'

'The answer's the same.'

Her smile lost some of its light. Tight creases appeared at the corners of her mouth. It was enough, Tallis thought. She'd briefly shown her cards; she hadn't banked on him refusing her kind invitation. 'Don't be too hasty, Paul. This could be your chance to redeem yourself.'

'Redeem myself?' Tallis scoffed. 'From what?'

Cavall leant forward. He caught a whiff of opulent scent. Her eyes were so dark they looked black. 'A man sleeps with his brother's wife and he doesn't need redemption?'

'How fucking dare you?'

'Your weakness for the opposite sex is well documented,' Cavall said in an even tone.

'Get out,' Tallis said, barely able to control the mist of anger that was fast descending on him, his desire to physically remove her crushing.

'I'll leave my card,' Cavall said smoothly, slipping one from the pocket of her jacket and placing it on the coffee-table. Her fingernails were short and unpolished. 'One more thing,' she added, rising to her feet, 'in certain matters, it's better to obey one's conscience than obey an order.'

Tallis stared at her. He suddenly felt as if his gut had been gouged with shrapnel.

'Don't worry,' she smiled, walking stealthily towards the door, 'I won't whisper a word to anyone about your doubts about shooting the black girl.'

CHAPTER FOUR

Tallis burrowed deeper beneath the duvet. After finishing the wine the night before, it had seemed the obvious thing to hit the Scotch. *Bad idea.*

He turned over, groaned, his head throbbing with the highlights of last night's conversation. He'd already come to the deeply unsettling conclusion that Cavall had used her Home Office contacts to get into his home. How she'd been privy to such personal and what he'd thought confidential information he was less certain, though that too seemed to point in the same direction. Clearly, someone, somewhere had talked. Not that he was denying Cavall's obvious powers of persuasion. Hers was a rare combination of cleverness and good looks. No point having those kind of attributes if she didn't exploit them. She'd done her homework well, using the intelligence with rapier-like precision. He was still bleeding from the final thrust.

The only person who could have betrayed him was Stu, but Tallis didn't believe his old friend would do such a thing, not even if he were absolutely trousered. Tallis pulled a pillow over his head, thinking that this was a morning when he really didn't want to go out to play. Budding Jimmy Paige next door wasn't helping. Perhaps if he lay very, very still, his head would stop hurting and his mind stop racing. But they didn't. Instead, his thoughts dragged him kicking and screaming to a period of time he didn't want to revisit, to him and Belle, to the exposure of their affair.

They'd been seeing each other intimately for about six months. On this particular occasion, Belle had told Dan that she was letting off steam in town with some of the girls from the Forensic Science Service where she worked. In truth, the two of them were meeting at a bustling country pub eighteen miles away. Later on, when Belle had called Dan from her mobile to let him know she'd be back later than expected, making the excuse that she was going onto a restaurant with the girls for something to eat, she'd accidentally left her phone line open. Worse, she'd left the phone on the table where they'd been sitting, exchanging sweet nothings. Dan had heard her every word, every promise, every declaration. He's also identified the man to whom she'd been making them. The fallout had been devastating.

'Don't you ever darken my door again,' his dad had spat in the aftermath. 'Know what's going to happen to you?' he'd added with breathtaking savagery. 'You'll end up walking the streets, holes in your shoes, stinking of piss, with a carrier bag in your hand. A useless nobody. Just like you've always been.'

And, yes, Tallis felt remorse, guilt about the affair, about the betrayal of his brother, but there had been extenuating circumstances. In reality, had either he or Belle exposed the truth, the consequences would have been cataclysmic.

Tallis struggled out of the covers and forced himself into a cold shower. Dried and dressed, he

46

downed a handful of painkillers with a pint of water, made strong coffee and picked up the phone. It was coming up for noon. The line rang for a considerable time before being answered. Tallis didn't dwell too heavily on the standard *hi, how are you* warm-up routine. He could tell from Stu's voice how he was – grim, sense of humour failure, depressed.

'You ever spoken to anyone about my reservations about the Liberian girl?'

'Fuck you take me for?' From sour to fury in 0.4 seconds.

'Fine,' Tallis said.

'Why?' Stu growled. There was a paranoid hitch in his voice.

'Nothing, nothing. Know how it is. Too much time on my hands, I expect.'

His poor-old-soldier act had the intended effect of softening his friend's prickly edges. 'No luck, then? Still doing the warehouse job?'

'Got one or two irons in the fire,' Tallis said, jaunty. Who was he kidding?

'Glad for you, mate. Does your *heed* in, not having a proper job. I should know.'

'But you're all right,' Tallis pointed out.

'Aye, pushing bits of paper around.' His voice was corrosive.

If Tallis had been a decent sort of a mate, he'd have told Stu that he was never going to get his old job back as long as he was on the sauce. Truth was, Stu wasn't in the mood for listening. Hadn't been for quite some time.

'You've got to stop thinking about the past, Paul. Won't do you any good.'

47

Tallis could have said the same. Why else was Stu drinking himself to hell in a bucket? 'You're right,' he said. 'Well, you take care, now.'

'Aye, have to meet for a bevy.'

'You're on,' Tallis said, eyes already scanning his address book for the next number on the list.

This time it was answered after the first ring.

'Christ, you're quick off the draw.'

'Right by the phone. How you doing?' Finn Cronin's voice was full of warmth and, for a moment, Tallis was reminded of Finn's brother, Matt. Matt had served with Tallis way back. They'd joined the army together, trained together, got drunk and pulled birds together. Matt had been the colleague he'd rescued under friendly fire. In spite of Tallis's best efforts to save him, Matt hadn't made it home.

'Good,' Tallis lied. 'And you?'

'Not bad. Carrie's pregnant again.'

'Christ, how many's that?'

'This will be our fourth. But that's it.'

'Going for the unkindest cut of all?' The thought made his eyes water.

'Carrie's idea. Doesn't want to spend the rest of her days on the Pill, screws around with her body apparently, mood swings, headaches, mostly.'

'Fair enough,' Tallis said, feeling awkward. 'I was wondering if I could ask a favour.'

'You want to doss down at ours for the weekend?'

'Smashing idea but no.'

'Pity. I'd hoped we could have a repeat of the Dog and Duck.'

'Only just recovered from last time.' Tallis let

48

out a laugh. 'No, it's...' He hesitated. Was he asking too much of Finn? Would it put him in a difficult position? Oh, sod it. 'I need something checked out.'

'Come to the right man. I spend my entire life checking things out.'

'Well, it's not a thing exactly, more a person, a cool-looking blonde, actually.'

'Tell me more,' Finn said, voice throbbing with curiosity. 'I can feel my journalistic streak stirring.'

That what these Southerners call it, Tallis thought drily. 'Her name's Sonia Cavall. She's connected to the Home Office.'

'The Home Office?' Finn sounded amazed. 'And you're asking me to check her out?'

'That's about it, yes.'

'Nice looking, you said.'

'It's not like that.'

'Not like what?' Finn laughed. So what's it really like? his voice implied.

Tallis held back. He'd known Finn for years. After Matt's death, they'd vowed never to lose touch so that whenever Tallis was in the West Country, he made a big point of seeing him. However long the absence, they always had a blast. Tallis was also godfather to Finn's youngest son, Tom. Tallis trusted Finn, but he was still a journalist and God knew what he might do with the information. 'She's tying up loose ends, you know, from last year,' he said elliptically.

'Right,' Finn said, his curiosity seemingly appeased. 'Timescale?'

'Soon as. Don't kill yourself for it.'

49

They talked a bit. Tallis sent his love to Carrie and the kids, double-checked Tom's birthday, which happened to be the following week then signed off.

In the two hours before he went to work, Tallis tidied up, pulled on some sweats and trainers, and went for a run in the hope that it would flush the last of the alcohol from his system. A shower and cheese sandwich later, and dressed in black trousers and a bright white shirt with the company logo emblazoned on the breast pocket, he drove the short distance to the out-of-town warehouse where he worked.

CHAPTER FIVE

The job mainly consisted of looking important and acting as a glorified car-parking attendant. His working environment was a sentry box complete with barrier to allow staff in and out. Tallis spent much of his time studying grainy images captured on the archaic CCTV system. The only highlights were the odd spot check, usually in the run-up to Christmas when theft was considered a good little earner, and the occasional request by one of the ops managers to frisk a member of staff suspected of stealing. If said suspect was found guilty, it was down to Tallis to liaise with police and escort the culprit, usually swearing and protesting innocence, off the premises. Big deal. Lately, if there was more than one security man manning the fort, he'd taken to hiving himself off and reading one of the many cookery books distributed through the company at knock-off prices. There wasn't much he didn't know about how to feed a family of four healthily, or the various types of power foods reputed to keep the aging process in check. There was no literature for sad, lonely bastards on a tight budget.

The shift, which finished at nine-thirty at night, seemed to drag more than usual. Fortunately, Archie, one of the other security blokes, broke the boredom by sneaking out to the fish and chip bar up the road and smuggling enough booty back for both of them.

When Tallis returned home he half expected Cavall to be there. She wasn't. All that lingered was the faint smell of her perfume, a pleasant contrast to salt and vinegar. He changed out of his work clothes and took a beer from the fridge, flipping off the top and drinking straight from the bottle. He'd barely sat down when the phone began to ring. He glanced at his watch. This time he felt no anxiety. There was only one person it could be: his mother.

She spoke softly so as not to wake his dad. Tallis asked after him.

'Not so good. Had another session of chemo yesterday. Always knocks him about.'

Tallis bit his lip. How long could his dad go on like this? he wondered. Did stubborn men take longer to die? 'And you, how are you doing?'

'Oh, I'm fine,' she said, stoic as usual. Only Tallis could detect the false note in her voice.

Early on, when the cancer had been diagnosed, he'd thought her nursing experience would help. Now he believed it a curse. She was far too aware of the medical implications. However viewed, his dad's condition was terminal, and his mother was in bits about it.

'Shall I come over?' he asked. 'To visit you?' he added nervously. His father had refused to see him since the blow-up with Dan and Belle. With his dad being so ill, Tallis didn't feel he could challenge the old man's decision.

'It's difficult at the moment,' his mum said, guarded. 'I really don't like leaving him.'

'What about the nurse? Couldn't she stay with him for a while?'

'He wouldn't like it.' No, Tallis thought. There was so much his father disliked – him, for a start. An early memory of sweating over maths homework flashed through his mind, his father standing over him, jaw grinding, demanding the correct answer and, in the absence of one, telling him he was no bloody good. For a long time Tallis had believed it to be true. They'd always had a strained relationship, probably because his dad had been a police officer and his youngest son had had a habit of running with the pack as a teenager. His dad had never been so pleased as when he'd decided to join the army. Of course, by then, Dan was already cutting it with West Midlands Police. Dan, the favoured one. Dan who never did any wrong.

'You need to take care of yourself, Mum, keep a bit back for you.' She hadn't done in almost forty years of marriage, so why start now? he thought. Except now it was more important than ever. How else would she survive when his dad was gone?

'I'm all right, son. You mustn't worry.' You have your own troubles was what she meant. 'Any luck with finding another job? Didn't you have an interview lined up?'

'Care of Max. It fell through,' he said honestly.

'Never mind. Something will turn up.' It just did, Tallis thought gloomily, but he'd have been mad to take it. 'I spoke to Dan yesterday.'

'Oh, yeah?' Tallis said with cool. 'All right, is he?'

'Fine. Settling in well, enjoying the new job. Seems to be finding his feet nicely. Says the other officers are friendly enough.' She sounded breathy and awkward.

'Good.' Not that it ever bothered Dan if colleagues liked him or not.

'He asked after you.'

'Did he?' Why? Tallis thought suspiciously.

'Don't you think you two...?'

'No, Mum.'

'But you can't go on like this.'

Why not? Tallis thought. His father hadn't spoken to his own brother for over twenty years. Vendettas must run in the family. 'The way it has to be.'

'Funny, that's what Dan said.'

'Did he?' Tallis said, genuinely taken aback.

'I hate all this. You used to be so close.' Her memory was cushioned by nostalgia, Tallis thought. He mostly recalled being beaten up and humiliated. It had been Dan who'd swung a spade

53

at his head from which he still bore the scar. 'Remember when you were kids?' she said brightly. 'You used to play removal men.'

'Doug and Kredge,' Tallis burst out, grinning in spite of his feelings. God knew where the names had come from. He'd have been about six at the time. Dan had played the foreman, bossy as ever. He'd been Doug, his oppo.

'You spent hours shifting stuff about.' His mother laughed.

His mother's laugh was so rare these days it made Tallis misty-eyed. 'No change there,' he told her.

'Still steeped in home alterations?'

''Fraid so. Not that I seem to be making a great deal of progress. The garden's a wilderness and I still can't decide whether I did the right thing, knocking the sitting room through to the kitchen.'

'Must be costing you a fortune.'

'It is.'

'Thought about getting a lodger?'

Only if they were dark-haired, thirty-six, twenty-four, thirty-six. Tallis smiled to himself. 'I don't think so, Mum.'

'Might help with the money.'

'The way the place is, I'd have to pay them.'

His mother laughed softly. 'Think you'll stay?' The question was floated like a feather on a mill-pond. He was aware that his father had suggested he sell up and divide the proceeds with Dan.

'For now,' Tallis said, noncommittal. 'Depends on work.'

This seemed to satisfy her. They talked a little more, briefly mentioned his sister, Hannah, her kids, but he could tell that his mum was anxious to end the call. Probably time to administer more drugs to his father. She promised to phone again towards the end of the week. 'Doug and Kredge,' Tallis murmured fondly, putting the phone down and returning to the sitting room.

'Jesus!'

Tallis started. He was freezing cold and mildly disorientated. Must have fallen asleep on the couch, he thought, looking blearily around him, blinking as his eyes adjusted to the unaccustomed light. Noise, he registered, noise from... Then it stopped. He staggered to his feet, went through the arch into the tiny galley kitchen and stared at the phone. Who the hell was calling on his landline at this time? Then another noise started, less intrusive. He dashed back to the sitting room to where his cellphone was vibrating on the coffee-table. He snatched it up, thinking it might be his mum, but didn't recognise the number, then, shit, he thought his dad had taken a turn for the worse, that... 'Max?' Tallis said, bewildered.

'Sorry to disturb you.'

'It's all right,' he said, dizzy with relief. 'I wasn't in bed.' He should have been, he thought, checking his watch. It was three-thirty in the morning. 'Something wrong?' Tallis said. 'Course it bloody was.

There was an uneasy silence as though Max hadn't quite rehearsed what he was going to say. 'Just had the police on the phone.' His voice was grave. 'They got my name from Felka's belongings.'

'Something happened to her?' Of course it had. He knew only too well how people dished up bad news. It started in increments.

'She's dead,' Max blurted out. 'Murdered.'

Tallis felt as though someone had drop kicked him in the kidneys. Four questions pounded his brain. Where? How? When? Why?

'Found in Lisson Grove near the Harrow Road Flyover.'

'What the hell was she doing there?'

'God knows.'

'But I gave her detailed instructions. She was supposed to take the tube from Euston.'

'There was some problem with the rail network, an incident on the line. She had to change trains so she arrived at Marylebone instead. I guess she got disorientated.'

'How was she killed?' Tallis said tonelessly.

'Stabbed.'

'You know why?'

'Does there have to be reason?'

'I was wondering whether it was a mugging, or robbery.' Then another thought occurred to him. 'Any sign of sexual assault?'

'Christ, not that they mentioned. Would they tell me a thing like that?'

'Maybe not.'

'They've arrested a guy, a fucking illegal, Somalian, the police said.'

Tallis briefly closed his eyes. Somalia was a country of extreme violence, some of which had been exported to Britain. Guy was probably zombied out on khat, a cheap, highly addictive drug, which had already crippled the Somalian economy and help fan the flames of civil war.

'Should have been deported months ago but went to ground,' Max continued.

Tallis swallowed. His throat was so tight it hurt. 'Her parents been informed?'

'Just coming to that. They're catching a flight to London later today, should arrive around five o'clock British time. I could get the next plane back, but...'

'You've already travelled halfway round the world.'

'Doesn't matter. It's not that. They don't speak a word of English.'

'You want me to meet them?'

'Could you?'

'Of course.'

'You sure? I know it's a lot to ask.'

'Not a problem, Max. Let me grab something to write with and I'll jot down the details.'

Tallis kept a night-time vigil. He didn't pray for the girl with the flame-coloured hair because, although brought up in the Catholic faith, he wasn't a believer, but he did plenty of thinking. As darkness made its slow and ponderous passage into the light, Tallis recalled their first meeting. He'd been having a drink with Max. Felka had bounced into the drawing room and introduced herself. She'd seemed so eager to please, to make a good impression. All sorts of other images flashed through his mind. Felka with the baby juggled on her slender hip, of her playing with the older boy, nursing the kids when they were unwell, cajoling them to eat their meals – quite the little mother. And only eighteen years of age. Snuffed out before she'd even got started. He frowned and drained the last dregs of the Scotch from the bottle into his glass. She'd once told him that her name meant lucky.

As the first rays of sun bled across a pale blue sky he thought of the balletic way in which she'd moved, how she'd spoken, that strange intonation on certain words, how she'd flirted. And, of course, he remembered the sensual way, the very last time he'd been with her, she'd whispered in his ear. Felka, he thought sadly, what a terrible, terrible waste of a life, and what a Godawful way to die – lost, alone, in pain in a strange land. He hoped her little brother would always remember her. Raising his glass, Tallis promised never to forget.

CHAPTER SIX

Tallis paid no attention to the design of Marylebone Police Station in Seymour Street. Copshops were copshops. He'd been inside enough of them during his career not to take much notice.

He approached the Formica-topped reception desk and gave his name to a female desk sergeant, stating the reason for his visit. Instructed to take a seat, he was informed that Detective Inspector Ashby would be with him shortly. Tallis sat down, staring at the various posters on the wall, reading them without digesting a word. All he could think of was Felka and the miserable way she'd died.

'Paul Tallis?'

Tallis started, stood up, shaking the hand of the man standing in front of him. 'Tony Ashby,' the DI introduced himself. He was mid to late thirties, small for a police officer, Tallis thought, but the world-weary eyes and the shadows underneath them were one hundred per cent copper. 'You're here regarding Miss Rakowski?'

'I'm collecting her parents from the airport.' Except the flight had been delayed due to a security alert.

'Ah, yes, they're catching a later plane, I understand.'

'That's why I came here.'

Ashby inclined his head. Confusion misted his eyes.

'Thought I could help,' Tallis said.

Confusion morphed to suspicion. 'In what way?'

Tallis met his eye. 'I used to be in the force.'

Yeah, yeah, Ashby's expression seemed to say. So bloody what? Then something happened, like a light flashed on in his head. *Tallis,* Ashby murmured, emphasising the syllables. 'You were one of the firearms officers got roasted in Birmingham.' He said it slowly, meaningfully.

Shit, Tallis thought. Should have kept my mouth shut.

Ashby suddenly beamed. 'Coffee?'

They sat down in an interview room. 'Bad luck, all that stuff in Birmingham,' Ashby sympathised, passing him a plastic cup of vile-looking brew. A couple of other officers wandered in and out for what seemed to Tallis fairly thin reasons. After the initial pleasure of being one of the guys again, he was starting to feel part celebrity, part animal in the zoo. 'Sugar?' Ashby said.

'Thanks.' Cop coffee was impossible to drink without sweetener. 'About Miss Rakowski,' Tallis said. Sounded strange to use her full name. He'd only known her as Felka. 'Any idea what she was doing near the flyover?'

'Fuck knows. Getting lost, I presume.'

Tallis shook his head sadly. 'She was given very specific directions to get to the airport, but from Euston. I even drew a map for her.'

'We found it. It was in her hand luggage. Thing is, there was an incident at Coventry, which meant a change of train and change of destination.'

'What type of incident?'

'Cow on the line.'

Tallis nodded for Ashby to continue.

'Know what kids are like. Any deviation and they panic. Can't find their way out of a paper bag, most of them, and what with her being a foreigner.'

Tallis cast Ashby a sharp look. He didn't think any offence was intended, probably just the way it had come out, and to be fair to the guy there was truth in the statement. He let his eyes drift and rest on a folder on the desk. Ashby seemed to recognise the manoeuvre. The shine went out of his good-natured expression. He threw Tallis a penetrating look. No, you don't, he seemed to say. 'Knew her well?'

60

'She'd worked for Mr Elliott, a good friend of mine. Yes, I knew her well. Good kid,' Tallis said, cringing at the phrase. 'I presume you've logged her movements from the station.'

'Witnesses are hard to come by. Nobody seems to remember her.'

'Could always do a scene reconstruction.'

'I don't think that will be necessary.'

'Because you have your man.' Tallis smiled. 'Fast result.' It sounded critical, even though he hadn't meant it to be.

Ashby smiled back, cool. He pushed the folder over to Tallis. 'Warn you, it's not nice. Stabbed five times and throat cut for good measure.'

Tallis didn't react, didn't miss a beat. He opened the file, took out the crime-scene photographs, studied them. The first frames displayed the outer perimeter of the scene, shots taken from a distance – the road, the sign for the car park, the outline of bottle recycling bins. Then he looked at the close-ups. She was on the ground at an awkward angle, face to one side, barely identifiable. Too much blood. Too much chaos. It was an appalling scene, even to Tallis's experienced eyes.

'Good job we've got the piece of shit off the street,' Ashby said.

'Post-mortem carried out?' Tallis said, looking up.

Ashby nodded.

'Any sign of sexual assault?'

'None.'

Thank God, he thought. Not that it made any difference. Felka was dead.

'There was extensive bruising,' Ashby said. 'She

61

put up quite a fight.'

'Weapon found?'

'Not yet. Serrated blade, judging from the nature of the wounds.'

'And the offender?'

'Fits the profile – young, opportunistic, disordered. Blood was found on one of his trainers and a substantial amount on his clothing.'

'So pretty conclusive?'

Ashby agreed. 'We're not looking for anyone else.'

'Think robbery might have been the motive?'

'Quite possibly. We've several reports from witnesses that he'd been hanging around the area, begging and behaving in a threatening manner to those not disposed to give him money. He was the last person to be seen with her.'

Tallis nodded, took one last look at the photographs. He didn't doubt Ashby. It looked like an open-and-shut case. 'Your suspect,' he said, 'still banged up here?'

'Waiting for his brief.' Ashby exchanged a conspiratorial smile with Tallis. Duty briefs were busy people. It could take time for one to materialise. In the meantime, they could sweat the Somalian.

Ashby stretched back in his seat. For someone in charge of a murder investigation, he seemed very laid-back, Tallis thought, probably because the investigation was buttoned down and there was a distinct lack of urgency.

'Possible for me to see her?'

Apart from mortuary staff and investigating police officers, only close relatives of the deceased got to see the bodies of their loved ones, mostly for identification purposes. As the Rakowskis spoke no English, and he was to act as interpreter, he'd be needed to accompany them to the mortuary, but he really wanted to see Felka alone. Somehow, he felt as if he owed it to her.

Ashby frowned, studied him for a moment, his look one of extreme doubt. 'Bit irregular,' he said.

'Not to worry,' Tallis began. 'It was–'

'But I guess, as it's you...' Ashby suddenly smiled '...we could stretch a point.'

Ashby drove. Conversation en route to the mortuary revolved around Arsenal, Aston Villa's performance under Martin O'Neill and the latest cricket score. 'Used to play a bit myself,' Ashby said, 'but don't get the time now.'

The formalities swiftly dispensed with, Tallis was shown into a viewing suite. The contrast from the crime scene shots was powerful. Cleaned up, Felka resembled a statue. Apart from where the gaping wound to her throat had been sewn up, and the bruising on her arms, her skin was the colour of old alabaster. In death, Tallis thought, she seemed childlike. He resisted the temptation to bend over her pale cheek and kiss her.

'That her?' Ashby said.

Tallis affirmed it was. 'Extensive cuts to her hands,' he murmured.

'Defence injuries.'

Tallis nodded sadly.

'Come on,' Ashby said, giving his elbow a nudge. 'I'll buy you a drink. You look as if you could use one.'

Tallis cracked a smile, allowed Ashby to guide him back out into the world, to cleaner air untainted by death and decay.

CHAPTER SEVEN

The Rakowskis eventually arrived six hours later. They looked like any other bereaved parents – shocked, red-eyed and frightened. Tallis did his best to convey his condolences, but there was no language in the world that could soften the blow of losing a child, especially in such horrific circumstances. He stayed with them at the police station, acting as interpreter, escorting them to the mortuary and eventually booking them into a small hotel nearby. As he left to travel back to Birmingham the following morning, Mr Rakowski, a small man with ginger hair and a wispy, greying moustache, clasped his hand with both of his, thanking him profusely. Mrs Rakowski, handsome in spite of the emotional drain on her features, tipped up on her toes, kissed him on both cheeks, just as her daughter had done less than forty-eight hours before. As Tallis walked away, he felt choked.

Driving back up the motorway, exhaustion started to play games with his concentration, the misery he felt at Felka's sudden and violent death inexplicably triggering thoughts of another long past miserable episode in his life when he and

Dan had engaged in a fistfight in the middle of their parents' kitchen. For weeks, Tallis had suspected that Dan had been stealing money from him. What had most upset him was that the loot had been so hard earned – he'd saved it up from many nights of laborious washing up in a rathole of a pub, then the only avenue to making money for a twelve-year-old schoolboy living out in the sticks.

He couldn't remember now on what pretext he'd challenged his brother. Try as he may, he'd had no hard evidence that Dan was stealing yet he could come to no other conclusion.

Dan threw the first punch. 'You little tosser,' he snarled, missing Tallis by inches.

'Tosser?' Tallis sneered back. 'You're the one with the mucky magazines. I'm surprised the whole village hasn't heard you jerking off.'

Dan's face contorted in rage. 'Why, you–'

But he didn't get any further. Tallis leapt at him like a lion taking down an antelope. The rest was a blur of shouts, blows, scrapes and fingernails in skin. That's why Tallis didn't realise that his father had stepped into the fray. Until it was too late.

'Come here, you little bastard,' his dad cried out, his cheek already beginning to swell where Tallis had landed one on him.

'What's going on?' Tallis heard his mother cry.

'Stay out of this, Sandra.' Dad never called her by her Croatian name, Sanja.

'Accused me of stealing,' Dan said, bloated with indignation. 'More likely, one of your mates. Right little tykes.'

'This true, Paul?' his dad demanded, eyes cold with fury, fists jabbing the electric air.

But Tallis's gaze was on his mother. A curled hand was pressed hard against her mouth, the white knuckles making indentations in her skin. Her eyes were full of anguish.

'What, Mum?' Tallis said, suddenly feeling his skin crawl.

His mum turned imploringly to her husband. 'I meant to put it back. I was going to,' she insisted. 'It was just to tide us over, money being tight,' she mumbled, apologetic.

His father stared at her with belligerent eyes for what seemed like minutes then everyone gaped at Tallis. He, the accuser. He, the one who'd hit his father in anger. Dan, by contrast, wore the triumphant expression of someone who'd just won a phenomenal game of poker.

His father ensured that his youngest son was sorry for making such a poor error of judgement with a beating cut short only by his wife's intervention. Neither of them noticed Dan looking on, mouthing *Stupid cow* in his mother's direction.

He spent the rest of the journey wishing he'd taken Max up on his offer of the BMW. The Rover had about as much acceleration as a snail, and there were too many lorry drivers playing boy racers. Knights of the road, he thought grimly as yet another beast of a vehicle veered out in front of him without warning in a vain bid to overtake a similarly sized juggernaut.

His thoughts meandered to Cavall, the visit, illegal immigrants, what Finn would dig up, if

66

anything. Questions that shouldn't have concerned him spiked his thoughts. How do people go to ground? If they want to become invisible and lead an invisible life, where do they go? How do they reintegrate into a society when they never had a stake in it anyway? Easy, he thought, they don't. They're much too hard-wired for bad. All right, but I'm good at bad, he thought. So how would I go about finding someone who is hell-bent on disappearing into the ether? No National Insurance number to check, no Inland Revenue, no bank accounts, no driving licence. All the usual routes blocked.

He pulled off at the next service station, got out, stretched his legs and bought a shot of high-voltage caffeine. Taking a thoughtful sip, he reckoned the best place to look for people on the run would be in the kind of traditionally low-paid industries where nobody asked questions – building and construction, fruit picking, food preparation, kitchen work. In spite of threatened government clampdowns, unscrupulous employers still exploited those ripe for exploitation. But this was all obvious stuff. The guys Cavall was talking about had either returned to their criminal careers or gravitated towards people of the same ilk: in other words, one and the same. That's why his skills undercover all those years before were important to Cavall, he realised. Infiltration was key to information.

He climbed back into the Rover, slotted Eminem into the CD player, jacking up the volume, and swiftly joined the M6. His first assignment undercover had been to chat up and gain the trust of a known drug dealer by posing as a dealer from another part of the country. For a short, adrenaline-spiked period of time, Paul Tallis hadn't existed. Whether it was because he'd been a tearaway as a kid, or the dark side of his nature had come to the fore, he'd slipped into the role with unsettling ease. Humans, even the male of the species, were predisposed to gossip, and most secrets were leaked not because arms were twisted up around backs but in the natural course of trading information and friendship, usually down the pub. Two important lessons he'd learnt were never underestimate the enemy and always treat them with respect. But that was all a very long time ago. Undercover was all right, but it was the buzz of firearms that had turned him on, which was why, as soon as he'd been able to get back into it, he'd leapt at the chance.

Eminem was cracking on about one shot, one opportunity when Tallis's mobile rang. He pulled over onto the hard shoulder, turned the volume down. It was Finn. 'Cavall's a political adviser with a formidable reputation. Educated at Cheltenham Ladies College and studied Political Science at Cambridge, where she was awarded a first class honours degree. Recruited by the Home Office, she worked for four years as a research officer before moving further up the food chain. Known to be a real babe with an obsession for meeting targets.'

Tallis scratched his ear. He couldn't imagine Sonia Cavall being anyone's baby, more the type of woman to freeze a guy's plasma. 'So you're saying she's above board?'

'As much as anyone in the department,' Finn said in a voice tinged with cynicism. 'Gather she's a bit of a cause merchant.'

Tallis thanked Finn and promised him a pint then pulled Cavall's calling card from his pocket. He had meant to chuck it away, but Felka's death had changed everything. Maybe a cause was what he needed.

After a hot shower and coffee, he rang Cavall's number and listened to the click and buzz of the call being rerouted.

'Cavall speaking.' Not Sonia, not hello.

'Paul Tallis. That job you wanted me to do, I'll take it.' Silence.

'Hello, you still there?'

'I am.'

More silence.

Suffering Christ, the woman was a ball-breaker. What did she want him to do, beg? 'Of course, if you've appointed someone else...'

'Why the change of mind?'

Change of heart would be more accurate, Tallis thought, but he wasn't going to discuss his motives with Cavall. 'Something to do with my bank balance. You're all that stands between me and penury.' Actually, he hadn't checked his finances for ages. He tried not to. Every time he did, he was deeper into his overdraft.

'So it's money.' Her tone was scathing.

This time Tallis said nothing. After suffering at the hands of his father, he was no longer easily humiliated, and if she were going to be sodding difficult, he'd rather forget the whole thing. 'I suppose I could fit you in tomorrow,' she said, finally. Sounded like a huge favour was being bestowed.

'Can't,' he countered. No apology, no excuse, no reason. He had nothing planned, but he was fucked if Cavall was going to exert that much power over him.

'All right,' she said crisply. 'Botanical Gardens, outside the Orangery, thirty minutes.' Click. Tallis closed the phone. Females for you, he sighed, unpredictable, capricious and utterly enthralling. No doubt about it, this was going to be a battle of wills. And in his experience, women always won.

He was three minutes early. Puffy clouds scudded across a sky the colour of a cormorant's egg. The air seemed quieter because of the sunshine. It was going to be a nice day, he thought. Well, maybe.

Apart from staff, there were few people about at that time on a Thursday afternoon. Tallis paid the admission charge and made his way through the entrance, following a designated route outside and across landscaped gardens skirted by vibrant borders of rhododendrons and azaleas. According to the information sheet, there were more than four hundred trees, a rose garden, rock garden and terraces, as well as cactus, tropical and palm houses, but all Tallis could think about was Cavall, the job, what lay ahead.

She was already there. Wearing a white fitted jacket over black trousers and top, she looked more formal. He glanced at his watch: she was bang on time.

Cavall acknowledged his presence with a minute

70

flicker of her eyes, and picked up her briefcase, which looked heavy. He immediately offered to carry it. 'Ever the gentleman.' She smiled with dry humour. 'But, no, thanks. I can manage. Walk and talk?'

He nodded, falling into step beside her. She had large feet for a woman, he noticed. 'Money has already been wired to an account for you, details in here,' she said, briefly lifting the briefcase. Tallis was impressed but said nothing. People only gave money away with that much alacrity if there was risk involved to the recipient. 'There are four individuals in total,' Cavall continued. 'All served sentences for violent crime, including murder. We want them found. To assist in your search, you'll be handed prison files and, in some cases, computer disks giving full profiles of each offender.' Tallis didn't break stride. He wondered how she'd got hold of the information. Home Office or no Home Office, prison files were seen on a read-only basis.

'And the mechanics?'

'How you go about finding each target is up to you.'

'But you want them alive?'

'Of course.' Cavall shot him a sharp look, clearly repulsed by the notion of it being any other way. Good, he thought, he wanted to get that absolutely straight from the start. 'As soon as the target's located, call the contact number,' she continued. 'It's your job to stay with your man until the handover.'

'That it?'

'Yes.'

Sounded simple. Too simple. 'What if there's a problem?'

'You call and wait for further instruction.'

'Who's on the rest of the team?' he asked. They were cutting through the palm house, steam rising, orchids and evil-looking insect-eating plants the only eavesdroppers on their conversation. It felt swelteringly hot. The damp air smelt of sap.

'There is no team.'

Tallis stopped. Cavall turned, met and held his gaze. He was trying to decipher whether one good man was good enough, or whether he was merely expendable.

'Think of me as your handler,' Cavall said, as if that should improve the situation. It didn't. 'Handler' was a word used for police who ran informers. Tallis was starting to feel grubby.

'Do I carry a warrant card?'

She shook her head, making her blonde ponytail rock from side to side. 'This is the equivalent of a black operation.'

'So I'm completely on my own.' There was no alarm in Tallis's voice. He just needed to clarify the situation.

'Think you can do it?' Her brown eyes drilled into his.

'Don't see why not.'

They carried on walking again. Tallis saw some kind of carnivorous plant swallow up a large bluebottle. 'Will I be armed?'

'What the hell for?' She looked entirely horrified.

To protect myself, he thought. Should the need

72

arise, he knew where to get hold of a weapon – not that he would do so lightly. After the Van Sleigh incident, he'd never wanted to carry a gun again.

'We really can't have any fuss,' she said, half-smiling, more conciliatory.

He stole a glance, bet she was a blinding fuck. Not that he had any intention of trying to find out.

They left the suffocating dome of heat and emerged into open air scented with roses. 'If this is unofficial, will I be able to talk to arresting and senior investigating officers involved with the case?'

'Up to you,' Cavall shrugged. 'You'll have to think of a cover story.'

Christ, this gets better. 'Former cellmates?'

'I'm sure something could be arranged.'

What and how? he wondered. 'And which prisons are we looking at?'

'The Scrubs, for starters.'

They walked in silence along a terraced area, Cavall's heels clicking on the gravel. Sunshine leaked onto the ground. Distant traffic hummed through a background of trees. Eventually they came to a bench. Cavall sat down, clicked open the briefcase, handing Tallis a thick buff-coloured folder. He stared at it. Another poisoned chalice, he thought. He was accumulating them like people collected supermarket vouchers. 'You realise these people might have reformed, gone straight. They could be trying to rebuild their lives.'

'Can't afford another crisis of conscience,

73

Paul.' She smiled but her voice was humourless. He noticed that whenever she used his first name, it served as a rebuke.

'They've done their time,' he insisted.

Cavall eyed him, her expression coldly remote. 'They're here illegally. They've already killed your fellow countrymen, women in some cases, and in the most horrific manner. In all probability they'll reoffend. But if you want out, say so now and stop wasting both our time.'

He felt tempted. Just get up, walk away, and pretend he'd never seen her. Then Tallis remembered Felka, thought of the wounds to her body, her fear, her pain, and the piece of scum who'd inflicted it. 'No,' he said decisively, 'I'll do it.'

'Good,' Cavall said, standing up. 'Oh, and, Paul,' she said with a dry smile, 'if you attempt to go public, or expose the plan, all knowledge of any link to me, and the department, will be vigorously denied. There will be no trail, no evidence, nothing to prove.'

Tallis looked up at her. 'And if it goes wrong?'

'It won't.'

But if it did, Tallis thought, watching her hips swing as she walked away, he'd be hung out to dry. Alone.

CHAPTER EIGHT

Back in his bungalow, Tallis stared at the folder as if it were an unexploded bomb. He must be cracked, he thought, taking a fresh bottle of single malt out of its bag and unscrewing the cap. Twenty-five thousand pounds' worth cracked, to be exact, and that was just a down payment, according to Cavall.

He poured himself a healthy slug, looked at it, changed his mind and poured it back into the bottle. Unlike Stu, he now had a reason to stay sober. Pulling the file onto his lap again, this time slipping out all the contents, he spread them on the knee-high coffee-table. There were prison documents, press cuttings, reports of the police investigation and details of court hearings, and, of course, mug shots of Agron Demarku, past and present.

Demarku was Albanian. His crime: torturing and beating a prostitute to death with a baseball bat. Tallis expected someone with broad shoulders and aggressive raw-boned features but the lad, for Demarku had been barely nineteen years old at the time of the offence, was a mere slip of a guy. He had kind-looking eyes and the type of small cherubic mouth Tallis had only seen on little children. He wondered how, after twelve years inside, prison had changed Demarku. Generally inmates went one of two ways: got lean or got fat.

Tallis turned to the latest recorded photograph of his man. Demarku had lost the freshness of youth. The hair was dirty blonde, skin more sallow. The blue eyes were dead behind the light. And he was thin, very thin.

According to the prison profile, Demarku had been born in Durres, an ancient port on the eastern Adriatic and more recently, Tallis thought, a focus for Albanian Mafiosi. Albanians, in spite of religious differences, had fought bravely, sometimes alongside Croatians, against a common enemy, the Serbs. As far as the Mafiosi were concerned, they maintained a code of silence to protect against betrayal. Like their Italian counterparts, they believed in honour.

A model prisoner, Demarku had spent much of his time reading and improving his English. He was also a devout Muslim. His medical records were without note, but a psychiatric report deemed him highly intelligent, manipulative and dangerous. In other words, Tallis thought, psychopathic. Demarku had expressed no remorse for his crime and maintained that his extreme actions had merely been the result of severe provocation. Had Demarku been a wife-beater, Tallis thought, something snatching inside as he viewed the crime-scene shots, Demarku's defence would no doubt have fallen into the *she made me do it* category. Scalds and burns inflicted on the twenty-three-year-old victim's body spoke another narrative.

The offender profile suggested that Demarku's viciousness towards women stemmed from a mother who'd abandoned him when he'd been four, leaving him in the questionable care of his older brothers and father. The shrink had stated for the record that Demarku's formative years had been blighted by regular beatings and worse. A strange, unwelcome thought formulated in Tallis's brain. He wondered what his own childhood would have been like without the restraining influence of his mother.

At the time of the killing, Demarku had been minding a small brothel in Camden, North London, which struck Tallis as unusual. Following the break-up of former Yugoslavia, the Albanians currently had a powerful hold on crime in the capital, but twelve years ago they'd been virtually unknown. Tallis considered how Demarku might have made his way to Britain: slipping away into the night on a fast boat and heading for the Italian coast as so many did. From there it would have been a relatively simple lorry ride to the UK. But why had he fled his native country? Not because of his vile family, surely? Tallis thought. And Demarku was far too young to have been caught up in the warm-up to the conflict that had engulfed the neighbouring region in the early 1990s. Educated guess, Demarku was on the run. A note by the senior investigating officer, a guy called Marshall, suggested that there was circumstantial evidence putting the young Demarku at the scene of a serious rape in which a middle-aged woman had been left a basket case only four months after Demarku's arrival in the UK. No wonder the big guys want you found, Tallis thought, feeling the blood pump in his veins.

Apart from his most recent visit to Marylebone Police Station, it had been many years since Tallis had last walked the streets of London. To reacquaint himself, he foraged through his only bookcase and, among a number of history books, found and pulled out an old *A-Z*. Plenty of scope for the ex-con to return to his old stamping ground, Tallis thought, locating Camden. He'd heard anecdotally that nearby Haringey was a first stop for ex-prisoners, and the chronically deprived borough of Hackney next door one of the most dangerous places in the UK for gun crime, but would Demarku return there? Would he even stay in the capital? With his fellow countrymen heading this way in droves, it still seemed unlikely he'd beat a retreat to his homeland, but Tallis had to admit that was more based on hunch than fact. And that, he supposed, was the beauty of this particular job. He was not constrained by police procedure. He did not have to abide by the rules of PACE – Police and Criminal Evidence Act. He could be a maverick and go with the flow. But against this, he had no back-up, no armaments, no fibre-optic cameras, no listening devices, battering rams, no body armour or respirator. No listening ear, no guiding light, no companion, he thought sadly.

Tallis returned to the map. According to the notes, Demarku, now thirty-one years old, had left Wormwood Scrubs two and a half months ago. He'd still have a young man's hunger, Tallis believed. Still have that burning desire to make up for the stolen years of childhood and time wasted in the nick. But the world would be a very different place to the one young Demarku had briefly left behind – more rush and thrust, more watching and checking, more pen-pushing and paper-chasing. Tallis rested his finger on the road outside the prison. Which route had Demarku taken? Via the bright lights of trendy Notting Hill in the hope of bumping into one of the beautiful people, or had he slunk off in the opposite direction to the lesser charms of Acton or Ealing? Which had it been?

He needed to get inside Demarku's head, to throw away his own values and adopt the attitudes of a psycho, a bit like learning a new language. People with great vocabularies and grammar often failed to convince because they lacked mastery of their accent. They continued to speak by using the same muscles and lip and tongue movements employed for their native speech. In learning a new language, you had to forget all that, and converse with new sounds, new speech patterns.

Tallis didn't doubt that the police had already done their homework and carried out the usual enquiries, talked to close associates and friends, visited Demarku's old haunts, so the only way forward was to look with a different eye and find something extra, something that would lead him to his man. Start with the obvious, Tallis thought. But first he needed to cover his tracks.

Across the road from the avenue was a long row of shops that included a mini-supermarket, newsagent's, an Indian take-away and launderette, a couple of charity outlets, anything-for-a-quid stores, and cheap-price booze emporiums.

79

The mobile phone shop was at the end next to a hairdressing salon called Wendy's. Twenty minutes later, he came out with the latest up-to-the-second gadgetry, not because he fancied a new phone but because he needed a new identity.

As soon as he returned home, he called the Met, and asked to be put through to Detective Chief Inspector Marshall at Kentish Town Police Station, Camden.

Several minutes later, he was told that DCI Marshall had taken early retirement. Tallis scanned the report, found the name of his right-hand man, DI Micky Crow.

'On a rest day. Can I take a message?'

Tallis exhaled slowly. 'Can you say Mark Strong wants to discuss an old case? Mention the name Agron Demarku.' Leaving his number, Tallis rang off, briefly considered calling Wormwood Scrubs, but decided that a black man stood more chance of attending a BNP rally than he had of pumping the governor for information. Instead, he phoned into work and said he wouldn't be coming back then rummaged in his bedroom for the weights he'd slung under a pile of blankets. Changing into a tracksuit, he gave himself a thorough workout, followed by a run to offset any stiffness in his joints. On his return, he showered, felt a million times better and checked out the train times from New Street to Euston.

Birmingham seemed small and parochial by contrast, Tallis thought as he stepped off the train and was swallowed up by a tidal wave of human traffic. It had been a while since he'd seen so many people, so many different shapes and sizes, nationalities and styles of dress. In the space of five minutes, and as his ear became attuned to his environment, he caught snippets of at least seven foreign languages, including Russian, Arabic and Portuguese. It was all so different to when he'd driven up a couple of days before. Cars, even crap cars, had a habit of sanitising one from the outside world and, given the circumstances, he'd been too zoned out to engage with it anyway. Here he felt a stranger, but he couldn't escape the undeniable buzz, the sense of being at the hub, that he was important again.

He caught a tube north, standing room only, swaying with the roll and clatter of the tube's manic flight through narrow tunnels, feeling like a human cannonball. The confined space strongly smelt of spices, body odour and unwashed clothes. Catching the eye of a pretty young woman, he smiled, his reward a downturned mouth and a look of distrust meshed with scorn. Most of the faces were tired looking, or disinterested, he thought. Bunched up with others, he was given the unsettling impression of fleeing refugees. Maybe they were in a way. Not fleeing from war or destruction but life.

He surfaced into wet air and schizophrenic weather – one moment sunny, the next clouding over and tipping it down. Instinctively, he scoured the faces, wondering if Demarku was among them, unsure that he would recognise the guy even if he were. For all he knew, Demarku could have radically changed his appearance. Detective Inspector Crow hadn't contacted him yet, but Tallis planned an ambush. First, he needed food.

He started walking, taking it all in – busy-looking car park, wheelie-bins, a skinny guy with a baseball hat on back to front crouched down on some concrete steps, unbelievably lighting a rock of crack in broad daylight, litter, dirty doorways, used condoms and spent syringes. He passed a fire station and a meeting house for Jehovah's Witnesses, shops and more shops, some run-down, some holding it together. At last, he found a café to suit his taste. He went inside and ordered an all-day breakfast from a youngish woman who definitely didn't want to be there. She didn't so much walk as slouch to the table.

'Fried bread?' Nasal whine. Eyes glued to the notepad.

'Please.'

'Tomatoes or mushrooms?'

Both, he wanted to say but thought it might further upset her day. 'Tomatoes are fine.'

'Eggs – fried or poached?'

'Poached would be good. Oh, and...'

'Yes?' Her eyes swivelled from the notepad. Never had he witnessed such an innocent word convey so much menace.

'Tea?' he said, giving her the benefit of his best smile. Without replying, she bellowed his order for all of London to hear, and did a nifty turn on her heel that must have taken hours to perfect. Miserable cow.

In spite of the waitress's distinct lack of customer-facing skills, the breakfast was surprisingly good, and fifty minutes later Tallis was

82

back on the street, halfway between Camden and Kentish Town, standing on the pavement in front of a battered wrought-iron gate. Almost off its hinges, it opened onto a stone flight of chipped steps leading to a raddled-looking basement flat. As Tallis leaned over, catching a strong whiff of dead flowers, a cat shot in front of him and darted across the road. He watched it skitter along the pavement before disappearing down an alleyway then returned his gaze to the tightly drawn and grubby curtains, felt the cloak of silence. Kitty, it seemed, was the only sign of life.

Walking away, Tallis wondered whether the current occupants knew that, just over a decade before, the place had served as a knocking-shop, that a young woman, tortured and beaten, had lost her life there.

Tallis didn't know who was more taken aback.

'Micky, short for Michelle,' the DI explained, as if she were talking to a deaf simpleton.

They were standing outside the police station, mainly because Crow, who had the build of an all-in wrestler, needed to smoke. She had short brown hair, and a rumpled expression that matched her trouser suit. Her complexion was that of a drinker, cheeks stick-of-rock pink and premature lines around her sagging mouth. She looked knackered, Tallis thought. He launched into his hastily prepared spiel, explaining that he was writing a book, non-fiction, and had an interest in the Demarku case.

'Why?' Her eyebrows moulded together to form a long, dark, hairy line.

'I'm partly Croatian,' Tallis said.

The look on Crow's face suggested that he'd just pissed in her vodka.

'Several generations ago,' he added with a reassuring smile. 'I'm British born, British bred.' Christ, it sounded like a strap line for meat traceability.

'Right, well, that's very interesting,' she said, puffing away, 'but I don't do chats with press unless I have to.' Her eyes flicked to her watch. He noticed her fingers were trembling. He'd observed the same symptoms in Stu. Drinkies, Tallis thought, Crow was counting the hours.

'But I've come all this way.'

'Shouldn't have wasted your time.'

'Off the record, that's all.'

Crow narrowed her puffy eyes. 'You're starting to annoy me. How can I put this nicely?' she snarled, squaring up to her full height so that her bloodshot eyes were level with Tallis's shoulder. For a worrying moment, Tallis thought she might lump him one. Time for one last roll of the dice, he thought. 'I'd love to take you for a drink after your shift.' He almost gagged at how charming he sounded.

Crow threw her head back and laughed. Sounded like threatened consequences. 'Persistent bastard, aren't you?'

'That's me.' Tallis grinned. 'So what do you say?'

'Tried the press office?'

So it wasn't a downright refusal. 'They'll only tell me what they want me to hear.' At least, that's what Finn always told him.

'Off the record, you said?' Crow's eyes narrowed against a cloud of cigarette smoke.

'You have my word.'

At that, she actually smiled. It was horrible, like a cheap, nylon nightdress. Tallis smiled back, he hoped with more sincerity than he felt.

'All right,' she said, won over. 'The Freemasons Arms, Downshire Hill, opposite Hampstead Heath. Meet me there at six.'

He did, but not before booking into a two-star hotel in Cardington Street, Euston. It was the wrong side of basic, but would fit the general image he hoped to convey. Sooner or later, he'd be mixing with criminals. Wouldn't look right to be staying at Claridges.

To maintain his new fitness programme, he went for a fast run through streets heavy with car fumes. He still reckoned he was better off than the lowly cyclist. At least people didn't try to actively kill you. After a shower and brush-up, he got to the Freemasons ten minutes early and ordered a pint of Fuller's London Pride. He liked the place immediately. Nice and airy, a little bit Eastern looking, and it had the most wonderful windows providing great views of the garden. The courtyard was already filling up.

After taking a glance at the sumptuously inviting menu and realising that he was hungry, he took his drink out the front into warm evening sunshine and managed to bag the last table. The crowd, he noticed, was young and well dressed, even the girls, which he found refreshing. He was getting tired of the bare belly and roll-up fags routine. He wanted his women, to look like

85

women not dockers.

Crow arrived, looking hot and sweaty.

'Get you a drink?' Tallis said.

'Large V and T. Been a fuck of a day,' she said, plumping herself down, dragging a crumpled packet of cigarettes from her jacket pocket.

Tallis went to the bar and returned with Crow's drink. She took a deep draw, as though she'd walked halfway through a desert for it. 'So,' she said, blowing two thin streams of smoke through her nostrils. 'What do you want to know? Presume you're already familiar with the details.'

'Most of them,' Tallis said. 'I understand after Demarku finished his sentence he was inadvertently released instead of being deported.'

Crow grinned knowingly. 'So that's your angle.'

'One of the angles,' Tallis countered.

'Fucking disgrace. If I'd had my way, he'd never have been let out.'

'But he was,' Tallis said, trying to keep her on track, 'and now he's on the loose somewhere.'

'Frankly, not my problem,' Crow said. 'We did our bit twelve years ago.'

'So no effort's been made to find him?'

'Seen my workload?'

'I'm not criticising.'

'Should hope not,' Crow said, taking another pull of her drink. At this rate, he was going to be making an early trip to the bar, Tallis thought. 'Put it this way, we've trailed likely haunts, talked to the usual suspects...'

'Informers?'

'Uh-huh.'

She didn't sound very convincing. Actually, it

cheered him. Demarku wasn't so much as eluding the cops as they weren't exactly busting a gut to find him. It meant he was in with more of a chance of unearthing his man. 'What about the guys he shared a cell with, all that kind of stuff?'

Crow cast him a withering look. 'Two words – targets, clear-up rate.'

'That's more than two.' He laughed.

'You get my drift. It's all about moving onto the next case,' Crow said, stubbing out a cigarette and lighting another. A young woman with a child in a pushchair cast her a venomous look, but Crow either didn't mind or wasn't taking any notice.

'What was Demarku like?'

Her face drooped then she began to cough, eyes watering and streaming, mouth opening and closing like a struggling perch as she tried to get her breath. Beating her large chest with one hand, she grabbed at her glass with the other, taking a large swig. It seemed to do the trick. 'Disturbing,' she croaked. 'Came across as being very polite, quiet, thoughtful even, the type of guy who most mothers would want as their son. If only they knew.' She frowned, taking a drag of her cigarette. 'Underneath the little-boy-lost facade, he was seething with fury. He'd as soon as slip a blade between your ribs as look at you. Probably smile while he was doing it.'

For the first time, Tallis registered a note of respect in Crow's voice, not born of admiration but fear. 'Another?' he said, gesturing at her empty glass.

'I'll get them,' Crow said, making to get up.

'Stay where you are, admire the scenery.' He wanted time to collect his thoughts, think about what he was going to ask next. He ordered another pint and the same again for Crow.

'Gather Demarku had also been linked to a serious rape,' he said a few moments later, putting their glasses down on the table.

'Didn't have the evidence to nail him.'

'No DNA?'

'No.'

'What about the victim? Couldn't she ID him?'

Crow shook her head. 'Never properly recovered.'

'Too scared to point a finger?'

'I'd say so, yes.'

'Think she'd talk to me?'

Crow snorted. 'You're a charmer, but I don't think so. She's had a shit time since the attack. Marriage collapsed under the strain. Kids went with dad.'

'Christ.'

'Christ indeed.' Crow picked a flake of tobacco from her tongue.

'Keep in touch?'

'Yeah, I do, actually. Not on a regular basis. Just call in when I can. And no, I'm not telling you who she is and where she lives,' Crow added, giving a deep, dirty, thirty-a-day laugh.

'Fair enough. Think Demarku might try and find her?'

'Have a hard time. She's moved twice in the last twelve years. Anyway, I don't think that's his game.'

'And what is his game?'

'Prostitution, and if he embraces our brand-new world and joins his brothers, people trafficking and drugs. The Albanians have cornered the market in London. Should suit you, if you're ever out of a job.' She laughed.

Tallis eyed her over the rim of his glass. He wasn't joining in.

'Keep your pants on.' Crow grinned. 'The Albanians trust no one but, at street-distribution level, they employ Croats. Fuck knows how they understand each other.'

Tallis quietly filed the information away. Crow obviously didn't know much about the Balkans. Croatians spoke and understood Serbo-Croat as did the Albanians, even if they didn't like to admit to it. 'Going back to the rape. Anything stick in the victim's mind about the attack?'

'Apart from its degrading nature?'

'Thinking more along the lines of Demarku himself, about his character, the way he behaved.'

Crow's dark eyebrows drew together. 'You into all that psychological stuff?' She didn't sound very enamoured.

'Just trying to find something original to say.'

'There was something, actually. I picked up on it too, so it's not exactly revealing a trade secret.'

'Yeah?'

'Cologne. The guy liked to smell good. Not any old cheap rubbish either. And he liked expensive clothes. Definitely got a bit of a flash streak.' She gave her glass a mournful stare. 'One for the road, I think. What's yours?'

Tallis told her. 'A half's fine,' he added.

Crow returned with a pint for him. 'No point in

89

pissing about,' she said, grinning happily. 'Thought of someone else you could talk to.' Tallis raised an eyebrow. Alcohol was definitely having the desired effect. 'Guy called Peter Tremlett. He was the probation officer involved in the parole board decision to release Demarku.'

Tallis knew enough about this most secretive of breeds to know that Crow was way off the mark. Probation officers had much in common with customs and excise officers: both kept their mouths shut. 'He won't talk to me,' he scoffed.

Crow winked. 'Twenty quid says he will.'

Tallis eyed her. She was definitely confident. 'All right,' he said, intrigued, taking two tens from his wallet. 'But, remember, I know where to come looking if you're telling porkies.'

Grinning from ear to ear, Crow leant forward, allowing her large bosom to rest upon the table. 'He's retired and resentful. Mad sod will talk to anyone who'll listen.' She laughed like a crazy cat, sliding the notes off the table and pocketing them.

After a night of very little sleep, Tallis got up early, went for a run then showered and dressed, but decided to stay unshaven. He took advantage of the hotel's all-inclusive breakfast. It wasn't a patch on the one he'd had the day before, but he was so hungry he wasn't complaining. At nine-thirty, he phoned Peter Tremlett, dropping Crow's name by way of an introduction.

'Christ, Micky Crow?'

'Yes, I–'

'Woman ought to be locked up.'

90

Tallis didn't like to dwell on what Crow had done to the unfortunate Mr Tremlett to elicit such a forthright response. He moved swiftly on. 'Thing is, it's about the Demarku case,' he said, feeding Tremlett the same line he'd fed Crow. 'Understand you were his probation officer.'

'Only in the technical sense. If you mean did I spend any time with him, the answer's no.'

Tallis scratched his head. 'But you had to work out a risk assessment for the parole board?'

'Oh, yes,' Tremlett said, voice packed with scorn. 'But things aren't as they used to be. When I first joined the probation service you spent time with your clients. Got to know them, got the measure of them. We did good work with some, prevented them from returning to a life of crime. Nowadays, we're so swamped with paperwork the client's the least of our problems. Know what happened in the Demarku case?' Tremlett's voice soared. 'I was given a sodding thick file to read and asked to talk to him via a video link to the prison. It's ridiculous. Body language is often key to working out whether someone is genuine or not. You can't pick up on a tapping foot or clenched fist if you're staring into a screen. I mean, it's laughable. There I was, having to make a judgement on a man without even being in the same room as him. And,' Tremlett said, anger convulsing him, 'it's not unusual. I'm just glad I'm out of it. You said you're writing a book?'

'That's right,' Tallis said, flinching at the slightly professorial tone.

'I'm thinking of doing the same. It will be a grand exposé.'

'Good for you,' Tallis said. 'Going back to Demarku...'

'Ah, yes,' Tremlett said, in an *I told you so* manner. 'Skipped deportation. Not that you can blame Immigration. They're even more swamped than us.'

'Any ideas where he might be?'

'The spit of land between Hounslow and Heathrow, I dare say.'

Spit? Tallis thought. How had he come to that conclusion? He asked him.

'My sister lives there. Says the place is full of his type of people.'

Except it wasn't. Thirty minutes out of central London, he expected to hear foreign accents, yet to say the place was overrun with Albanians was a myth.

Hounslow reminded him of parts of Moseley but with riverside walks and open spaces. According to the guide he'd picked up, it was supposed to play host to five historic houses, not that he'd seen much evidence of deep cultural heritage. The high street looked similar to hundreds of others: unremarkable. The only place of interest was a small trashy-looking letting and estate agency off the main drag. Some of the homes on offer, Tallis thought as he studied the window, he wouldn't want to put a dog in. He wandered inside. A large black guy sprawled in front of a computer with a nervous-looking couple caught his eye and smiled, said he wouldn't be a moment.

'We have no references,' the woman was saying in halting English.

92

'No problem.'

'But without references, we cannot get a mortgage.'

'I can get you a mortgage,' the black man said confidently. 'I can get you anything.'

Passports, visas too, Tallis thought, ticking off the mental list. 'It's all right, I'll come back later,' Tallis said, walking back outside, narrowing his eyes against a bright sun and sky veined with light. From there, he made his way back to central London where he trawled the outside of two mosques. Studying the faces of the faithful leaving after Friday prayers, he was met with a wall of dark suspicion. As an antidote, he headed for Soho.

Six hours later, footsore and weary, Tallis returned to the hotel. Many years before, he'd gone out with a girl who'd worked in Great Marlborough Street, something in public relations, he thought. She'd invited him down for what he'd hoped was a dirty weekend. He'd met her at her office after work full of expectation. She'd taken him on a whistle-stop tour around Soho – maybe it was to get him in the mood. He'd been gobsmacked by the place. It had seemed like the centre of the universe, bursting with life and colour. It hadn't been the vice trade that had captured his attention, the restaurants, or the swirl of scandal boiling in the streets, but the presence of the film and television industry, all the small independent production companies, theatrical agents, actors' support groups. There had been people like he'd never seen them before;

with attitude, daring, assertive, look at me, darling. He'd loved the smell of success and, yes, the sometimes seediness, even liked the street names – Berwick, Frith, Brewer. It had seemed dangerously intoxicating to a poor lad brought up in the sticks. But that had been then. This time he looked with fresh eyes, jaded eyes maybe. When he spotted a small cinema it was one promising adult viewings, cards in windows advertised the prospect of a *good time*. It made him think only of Demarku and pain and exploitation, and no amount of gawping at astonishingly priced menus in staggeringly inviting eateries was going to change all that.

The following day he visited gyms, clubs and cafés. He hung out in several bars, eavesdropped on any number of conversations, flashed Demarku's latest mugshot to a couple of likely looking sorts and came up empty. As a devout Muslim, Demarku was unlikely to be found in a back-street boozer, but Tallis hoped that it might spark a connection, cause a chain reaction. With the aid of Google Earth, it was possible to locate a guy by the brand of condom he used. All you needed was an address in a suburb. Via a computer, you could trace a mobile-phone user, even with the phone on sleep mode, to within five hundred yards. But he had no address, no phone, no nothing, in fact. He was beginning to feel the awesome nature of the task ahead of him, wondered how he was going to get that one lucky break. Around four, he found himself in a bar full of old people and dispossessed-looking men and women on benefits, drinking their way to oblivion.

The old folk had red eyes and red faces, the younger lines and heavy jaws. The talk was of soap stars and TV shows and somebody's latest operation. Nobody spoke of politics or the state of the nation. Afterwards, he took a detour through Chinatown, eventually picking up the underground at Tottenham Court Road back to Euston. Not a very productive day.

But tomorrow would be different, he promised himself. Tomorrow he was going to a pub in Earl's Court. According to a snippet of conversation gleaned from two unsuspecting Croats rabbiting away on the tube, the place was well known for its eclectic clientele.

CHAPTER NINE

Sunday morning in London, beautifully warm and sunny, with only a few wisps of cloud in a sky panelled with light. Perfect. Resisting the temptation to visit the Imperial War Museum, Tallis decided to meander down the Kings Road, and eventually found himself staring into the branch windows of some very expensive estate agents. Their business cards, he noticed from a display, were printed in both Russian and Arabic. He wondered where the average well-heeled Albanian was buying property these days.

Walking up to Sloane Square, Tallis took a tube to Earl's Court. By one o' clock, he was sitting in a ratty-looking pub on the corner of Earl's Court

Road. Two days without a shave, his clothes slightly rumpled, he blended into the scenery well. The pub was crawling with down-and-outs and those whose dissolute hue suggested that they were recovering from last night's hangovers. Not easy, Tallis thought, when your head's throbbing with the blast of sound from Big Screen Sky TV and three pool tables.

Tallis took his drink and sat down at a beer-stained table overrun with last night's empties. Scouring the blunt-featured clientele, it wasn't long before Tallis heard the sound of *hrvatski*, the official language of Croatia, and traced it to two men standing at the bar. They looked to be in their mid to late twenties. Both had shaved heads. Both had flat, slanted cheekbones. One had the triangular physique of a bodybuilder on anabolic steroids. The other was smaller, less pumped up. They were rattling away, joshing one another, excited about something. Tallis pushed his way through to get closer. They were talking about a VAT scam with mobile phones. After five minutes or so the conversation switched to drugs: heroin and amphetamines.

Tallis listened. From the way they were talking it was clear they were small fry, runners for someone else. Tallis wondered who their supplier was. He listened some more but no name emerged. *'Oprosti!'* he said, breaking into the conversation. 'Excuse me.' The two men threw him slow, suspicious looks. Keeping his voice low, he asked whether they could supply him with some cocaine for personal use. He was careful to ask only for a small quantity so that he didn't alert their suspicions. The triangular-shaped guy ignored him. The other issued a flat, *'Ne razumijem'*. I don't understand.

'Come on, guys,' Tallis said persuasively, continuing to speak in their native tongue. 'I'm off my own patch. It's just to keep me going. Blood brothers and all that.'

Triangle shape burst out laughing.

Tallis looked him straight in the eye. 'If you can get more, I'll take it.'

The big guy stopped, stared. His sludgy-coloured eyes were unblinking. 'Where are you from?'

'Vukovar.'

Both men exchanged glances. As Tallis already knew, Vukovar struck an emotional chord in the heart of every Croat. It wasn't a place readily forgotten. A prosperous pretty little town on the Danube, Vukovar had once been the showcase for baroque architecture. No more. In the early 1990s, it had become a battleground, laid siege to by Serbian forces, a siege in which more than two thousand people had died, many more afterwards, a lot of them buried in mass graves. Tallis had visited once. The weather had been cold and damp and miserable, yet even if the sun had shone, the place would still have felt tainted. He thought of the town as a beautiful woman who'd had the misfortune to catch smallpox. Every street corner was pitted and made ugly by gunshot and mortar. Tallis remembered his grandmother weeping over its destruction.

The triangular-shaped man clapped a thick and meaty arm around Tallis's shoulders. 'Drink, my friend,' he said, ordering brandy. 'A pity it isn't *slijvovica,'* he added, referring to the fierce plum brandy traditionally drunk in Croatian restaurants. 'My name is Goran,' the big guy explained. 'This is Janko,' he said, indicating his waxy-faced friend.

'Marko Simunic,' Tallis said.

Two hours later, they were all drunk and the best of mates. Goran and Janko were originally from Split. Both had come to the UK at the start of the hostilities in Kosovo in 1999. Lying about their ages, they'd worked as bartenders for a couple of years before getting into a more lucrative line of business. As Tallis had guessed, they were runners for someone else. In return, Tallis told them that he'd been involved in a drug smuggling operation in the South-West. At this, Goran's flat, almost Slav features twitched into life. 'All you need is a fishing boat, a dinghy and some lobster pots.' Tallis laughed. He wasn't so drunk that he didn't know what he was saying. 'There are many small beaches, all of them accessible.'

'What about Customs?' Janko said.

'Non-existent.' Tallis grinned. 'They used to run small inshore boats but they got sold off. Officers now spend most of their time patrolling Dover, the major airports, this neck of the woods.'

'So you think it would be a good way in?'

'Oh, sure.'

'And you have contacts?' Tallis decided that Janko was the smart one.

'Yes.'

'Then what are you doing here?' A cunning light in Goran's eyes suggested that the brandy had not even begun to seep into his brain.

'Lying low.'

'From what?'

'A guy I pissed off.'

'How?'

'I wanted a slice of his action. It's being sorted.'
He's being sorted was the implication.

Janko seemed to accept the story. Goran didn't.
'Why do you choose to do business with us?'

'I told you.'

'Why *us?*' Goran persisted, evil-eyed.

'Hey,' Janko said. 'This is our friend, our brother.'

'More drinks,' Tallis said, standing up, feeling the heat.

'Sit down,' Goran snarled.

'Fuck you.'

The air was electric. Tallis had visions of thrown fists, thrown chairs.

Janko stepped in. 'Guys, guys, calm down. We are as one. Our enemies are the same.' He meant the Serbs, Tallis thought. 'Go get the drinks, Marco.'

Tallis felt more rattled than he should have done as he pushed his way to the bar. He took a few deep breaths. Told himself not to be so bloody unprofessional.

On his return, Goran had softened. 'This operation in Devon, it's easy to import the goods?'

'Dead easy.'

'We know someone,' Goran said, trading a look with Janko, 'someone we work with. He might be interested.'

'Yeah, who?'

'Our boss,' Janko chipped in. 'We need to run it past him. We'll let you know what he thinks.'

'Sounds good to me.'

'*Zivjeli!*' Goran said, raising his glass. 'As a sign of good faith, Janko has a tester for you. You like it, we can discuss more.'

Without a word, Janko stood up. Tallis knew the routine. They both headed for the toilets. Janko discreetly passed him a wrap, which Tallis pushed into his trouser pocket. Job done, they went back to Goran. 'You like girls?' he said.

Tallis grinned in what he hoped was a convincing manner. These guys were into machismo. To state otherwise would have displeased them.

'We fix you up,' Goran said, knocking back the rest of his brandy. 'Come.'

Tallis stood up and followed him. He didn't feel he had much choice.

They travelled in a bottom range Mercedes-Benz E-Class, still an impressive ride. Janko drove and broke into raucous song. Goran turned round, laughing. Tallis joined in, more as a cover than amusement. He was watching where they were taking him. They were headed for Hammer-smith. Tallis thought they'd go over the flyover and join the Great West Road. Instead, they dropped down underneath it.

Traffic seemed heavy for a Sunday. The sky was losing some of its light, the day its energy. The brandy was starting to kick in just behind Tallis's eyes. He closed them for what seemed a fraction of time. When he opened them they were outside a chip shop. Great, he thought. It would soak up some of the alcohol. The boys had other ideas.

Exchanging greetings with two men behind the counter, Janko and Goran led the way. Tallis followed them through a scullery and into a small, enclosed, paved yard. Encased in glass, fruitless vines hung from the roof, it smelt like a greenhouse. Instead of tomatoes growing, big hessian sacks of potatoes lined the walls. The yard formed a bridge between the chip shop and another building in which there was a closed door with an entry phone next to it. Goran pressed a button and spoke his name. There was a click and the door sprang open, leading into a narrow hall with a flight of stairs leading steeply up to a short landing. Carpeted in worn deep purple, the stairs had seen some action. They went up another flight, and through another door which opened out onto a dimly lit bar with barstools in faded leather. Tallis took it in at a glance – furnishings dark and indecipherable, three sofas, one of which looked badly sprung, door off to the right, one man, nervous looking. And no surprise, Tallis thought as a fat woman emerged from behind the counter. Well, not fat exactly. Not even overweight – more a human hulk with a pockmarked jaw and teeth like an Orc.

'This is Duka,' Goran said, grinning like a demented hyena.

Tallis looked at Goran, looked at the woman, stunned, thinking, Please, God, no.

'Duka looks after the girls,' Janko explained, with a laugh.

'Oh, right,' Tallis said, grinning now, sharing the joke.

'You want girl?' Duka probed a tooth with a dirty nail.

'Give him the new one' Goran said. 'On the house,' he added, a sly expression in his eyes. Tallis wondered what was expected in return for the favour.

Duka waddled along the length of the bar and out of sight, flesh sliding over flesh. Tallis heard a grunt, a curse then a jangling sound of metal. When Duka returned, she was sweating like an elephant on heat. 'Eleven,' Duka said, belligerently handing him a key.

'Through the door,' Janko explained. As Tallis pushed it open, he heard Goran order more brandy.

He stepped into a dingy corridor, doors off, not unlike a cheap hotel. He could hear nothing other than his own feet creaking on the thinly carpeted floor. Either business was lax or, as he suspected, the rooms were soundproofed. Number eleven was at the very end. He waited outside, collecting his thoughts, then slipped the key in the lock, turned it, tapped on the wood with his free hand as he entered, the sound hollow in the surrounding silence.

Inside smelt of cheap perfume and damp. A double bed dressed in black satin sheets, more funeral pyre than love nest, rested in the middle of a room that took seediness to another level. There was a cracked sink in the corner with a bottle of baby oil resting on the ledge. The window, from which hung faded brown polyester curtains, had bars. To the right of the window was a single wooden school chair on which a girl was seated.

Dark-haired, pallid, she gazed straight ahead with big eyes, seeing but not seeing. Tallis recognised the expression. He'd witnessed it before in the eyes of war-hardened civilians who had lost everyone and everything. The girl, no more than Felka's age, wore a black bra and panties. Her feet, resting square on the floor, were bare, nails polished but chipped. She possessed a full figure, the skin close knit and youthful. Her right arm was crossed over her left breast as if to protect herself, the fingers of her hand resting on the shoulder strap. She had a large, recent bruise on her thigh. She was breathing fast.

He approached her softly. She turned to him with large eyes and pushed the strap off her shoulder, allowing him a tantalising glimpse of her nakedness.

'No,' he said, looking around him for something to cover her with. Seeing nothing, he took off his jacket, put it round her shoulders. For the first time, she lifted her eyes and looked at him, whispering something he couldn't make out.

'It's all right,' he said, sitting down on the bed. 'I only want to talk.'

She swallowed hard, nodded.

'What's your name?'

She didn't answer, wouldn't answer. He wondered how long it had been since she'd felt like a person instead of a thing. 'Where are you from?'

She shook her head, sudden fear in her eyes. She glanced at the door. 'Nobody will hear us,' Tallis assured her.

Still the big-eyed stare.

'Do you understand me?'

The flicker of light in her eyes told him she did. 'Were you brought here?'

She opened her mouth very slightly, closed it.

'Against your will?'

Her dark eyes filled with tears.

'I can get you out of here,' Tallis said urgently, 'but first I need your help.'

Her face sagged. She looked down at the floor. He'd blown it, he thought. 'My name is...' He wanted her trust but knew that telling the truth could get both of them into a lot of trouble. He started again. 'The guys out there know me as Marco,' he told her, 'but my real name is Max.'

'Max,' she said softly, as if committing his name and her lifeline to memory.

'Yeah.' Tallis smiled warmly. 'I have a wife and kids and I live in a lovely big house in a village called Belbroughton, not far from Birmingham.' Then, meshing fact with fiction, he told her about where he'd grown up, that he hadn't always been so successful, that he, perhaps like her, had come from humble beginnings.

She gazed at him in awe. 'Thing is,' Tallis said, wondering how long he'd got before the others became suspicious. 'I need to find this man.' He pulled out the most recent photograph of Demarku, showed it to her. 'You recognise him?'

The girl drew back, shook her head sadly, disappointed that she couldn't help.

'His name is Agron Demarku. He's an Albanian with a history of violence towards prostitutes.'

Again, the closed-down expression.

'Do you talk much with the other girls?' Tallis said.

She gave a mournful shrug.

'All right,' he said, gently slipping the jacket off her shoulders. 'See what you can find out. I'll return tomorrow night.' Without looking back, he left the room.

There was no sign of Janko or Goran. 'They left,' Duka said tonelessly.

'They say anything?' Tallis said.

'Nothing.' Duka glowered.

Retracing his steps, Tallis found his way back to the chip shop. He caught the eye of one of the two men who'd greeted Goran and Janko. 'Here,' the man said smiling, handing Tallis a portion of fish and chips in a small plastic tray. Small and wiry, he had a broken front tooth and blunt features. He spoke Croatian, his accent suggesting that he, too, was from the north. 'Goran says to meet him back at The Courtfield tomorrow night at eleven.' Tallis thanked him and began to eat. Food customers came and went. Other punters, knowing the ropes, walked straight through. Tallis dismembered a piece of fish. The batter was chewy, but he was hungry and didn't care. During a lull Tallis turned to the small guy.

'Known Goran long?'

'Three years.'

'Good guy to do business with?'

The small man leant over the glass, the genial manner gone. 'No questions.'

Tallis smiled a *fair enough*. 'Thanks again for the chips. Be seeing you. She was good, by the way,' he called over his shoulder.

The evening was spitting with rain. Logging the exact location of the chip shop, he began to walk, finishing his supper on the way. He soon found himself in a mixed sprawl of residential and industrial estate. Low-flying aircraft indicated he was near the airport, the sheer density of houses suggesting that they'd been there first. A gang of kids shambled along the road towards him. One was on a bike, zigzagging along the pavement, the others larking about behind, effing this and effing that. On seeing two girls walking up the other side of the road, they let out a stream of sexual abuse. The oldest lad, who happened to be of mixed race, looked to be about fourteen years old. Tallis wondered if this was the future, if they were the next generation of thugs. Drawing near, it became clear from the feral expressions on the boys' faces that nobody was going to step aside, nobody was giving ground. He should have done the simple thing and walked round them. Better to be safe than wind up dead with a knife in your stomach, but Tallis felt in a perverse mood. He kept on walking, calling their bluff, his eyes fixed on the ringleader riding the bike. As Tallis predicted, the lad swerved at the last minute to avoid him, the others following suit. Not quite so hard as you think you are, Tallis thought with a smile.

The urban landscape was changing. Roads were wider and busier, the concrete more connected and commercial, less grim. There were airport hotels where you could walk into Reception and catch a glimpse of people in swimming costumes kick-starting their holidays, sipping pina coladas around bathtub-temperature swimming pools. Maybe Tremlett, the probation officer, was right, Tallis thought, if not about the ethnicity of the inhabitants, about the location. On he walked, occasionally glancing over his shoulder, for an irrational moment feeling as if he were being followed. Eventually, seeing a taxi, Tallis stuck two fingers in his mouth and whistled. Dropping the plastic tray in a nearby bin, he sprinted across the road and instructed the driver to take him to Euston.

'Fair way to go,' the cabbie said, dubious.

Tallis suddenly realised how dishevelled he looked, unshaven, smelling of booze and fish and chips. He pulled out a wad of notes. The driver told him to hop in. 'You often do this run?' Tallis asked.

'Several times a day, usually pick-ups from Heathrow.'

'Know the area well, then.'

The cabbie laughed. 'Stating the bleeding obvious, if you don't mind my saying.'

'What about the people living here?'

'What about them?'

'Good mix of cultures?'

'You mean how many immigrants we got here?'

'Well, I wouldn't...'

'Answer to that's bloody hundreds of them. Slough's an Asian stronghold. Here's full of Eastern Europeans and Polish. Well,' the cabbie said, blowing out between his teeth, 'don't get me started. Poles all over the bleedin' place, ain't they? Begging, and doing us out of a living and all that. Me, I live in Dagenham. Know where I belong.'

Bet you vote BNP, Tallis thought. 'Many Albanians live here?'

'Shouldn't wonder. Know how to use guns,

107

don't they?'

Everyone from the Balkans knows how to use a gun, you prat, Tallis thought.

They pulled up at some lights. Tallis whipped out the photograph of Demarku, held it up for the driver. 'Seen this guy before?'

The cabbie looked in his rear-view mirror. 'Not a clue, mate.'

'You sure?'

The cabbie eyed it again. 'Mate of yours, is he?'

'No. Someone I need to find.'

'Right,' the cabbie said, looking again. 'Bit of a sort, ain't he?'

'Think so?'

'Know so. Looks like a bleedin' foreigner.'

CHAPTER TEN

Dog-tired, Tallis slept most of Monday. After his customary run and shower, he left the hotel around two, ambled down Tottenham Court Road and found a café where he ordered and ate a sandwich before making his way across London and over the river to the Imperial War Museum. Some hours later, sobered and not a little depressed, he retraced his way back, walking through St James's Park to clear his head then catching the tube to Westbourne Grove to an Italian restaurant he'd seen advertised in a free newspaper. After downing a plate of prosciutto and pasta with clams, washed down with two glasses of house red and finished off with a heavy-duty espresso, he took another tube to Hounslow West, changing once.

It was after nine when he reached the chip shop, two hours before his meeting with Goran in Earl's Court. Tallis walked in, exchanged a glance with the small, wiry guy who'd given him the chips the day before. This time there was less warning in his manner: he came across as relaxed, bordering on friendly. 'Back already?' Then with a leer, he said, 'That good, huh?'

'The best, but this time I pay,' Tallis said with a grin, taking out his wallet.

'Duka takes care of it. Go on through,' he indicated with his thumb. 'Know where to go.'

Duka was mean and malodorous. She turned her slow eyes on Tallis who explained he wanted the same girl as the night before. 'No,' Duka said without explanation.

Tallis smiled as though he didn't understand, part of his brain racing. Had the girl talked? Had she betrayed him? 'She with someone else?'

'Yes.'

'Then I'll wait.'

'No,' Duka said again, emphatic.

Tallis raised an eyebrow. This time he wasn't smiling. Duka shrugged. 'Take another girl or come back tomorrow.' Who gives a shit? her expression implied.

Tallis walked straight up to her, put his face close to her face, inhaling breath foul with garlic and tooth decay and hostility. 'I'll come back tomorrow afternoon at two. Make sure she's here.' Then he turned on his heel and walked back the way he'd come.

Tallis was three hundred yards from the pub when two blokes in hoodies appeared from nowhere and jumped him. The biggest bloke was in front of Tallis, the other slighter figure moving to the left, catching Tallis on his blind side. It was a typical pincer movement and one he was familiar with. Had it been one assailant, he would have reacted differently, perhaps tried to talk him down, but with two, the odds were greatly against him. Only one thing for it, he thought. Attack.

Eyes flicking to the right, locating the bloke's jaw line, Tallis pushed off his back leg, letting out a blood-curdling scream and simultaneously lashing out with an elbow. His reward a gratifying snap as he connected with the man's jawbone, felling his attacker and knocking him into the side of a car parked illegally in the road. A split second later, the bloke built like a brick wall had landed a right hook heavy enough to make Tallis's brain rattle around his head. Immediately, Tallis grabbed the man's hood with both hands, forcing him down, and brought his own knee up sharply, smashing into his opponent's head. The man rocked backwards momentarily then pulled out a blade. Suddenly, everything slowed. Tallis knew that the situation could cut up very dirty, very quickly and wondered whether the guy was pumped up on drugs.

Almost crouching, his attacker sliced the air with his knife hand, feinting with the other. Tallis, eyes fixed on his assailant, waited for the strike then blocked the guy's knife hand with a forearm

110

punch. Kicking out with his foot, and hooking it round the guy's thigh, he knocked him off balance. As he crashed to the pavement, knife flailing, Tallis moved in to stamp on the guy's chest. To his astonishment, the man raised his hands, and let out a laugh. The hood had slipped back, revealing a face: Goran.

'Fuckin' weird sense of humour,' Tallis said in Croatian, grabbing Goran's arm and pulling him up. 'Oh, Christ,' he said, looking at the staggering figure unpeeling himself from the wing of a Mini. 'That Janko?'

'You fight good,' Janko said, eyes rolling, still dazed.

'Come,' Goran said, slapping his arm around Tallis's shoulder. 'We drink. We celebrate. Then we meet Iva.'

Iva had the bearing of a rattlesnake. He was tall and thin with deep hooded eyes that never let you know what was going on behind them. As Tallis had clearly passed his little initiation ceremony with flying colours, he seemed affable enough, but Tallis wouldn't have trusted him as far as he could have thrown the mighty Duka. By now, Janko and Goran had melted into the background. This was Iva's show.

Iva was from Osijek, a large town on the south bank of the river Drava. Like Vukovar, its near neighbour, it had suffered heavy bombardment during the hostilities in 1991. Tallis prayed Iva wasn't going to quiz him about his so-called homeland and his alleged activities during the war. Fortunately, Iva appeared more curious

111

about Tallis's commercial interests.

'The boys say you have contacts in the South-West,' Iva said, taking a sip of brandy, his lazy eyes focused on Tallis.

'That's right,' Tallis said. 'We like to make extensive use of the region's natural resources.'

Iva inclined his head.

'Fishermen are key to the success of the enterprise,' Tallis explained.

'And heroin is so much more lucrative than cod, I think,' Iva said with a slow smile. 'Tell me how it works.'

'Drugs are generally imported through larger foreign vessels coming from the usual routes – cocaine either from the Caribbean or Colombia, cannabis from North Africa through Morocco and Spain. We have a deal going on at the moment with one of the cross-Channel ferries, but that's a separate venture,' Tallis said, hoping that this would tempt Iva to take him seriously and realise that he was playing with someone in a bigger league. 'Smaller craft meet the foreign vessels out at sea, take the goods and land them in one of the many coves along the coast. It's an old-fashioned technique, once used for smuggling contraband, and known as coopering. Goods are recovered and driven up the motorway to wherever you want them.'

'And police?'

'When did you last go to Devon?' Tallis snorted. 'Plods are only concerned with boat theft and CD players nicked from cars.'

'I have never been to Devon.'

'Well, now's your chance. I'll show you the

112

sights,' Tallis said with a smile.

Iva didn't react. This bloke was nobody's mate, Tallis thought.

'I understand you've pissed someone off,' Iva said.

'He pissed me off.'

Iva gave a thoughtful nod. 'You work alone?'

'Does anyone?'

'What would your colleagues think?'

'About what?'

'Doing business with us.'

'As long as there's money in it, they'd be happy,' Tallis smiled.

'So you can effect an introduction?'

'Naturally.'

Iva nodded again and asked Tallis where he could be contacted. Tallis gave him his number and they agreed to talk some more the following day.

This time there were no problems. Tallis paid Duka and went straight to room eleven. The girl was sitting in exactly the same place. Only her face was different. A bruise was blossoming on one of her cheekbones and her bottom lip was puffy and split. Tallis moved silently towards her, rested a hand on the top of her head, making her flinch. He kept it there, stroked her hair, talking softly. 'Tell me your name.'

She looked up at him. A tear rolled down her cheek. 'Elena.'

'Why are you crying, Elena?'

'Nobody asked my name before.'

Tallis crouched down so that his eyes were level

with hers. 'It's the perfect name for a very pretty girl. Here, I've brought you this.' He reached into his jacket pocket and handed her a bar of chocolate. She took it shyly, with caution, as if she expected him to snatch it back. 'Go on, eat,' he said.

She looked up at him and smiled for the very first time since he'd met her. It reminded him of light on clear water. Reminded him of Belle.

'Where are you from?'

'Lithuania,' she said in a small voice, biting a chunk off and offering the rest to Tallis who politely refused. She ate carefully, with great self-consciousness, as though embarrassed. When she'd finished, she said, 'Take me away?'

He didn't know how he was going to do it but he knew that it was impossible to leave her there. Again, he was reminded of Belle. 'Trust me?'

She nodded.

'Good.'

'I have something for you, too,' she said, her voice not much more than a whisper. 'The man you are looking for. He is sometimes known as Mickovic. He lives in Belgravia.'

Tallis gently smiled. 'Can't be right. This man has only just come out of prison. It's a very expensive part of London. How could he afford to live there?'

'It is true,' the girl said firmly. 'He travels in a Mercedes, new plates, black.'

Sounded like everyone's idea of a gangster's mode of transport. 'How do you know this?'

'One of the girls remembered him. He's very cruel, brutal. He hates women.'

'She say anything else about him?'

'She said he smelt of trees.'

Cedar, a classic fragrance in men's aftershave, Tallis thought, remembering what Crow had said. 'All right,' he said, getting up. 'Act normally. I'll come and get you when the time's right.'

'Soon?' she said, grabbing hold of his arm, her eyes pleading.

He put his hand over hers. 'I promise.'

'She's just one girl, for Chrissakes.'

'My point entirely,' Cavall said.

'I'm not asking you to send in an army.'

'Look, when I told you to call this number, it was specifically for problems. This is not a problem. This is you thinking with your dick.'

Tallis bit down hard. He wanted Cavall's help too much to rise to a jibe like that. 'The girl's given me valuable information.'

'Checked it out?'

'Not yet, but I'm onto it.' He was sitting in a taxi, heading for Belgravia.

'*If* the intel's good, we might be able to do something.'

Might? Tallis stared at the floor. 'Forget it. Sorry I asked.'

'Good,' Cavall said crisply. 'Glad we've got that out of the way. Can't afford to be sidetracked...'

'But—'

'Put it like this, we send in the cavalry, she goes home, next thing you know she's retrafficked to Greece. All a bit of a waste of our time.'

'Sure, thanks.'

'Call me soon, Paul. We're counting on you.'

Tallis closed his phone and looked disconsolately out of the window. Streets and shops and people rushing about in a game called living. Without exception, the women were slim, attractive and well maintained, the men taut and ambitious, the cream of the gene pool. Then he had an idea. He slid open his phone again and called Micky Crow.

Tallis didn't make it to Belgravia. He was intercepted by a phone call from Iva who told him that they were on for a meet at the pub. Tallis thought it an unlikely venue but didn't argue. Instructing the cabbie to drop him off at Hammersmith, he walked the rest of the way. A prickly feeling in his gut told him that something was off. As a precaution, he took out the photograph of Demarku, shredded it and pushed it into the nearest rubbish bin.

Goran and Janko were waiting for him at the bar. They went through the usual comrade routine– *'Bok, kako si?'*, *Hi, how are you?* – and ordered drinks, though on this occasion Tallis was careful to pick Pepsi. He explained to the boys that he had a bad stomach. After two hours of chatting about cars and football and the fact that the actress Sharon Stone had a home on the Dalmatian coast, Iva appeared. As expected, Goran and Janko made themselves scarce. Obviously, the boss liked to do business alone.

'Drink?' Tallis said.

Iva looked at his watch. 'No time. Ready?'

'Sure.'

He followed Iva outside where a black Mercedes with new plates was waiting. Iva opened the door for Tallis in a curiously hospitable gesture that made Tallis nervous. Tallis smiled a thank you and climbed in. Iva, next to him, instructed the driver to start driving, and fell silent. Tallis took his cue from Iva and didn't utter a word.

They arrived in Knightsbridge, pulling up outside a smart perfumery. Iva got out and Tallis followed. The shop was all bright lights and whiteness, like a space-age pharmacy. A heavily made-up young woman stood behind a counter. She, too, was dressed in white, although there was nothing virginal about her manner: too pouting, too come and get me. Tallis flicked his eyes to the rows of clear glass bottles filled with varying shades of oil and scent and read the names, ylang-ylang, rose otto, bergamot, neroli...

Iva leant towards the woman, murmured something in her ear. Nodding in agreement, she walked to the front of the shop, locking the door, turning the open sign to closed then led them through a door at the back and into a warren of rooms, each connected like a spider's web. There were boxes and boxes of top-brand mobile phones. Tallis felt a sense of creeping unease as door after door closed behind him.

He heard the voice of the man before he saw him. 'Did you know that musk is gathered from the balls of musk deer, Marco?' The man, who had his back to him, turned round with a blinding smile. Two months in the outside world had put weight on his body and colour in his cheeks. His hair, tinted blond, was well cut. His hands looked manicured, clothes expensive. In short, his manner and bearing were regal. But there was no mistake. This was definitely Demarku. Tallis could hardly believe his luck. 'Musk forms the basis for nearly every fragrance,' he continued, speaking in heavily accented English.

'Brings out the animal in us, I guess,' Tallis said.

'Very good.' Demarku let out a laugh. 'You speak good English, too.'

'Have my mother to thank for that. She's British but married a Croat.'

'Unusual,' Demarku said, still smiling. Tallis remembered what Crow had said. *He'd as soon as slip a blade between your ribs as look at you. Probably smile while he was doing it.* 'Does it trouble you that I'm Albanian?'

'Why would it? I have great respect for your people.'

'Our two nations have suffered much together,' Demarku said, his voice sombre.

'What has happened to our people is indeed shameful,' Tallis agreed.

'I hate the pig-eating Serbs, and their ethnic-cleansing campaigns,' Demarku said, his eyes dark with hatred. For a moment, he seemed lost in time. Was he thinking of all the days he'd spent helplessly in prison when his fellow countrymen in nearby Kosovo had been slaughtered? Tallis didn't know.

'Drink?'

'No, thanks,' Tallis said. 'Unless you have water.'

Demarku flashed another smile of approval. Without order or invitation, the woman scurried off, returning minutes later with a tray of bottled mineral water and three glasses. After obediently pouring, she left the room. Iva, meanwhile, took up a position at the back, one foot resting on the wall. Tallis wondered whether it was intended as a veiled warning.

'Please, sit,' Demarku said, indicating one of two leather chairs. There was a weird graciousness about the man, Tallis thought. He seemed capable of exuding warmth but in the same way an electric fire heated a room while sucking all the air from the atmosphere. 'Iva tells me you have an operation in place that might interest us.'

'Correct.'

'We have our own suppliers,' Demarku said – rather sketchily, Tallis thought. 'But we're always looking for new ways to import.'

'I understand.'

'I gather you use small craft to land the catch.'

'Yes.'

'And you have runners in place to do the pick-ups? We wouldn't want some beach bum freeloading on several kilos of amphetamines.'

'This can all be arranged – for a price.'

'Ah, yes,' Demarku said. 'Everything and everyone has its price.' He studied Tallis for a moment. Tallis was reminded of the great Brazilian footballer, Ronaldhino. He had a wonderful knack of looking one way while kicking the ball the other. 'We like to build good working relationships with the people we decide to do business with,' Demarku continued. 'Trust is essential. Can we trust you, Marco?'

'I think Iva can vouch for me,' Tallis said, glancing over his shoulder.

Demarku laughed. It was strangely high-pitched. 'Iva trusts no one.'

'Don't blame him.'

Demarku threw back his head and laughed again. Tallis found it contrived. There was no humour in the man, only vanity.

'Agreed, but enough business,' Demarku said, getting up. 'I understand you enjoy women.'

For fuck's sake, this was getting beyond a joke, Tallis thought. 'Well, I...'

'I've planned something special,' Demarku said, sharp-eyed, the sub-text: do not disappoint me. 'Please, join us.'

Tallis felt his smile wasting away. He didn't like the sound of *us*.

He felt nothing but horror.

The room was small and airless. Even Demarku's aftershave couldn't mask the smell of sweat, blood and fear. Throughout the entire ordeal, Tallis was in conflict: save the woman or punish the men?

Apart from two chairs and the camera spotted when he first entered, there was nothing else. No need. Everything was attached to the walls – restraints, whips, handcuffs, knives.

The woman was absolutely terrified. As they ripped her clothes from her, she pleaded and begged then screamed, and the more she screamed, the more Demarku smiled.

Tallis was invited to join in with the rape but he fell back on an old excuse he'd learnt while undercover. 'Sorry, some tart gave me the clap. I'm on pills the size of an ostrich egg.'

'And why you're not drinking,' Demarku

commented shrewdly. 'Another time, then. Take a seat. Watch. Enjoy.'

Iva took his turn first, followed by Demarku. Then they 'spit-roasted' the woman, one having sex in front while the other sodomised her. It was cold, savage and brutal.

Skin crawling, bile rising from his gut, Tallis used every mental weapon to feign enjoyment, knowing that to fail would blow his cover. When they started on her with knives, he feared they were going to kill her, that he was watching a snuff movie in the making. What would it take to make them stop? he roared inside. Could he rush Iva, by far the more dangerous, and take on Demarku? Could he bag him and call Cavall? Should he die trying? When approaching a dog, if you surprise it, it's more likely to bite. It was the same with humans. He didn't want either of them reaching for a knife or a gun, and the brief stated that the handover should be with absolute discretion and a minimum of fuss, with no other parties involved. No other witnesses, Tallis suspected grimly. Like it or not, he felt forced to sit it out.

By the time they finished, the white-painted walls were spattered red. The woman, in great pain and barely conscious, was like a piece of raw meat.

Afterwards, both men having showered and changed, Tallis walked with Demarku out onto the street. Rain lacerated the pavement. The air felt dense with traffic fumes, but it felt good, so good to be out in the open, to be back in the real world instead of the stuff of nightmares.

121

'You look pale, my friend,' Demarku said.

'Really?' Tallis smiled. He took Demarku's hand, clasped it in both of his, thanked him warmly and promised to be in touch.

Demarku wished him goodbye, turned to leave then turned back. 'Oh, Marco,' he called.

'Yes?'

'Something you haven't asked me.'

Shit, Tallis thought. He'd slipped up and Demarku was on to it. 'What's that, then?'

'My name.'

'Never remember names,' Tallis bluffed. 'Now faces, especially memorable faces...'

'My friends call me Agron,' Demarku said, obviously delighted by the implied compliment.

As soon as Tallis was clear of the perfumery, he vomited into the gutter.

CHAPTER ELEVEN

The next morning, haggard from guilt and loss of sleep, Tallis returned early, and staked out the perfumery from a café on the opposite side of the street. Rain was pouring down, making the roads look like polished slate. He'd followed Goran and Janko's example and thrown on a hoodie, not because of the weather but to protect his identity.

At eight-thirty, a white van drove up outside the shop. Goran and Janko got out, went in, came out an hour later with a roll of carpet under their arms, struggling with it before throwing it in the back of the van. Tallis's alarm bells rang. As the two men drove away, he thought the poor, unfortunate woman from the previous afternoon had been inside. What to do? Stick rigidly to the brief, risk upsetting Cavall, or contact Crow again? And tell her what?

He pulled out his phone. Demarku had to be picked up. Nothing could jeopardise the plan. But neither could he simply leave the woman to the tender care of Goran and Janko. After a moment's deliberation, he made an anonymous call to the police, giving the registration of the white van.

At ten, Demarku arrived, spent an hour talking to the woman in the shop then left. Tallis followed.

Demarku's first stop was a jeweller's shop where he spent fifteen minutes trying on several watches before leaving empty-handed. He spent an hour in a gent's outfitters and walked out with a pale grey single-breasted suit and several shirts. Next, he asked to see a pair of black shoes with a two-hundred-pound price tag. After he'd tried them on he paid for them in cash. The man was an out-and-out narcissist, Tallis thought. He didn't simply care about looking good – it was his reason for being. As for funds, either he'd managed to acquire some wealth before he'd gone inside and had hung onto it, or there was a big fish somewhere, acting as Demarku's paymaster.

Tallis dropped back, heart racing, and followed Demarku down Lowndes Street. The rain was lighter now but still persistent, yet Demarku was walking as if he hadn't a care in the world. For all his guile and cunning, Tallis thought grimly, Demarku was oblivious to the man stalking his every move.

There were more trees, more greenery, giving him cover as he followed his prey through leafy Belgrave Square through streets that were tranquil and moneyed. He passed four-storey Georgian houses with chandeliers and huge drapes at the windows and black-painted railings outside. How many millions of pounds would it cost to live in a place like this? Tallis wondered, incomprehensibly. Then Demarku turned. Instinctively, Tallis turned, too, cupping his hand, pretending to light a cigarette, watching out of the corner of his eye as his man ran up three stone steps to a house and let himself in. Now what? he thought. Make the call or wait? He knew from his time on close-target reconnaissance that if an arrest was to be carried out, it's imperative you got the right premises. And he just wasn't sure.

Tallis crossed over the road, hoping that Cavall's people were ready to move in, that they were on permanent standby. But there was every chance that this was not Demarku's home. Perhaps he had powerful friends or a rich lover, someone with a heavy taste in S&M. Either that or he was squatting. While Tallis was deliberating, the front door swung open. Out came Demarku. He'd changed into jeans and a black roll-neck sweater, the shopping left behind. Looking left then right, he turned back the way he'd come. Tallis waited ten seconds then slowly picked up the chase.

The Albanian Embassy in Grosvenor Gardens came into view. Demarku slowed his pace. For a confused moment, Tallis thought he was actually going inside, but Demarku walked past, moved on. Perhaps it was nothing more than an instinctive connection with the fatherland.

Turning into the tube station, Demarku took the Victoria line to Warren Street, changing to the Northern line. Tallis, travelling in the compartment behind, kept pace, his focus only on the man, any qualms he had about the ethics of what he was doing dispelled by the events he'd witnessed the day before and his inability to prevent them. When Demarku got off at Camden Town, Tallis followed.

They were in a matrix of grubby streets and worn-out buildings, where the pub windows were mostly boarded up and there was dog shit on the pavement. Demarku was ten metres in front and slowing. A man in a crumpled suit nodded to him and he nodded back. Home territory, Tallis registered.

'Oi, Paul, you old bastard,' a voice yelled, 'what you doing here?'

Tallis resisted the strong instinct to jump. He didn't even turn, kept on walking. Demarku, however, had turned round and was looking intently at them.

'Hey,' the voice yelled again, angry now. 'You ignoring me or what?'

Tallis whipped round, keeping his back to Demarku, thanking God for the added protection afforded by the hoodie. 'Keep your voice down, Stu,' he snarled quietly.

125

Stu stared at him, red-eyed and dissolute. His breath reeked of so much lager Tallis thought he was probably flammable. Unsteady on his feet, loose-mouthed, Stu had the drunk's typical loss of volume control.

'I'm not supposed to be here,' Tallis snarled.

'Wha' you mean?'

'For Chrissakes, shut up.'

Stu looked shocked, then confused, then furious. He poked Tallis in the chest with a finger. 'Fuck you think you're ordering about? You're not in the—'

'How much have you had, Stu?' Tallis said, touching his arm, desperate to steer Stu away. Out of the corner of his eye, he saw Demarku still looking.

'Nothin'. Me, I'm on the wagon.'

On the wagon to Stu meant low-strength lager. Fifty shots usually achieved the same hit as several normal pints. And it wasn't even lunchtime. 'Look,' Tallis said softly, eyes drilling into his friend's face. 'This is condition red.'

Stu blinked, nodded, sobered up. Condition red was the phrase used for when an arrest was imminent.

'I'll meet you at that pub,' Tallis said, gesturing to a decrepit-looking place on the opposite side of the road. 'Give me an hour.'

Stu shuffled away. When Tallis turned round, Demarku was nowhere to be seen.

Fuck, fuck, fuck. The streets all looked the same. The houses all looked the same. Even the bloody road markings were the same. In spite of scanning every building, every alley, the guy had

126

vanished into the urban ether. He only hoped to God that Demarku hadn't rumbled him.

Finally, retracing his steps, and about to cross the road, he saw something that brought him up short. The street was a dogleg and easy to miss but, parked on the corner, was a gleaming black Mercedes with new plates. Tallis sauntered over, noticed the heavy-duty sensor winking at him from the dash. Taking a step back, he kicked the passenger door, putting his full weight behind it. As predicted, the alarm went off, emitting a high-pitched screeching noise that made the leaves dance on the trees. Swiftly crossing the road, Tallis ducked behind a wheelie-bin and watched. Thirty seconds later, Demarku emerged from a tall squalid-looking house several metres down the road, a clutch of keys in his hand. Pointing at the car's sensor, he switched off the alarm and inspected the car, cursing and spitting with fury at the damage. Tallis swallowed hard, felt his palms itch with suppressed rage. The guy could get steamed up about a dent in a car wing, but gouges and cuts and bruises on a woman's skin only moved him to laughter.

Demarku spoke urgently into his cellphone, rattling orders in Albanian. Tallis listened. Demarku neither made mention of being followed nor of being betrayed. As Demarku returned to the house, Tallis pulled out his own phone and made the call to Cavall.

Ten minutes later, a black BMW turned into the street, a man and woman inside, and double-parked in front of the Mercedes. Tallis straightened up, made his way towards them, exchanging glances. 'You Tallis?' the man said. He was dressed casually, as was his companion. They looked so ordinary and unremarkable, Tallis wouldn't have given either of them a second glance, apart from the fact both were wearing leather gloves, which on a summer's day seemed distinctly odd.

Tallis agreed with his eyes. 'You must be the immigration officers.'

The woman answered. 'That's right.'

'Target's in number twenty-nine.'

'Thanks. We'll take it from here.'

'I'd like to come with you.'

'Not necessary, sir.' The woman spoke again. She had pale blue eyes, plain, vapid features.

'How are you going to get him? Knock on the door and hope he comes quietly?' Tallis smiled a warning, eyes level with hers. 'This guy knows me. He'll respond without any aggro.'

The man looked at the woman who looked at Tallis then gave the go-ahead. Interesting, Tallis thought. The woman was the decision-maker.

The house was split into three flats. The first button on the entry phone was marked Patel, the second Cookley, and the third nothing. Tallis pressed the button for the third flat.

'*Po?*' Yes.

'Agron? Marco.'

'What are you doing here? How do you know where I live?'

Tallis imagined his face, imagined the lines of suspicion etching his eyes. 'You have a problem.'

'What sort of problem?'

'Iva.' Tallis stared into the eyes of the man

128

standing next to him – unreadable.

Silence. Now there'd be confusion, Tallis thought. After what seemed like an interminable time, Agron spoke. 'OK.'

Tallis looked at the others, giving them a good to go expression as they sneaked in behind him and ascended three flights of stairs.

The door to the flat was ajar. Tallis recognised it as a possible killing ground. Doorways or any point of entry were known as coffin corridors. Tallis scanned the entrance, stepped in. Agron greeted him with a smile on his face and stiletto in his hand. Tallis went to step forward to disarm him but the agency people swooped like a pair of Valkyries, knocking the blade onto the floor, the guy head-butting Demarku and pushing him to the ground. No ordinary immigration officials, Tallis thought, wondering what section they worked for.

Pinning Demarku's hands behind his back, the woman clapped on a pair of handcuffs and hauled him up onto a chair. Tallis squatted down in front of him. 'When was the last time you got it up without beating a woman senseless?'

Demarku smiled, threw his head back, and spat into Tallis's face. Tallis wiped the spittle from his cheek, returned the smile. 'Get him out of here,' he said, straightening up, striding out.

He told the woman what he would do to her, physically and sexually, in explicit detail. He said that she would never be safe, that he had friends in high places, that they would come for her in the night and take her and torture her, and that

129

she would pray and plead for death.

She did not speak. She showed no emotion.

The man returned, carrying a bottle of whisky, which he gave to the woman who unscrewed the cap. The man clamped both hands on his mouth, wrenched at his jaw. Demarku twisted and struggled, would not open his mouth. The man hit him, knocked him almost senseless. Next thing, the woman was pouring the contents down his throat, choking him, drowning him, some of the fiery infidel liquor spilling down his neck and sweater, the stink of it strong in his nostrils. He retched and gasped, tasting the bitterness on his tongue, feeling his eyes swell, his brain uncouple. When they were done, they took off his handcuffs, dragged him to his feet, pulled him through to the bedroom and over to the open window.

He began to curse and kick and struggle. For a second, he broke free, fleeing to the bathroom, locking the door after him, trying to escape through the locked window, nails tearing blindly at the frame. He couldn't think, or focus, the alcohol making everything swim before his eyes. He felt sick with the violation, sick with terror. Then they broke down the door, came for him, hauled him back out, dragging his body mercilessly across the floorboards, battering it against the doorframe. He saw the open window and screamed.

Falling and falling, his final vision was of the railings coming up to meet him.

Tallis didn't meet Stu as arranged. Three hours in

the company of a tanked-up Glaswegian wasn't his idea of a good time. Instead, he returned to the hotel, took a shower, and shaved for the first time in days. His cellphone went just as he was coming out of the bathroom. It was Crow.

'Word of advice – leave the intelligence gathering to us?'

'This supposed to be cryptic or witty?'

'She wasn't there.'

'What do you mean, she wasn't there?'

'You dim as well? She wasn't fuckin' there. In fact, nothing and nobody was there other than several portions of cod and chips and the odd saveloy.'

'Oh, for Chrissakes.'

'Don't get shitty with me,' Crow said. 'I've just made myself look a complete fool. In fact, I'm thinking of doing you for wasting police time.'

Tallis put his hand to his head. It was like living in some horrible parallel universe. 'But the rooms, the bar, the girls.'

'The rooms were just rooms. No sign of elicit goings-on. No evidence.'

Tallis fell silent. Perhaps Elena had talked. Maybe Duka had got wind and sounded the alarm. Certainly, someone had got there first. Maybe Cavall had relented, or maybe that was wishful thinking. He couldn't bear to imagine what might have happened to Elena.

'Something else,' Crow said menacingly.

'Yeah?'

'Know anything about the abduction of a badly mutilated woman this morning?'

'Mutilated?'

'Cut to ribbons. Poor cow was barely alive.'

Alive. Thank God, Tallis thought. Then a worrying thought struck him. Would she be able to identify him as one of the men in the perfumery?

'We caught the blokes responsible red-handed,' Crow continued.

'Congratulations.'

'They were both Croats.'

'So?'

'So,' she said, a penetrating note in her voice, 'you deny all knowledge?'

'I do.'

'You know nothing about an anonymous tip-off?' Crow pressed.

'Nothing.'

An uneasy silence prevailed. Tallis knew he wasn't believed. He had the unmistakable impression that this was not the last he'd hear from the woman, and instantly felt bad for dragging her into his mess. 'You really in trouble?' he said, contrite.

'Been in worse.'

'I'm really sorry. I–'

'Forget it,' she said, sounding more pissed off than angry, 'but this thing with Demarku, you should leave it alone. He's like the Scottish play. One mention of the name and all manner of disaster follows.'

CHAPTER TWELVE

Tallis paid his bill and checked out of the hotel with the intention of catching the next train back to Birmingham. Cavall had other plans.

'Nice work,' she said, congratulating him. Was it? he thought. A girl lost, a woman desperately injured, and he'd done fuck all to save either of them. He should have just taken Elena, kicked Demarku's and Iva's heads in, and to hell with the consequences, but, no, he'd just had to follow orders. 'Handover go all right?'

'With Bill and Ben?' he said humorously.

'Bill and Ben?' Cavall, not getting the joke, sounded confused.

'The immigration officers. Yeah, I'd say so. Fortunate as Demarku pulled a knife.'

'Naturally, you'll be properly remunerated. We'll meet for a debrief tomorrow morning, early.'

'How early?'

'Six-thirty.'

'Where?'

'Epping Forest.'

'That wise?'

'Why?'

'Gangster land. Someone might be burying a body.' His second cheap attempt at some badly needed humour went unnoticed.

'These are the co-ordinates, Paul.'

He destroyed and got rid of the phone, hired a

133

Jeep and spent the night in a dull, featureless boarding house in the small market town of Epping where the owners were glad to take his money for very little effort on their part.

Setting out at four in the morning, it took him over an hour to find the exact location. Only twelve miles from central London, one of the most ancient forests in the country, a vast crescent shape covering over six thousand acres and crossed by dozens of roads, trying to find a way through Epping Forest's hidden depths was no easy task.

The rendezvous turned out to be a clearing deep within the forest, though heavy ruts in the path signified that farm machinery or a 4x4 had recently passed that way.

The air smelt of pine and earth. Light sifted through trees heavy with leaf and bladed the ground. A sky of apricot and Prussian blue suggested more rain to come. Apart from the sound of his footfall, there was nothing other than birdsong.

Tallis waited and watched, hidden. Something about the scenery, the trees shimmering in the early morning, reminded him of a long-distant memory, of him and his brother playing in some woods with another boy – not one of their kind, his dad had told them afterwards. Couldn't even remember the lad's name now. There'd been some spat. Dan had lost his temper and pushed the boy out of a tree. Fortunately, he hadn't broken anything, though he had been badly winded and bruised. That evening, when the father of the lad had come round to complain, their dad, rather than apologise, had castigated him, told the proud-looking man with the swarthy skin, coal-black hair, the gold earring in his ear, that he was nothing but a dirty gypo, a layabout, told him to bugger off, remove himself from his land. Tallis, cowering in the corner, had watched the man's expression. He'd seen the proud mouth crease with contempt, the flare of anger in his eye. Tallis had felt real shame. Once the door had closed, the witch-hunt had begun. Dan had put the blame on him, and Dad, like he always did, had believed his eldest son. Tallis had gone to bed hungry that night, but he hadn't cared. He'd been on the side of the gypsy.

In the distance, he heard the drone of a vehicle's approach, the engine note suggesting an off-roader. The noise died some distance away followed by another, muffled by foliage, perhaps a door opening and closing, and the sound of one pair of feet moving along the track. He suddenly realised how vulnerable he was. Perhaps this wasn't Cavall at all. Perhaps...

She stood like an archangel in the centre of the clearing, sunlight flickering through the trees and playing on her hair. Her face was scrubbed of make-up and she wore a simple shirt over jeans. She looked fresher, younger, innocent.

Tallis stepped out to meet her. She smiled in greeting, handed him a file. 'Thought you wanted a debrief,' Tallis said, taking it.

'As long as we got our man, we're happy.' She didn't particularly look it, he thought, puzzled.

'Not interested in the method?' Not interested in the fact I watched and allowed two women to

135

suffer, that an old pal nearly blew my cover, that Demarku tumbled me?

'Should I be?' She had a curious glint in her eye that didn't quite square with the question.

'Ends justifying means and all that.'

'You must be tired, Paul. You're not usually so cynical.'

Oh, I am, he thought. I just don't always show it. 'The girl I spoke of.'

'What of her?' Annoyance creased her features.

'Doesn't matter. You should know that Demarku almost killed a woman in front of me, that he's into VAT fraud involving mobile phones, that he deals in amphetamines and heroin.' He went on to name Demarku's colleagues. 'Two of whom were picked up by the police yesterday morning.' He added that he thought there was a Mr Big involved somewhere, probably hanging out at the house he'd seen Demarku enter in Belgravia. Cavall expressed little interest, the next job her only apparent concern.

'Your next target's a woman.'

Tallis shot her a sharp look. 'You never said anything before about a woman.'

'Didn't I?'

'No.'

'What difference does it make?'

A lot he thought, wanting to slap the scheming smile off her face.

'Oh, I get it,' Cavall said. 'Too much like déjà vu. Can't afford to be squeamish, Paul.'

He stared at her. 'If you'd seen what I'd seen, you wouldn't be making such uninformed statements.'

Cavall bridled. 'Witnessing the depths of depravity is part of the job.'

'Then I quit,' he said, shoving the file back hard into her small chest.

'Can't do that, Paul.'

'And stop calling me Paul,' he said, angry now. 'Only my friends call me that.'

The smile faded. 'I apologise. It was presumptuous of me.' She studied his face for a long moment, let out a sigh as though she didn't know what to do with him. 'Here,' she said, taking the file and offering it back.

'Why should I?'

'Because you know it's right. Because you need to.'

He didn't move, simply looked into her lovely face. Did she know him better than he knew himself? 'You're taking a big risk with me.'

'A calculated risk.'

Tallis shook his head. 'You've informed me of a plan that contradicts everything I've ever learnt about law enforcement. You're giving me classified information. You're allowing me to turn a blind eye when I should be singing like a canary. What's really going on?'

A slow smile played on Cavall's full mouth. 'You always been a conspiracy theorist, or is this a recent development? Surely you're not saying you retain sympathy for the likes of Demarku?'

'Not the issue.' In fact, Tallis nursed fond hopes that Demarku would be dropped at high altitude from the cargo hold of a jet somewhere over the Atlantic.

'Can I make a suggestion?' she said, touching

137

his arm. It was the first time, he realised, that she'd shown any sign of physical contact.

'Feel free.' He suddenly felt weary.

'Go home.'

Home? Not his grandmother's bungalow, or his mum and dad's house, the dwelling where he'd grown up, the place from which he'd been exiled. Home, once, had been Belle, Tallis thought, and he could never go there again. An image of her lovely face blossomed in his mind, and he remembered how they'd sneaked away for three precious days together, before things had got complicated. Dan had been away on a course, and they'd gone to Cornwall, found a lover's retreat. It had poured with rain day and night. It hadn't mattered. They'd hardly ventured out of their room except to eat and gaze into each other's eyes in wonderment. For the first time in years, she had felt truly safe, without fear of saying the wrong thing, of causing unwitting offence, of living life on a knife-edge. He had felt more complete than at any time in his life either before or since.

Cavall was still talking. 'You look tired. Get some sleep, rest, then read this,' she said, gently taking his hand, slipping the file into it and walking away.

CHAPTER THIRTEEN

Tallis took Cavall's advice literally. From an early age he'd known how to take care of himself, to make himself feel better. It was all about creature comforts. He spent the first twenty-four hours either asleep or vegetating in front of the television, and the next pottering around the bungalow, and making sure he had decent food to eat. He worked out once, but was already up to a much higher level of fitness than only a week before. He knew it. Could feel and see it. Twice he called Belle to listen to her voice on the recorded message before hanging up the phone.

By Sunday, he felt more ready, or as ready as he was going to feel. Taking out the file, he saw that his next target's home of origin was Romania, a country in southeast Europe caught between Bulgaria and the Ukraine, bordered by the Black Sea on one side and the Transylvanian Alps on the other. Shades of Dracula, Tallis thought with a wry smile.

The offender's name was Ana Djorovic. Born in Romania forty-three years before, she was Serbian by blood and belonged to the significant ethnic minority that existed in the country, but Djorovic had long ago turned her back on her roots and chosen to reinvent herself. Deeply superstitious, she professed to be a gypsy, a fortune-teller, specialising in removing curses from gullible clients and conning desperate women to give up their babies in return for money and the promise that they were going to childless couples with good homes. Tallis had heard somewhere that there was a vibrant baby-trafficking trade between Bulgaria and Greece where children were, apparently and for reasons he didn't like to think about, in heavy demand. According to the notes, three babies, two girls and one boy, were taken from British women and sold by Djorovic to an unknown destination, though Greece was suspected. Djorovic might have got away with her crimes had it not been for one simple, fatal mistake. A woman conned by Djorovic had had a change of heart, a choice for which she was to pay with her life. Tallis studied the crime scenes and winced. Djorovic had plunged a viciously sharpened fingernail into the heavily pregnant woman's neck, puncturing the carotid artery. A crude attempt was made to cut out and remove the baby from the woman's body, but it failed. The unborn child died with his mother.

Ana Djorovic had been sent to Holloway with a recommendation that she be deported on release. But she hadn't been. Tallis studied her photograph. A dark, thin-featured woman stared back at him. Her eyes were black seed pearls, her mouth small and unforgiving, nose Roman and too big for her face. Cunning, devious and calculating for certain, but worst of all, to Tallis's mind, she had no heart, no soul. This wasn't some woman blinded by infertility or bereavement or the deep desire to shore up a faltering relationship – she was doing this out of greed. For a man to trade in babies was barbaric. That a woman should betray her own sex was unthinkable. He read on. Distinguishing features – a tattoo of five dots, four in the shape of a rectangle with one in the middle, like dice, or quincunx, on the flange of skin between thumb and forefinger. Tallis rubbed his chin. Somewhere, in the part of his brain labelled useless bits of information, he recalled that that type of tattoo was popular with Romanian inmates. It meant alone between four walls. Intriguing, Tallis thought, sliding the photograph into his wallet. And where are you now?

Needing to get out into the open to think more loosely, he grabbed his house keys and headed for the playing fields near the high school. Once, when he'd been on his way to train at the National Firearms School at Hindlip in Worcestershire, he'd taken the wrong turning and wound up at a travellers' encampment. Close-knit, feudal and loath to inform on each other, the travellers had stared at him with open hostility. Even the kids had narrowed their eyes, unsmiling, and who could blame them? Tallis thought, remembering how his father had treated the gypsy at their door. He didn't know much about gypsies other than they had a hang-up about mirrors, and a real fear of the dark, which explained why those engaged in criminal activity often carried out their crimes during daylight hours only. They also preferred the con trick to blatantly breaking into a property.

Twenty minutes later, he was watching a group of kids having a kick-about with a football. One had ripped the seat out of his trousers but played

141

on, oblivious. All were covered in grass stains. When he and Dan had larked about in the back garden, they'd made temporary goal-posts with dustbins. Must have been fourteen at the time, he thought, gut griping at the memory of the football going through next-door's greenhouse. Too young to take the blame for someone else's mistake, too old to receive yet another beating from his old man. Tallis smiled. He hadn't known it then, but the dynamics between father and son were quickly to change. About twelve months later, his father had come looking for him after a tip-off from Dan. Tallis had been out smoking with some of his mates, a cardinal sin. His dad had marched into the bus shelter, yelling as usual.

'I've been looking all over for you. What the hell do you think you're doing?' he said, making a grab for Tallis in a bid to humiliate him. From the look in his eye, Tallis was in no doubt that his dad was going to give him a hiding, but by now Tallis had grown another three inches. He was starting to bulk out across the shoulders. He was beginning to feel his place in the world, outside the constraints of his family. Before his dad could touch him, he was up off the seat, facing his father, eyes boring into his.

'Did Dan grass me up?'

'You leave Dan out of it,' his father snarled, taking a step towards him, one arm swinging back ready to land the first blow.

'You fucking lay a hand on me and I'll come back for you, I swear.' He didn't know where the words came from. He hadn't thought about them, hadn't planned for the moment. They were simply the product of years of mental and physical abuse. For the first and only time, he saw fear flicker in the older man's eyes, felt a stir of triumph in his own heart. When his father walked away alone and empty-handed, Tallis knew a landmark had been reached. From that day on, his dad never laid a finger on him, barely exchanged more than a few words with him. Until Belle.

The sky was darkening, and he heard the faraway sound of thunder. He set his chin down and walked on, felt the spit of warm rain against his face. A couple exercising two nutty English springer spaniels exchanged good afternoon with him.

His mind returned to Djorovic. She was a traveller by nature so he guessed she'd be more likely found in a rural location, her stamping-ground country fairs, mystic conventions, places where she could easily drift in and out. Christ, he groaned inside, realising the extent of the search – she could be anywhere.

Returning home wet a couple of hours later, the bungalow seemed to cast a brooding presence, as if someone had disturbed its peace. Maybe it was the beeping sound on the answering-machine. For a delirious moment, he thought it might be Belle. It wasn't.

'Mum here. Wondered whether you're free tomorrow. Dad's feeling a little better and going out for lunch in Ludlow with an old police colleague. Thought we might get together. If you can make it, phone me ... after nine.'

Tallis changed into dry clothes, jemmied open

143

a can of lager, put the chicken he'd bought for dinner in the oven and slotted a Robbie Williams CD into the player. Belle couldn't stand the singer, Tallis remembered with a smile. Her dislike was rabid, especially for someone who wasn't given to irrationality. They'd once had a terrible row about it, though he suspected now it had been more connected to the stress they'd both been under rather than it being poor old Robbie's fault. That was the funny thing about broken relationships. Not only did you miss the person you loved, you missed all the things you hated about them, too.

They met in Hereford outside the cathedral. His mum looked very small and lonely, he thought as he crossed the grass under a beating sun. She was wearing an old linen shift dress that she'd had for as long as he could remember. Once dark blue, it had faded to the same colour as her tired eyes.

'You look well. Lost weight?' she said, kissing him on the cheek.

'Dunno. Not consciously.'

'Suits you,' she said, slipping her thin arm through his.

He squeezed her hand. 'Any ideas for lunch?'

'How about The Church? It's a lovely day. We could sit outside.'

The Church lay in the centre of the city. Converted to a restaurant, it served no-frills food at reasonable prices – right up his mother's street. She ordered home-made lemonade and quiche with salad. Tallis ordered coffee and a sausage sandwich – he'd never been much of a quiche merchant – and took their drinks and lunch outside to an outdoor table so that they could soak up the good weather and watch the world go by.

To start with there were more silences than words, and Tallis was glad of the distraction food provided. 'Any news on the job front?' his mother asked at last.

Tallis swallowed the last of his sandwich and reached for his coffee. 'Not really. Maybe a chance of a bit of private work.'

'Oh?'

'Investigative stuff.' He'd never been able to lie to his mother. His father was different.

'Sounds very mysterious.' There was a slightly disapproving note in her voice.

Tallis shrugged.

'You won't do anything stupid, will you?'

More stupid than he had already? he thought. ''Course not.' He smiled. 'Anyway, enough of me. What about you? Anything new?'

'Not really. Invaded by the usual influx of fruit-pickers. I don't mind so much but it upsets your dad. He's written to several farmers about them, but they don't take any notice. Must say I'm very disappointed in Harry Alder,' she sniffed. 'Thought he'd understand.'

'They have to make a living, Mum,' Tallis pointed out reasonably. 'And as long as their workers aren't causing trouble, where's the problem?'

His mother leant forward and dropped her voice a register. 'Dad was horrified the other day. I'd only nipped up the road for a paper otherwise I'd have answered the door. Anyway, there was

145

this young woman on the doorstep, didn't speak a word of English. She carried a card, which she held up for him to read. It was written quite poorly, in capitals, according to your dad. It said that she was from Poland, or some such country, and her family were destitute. She had some drawings she wanted to show him, I presume to buy, though they couldn't have been much good, your dad said, because they were rolled up underneath her arm. No better than door-to-door begging. And she was pregnant.'

'What did he do?'

'Told her to go away and phoned the police.'

'Right.' Not from concern, Tallis thought. Not because she was breaking the law. Not even because of the fear of crime. The woman was a foreigner, his dad would complain loudly, and she was on his bloody patch. For as far back as Tallis could remember, his father had tried to inculcate his children with his racist views. Tallis felt baffled by his dad's closely guarded prejudice. It seemed so illogical. His father had been born and bred in the countryside. Back then you didn't see too many black people. Didn't see too many of them now, come to think of it. It had been the source of a lot of heated argument between them. Tallis had once completely lost it and accused his father of being a hypocrite. 'You married Mum and she's half-Croatian.' For his pains, he'd received a clip round the ear. Thing was, his mum was white not black, not even vaguely foreign-looking. Tallis had seen some early photographs. With her blonde hair, fresh, pink-cheeked, even features, she looked every inch the Englishwoman. It was understandable that, initially, his dad had been hoodwinked.

Their paths, according to his mum, had crossed in the line of duty when a stabbing victim had been taken to the hospital where his mother had worked. Tallis's dad, a young PC just starting out, had been ordered to take a statement from the victim. The pretty young nurse who escorted him to the ward had been none other than Tallis's mother. The attraction, by all accounts, had been instant. His dad had asked her out on a date. She'd accepted. A whirlwind romance ensued.

Regarding herself as British born and bred, his mother never thought to inform her new love about her true origins. By the time he found out, he was too smitten to care. It wasn't so unusual. In affairs of the heart, men and women could be fickle and inconsistent. Principles were often sacrificed. Even racists could be choosy with their labels. Problem was, the prejudice never truly went away. Like cancer, it could go into remission and resurface later. As Tallis grew up, he learnt to avoid the subject, or not to take the bait. To his frustration and annoyance, his mother always defended his dad, insisting that theirs was simply a generational misunderstanding, a mismatch. Things were different when his father was growing up, she'd say.

'These fruit-pickers you mentioned,' Tallis said.

'What about them?'

'Where are they from?'

'Abroad, I don't know. Why?'

'Just wondered,' he said, an idea formulating in his head.

147

While his mother went to powder her nose, as she so quaintly put it, he called a mate who, after leaving the army, had joined the police as a civilian working on the desk at the main nick in Hereford. Darren Mason steadfastly resisted the invitation to train as a copper, even though he was constantly moaning about the low pay. Thing about Darren, he was a fount of information.

After negotiating his way through the telephonic equivalent of an obstacle course, Tallis was eventually put through.

'Paul, my old mate, how you doing?'

'Good, thanks. Darren, I won't take up too much of your time. Know how busy you are.'

'It's like a sodding lunatic asylum here. Probably not allowed to say that any more,' Darren gave a husky laugh. 'Somehow *a home for those with learning disabilities and personality disorders* doesn't really do the business.'

Tallis grinned. Although he badly missed his job, every cloud had a silver lining. Lately, the political correctness thing had got a bit absurd. 'Do you come across many foreign fruit-pickers in your neck of the woods?'

'Only those engaged in criminal activity.'

'Such as?'

'Minor theft, getting pissed on wages day and falling into fights – mostly triggered by hostile locals.'

'Which nationalities are we talking about?'

'Eastern Europeans.'

'Be more specific.'

'Albanians, some Poles, Lithuanians, Romanians, Hungarians.'

'Come across many women?'

'Only those who find themselves pregnant and want to go back home.'

'Pregnant?'

'Up the duff, in the club...'

'Yeah, yeah, I know what it means, Darren.'

'Then why all the questions?'

'I'm looking for a forty-three-year-old woman by the name of Ana Djorovik.'

'Go on.'

'She has a penchant for conning desperate women into giving up their babies.'

'Bloody hell. Got form?'

'Did time in Holloway for murder.'

'What makes you think she's here?'

'I don't. Just following a hunch.'

'I'd normally say instinct's highly overrated but, in this instance, you might be onto something. The beauty of fruit-picking is that it's still pretty unregulated, doesn't have the same risk attached to it as cockle-picking, and doesn't require much skill. If you want to disappear under the radar, it's as good an environment as any. Want me to keep an ear to the ground?'

'I'd be grateful.' Tallis furnished his old friend with a full description, including details of the tattoo. 'And, Darren?'

'Yeah?'

'I'd appreciate it if you didn't mention my enquiry to anyone.'

'No problem, mate. Mum's the word.'

They parted in the main car park in town with the promise to talk again soon. Tallis followed his mother out of the city, flashing his lights as she forked right to go and pick his father up and he forked left, following the route to Harry Alder's place. Tallis didn't know exactly how many acres were cultivated, but it was one of the largest farms in the area, a mix of arable and dairy, cider production in the autumn, strawberries in the summer. Like most successful farmers, Alder had diversified. The handsome black and white farmhouse provided bed and breakfast for tourists, and Alder's wife was a frequent presence at farmers' markets supplying the discerning shopper with home-grown meat, cider, perry, fruit and jam.

At last, Alder's place snapped into view. Flanked on both sides by orchards of apples and pears, the road was a switchback. Turning off at the sign, Tallis drove down a long beaten-up track, pitted and rutted with potholes.

As Tallis rumbled up and down the gears in the Rover, he wondered if the suspension would hold.

Parking next to Alder's Range Rover, Tallis climbed out of the car into a day that seemed to be getting hotter and hotter. On hearing his arrival, two Jack Russell terriers scooted out of the house and snapped at his heels, followed by a red-faced Alder. 'Kick the little bastards,' Alder roared.

Sorely tempted, Tallis managed to resist.

'Mitch, Chalkie, get your arses here. *Now!*' Alder bellowed, his face the colour of a burst tomato. Mitch and Chalkie had other ideas. Breaking off in different directions, they did a quick circuit round Tallis's car, peeing up the wheels, and came back, nipping and snapping at his legs before finally disappearing back inside.

'Sorry about that,' Alder said.

'Good guard dogs.'

'It's their size. Makes them bolshie. Bit like people,' Alder gave a wheezy laugh, both shoulders shuddering. Pint-sized himself, his wide girth supported by extraordinarily bandy legs, Alder was no stranger to aggression, particularly when he'd had a few. 'You here on your dad's behalf?'

'No.'

'That's all right, then.' Alder's cheeks puffed out like a pair of bellows. 'How is the old man? Heard he wasn't too clever.'

'Not so good,' Tallis agreed.

'Fancy a snifter? Got a nice glass of cider on the go and the missus won't be back for hours.'

Tallis didn't particularly care for the stuff but thought it the best way to pump Harry for information. They walked inside to a wide, flagstoned hall with doors off both sides. Fortunately, the dogs were nowhere to be seen.

'In here,' Alder said, showing Tallis into a vast kitchen with a big refectory table and chairs running down the middle of the room. Alder gestured for Tallis to sit down while he fixed the drinks, but Tallis wandered over to the window. The views extended across much of Alder's land and a fair slice of Herefordshire.

'Those new buildings over there?' Tallis said, narrowing his eyes against a brilliant sun.

'Converted pig pens.'

'Converted to what?'

'Accommodation,' Alder said, handing him a glass of what looked like a urine sample.

'Really?' Tallis frowned, taking a cautious sip of liquid so strong it felt as if his salivary glands had been grabbed and squeezed dry.

'For the workers.' Alder grinned.

'Locals?'

'Must be joking. Won't get out of bed for less than a fiver an hour, lazy buggers.'

'Where from, then?'

'Poland and Hungary, mostly.'

'No Romanians?'

'Wouldn't have a clue.'

'You don't check?'

Alder's piggy eyes suddenly narrowed with suspicion. 'What's this all about, Paul?'

'Sorry, Harry,' Tallis said with a wide smile. 'There's me rolling up without any warning, taking your valuable time without a word of explanation. Thing is, I'm looking for someone – a woman.'

Alder smirked and slapped Tallis's arm. 'Always appreciated a bit of skirt, right from when you were a lad.'

Tallis did his best to smile. Alder was just another in a long line who'd fallen for Dan's crap about his so-called womanising. 'Not like that, Harry. This is work. Thing is, she's here illegally, in trouble with the law.' A worried look sped across Alder's face. 'It's all right.' Tallis smiled. 'Nothing for you to worry about. Strictly between you and me.'

Alder's piggy little eyes examined him over the rim of his glass. 'Heard you left the police.'

'Yes.'

'So it's not official.'

'A private job.'

'Got you.' Alder grinned sagely, taking a deep pull. 'And you think she might be here?'

'It's a real long shot, to be honest.' He pulled out the photograph from his wallet, showed it to Alder who shook his head doubtfully.

'What sort of trouble she in?'

'Theft. Bit handy at casing joints, houses where it's assumed there's stuff worth taking.'

'Bloody hell,' Alder said, looking around him, suitably alarmed.

'All right if I go and take a look, talk to a few people?'

'Be my guest,' Alder said, downing his drink. 'As long as you don't keep them too long from their work,' he added with a grin.

There was no shortage of workers eager to talk to him about the fifteen-hour days they were forced to work, the inadequate food, the denial of proper dental and medical care when necessary, but nobody had either heard of Djorovic or seen her. That would be too easy, Tallis thought as he made his way past the bank of strawberry fields and back to the farmhouse.

He found Alder sprawled out in an easy chair on a veranda, half-dozing in the afternoon sun. 'No luck?' Alder murmured sleepily.

'Thanks, anyway,' Tallis said, making to leave. 'Oh, one thing, Harry.'

'Yeah?' Alder said, prising open one eye.

'Word to the wise,' Tallis said, tapping the side

153

of his nose. 'Make sure your workers get a better deal. They might not live here but they still have rights. Wouldn't like Health and Safety or one of those rabid trade unions getting wind of their conditions.'

Alder was still gesticulating and swearing as Tallis drove down the drive. Looking into his rear-view mirror, Tallis laughed at the fat little man jumping up and down like a spitting gremlin. The only surprise was that Alder hadn't set the dogs on him.

The rest of the afternoon and the next three days were spent travelling around fruit farms in Herefordshire, Shropshire and Worcestershire. Rolling countryside, fabulous weather, response mixed, result negligible. Some farmers were cagier than others. Of those who were helpful, a few allowed him free rein to talk to their workers, but nobody could give him the information he wanted. Driven mad with frustration, Tallis was resigning himself to scouring Kent, Somerset, half of Cambridgeshire, maybe even Perth for the raspberry season, before ditching the entire idea and going back to first principles when he experienced a minor breakthrough. It was right at the end of Thursday afternoon. He was talking to a local woman called Chrissie at a small fruit farm in Great Witley, twelve miles from the cathedral city of Worcester.

'I've seen someone like her, but not here.'

'Where?'

'The village shop up the road.'

'You think it was her?'

Chrissie nodded. 'The woman I saw had dyed chestnut hair, but you don't see many tattoos like the one you described,' she explained.

'When was this?'

'Month ago, maybe more.'

Tallis's heart sank. A month was a long time. She could be anywhere by now. 'Remember what she said?'

'Only that she was looking for work.'

'What kind of work?'

'Picking, farm labouring, that kind of thing.'

'Say anything else?'

Chrissie smiled. Late thirties, maybe older, she had a lived-in face, worn, weather-beaten features, like she spent a lot of time outdoors. She had a nice way about her, sexy with it, Tallis thought appreciatively. 'She offered to read my palm.'

'What – just like that?'

'Not quite.' Chrissie laughed. 'Ever been to a village shop?'

Last time had been twenty years ago. 'I'm more of a city dweller.'

'You can spend all day there talking about nothing and everything. It's quite an education.'

'Take your word for it.' Tallis grinned. 'So you got talking?'

'Yeah. She seemed all right.'

'All right?'

'You know. Not spooky, like those gypsies who shove a piece of heather in your hands and ask for money, or visit a curse on you.'

'Notice anything else about her?'

'One of her hands was bandaged.'

'The left one.' The one with the sharpened nail,

155

he thought.

'Yeah,' Chrissie said, surprised. 'How did you know?'

'Because you saw the tattoo,' Tallis said, quick thinking, 'and that's on her right hand.'

'Right.' Chrissie laughed. 'There's me starting to think you're the mind-reader.'

She leant forward showing an impressive expanse of cleavage. Tallis caught a whiff of strong scent, vanilla and rose at a guess. 'So what did she say about your palm?'

'Oh, no, I'm not into all that stuff. Have a hard enough time dealing with the past without knowing where my future lies.'

It was the classic tell-me-more trap, Tallis thought, and he wasn't falling for it, no matter how wide and inviting her smile. 'Mind, there was something else,' Chrissie said, this time less enigmatically.

'Yeah?'

'Told me I hadn't got any kids.'

'And have you?'

'No.'

'Fifty per cent chance either way.'

'No, you don't understand. I had an accident when I was younger. I actually can't have children. She said she knew.'

And that wasn't spooky? Tallis thought. He'd never understand women as long as he lived.

'Any idea where she was heading?'

Chrissie shrugged. 'Annie in the shop mentioned her brother's place near Evesham. He farms there, always looking for casual workers this time of year. Don't know whether she fol-

156

lowed up on it, though.'

'Got a name?'

'Roger Addison. Honeysuckle Farm. Sounds quaint, doesn't it?' She laughed. Lots of little ridges appeared on the bridge of her nose. Made her look cute, Tallis thought.

'Thanks, Chrissie, you've been really helpful,' he said, climbing back into his car.

'Wait,' she said, scooting round to the driver's side. 'Got a phone with you?'

'Well, yeah...'

'Take my number in case you need another chat.' She beamed invitingly.

The land surrounding the vale of Evesham was flat and peppered with landfill sites, the town itself a cobbled-together mixture of ancient and modern. Tallis preferred the older part, he thought, admiring the black and white half-timbered buildings and remnants of original medieval wall. It wasn't hard to imagine the scene of the great battle that had taken place there between Henry III's son and a rebel group of barons led by Simon de Montfort. De Montfort had been annihilated. Over four thousand men had died that August day in 1265.

Honeysuckle Farm lay several miles outside the town near the charming picture-postcard village of Fladbury. On arrival, Tallis made out he belonged to a private agency responsible for locating Ana Djorovic. 'The information I have to relay to her is of a personal nature,' he added obtusely. Addison, a tall giant of a man with a big smiling face and a gentle disposition that belied

157

his size, was keen to help. 'Yeah, that's her all right,' he said, looking at the photograph in Tallis's hand.

'She on site?' Tallis said, hardly daring to believe his luck.

'Too late, I'm afraid. Moved on a week ago.'

'Reason?'

'I fired her.'

'Oh?' Tallis said, casual with it.

'She wasn't a good worker. Spent too much time talking.'

'About what?'

'What most women talk about.' Addison grinned loosely. 'Men.'

'That it?'

'Not quite,' Addison said, sudden seriousness in his expression. 'My wife, Jackie,' he said, concern in his voice. 'Ana bothered her.'

'Bothered?'

'Jackie's pregnant with our second child. Ana was always pestering her about the baby – when it was being born, where, what plans she'd made, whether she was going to hospital or opting for a home delivery.'

'An unhealthy interest,' Tallis interposed.

Addison nodded. 'Sometimes my wife would catch Ana staring at her. Made her feel uncomfortable.'

'Threatened?'

'Really upset her.'

'Can I talk to your wife?'

'She's in the sitting room, feet up, doctor's orders, but I'm sure she wouldn't mind. Let me have a word first.'

Addison disappeared, leaving Tallis in the large quarry-tiled hall that doubled as an office. A battered old filing cabinet stood in one corner, and a table littered with papers, mugs and an ancient-looking computer butted up to the far wall. Addison reappeared moments later. 'Go on through,' he said, indicating a door. 'Sitting room's on the left.'

Jackie sat resplendent. Dark-featured, she had the typical bloom of a woman in late pregnancy. One dainty hand rested casually over her large tummy in a sweetly protective gesture. Kind eyes, Tallis thought as he went inside and asked if it was all right to sit down.

'Help yourself.' She smiled. 'Nice to have some company. Gets a bit dull, sitting here like a beached whale. Rog said you're looking for Ana Djorovic.'

'That's right.'

'Why?'

'Because she's working here illegally.'

Jackie's face clouded. She put a hand to her breast. 'Rog isn't in any trouble, is he?'

'No, not at all.'

She shook her head. 'My husband doesn't always ask the right questions,' she said apologetically. 'He's way too trusting.'

Tallis did his best to reassure her. He knew nothing about pregnant women but the last thing he wanted was to upset her and send her into labour. 'Tell me about Ana. I understand she intimidated you.'

'So stupid of me.' She smiled with embarrassment.

'Stupid?'

'Pregnant women are prone to strange ideas.'

'Really?'

'Really.'

'But?'

'I felt as if I were the only reason for her being here. Ana's ghoulish interest in the state of my health went way beyond ordinary curiosity. Sometimes,' she said, leaning forward, anxiety imprinted on her face at the memory, 'I'd catch her looking at me.'

'Uh-huh?'

'She'd have this sly smile, like she knew something terrible was about to happen.'

'You felt in danger?'

'Not just me, but my child,' she said, patting her tummy. 'You read such terrible things these days about women who attack pregnant women so that they can steal their babies. And when Rog fired her, my God, Ana called down every curse imaginable upon us.'

'Just as well she's gone, then.' Tallis grinned, wanting to defuse the tension in the room. 'No idea where?'

'Didn't leave a forwarding address.' Jackie Addison laughed.

That was better, Tallis thought. He didn't think a sensible woman like Jackie was going to suffer any lasting repercussions. Problem was, what next? He was still no closer to finding the wretched woman. Looked as though his luck had finally given out. 'The rest of your workers, where do you recruit them from?'

'Not recruit exactly. You make it sound like

we're far more organised than we are.' She laughed again. 'A lot of them are school-leavers or students who come back every year. Good way to make some easy cash. And, of course, we're always inundated with foreigners.'

'Work must be fairly backbreaking.'

'Have to be fit,' she agreed, 'but a lot of them enjoy it. Rog doesn't run a terribly tight ship. I think most of them feel it's a bit of a laugh.'

'Ana associate with anyone else?'

'Kept herself to herself.'

'Not that popular?'

'She was a good deal older than the rest of the pickers. Don't suppose she felt they had much in common.'

'Not unless they were pregnant,' Tallis reminded her, smiling.

'Yeah,' she agreed, her dark eyes flickering for a moment. 'Actually, now you mention it, there was a girl, Kelly, I think her name was. Came from the West Country, pretty little thing, all blonde hair and smiles. Like a lot of kids her age, she had boyfriend problems, packed her bags one night and left.'

'And Ana was friendly with her?'

'Overstating the case. I saw them talking together on a couple of occasions, that's all. I don't know.' She shrugged. 'Maybe Ana was offering advice.'

Acting maternal, Tallis thought, another idea formulating in his mind.

'When did Kelly leave?'

'Two weeks ago, maybe more.'

'Know where she went?'

161

'Back to Plymouth, I suppose. One of the other girls mentioned something about a festival or carnival.'

Madness, he knew, but with no other lead, Tallis thought it his only option. Any excuse to cruise down the motorway in Max's Z8. Returning to the house in Belbroughton, however, stirred up an avalanche of emotions. All he could think about was Felka, her smile, her laugh, the way she'd looked that very last time: happy and excited. He wondered if he'd ever be able to go back to Max's place without feeling taunted by her spirit.

After the initial thrill of stabbing the ignition and hearing the sumptuous roar of the V8 spring to life, he slipped out of Max's drive, eventually joining the dual carriageway at a speed normally reserved for Formula One racing drivers. Fortunately, the left-hand drive meant that he had a better view than most of what looked like a police paddy wagon tucked up on an incline with the miserable title SPEED ENFORCEMENT UNIT emblazoned on the side. Slowing to a respectable forty miles an hour, he almost waved to the boys as he drove past, his eyes riveted upon the driver watching him while talking urgently into a radio – marking my card, Tallis registered.

Traffic was typical of a Friday in late July – dense, sweaty and slow. Although the car had a sport facility for a sharpened response, there was sadly no facility for the elimination of caravans and roadworks. Arriving in Plymouth around noon, he booked into the only available room at a Travelodge near the city centre.

Flattened during the Second World War, Plymouth had been rebuilt with little sympathy, Tallis thought, walking up the broad road that swept up to The Hoe and gave a brilliant view of Plymouth Sound. In spite of its historic links to Sir Francis Drake and the Pilgrim Fathers, much of the city seemed to have fallen prey to architects and designers who seemed to find concrete alluring. Fortunately, the Barbican, an area around Sutton harbour, had escaped the onslaught of architectural vandalism.

Blisteringly hot, the air distilled with salt and the rowdy caw of seagulls, Tallis was suddenly reminded how hungry he felt. There were any number of small eateries and bistros in the shape of former warehouses around the harbour. Without much thought, Tallis decided on a pub that served fresh crab and lobster. Ordering a pint of Heavitree, he went outside and watched the fishing boats bobbing up and down on water the colour of deep purple. As he listened to the ebb and flow of passing chatter, he became acutely aware that for every second wasted Djorovic was on the run for that little bit longer, that there was an increased risk of some innocent girl falling victim to her obsession.

Within the hour, and vaguely suffering from indigestion, he was back on streets that were higgledy-piggledy, and cobbled underfoot. It was like walking around a *souk* without the guttural backdrop of Arabic, Tallis thought. In fact, he heard no foreign accents at all, only the warm burr of West Country competing with the odd

163

blunt nasal of West Midlands. Most shops were geared to tourists, and sold local art, pottery, bric-a-brac with fishing themes, gaudy trinkets, home-made pasties, clotted-cream fudge and ices. A design centre with more up-to-the-minute creations vied with the late Robert Lenkiewicz's now defunct art gallery, both mausoleum and memorial to the great painter's art.

Avoiding yet another band of holidaymakers, he questioned what the hell he was doing there. Djorovic was hardly going to pop round the corner and slap into him, however much he willed it to happen. His was an absurd idea and it was time to face the horrible truth that his hunch was nothing more than that. Worse, without it leading anywhere, he was finished. He was just debating what to do when his mobile rang. It was Darren.

'Got something for you.'

Tallis had the feeling that Darren was about to become his new best friend.

'Been doing a bit of careful asking around. Turns out your woman's been sighted.'

Where? How? Had she been arrested? Tallis asked none of these things, simply listened.

'Got a mate who works in Stonehouse, rough end. He was called out to a pub where a stabbing had taken place. Usual procedure: pub closed off and everyone at the bar interviewed.'

'Djorovic was a witness?'

'Not exactly. Just happened to be there. Said she was from Slovenia, on holiday there, staying with a friend.' Darren paused, clearly reading from his notes. 'A Kelly Anne Simmons.'

'This Kelly, she was with her?' Tallis asked, hardly daring to hope.

'Yup, bit the worse for wear, I gather. Pissed as a fart, Dean said.'

'And Dean didn't think to investigate Djorovic's credentials?'

'To be fair, not exactly uppermost in his mind. What stuck with him was her tattoo.'

'Don't suppose you've got an address for Miss Simmons?'

'Just about to give it to you, my son.'

Tallis took it down, thanked Darren profusely and promised that he owed him big time.

'Don't talk so soft,' Darren said. 'Remember Desert Storm? If you hadn't come to the rescue, I'd be playing a fucking harp.'

It took him longer than expected. Terrified he'd scratch the Z8's beautiful bodywork, he spent a lot of time in reverse, making way for caravans and trailers and people who didn't know how to drive. Some clown had driven down one of the narrow lanes at speed and straight through a tribe of ducks that had somehow lost its way and ended up on the road. Tallis pulled over, helped another driver gather up the remaining ducks and shoo them into a field and safety. Afterwards, he swiftly dispatched the dying.

By the time he found a free slot in the car park at the top of town, parked and walked down the road towards a street market, traders were already packing up, though it was still quite busy. A dark-skinned man selling rolls of brightly coloured fabric flashed him a gold-toothed smile.

165

He had an impressive leopard-print pattern tattooed onto his head.

Stepping into a lane littered with people, Tallis was immediately struck by the alternativeness of Totnes, mostly in the way the inhabitants dressed. It was as if he'd gone back in time to the hippie generation, except these folk appeared more grounded; there was a lot of talk of organic food and drink, bartering goods in return for favours.

Armed with the address, he walked into the nearest shop, a greengrocer, and asked for directions.

'Walk down the hill and there's a turning to your left, about halfway down, leads you into a courtyard with a café. Go past there, past the supermarket, out the other side and you'll find a row of houses tucked away in a cul-de-sac. Kelly's ma lives in the double-fronted last but one from the end, number five.'

Tallis thanked him and walked on. His initial impression of the town was further confirmed by his journey down the high street. Shops on dark arts and crystals, mystic therapies and homeopathy cuddled up to organic greengrocers and second-hand bookshops, and places selling hippie kitsch. The faintest whiff of aromatic oil and cannabis mingled with sea air. Half the population must be stoned, Tallis thought.

Number five was exactly as described, handsome, tended, everything in its place, except Tallis thought, glancing to the left, the green aspect as it was known in firearms speak, something wasn't quite right.

He went up the short gravelled path and knocked at the door. If Djorovic was there, he was going to come up with an excuse about getting lost while delivering goods in the area then turn her in. If she wasn't, he intended to find out where he could locate her. He knocked again, took a step back, looked briefly up at a bedroom window.

'Help you?'

Tallis turned. A thin, reedy-faced man was standing over the other side of a small picket fence in the next-door front garden. Tallis walked over. 'Looking for Kelly or Kelly's mum. They in?'

'Kelly's mum isn't – on holiday in Ibiza. Not sure where Kelly is. Got a friend staying with her, foreign woman. Some talk about them going to the music festival in Salcombe, last I heard.'

'Right, thanks.'

'Take a message for her?'

'No worries. I'll maybe call back later.'

Tallis made to go, moving slowly, waiting for the sound of the neighbour's retreat, the slam of the front door. Alone again, he went back up the path, noiselessly, followed it round the side of the house to where the garden gate had been let open. The bolt, he'd already noticed from when he'd first observed the property, hadn't been shot.

Glancing behind him, making sure he was unseen, he walked inside and across a minimalist area of coloured gravel and tropical-looking plants and into a walled garden with vines and fig trees and bamboo, each small section broken up by statues, an ornamental waterfall, a table with

167

two chairs and a brick-built barbeque. It seemed as if a great deal of thought and love had been lavished on it, Tallis thought, glimpsing an old swinging garden seat. Like one his mum had, it had metal supports with a candy-stripe canopy and tasselled side panels to enclose and protect anyone seated inside from too much sun. It was set in an arbour near the boundary wall.

Tallis entered the cool swathe of green, the enveloping darkness, hearing the buzz of insects, and stopped. Something was wrong, badly out of place. Heart bumping in his chest, all his senses alert, he dropped his gaze, saw where the grass was roughly flattened and bent, the ground disturbed. A light warm breeze picked up, travelling through the tunnel of green, rocking the covered garden seat. Next, he saw blood.

He knew before he saw. Wasn't mind-reading, wasn't sixth sense or instinct, or clairvoyance. As he began to unzip the awning, experience confirmed that inside was a body.

He looked down. No gasp, no muted cry, only pity and fury.

The girl was on her back, eyes half-open, chest a mess of stab wounds, some deeper than others. The weapon, a vicious-looking barbeque fork, was impaled in the swell of her stomach. Jesus, Tallis thought, feeling faintly sick. Not just one victim, two. In no doubt that the dead girl was Kelly Simmons, he wondered how long she'd been there, wondered if he could have moved sooner... Perhaps if he hadn't rested that weekend, hadn't trolleyed about the countryside, consumed that pint...

Now what? Tallis thought. Ought to report it to the police but, fuck, I'm not supposed to be here, double fuck, I've been seen by the bloke next door, and my dabs and footprints are all over the crime scene. Pulling out his phone, he contacted Cavall, explaining the situation.

'Shit, shit, shit,' she cursed. Tallis said nothing, wondering if her ire was for him or the situation. Certain police departments viewed firearms officers as thugs without brains. Was Cavall thinking the same? He waited for her to calm down, which she did in less than a heartbeat. 'Move out of there. Find Djorovic.'

'I can't just leave.'

'You can.'

'But the police…'

'You have to find her.'

Tallis ran a hand over his chin. He hadn't a clue where to look. 'Put out an alert on ports and airports.'

'Don't tell me my job – just find the fucking woman.'

Ordinarily Tallis found the combination of upper-class accent and obscenity a turn-on. Not this time. 'What about the stiff? My DNA's all over the place.'

'I'll take care of it.'

How? Tallis wondered. Cavall wasn't above the law, even if she thought she was. 'Look, something you should know – both women were recently interviewed by Devon and Cornwall police. They were in a pub in which a stabbing took place. Somebody is going to make the connection.'

'How many more times?' she railed. 'I told you,

169

it will be taken care of.'

'The woman's committed murder, for God's sake. She needs to go through the judicial system.'

'Tallis, I don't have time for this.'

'Well, have time for this,' he snapped, staring at the body. 'The girl was pregnant.'

The seaside resort of Salcombe was heaving with musos, wannabes, locals and luvvies. Finding nowhere to park, Tallis left the car at the top of a hill in a residential area of whitewashed houses and walked down a steep incline, curved like an upside-down coat-hanger, and into the town. A favourite with yachtsmen and holidaymakers, Salcombe's tiny streets reeked of history and smugglers' tales of derring-do, the natural harbour providing a dramatic portal to hundreds of creeks, making it, Tallis thought, a drug importer's dream. But would Djorovic be there? If he were Djorovic, he'd be legging it up the M5. Jesus, maybe he'd gone the wrong way entirely. Maybe he was wasting more precious time. Then he thought of Cavall. Would she have the sense to have the motorway covered? He looked around him in an agony of indecision, trying to focus. Who the hell in their right mind would go to a music festival when they'd just committed the most appalling act of murder? Conversely, Djorovic didn't strike him as a particularly sane individual. To catch her, he needed to think with her illogical, superstitious mindset.

Tallis pushed his way through crowds of people, and inhaled the strong smell of salt and alcohol mixed with sweat and high spirits, the vibrant sound of salsa music pulsating and growing louder and louder in his ears as it funnelled down the narrow street. Mums and dads clutching their children close to them, it was as much a family event for locals as it was for marauders, Tallis thought, watching a bloke wearing shorts and flip-flops do a moonie in front of some shrieking teenagers. Further on, drunken nautical types cavorted with braying women spilling drinks with lots of greenery in them while a couple of coppers looked on, benign. Would the sight of the law be enough to spook Djorovic?

Slowly and tenuously, Tallis found his way to the centre of town and a square used routinely as a car park, judging by the location of some toilets. At the end was a quay signposted Whitestrand.

Set against the exotic lackdrop of Salcombe Harbour, a large stage, where a ten-piece band were belting out a hip-twisting number to the obvious delight of the crowd, formed the main attraction. Tallis pushed, cajoled, smiled his way to the front near the music and turned round and faced the assembled crowd. Combing through any number of eager-looking faces, he came to one painful conclusion: he'd have difficulty identifying his own mother in the crush. After a few lame attempts at *'Have you seen this woman?'* and flashing the photograph, he beat a retreat and walked past the ferry steps and a pub of the same name, up the hill away from the noise and clamour, trying to think.

171

The shops looked more expensive, as did the restaurants. A smell of garlic and cooked onions in wine pervaded the salt sea air. As if to illustrate the cultural divide, a high-class estate agent, with windows lit by soft halogen, displayed vast seaside retreats at eye-watering prices. Tallis walked up to the furthest end, where the road dipped and narrowed and led past a yacht club and the Marine Hotel, sensing that he was going nowhere. Turning round, retracing his steps, his mind nauseously flashbacked to the girl on the garden seat.

By now the band had finished one set and was about to embark on another. Tallis walked back down the main street, ignoring the route he'd first taken into the town. After exploring a short quay and peering into the windows of the Custom House, he continued past a shop selling rock and ice creams, a deli and restaurant, past The Fortescue pub at the end, weaving his way along by the harbour wall, feeling a light evening breeze play upon his face. The sun looked as if it had fallen and dashed itself on the ocean, shards of gold and red shooting up into the darkening evening sky.

He found himself in a quieter zone of seaside flats and terraced hideouts with gardens lit by lamps and candles, their owners sitting drinking wine, territorial. The less privileged congregated on the few available wooden benches along the quay, eating pasties and listening to the soothing beat of small boats bobbing against the sea wall, threads of light casting a silver sheen across the water. Hearing a mewing sound behind him,

Tallis stopped, turned, stepped aside with a smile to allow a woman pushing a pram to get by. As the pram drew level, he glanced down at the crying child, a newborn by the look of it, not that he knew much about babies other than his sister's brood. This one was blotchy-faced with a milk spot on its lips. Weeny, he thought. Then he saw the hands that pushed the pram. He looked up, met the stranger's eye, felt as if someone had thumped him with a cattle prod. Part of him wanted to grab her then and there but, aside from the child, those weren't his orders. Instead, he watched, slipping into the shadows behind her, and called Cavall.

Wide road of terraced houses, junk shop on the opposite side, nameplate: Island Street. He relayed the information. 'There's a problem. She has a baby.'

'Fuck,' Cavall said. 'Stay with her. Team will be with you asap.'

'What about–?'

'Do it.'

'But–'

'I forbid you to make an approach, under-stand?'

Tallis closed the phone, kept moving. The baby was really crying now. Djorovic, seemingly oblivious, wearing a long flowing coat too warm for the time of year, walked with a sure stride, heading, it seemed, to a chosen destination. Either that, or she was trying to escape the night. Tallis wondered how long he'd got to spring her, how difficult it would be with a baby involved, how soon Bill and Ben would reach them.

The landscape was changing – houses one side, boat-builders' yards, sailing shops the other. Something inside told him that Djorovic knew he was in pursuit. At any second he expected her to veer off down one of the side streets or alleys, into one of the nooks and crannies, and face him down. Maybe some of the superstitious nonsense had rubbed off on him. Suddenly a flurry of teenagers appeared from nowhere, jostling and leaping like frogs on speed. Without warning, Djorovic shoved the pram hard into the middle of the group and took to her heels. In slow motion, Tallis imagined the pram spin, keel over, throwing the child headfirst out onto the road. He broke into a run, shouting. One of the lads made a grab, catching the pram inches from hitting a brick wall. Another lad was already lifting the screaming baby out, comforting it. Tallis yelled at them as he flew past, told them to contact the police.

Another wave of late-night revellers rounded the corner, not too pleased to be forced aside by a man perceived to be running full tilt after a woman. Fortunately for Tallis, they were too apathetic to do anything about it. But his momentary lapse in concentration had cost him. He found himself in a boat park, Djorovic nowhere to be seen. Christ, he thought, regretting the call he'd made to Cavall. Bill and Ben wouldn't be too pleased at a no-show.

The man drove the car at speed. The woman followed the map reference and issued instructions. Belonging to MI5, they were playing the

174

role of immigration officers, taking their orders directly from the Home Office. Unlike real officials, both were armed. They didn't want another screw-up like last time.

Their mission was crystal clear – pick up the woman, without force, weapons only to be used in exceptional circumstances. More crucially, they were to be as convincing as possible to those they encountered, their brief to identify, watch and observe the players, find out their contacts and see where they led.

'What's that ahead?' the man said.

The woman glanced up. 'Shit, looks like a car's gone off piste and into the wall. Slow down, there's a body lying in the middle of the road.'

'Fuck, we don't need this.'

'Can't just drive away.'

'All right, you call an ambulance. I'll check it out. Be two ticks.'

The man stopped the car, got out, and ran towards the body. He didn't make it. Only saw the flash and black. Startled, the woman reached for her weapon, the last thing she did before she, too, was shot in the head at point-blank range.

Footsteps masked by the eerie clank of halyards, Tallis darted up and down, hugging the boats for cover, peering behind yachts, dinghys, gin-palaces, fishing craft, sensing that Djorovic was near but unable to locate her. At any moment police would arrive, he thought, worried. Deciding his only option was to hide and sit it out, he positioned himself behind a large yacht lying like a sleeping dog waiting for its master's return.

Minutes thudded by. With the only light from a blossoming moon, Tallis adjusted his eyes to the shifting shadows, hunkered down, kept absolutely still, letting his breath out in short, shallow bursts. In the distance, he heard the sound of a car engine and saw two gauzy beams of light spread over the hill and power across the horizon. The cavalry, he thought, conscious of the net closing and Djorovic hidden. Somewhere. Shifting his gaze desperately back to the boats, he heard another noise, a popping sound, like gunfire, followed by an almighty explosion that made him jolt. As he gazed up towards the hill, great flames of light flashed into the night, illuminating the sky. Must have been wrong, he thought. Not the cavalry at all, just lads torching a car, having a laugh.

A scuffing noise, the briefest sound, nothing more, suggested someone else had heard.

Tallis tuned his ear. Unfurling his body, he snaked to the left, eyes scanning a ramp that led down to the water. Heart beating, a warm glow radiated in the pit of his stomach. She was there. He knew it. To hell with containment, he thought. If he didn't get her, she'd escape.

He moved noiselessly, almost within reach of the ramp when, screaming like a banshee, she exploded from behind a pile of wooden crates and lobster pots and came straight at him, splitting his cheek open with one flick of her wrist. In pain, and with blood pouring down his face, he lost the advantage, and she came at him a second time, hand stretched out, nail glinting in the moonlight, sharp as a razor, this time aiming for his eyes. Tallis countered by twisting his head, flicking blood into the fast-cooling air and following up with a straight finger jab to her throat that felled her and sent her to her knees. Her weapon arm partially paralysed, so great was the damage to her throat, she flailed wildly, staring at him, eyes rolling, voice guttural, cursing. Only the sound of a car racing across the yard prevented him from giving Scissorhands a follow-up blow. He turned: Bill and Ben. The bloke, Tallis noticed, seemed a little out of breath, as though he'd had to bust a gut to get there. A smell of petrol hung in the air.

'Should get that looked at.' the woman said, jumping out and marching past him, seizing hold of Djorovic. Her colleague followed and clamped on the handcuffs.

'Should get *her* looked at,' Tallis said, trying to staunch the flow of blood from his cheek, which hurt like fuck. 'Don't suppose either of you carries a pair of nail scissors?'

'Could just pull it out,' the man said deadpan, manhandling Djorovic to her feet.

'Joke,' the woman cut in, amused by Tallis's perplexed expression.

From somewhere, he heard the distant sound of police sirens. Shit, he thought. Strangely, neither Bill nor Ben seemed concerned. The woman pushed Djorovic towards the car.

'She had a baby with her,' Tallis said. 'Some lads rescued it. They called the police.'

The man traded glances with the woman. Tallis picked up on it. 'See any?'

'No.'

177

'Hadn't we better check?' Tallis said. 'Make sure the child's all right.'

Another exchange of glances.

'Can't.'

'But–...'

'Don't worry,' the woman said smoothly. 'We'll call Cavall, get her to follow it up.'

'Right,' Tallis said, uncertain.

'Anyway, looks like you need some hospital attention.'

He was already coming to that conclusion. Gently probing the wound told him that he needed at least three stitches. 'Cadge a lift?' Tallis said. He didn't fancy walking back through town again, even if most of the revellers had gone home.

'Jump in,' she said.

The woman drove, Tallis riding passenger, Djorovic in the back with the minder. Silence descended, punctuated only by Djorovic raining down a curse on all of them.

They dropped him off by the Z8. His last vision as their car disappeared from sight was of Djorovic and the hatred alive in her eyes.

Suspecting fish hooks, heat exhaustion, sunburn and alcohol poisoning were more their line, Tallis took his chances and turned up at South Hams Hospital in Kingsbridge, hoping to find and per-suade a young, good-looking nurse to sew him up.

'Looks nasty,' a nurse said, neither young nor good-looking. She prodded the wound as if he were insensate to pain. 'How did you do it?'

'Slipped with a razor.'

178

'You'll be telling me next the moon's made of cheese,' she said, eyeing him perceptively.

Tallis said nothing. She could think what she liked. He wasn't budging.

'Been quite a night of it,' she said, ruthlessly fishing. 'Mothers mislaying their babies, drunk and disorderly, scuffles, road accidents...'

'And here's me thinking Devon's such a sleepy place.'

'Not local?'

'Passing through. Thought I'd catch some sounds.'

'Ah, the music festival.'

'Most enjoyable.'

'So you went back to wherever you're staying and decided to have a shave.'

'That's about it.'

'Don't want to talk to anyone about how you got that injury, then?' she said, making one last valiant attempt.

'See it was like this, Constable,' Tallis said with a grin. 'Just me, the shaving brush and the razor...'

'Fine.' The nurse grinned, playfully slapping his arm. 'We'll get you cleaned up but it'll need suturing by a doctor.'

'Can't you do it?' Tallis didn't fancy another round of interrogation.

'It's policy with facial injuries, I'm afraid. Doctors always deal with them.'

'What about steri-strips? Easy enough to slap on.'

'I'm sure you'd love that.' She laughed again. 'No, sorry, there's no getting out of it. It's way too deep. Needs several stitches.'

179

The local anaesthetic inserted in his face was a lot worse than the stitching. By the time they'd finished with him, it was coming up for three in the morning. He wondered how the Travelodge would feel about him sneaking in shortly before dawn.

Outside, Cavall was waiting for him.

'Didn't know you cared,' he said.

She gave him a cold look. 'I was told you were here, thought I'd come and see for myself.' She sounded angry and less composed than on previous occasions.

'Where did you think I was? A lap-dancing club?'

She said nothing.

'Baby all right?'

'What baby?'

'Fuck's sake, the baby in the pram. Didn't Bill and Ben, or whoever they're called, contact you?'

'Oh, yeah, sorry.' Cavall twitched a smile. 'Baby's fine. Reunited with its mother.'

'And the girl?'

'What girl?'

'The dead girl,' Tallis said, thinking, For Chrissakes.

Cavall flashed one of her rare smiles. 'No need for you to worry.'

'About the fact we screwed up, or that a mother's lost her daughter?'

'Don't go sentimental on me, Paul. Doesn't suit you.'

He turned on her. 'You always been a hard-faced cow, or does it come with the job description?'

Cavall cast him a venomous smile. 'Talking of job descriptions, where did you go after you called?'

'What?'

'Want me to repeat it?'

'You know where I went.'

'I know the transaction was carried out.'

'Transaction? This isn't a bank negotiation. This is someone being picked up for murder who, incidentally, should face the full scrutiny of the law.'

'That's your considered opinion?'

'Yes.'

'Think you should take a couple of days off.'

'Why?' He was really pissed off. He'd done his job, risked his life, got his face sliced up, and Cavall was behaving like a spank-arsed school-girl.

'On second thoughts, make it a week.'

What the hell was the matter with her? He smiled, decided on a charm offensive. 'Bet James Bond never got told to take it easy.'

Didn't work. 'You might have the car,' she said, looking at the Z8 scathingly, 'but that's as far as it goes.' She slipped a folder from out of her shoulder-bag and handed it to him. 'Some light reading. Could be your hardest case to date,' she added, stamping away into the remains of the night.

She'd wet herself.

Sick and giddy, she'd tried to run away on legs that refused to obey the scrambled impulses of her brain. Her skin itched and burnt with heat.

Each time she opened her mouth to scream, her throat closed over. She could no longer see, her vision blinded by the booze. And her memory was shot. Nothing to hook onto.

The man and woman were dragging and bumping her along a track. Should have hurt but she felt too numbed to notice. There was a far-away noise in her head, rhythmic and soothing, repetitive, like waves breaking on a beach. She wanted to lie down and sleep, to lose herself. They told her she could. Soon. Funny how life depended on these two strangers, she thought, this man and this woman, her nemeses.

She glanced up, stared into the borders of a starless sky, shivered helplessly with fear. The night was an omen. Like a vast black cloak, it smothered and choked her. She wondered what would become of her lost and abandoned soul.

CHAPTER FOURTEEN

Tallis slept in the car. Shortly before seven, he returned to the Travelodge, showered, changed his clothes and had breakfast – full Monty – then checked out. Rather than beat any speed records, he drove at a sedate pace, stopping at midday for petrol and a cup of inky-looking coffee and picked up several copies of daily newspapers, including the Plymouth-based *Western Morning News*. He wanted to see if any had carried the story on the murder. A quick flick-through suggested they hadn't. He'd probably missed it, or maybe it was in a small stop-press section, he thought, folding them up and driving back to Birmingham.

Home was much as he'd left it, apart from the ear-grinding clamour emanating from the next-door neighbours. The house didn't shake with sound. It was pulsating, like the whole construction was going to take off and disappear into the ether. If only, Tallis thought, tight-lipped. Marching up the drive, he had his hand out ready to knock and complain before realising he'd never be heard over the din. Only one thing for it, he thought, noticing that neither car was on the drive, leaving little Jimmy at home alone.

He crept round the back. Really was about time they got a gate or took some sort of security measure, he thought. First rule of MOE – method of entry – was to check whether the door was locked. Luck was on his side. In fact, the door was slightly ajar, a pair of muddy trainers and a football suggesting that little Jimmy had been having a kick-about in the garden. Tallis walked inside, grateful for the blanket of noise encompassing him and masking his movements. He advanced towards the fuse box, which was in a small utility room just off the kitchen. He knew the exact location because, on a previous visit, shortly after he'd moved in, his next-door neighbour's fat wife had asked him round, ostensibly to trace the source of a power cut. The see-through negligee had suggested something else, he remembered with a smile, as had the look on her face when he'd calmly opened the fuse box, flicked the trip switch, power back on and made a getaway, declining the offer of coffee or anything else.

Opening up the clear plastic panel, he located the main supply and threw the lever. At once, there was silence. Job done, he slipped back across the kitchen, out of the back door and crossed into his own drive.

There were two messages on his phone. Stu was in a rage, his message along the lines of where the fuck did you get to, you tosser? Max sounded despondent. 'Hi, Paul. Hope you're OK. Gather the guy picked up by the police for Felka's murder has been formally charged. Understand the parents have requested her body to be flown back to Poland for burial. Thought we'd try and arrange to attend the funeral. What do you think? Think it's appropriate?'

Tallis listened to the rest of the message, which largely concerned Max's holiday though his friend didn't sound as if he had much of an appetite for it. He deleted Stu's message and saved Max's, letting out a sigh, badly needing someone else to talk to. And not just anyone. Did he have the courage to phone Belle?

Hand hovering, sparks of excitement exploding in his stomach, he imagined hearing her voice. In passing he could find out how she was, how work was going, if she was happy, if she was miss– No, he thought, riven with disappointment, it wouldn't be right. Moving his hand from the receiver, he stared at the phone as if it was the cause of his heartbreak.

Without any great enthusiasm, he unpacked, shoved a wash into the machine and dealt with the dirty dishes stacked up on the draining board, wishing he'd made more of an effort to clean up before he'd left. Afterwards, he took out something unlabelled and unidentifiable from the freezer and made himself a sandwich from the remnant of some sweaty Cheddar, spooned two large shots of instant coffee into a mug and, while the kettle boiled, pulled out the folder Cavall had given him.

It felt much thicker than the others, the reason for which soon became obvious. In addition to the investigative reports, there were a number of witness statements and a CD based on film taken from a CCTV camera, which he put to one side, preferring to scan the text first. The salient points were: Mohammed Hussain, Mo to his mates. Sometimes known as Mo Ali or Mo Rahman, or Saj Rahman. Pakistani. Thirty-five years of age. Had fled from Islamabad and gatecrashed the UK at the age of sixteen. History of living on the streets of Greater Manchester, engaged in petty theft, working up to armed robbery with violence. Dangerous obsession with guns. Always operated in a gang. So he's a team player, Tallis thought. Hussain had taken part in holding up a post office in Manchester during which a postmaster had been shot and killed and for which Hussain had received fifteen years at Her Majesty's pleasure after a trial that had lasted several weeks at Manchester Crown Court. Hussain had served most of his sentence at Strangeways, a massive Victorian complex, grimy and depressing, renamed Her Majesty's Prison Manchester in an attempt to rebrand it after serious rioting broke out in 1990.

Tallis broke off to pour hot water into his mug. There was no milk so he settled for two sugars instead. As an afterthought, he snaffled the last biscuit from the tin. Taking both to his desk in the corner of the living room, he powered up his PC, and put the CD from the file into his machine. Within seconds Tallis was looking at a series of flickering black and white images. A slot on the upper left-hand side told him the date and, underneath this, the timeline.

The focus was angled at the counter and the terrified man standing behind it. Three other figures wearing balaclavas, their backs to the camera, brandished sawn-off shotguns, an evil and underestimated weapon in Tallis's opinion – the sheer damage it could inflict on the human body was awesome. All three figures formed a human shield, preventing the postmaster from fleeing or anyone from coming to his rescue. There were two others in the frame, both women, one on the floor with hands clamped over her ears, another screaming by the look of her, her long hair grabbed by the robber on the left while the guy in black on the right clearly threatened to do something awful to her if the postmaster didn't comply. And he had the means, Tallis saw. At the guy's feet was a small can of what looked like petrol. The guy standing in the middle passed him a lighter. All this while issuing orders to the post-master, who seemed too petrified to move.

As with a lot of firearms incidents, it escalated quickly, what happened next unpredicted. The guy on the right quickly lost it, leapt over the counter and grabbed the hapless postmaster round the throat, issuing him with a final ultimatum. Snapping out of his mute state, the postmaster, rather than giving in, began to struggle. A fight ensued. The gun went off. Tallis's eyes flicked to the timeline. It read 17:29:19 p.m. Rather than fleeing immediately, Hussain, cool as you like, frisked the dying man, grabbed some keys from his pocket and raided the safe. The robbers made off with several thousand pounds between them before being picked up travelling in a stolen car two hours later.

Tallis ran the tape a second time, pausing it, rewinding it, running it again, watching the action, seeing who did what when. The pecking order between the villains soon became clear. Both guys on the left and in the middle deferred to the figure on the right at all times. While they seemed nervy, pumped up maybe with drugs, Hussain was coldly calm, the father figure. Tallis studied him again. He was, by any standards, a tall guy. Maybe six-three, six-four. Tallis smiled. No matter how much Hussain might try to disguise himself, he couldn't conceal his height. And he was well built, dwarfing everyone else in the room. He was the man with the power. He called the shots. Literally.

Tallis rechecked the length of Hussain's prison sentence. Fifteen years didn't seem an awfully long time but he supposed Hussain's brief had argued that the gun had gone off by accident. As was standard practice, Hussain had been released at the two-thirds mark, coming out after serving ten years. Refilling his mug, he read through the witness statements once and then again. Understandably, the woman threatened with death by fire had given a harrowing account, the other woman a slightly less traumatised version. Neither of them was in any doubt as to the identity of the ringleader and main offender. Both witnesses confirmed what the police already knew: Mohammed Hussain had threatened to torch the woman. Gunshot residue found on Hussain's clothing confirmed that his weapon alone had discharged the fatal shot that had killed the unfortunate postmaster.

Tallis slipped out a newspaper cutting current at the time.

ARMED GANG SHOOT AND KILL POSTMASTER

Manchester Evening News

Forty-year-old Raymond Clarke is the latest victim of a spate of armed robberies in the city. The postmaster was shot and killed shortly before closing time on Tuesday when an armed gang broke into his post office and shop at Salford and demanded he hand over the takings.

Mr Clarke, a married father of three, was brutally murdered by one of the gunmen after putting up a spirited defence. Two women, in the shop at the time, were also threatened, one of them with being set alight and assaulted by gang members. A can of petrol was later found at the scene.

It's believed the gang made their escape in a stolen red Ford Escort found abandoned just outside Prestwich, the gang believed to have switched vehicles with the intention of heading for Yorkshire. Three men have since been arrested in connection with the incident after a police chase along the M62.

Detective Chief Inspector Sean Hutchinson said, 'This was a vicious and brutal attack on an unarmed and defenceless man. It was carried out with complete disregard for life and we believe that it was only Mr Clarke's bravery that prevented a young woman from sustaining very serious injuries. Without his intervention, the outcome could well have resulted in further tragic consequences.

'I can confirm that three men of Asian origin were arrested at 20.45 hours on the outskirts of Huddersfield and are currently helping us with our enquiries.'

A later article included photographs of all three individuals. Tallis tried to look beyond the posed exteriors to the men. In Hussain's case, it wasn't easy. He had a face that exuded threat. His spatulate nose suggested it had been broken at least once and his eyes were flat and dead. Glossy hair tied back, in popular fashion at the time, he had deep sideburns that crept down his face like large hairy caterpillars. A later photograph suggested he'd ditched the ponytail, possibly because he'd been going bald on top. The eyes remained the same, shifty, skin pitted and lined due to prison conditions. A medical report confirmed that he suffered intermittently from smoking-related bronchitis. Guess I'm looking for a tall guy with a cough, Tallis concluded, looking for notes on visitors and seeing none, which struck him as odd.

He returned to the personal file again. He didn't think it a stereotypical view but most individuals he'd come across of Asian origin had reams of relatives. There'd been a standing joke at the warehouse where he'd briefly worked about the time taken off by certain colleagues to attend funerals. There always seemed to be an uncle or aunt pegging it and it was never a simple afternoon or morning's absence. There'd be days of preparation and fasting and prayer. Yet Hussain seemed absolutely alone in the world, both inside prison and out.

Tallis turned to the interview records. Hussain revealed nothing. He employed a deliberate policy of not answering questions and refusing to confirm his real identity. Interestingly, it was never actually proved which one was really his. For some reason, Hussain was settled on, through what reasoning Tallis didn't find out. Of no fixed abode, it was discovered that Hussain had, at one stage in his life, been living at an address in Moss Side, an area engulfed in gun culture and home to Yardie power.

Tallis took out a pad, reviewed everything once more and jotted down some notes. It didn't take him long to realise that this time he was sunk. His Urdu was about as good as his Chinese: in other words, non-existent.

He took it easy for the rest of the day, thought about returning the Z8 to Belbroughton and decided he couldn't face the silence. As a precaution, he put the car in the carport, and hoped not too many undesirables would notice. He had no intention of taking Cavall's advice. The

190

stitches didn't need to come out of his face for several days so there was no time to be lost, if only he knew where to start looking. Start with the obvious, he supposed. It amazed him how often criminals felt compelled to return to their old haunts. If Hussain, or whatever he called himself, had survived for several years in the Greater Manchester area, Tallis had no reason to believe he would be in a tearing hurry to leave. Which left him with a problem. Tallis's only connection to the city was with a bloke he'd met on a training course who was serving with Greater Manchester Police. He didn't know the city and its environs at all. The thought of walking straight into his brother's new stamping ground left him feeling cold.

CHAPTER FIFTEEN

After a beer and a strange dinner of pasta bake with a sausage chucked in, he took a long hot shower, turning in for the night with the newspapers he'd bought in Devon. Spreading them out on the bed, he read, paying more attention. Nowhere could he find any mention of the events of the weekend. To be certain, he combed through the *Western Morning News* again. The lead article highlighted the case of a man who preyed upon young homeless boys in the city of Plymouth. Several short pieces covered a stabbing in Union Street outside one of the nightclubs and various other assaults at different locations. There was no reference to the abducted baby that had gone walkabout, not even as a slice of late news, although there was a short piece about a road accident in which a car had been turned into a fireball, incinerating its two unfortunate occupants. So that's what all the shock and awe had been about, Tallis thought. Then his eyes hooked on something.

WOMAN'S BODY FOUND ON RAILWAY TRACK

Western Morning News

Transport police are trying to identify the body of a woman who was found on a section of track outside Totnes station in the early hours. The woman, believed to be in her late forties to early fifties, had one distinguishing feature, the tattoo of a dice on her right hand between her thumb and forefinger.

A substantial amount of alcohol was found in her bloodstream and police are wondering if anybody noticed an inebriated woman fitting her description. A spokesperson for the police said: 'This lady was probably quite distressed and agitated. Clearly somebody knew her. She might be someone's mother or aunt, sister or daughter.

'Fortunately, we have very few deaths of this nature but we have noticed a recent rise in the number during this time of year. We remain open-minded as to whether the lady was local or visiting the area. It's not uncommon for people to take their own lives some distance away from where they normally live. In this instance, no foul play is suspected. We are treating the death as a suicide.'

With a slight lurch, Tallis wondered how clever Cavall had been and, if not, how long it would be before an association was made between the woman who'd been present at the pub on the night of the stabbing in Stonehouse and the one now lying in bits in a mortuary. With luck, it could take time before the Transport Police linked up the information with Devon and Cornwall. But that wasn't really his main concern.

Without hesitation, Tallis contacted Cavall. The number rang and rang. Doubt worming in his mind, he made three more attempts during the night. Still no reply.

It was just possible, he supposed, that Djorovic had made an escape and ended up beneath the wheels of the train, or perhaps she'd been escorted onto the train and fallen by accident. No, he thought, that wouldn't work. There'd be some record of Djorovic buying a ticket and boarding with the immigration officials in tow. And why would they be catching a train in any case? They had a car.

He got up, flicked on the kettle, made himself some coffee. What if it wasn't suicide? What if she'd been taken to some secluded stretch of land near to the train track, filled up with alcohol and pushed? Jesus, he thought, was that why Cavall wasn't answering his calls? What happened now?

He took a gulp, almost scalding the roof of his mouth, suspicion gnawing at him. He still had no idea what had happened to the murdered girl's body, how much his tracks had been covered at the crime scene. Enough? Or was there a little bit of evidence that could be used against him as some kind of lever or bargaining chip? Was it even possible to forensically sweep and clear away so much blood? Should he continue, or should he ditch the entire operation? What would be the consequences? Did he already know too much? And if he shared it with someone else, would they, too, be at risk?

As soon as it was light, he called Finn Cronin from his mobile phone. He'd taken the precaution of wandering outside into what passed for his back garden.

'Fuck me, you're up with the lark.'

The lark hasn't slept, Tallis thought grimly. 'Early bird and all that crap. Anyway,' he said deliberately sounding upbeat, 'it's too nice to be lying in bed.' In fact from where he was standing, it looked as if it were going to be a glorious day.

'And you thought you'd call to tell me about it.'

Tallis smiled. Didn't feel too convincing. Time to cut to the chase. 'Finn, I need your help.'

'Go on.'

'Cavall – can you dig deeper?'

Finn let out a sigh. 'Not sure I can, mate.'

'It's important.'

'Why?'

Tallis hesitated. 'What I'm going to tell you next has to remain between you and me.'

'Discretion's my middle name.'

'Discretion's no good. This requires secrecy. Can't breathe a word, use the information or leak it. And no questions.'

'You in trouble?' Finn's voice was ringed with concern.

'Maybe. I don't know.'

'Fire away.'

'Can you run a check on deportations, one in particular, a guy called Agron Demarku, an Albanian. He's served life for the murder of a prostitute. Immigration officials were supposed to be putting him on a plane back to his homeland.'

Tallis could hear Finn scratching a pen across a pad.

'Run to appeal?'

'Erm, not that I'm aware of.'

'OK.'

'Next, a girl was murdered in South Devon at the weekend, place called Totnes. I can't find any record or any news coverage of the killing. Not even sure the police were called in.'

'Not called in?' Finn let out a laugh, 'they must have been. People don't get bumped off and disappear. Well, not in this country anyway.'

Unfortunately, Tallis suspected they did. 'You need to tread very carefully. This is all highly sensitive. I shouldn't even be discussing it.'

'And Cavall's in the mix?'

'Uh-huh. Kind of.'

'Fuck,' Finn sighed. 'All right, let's recap.'

Forty minutes later, Finn began to wrap up the call. He didn't have a question, only a statement. 'Sounds as though you're really in the shit this time.'

Without a trace of humour, Tallis couldn't help but agree.

He spent the next few days in a state of partial paralysis. Part of him wanted to operate like normal, the other found he couldn't. It was just like before, after the shooting in the shopping mall. He had spent whole days obsessing about the girl with the midnight eyes.

Finally, his fear was replaced by the hope that either Finn or Cavall would phone and clarify everything so that when Cavall eventually called back, in the middle of him performing a home surgical to remove the stitches from his face, he was taken by surprise.

He came straight to the point. She didn't deny it.

'Collateral damage. Djorovic employed the oldest trick in the book. Said she had to have a pee then made a break for it. The rest you already know. How did you find out, by the way?'

'Newspaper,' he said dully. It sounded plausible even if Cavall was cold-blooded about it. 'What about the alcohol?'

'What about it?'

'Where did she get it?'

'Must have been tight when you picked her up.'

'She wasn't. And she had nothing to drink in the car.'

'You were with her?' Cavall suddenly sounded as suspicious as he did.

'Briefly. The immigration guys gave me a lift.'

'How many of them?'

'Same as last time, one bloke, one woman.'

'Where did they take you?'

What is this? I'm the one supposed to be asking

the questions, he thought. 'To collect my vehicle.'

Cavall said nothing. He could almost hear the cogs in her brain revolving. He pressed her again. 'Basically, you're telling me it was an unfortunate accident.'

'And we have to move on,' she said firmly. 'The reason I called, there's been a sighting of Hussain near Stockport.'

'Where exactly?'

'In the main shopping centre.'

'When?'

'Two days ago.'

'Makes my job easier.'

'Not too easy, I hope.'

'You're still getting your money's worth. One other thing.'

'Yes?'

'The murdered girl.'

Cavall gave a silvery laugh. 'You really worry too much, Paul. By the time we'd finished, nobody would have had a clue you'd been there.'

He knew from Belle that it was an impossible task to remove all evidence. It only took one spot of blood, one hair, half a footprint impression...

'But what about Kelly?' he persisted. And the dead baby, he thought.

'Unwise to get on first-name terms with victims.'

'She wasn't *my* victim.'

'No need to be defensive, Paul,' she soothed. 'All taken care of.'

That's what bothered him.

197

CHAPTER SIXTEEN

Tallis's first impression of Stockport was that it hadn't moved on since the Industrial Revolution. A huge hat museum, and testament to the city's millinery credentials, formed the main tourist attraction. Other than that, there were the usual types of shops with the usual types of people, the overall impression one of suppressed criminal activity, judging by the hard-looking shaven-heads prowling the town's precincts. But first impressions were deceiving. In among the mills and chimneys, there were some very fine examples of thirteenth- and fifteenth-century architecture. A huge brick-built nineteenth-century viaduct, a determined suicide's dream, dominated the town.

Having switched cars before the journey, Tallis parked the Rover in a multi-storey car park, a concrete construct that smelt of piss, within a short walk of the Merseyway Shopping Centre. The journey to Stockport would have been made in half the time in the Z8 but he didn't dare risk Max's car in an area where the criminal scene was heavier. He'd already seen one parked car on his way in with its window smashed, bits of windscreen over the passenger seat. If someone nicked the Rover, they'd probably be doing him a favour.

He started off by trying to get a feel for the place, the territory, to check the pulse beneath the surface. He went into various shops, bought an *A-Z* of Manchester and a basic guide, talked to people, showed them Hussain's photograph and was met either with indifference or hostility. After a couple of hours he started a trawl of the pubs. Same reaction. If Hussain had been there two days ago, he wasn't now. And nobody was telling anyway.

Walking down a street, he saw two ugly-looking white girls being chatted up by four Turkish Lotharios. As he passed, catching a drift of the Turks' native tongue, he wondered if the girls realised the depth of depravity on offer. From the coy smiles on their faces, he guessed they had no idea. Further on, a paramedic on a motorbike was cheerfully driving across a pedestrian walkway. Maybe he was looking for prospective patients, Tallis thought drily.

Getting nowhere, Tallis gave up and headed for Manchester and found a modern, comfortable hotel at Salford Quays, not far from Mighty Manchester United's Football Club. He fancied he could almost hear the victorious cries of Man U. fans as he stepped out of the car.

After checking in under an assumed name, he took a trip round Salford and was surprised to see that it was a fairly affluent neighbourhood, or at least not as rundown as he'd expected. There were several blocks of newish-looking flats. Streets were lined with trees, not too much evidence of graffiti or litter. The women looked groomed, make-up immaculate. Some bordered on flashy and cashed up. Fake tan was popular with both camps.

199

Salford Crescent Police Station, he noticed, was closed, enquiries directed to the new twenty-four-hour police station in Chorley Road at Swinton. Not that he had any intention of popping in.

The sub-post office looked as though it had been the subject of a facelift. Clean and modern, it was hard to imagine the place as the scene of so much misery ten years before. Following the map he'd sketched in his head, he crossed over the road to where the stolen Escort had been parked for the getaway and where parking restrictions now marked the spot. Glancing at his watch, it would have been roughly the same time. Traffic lighter than it would be now. He wondered how Hussain had felt at the prospect of getting his hands on the money. Excited, pumped up, apprehensive that his plan might go wrong? No, Tallis thought, there was nothing nervy about the man with the gun. If he shouted and screamed orders, it was to intimidate, to display power, not because his was a disordered personality.

So where would Hussain go? Back to where he'd come from, where gun law was king, Tallis thought, but Moss Side could keep for the morning.

He started early when the crack dealers were still asleep. Armed police with bulletproof vests routinely patrolled the area, though he saw none. Walking down streets disfigured by poverty, the grinding atmosphere of criminality and decay was inescapable. Acutely aware of his surroundings, Tallis ran a mental commentary – hidden doorway to the right, alley up ahead, wasteland, two black guys wearing woollen hats giving him the look. It was the kind of place where outsiders were viewed with deep suspicion, where you never met a stranger's eye. Even the sun seemed reluctant to make an appearance, the sky opening up a crack, enabling it to take a peep and decide, no, thanks.

Terraced houses were numbers with no name, down at heel, deprived, gardens more concrete and gravel than flowers. Even the pavements felt lethal beneath his feet. Cars in assorted states of abuse lined the road, some torched, some bent, some abandoned, and those on drives were swathed in tarpaulin, though this rarely protected from vandalism. Graffiti adorned walls and hoardings made play of the gangster culture that had come to dominate the area, reminding him of Northern Ireland. The site of the Old Maine Road Stadium, bulldozed and awaiting re-development, lay like a permanent scar, providing a magnet for more crime. A bank of freshly laid flowers in a local park marked the spot where a teenager had been shot dead, another mother losing a son.

All attempts to talk to newsagents, café owners, taxi drivers, people selling Halal food were deflected and crushed. Tallis shouldn't have been surprised. Witnesses who testified were as rare as witch's blood. Reprisals were real.

Crossing the divide from Moss Side to the edge of the city centre, Tallis found himself off a roundabout in a street of mostly boarded-up shops, the sole survivors an old-fashioned barber's with the red and white striped insignia outside, a boutique selling saris and a military surplus store, glorifying the paraphernalia of combat. A downtrodden-looking bloke confronted him with the usual plea for small change, his accent pure Birmingham. Why did homeless people go to other cities to be homeless in, Tallis thought, chucking him fifty pence in a vague symbol of solidarity, though suspecting that it would contribute to his next fix.

Tallis entered the surplus store, looked around, checking it out, noting the clientele, mostly little men posturing as big men. The goods were laid out on two floors. Downstairs flak jackets, boots, Bergen rucksacks and camouflage trousers; upstairs air pistols, devices to catch rats and squirrels, shotguns in display cabinets and a terrifying array of ceremonial swords. Millets meets Territorial Army, Tallis thought. Near the back of the till a lethal-looking crossbow hung in sinister splendour. An urbane-looking man with short silver-grey hair and a moustache, more accountant than gun dealer, approached Tallis. Tallis wished he could show his warrant card, not that it ever proved a barrier to lies. He smiled, flashed the photograph of Hussain.

'You police?' The man's eyes were dark and deep set. There was a trace of a foreign accent, not one Tallis could easily identify.

'No.'

The man shook his head, handed back the photograph. 'We have many customers.'

'But you'd remember this guy. He's big, six-three, -four. Passionate about guns.'

The man smiled. 'You'd be surprised the

number of people fitting that description.'

'So you haven't seen him?'

'No.' Those dark eyes said something else, Tallis thought.

'Tell you what you could help me with.' Tallis smiled. The man smiled back, glad of the change of subject, it seemed. 'I'm new to Manchester. Where's the rough part of town so I can avoid it?'

'Which way did you come?'

'From Moss Side.'

'Doesn't get much rougher,' he said. 'It's a shame. The older generation are largely upstanding and God-fearing. It's their children who pose the problem. They have no respect for anyone or anything. We had a couple of stabbings here a few days ago.'

'This street?'

'Uh-huh, one fatal.'

'That usual?'

'What's usual? People who live in nice areas get knifed outside their own homes these days.'

Tallis thanked the man for his time and went downstairs. Walking out, he overheard some old fat bloke dressed from top to toe in camouflage gear extolling the virtues of semi-automatics for 'taking out'. Sliding a pie out of an oven looked the closest the man ever got to taking out, Tallis thought. He just didn't get the fascination with killing people. When you'd done it for real, it was hard to comprehend anyone wanting even a vicarious slice of the action.

Like Plymouth and Coventry, Manchester had suffered its fair share of bombing during the

Second World War. Fortunately, many of its oldest buildings remained untouched. Tallis was struck by the successful blend of old and modern architecture. In common with Birmingham, Manchester provided a shoppers' dream location, and there was more. The hotels were bigger, the sense of glamour stronger, yet no matter how many architectural facelifts, he was aware of a stronger undertow of criminality. He could almost touch it.

Feeling hungry, he found a bar in Bridgewater Street. Split into two rooms, classy upstairs, basic downstairs, he ordered a pint and a steak sandwich and took his drink to a quiet corner. Still quite early, most punters tended to drift outside and sit by the canal and soak up the sun.

For the first time since he'd become embroiled in Cavall's plans, he felt lonely. In a strange city, with no leads, he wondered whether this time his luck had run out, whether he'd fail, and whether he really cared. He imagined Cavall's reaction, the curl of her full lip, the expression of disdain on her face then, with a sick twist in his stomach, he remembered the precariousness of his situation. One of the last to see Djorovic alive, the first to find the girl dead, he couldn't afford to fail. Dared not fail. If he did, Cavall had enough on him to throw him to the lions.

'You look troubled, my friend.'

Tallis looked up. The man standing before him was dark-skinned with sharp, intelligent-looking eyes. He might have been Indian, Pakistani or from the Middle East. Tallis suddenly realised how easy it was for a white man to confuse one race with another. An image of Rinelle Van Sleigh flashed through his mind.

Smartly dressed in pale denim jeans, the man wore a casual lemon check shirt, open neck, short sleeves. His build lean, he was probably no more than five-ten in height. He held a glass of what looked like whisky in his hand, which struck Tallis as out of place. No devout Muslim, then.

'Mind if I sit down?'

Tallis shrugged. 'Free country,' he muttered. He really didn't feel like being someone's mate. He took out the newspaper he'd bought earlier in the day, making a show of unfolding and reading it. The man pulled up a chair. He sat close enough for Tallis to notice his aftershave. Part of him felt queasy. It reminded him of Demarku.

Tallis's sandwich arrived. He took a hungry bite, and looked around the bar, saw that it was steadily filling up with drinkers.

'Understand you've been asking questions.'

Tallis didn't flinch, kept on chewing. Intelligence must be exceptionally good in these parts. If the guy had come to warn him off, however, he could go to hell. There was more at stake than the mission.

'I may be able to help.' The voice was perfectly modulated, like he'd done a stint at Eton, Tallis thought, thinking of his rather humbler roots. He held his silence, avoiding eye contact, thinking this was a set-up. The man smiled, extended his hand. 'My name is Asim.'

Tallis eyed him warily, took another bite of his sandwich, chewed, and swallowed. 'And why would you want to help me, Asim?'

205

'Not help exactly.' Asim smiled. 'Trade.'

'For money?'

Asim nodded, eyes bright with fire.

'Strange line of business to be in.'

'Popular,' Asim corrected him. 'Trading people is one of the oldest professions.'

'Like prostitution.' Tallis twitched a smile. 'You make it sound almost noble.'

Asim laughed. 'Trade, not traffic.'

'What makes you think you can find my man?'

'Nobody can hide for ever.'

'Bin Laden seems to be making a pretty good stab at it.'

Asim smiled engagingly. 'It's a question of knowing the terrain and who to talk to. You've been talking to the wrong people.'

Tallis gave him a sideways look. There was something about the guy he liked. He didn't seem dodgy, even if he was. He had a presence – confident, authoritative, trustworthy. And what, Tallis thought, do I have to lose? He extended a hand. Asim took it in his warm and steady grip. 'Craig Jones,' Tallis said.

'Get you a drink?' Asim said.

He was tempted to ask for another pint, but decided it was better to keep his wits about him. 'A Coke's fine.'

Tallis's mind tumbled with questions. Who'd put out the word? How had Asim found him? Was he really a guardian angel or devil in disguise? He'd heard somewhere of a company with an A-list celebrity membership who guaranteed to attain the unattainable – tickets for World Cup Finals when there were none to be had, dinner in an exclusive restaurant with a six-month waiting list. Were they in the people game, too? Was Asim part of their team?

'So Craig, can we do business?' Asim flashed a winning smile, returning to the table with Tallis's drink.

'That depends on whether you can find him.' Tallis pulled out the photograph. 'Mohammed Hussain. Sometimes known as Mo Ali or Mo Rahman or Saj Rahman.'

Asim's face darkened. 'This man is protected.'

'By whom?'

Asim's black eyes glanced away. From the grind of his jaw, he seemed to be weighing something up in his own mind. For some reason Tallis noticed that he'd barely touched his drink. 'When people are sent to prison, they become vulnerable to causes,' Asim said. 'Prisons, like universities, are recruiting grounds for extremists of all denominations.'

'You saying that Hussain is involved in terrorism?' Christ, whose toes was he going to be treading on? Tallis thought. And Cavall had assured him that all four illegals had no terrorist links.

'He moves in interesting circles, which is the reason I will try to help you. I believe in peace, and people like Hussain give the rest of us a bad name.'

'You Pakistani?'

Asim shook his head. 'Egyptian. Not that many can tell the difference. To most, we're all the same – would-be suicide bombers and murderers.'

Tallis felt something murky stir inside. He was

as guilty as the next man for harbouring prejudice. Asim seemed to read his mind. He flashed a benevolent smile. 'Think of me as your protector, Craig.'

'My protector?'

'It's what my name means.'

He'd need more than a name to protect him. 'Think you can find him?'

Asim smiled again. 'I will make enquiries,' he said courteously.

'And the money?'

'No hurry,' Asim stood up. 'Let's see where things lead.'

'How will I find you?'

'At Mavericks, tomorrow night at ten.'

Asim never asked once what he was going to do with Hussain when he found him. Maybe he didn't care.

CHAPTER SEVENTEEN

Tallis spent the rest of the afternoon and the following day people-watching. He spotted a couple of footballers, the odd soap star and several famous but irritatingly unidentifiable faces among the crowd. Hussain's wasn't one of them.

Impressed by the scale of redevelopment in the city, Tallis felt churlish not to admire the swanky hotels and clubs, the massive shopping centres and malls, museums and art galleries, the sheer volume of human traffic, yet by the end of the second day he was glad to escape the madness and settle in Piccadilly square, an oasis of lawn and flowers and peace. Sitting on the grass, soaking up the sun, he remembered a fabulous afternoon spent sprawled out in Montpellier Gardens. He and Belle had sneaked off to Cheltenham where a mate of his had lent them his flat for the night. It had been an incredibly hot day. They'd had some lunch on the promenade in a lovely Italian restaurant and, after trawling around the shops for a bit, they'd parked themselves on the green, his head resting in Belle's lap. Out of the blue, her mood, which had been euphoric, suddenly changed.

'Paul?'

'Mmm?'

'You know we can't go on like this.'

'Like what?' He looked up at her. He knew exactly what she was talking about, but he felt such a sudden chill of fear that he didn't want to put words to it.

'Sneaking off, illicit phone calls, lying. One of us, sooner or later, is going to be found out.'

'Not if we're careful.'

'It's not just that.' She sounded unsteady.

She was asking where they were going. She was asking about futures. He'd asked himself the very same questions over and over. So far, he'd failed to come up with answers. 'We could come clean, I suppose.' The thought was terrifying.

She shook her head. 'I know what you think of your father, but it wouldn't be right. Your dad's a very sick man.'

Not right, he thought bitterly. Trouble with the

209

whole damned situation there was so much that wasn't right. Whenever he thought of his father, he thought of his brother and vice versa. His, and theirs, was a constant story of betrayal and revenge. Belle was spot on. To reveal their secret affair could only court tragedy. 'So what are you saying?' He rolled over onto his knees, put his hands on her shoulders. He felt sick.

'Nothing,' she said, biting her lip. The tears in her eyes mirrored his own.

Then he put his arms around her, held her close and kissed her.

Tallis blinked and experienced the oddest sensation. Glancing around him, he got up, walked away, down one street, into another, nice and easy, no quickening of pace, no hesitation. He went through entrances and emerged through emergency fire exits, surreptitiously checking to see if he was being followed. Either, he concluded, he was imagining it, or his tail was extremely gifted in the art of surveillance.

With several hours to go until his meeting with Asim, Tallis returned to the hotel and went for a run, showered and changed then ate a plain dinner in the dining room. Shortly after nine-thirty, he made his way to a club in Canal Street, affectionately known as Anal Street, according to some blurb he'd read. It was the centre of Manchester's gay community. The bar was a crush of people and colour. He had to queue for several minutes to order a drink, giving him ample chance to ponder the choice of unusual location. Was Asim gay? Was he suspicious of Tallis's sexuality? Christ knows why, he thought, nobody else seemed to be in doubt.

An hour and a half later, Tallis was considering none of these things. He was thinking set-up and wind-up. Downing his third soft drink, he returned to the hotel, severely pissed off and, giving in to temptation, took full advantage of the mini-bar in his room while rewinding the conversation and events of the previous day. Asim had positively identified Hussain. No doubt about it. Knew who he was and for whom he worked. Terrorist connections had been implied rather than asserted. Either way, Asim was playing with fire. Maybe he'd made one too many enquiries. Maybe he was lying somewhere with a bullet in his head. Or, Tallis thought, maybe Asim was the problem. The whole coincidence of Asim stumbling into him, the way he'd engineered the meeting. Christ, Tallis had done the very same himself on the few occasions he'd worked undercover. And the friend line was pure textbook. Asim gave the impression of working alone, of touting for business, of doing him a favour, of helping world peace. Which was it? Tallis wondered sleepily. Next thing he knew it was morning, his neck stiff as hell from spending the entire night asleep in a chair.

Stubborn by nature, Tallis went back to the club that night and the following night. Still no Asim. Dividing the *A-Z* methodically into sections, he spent the intervening daylight hours pounding the pavements, hanging out in dark bars, visiting a couple of shops that purported to legitimately sell shotguns, air guns, knives and swords, tuning his ear for any criminal under-

211

current. During his reconnaissance, he overheard deals in Russian and Jamaican patois, both conversations conducted openly in city-centre pubs. Same old: heroin. There wasn't even a sniff of information on Hussain. And of Asim there was no sign. Furious, not simply for having his time wasted but for having such dangerously poor judgement, Tallis resigned himself to continuing his search alone.

Unable to sleep again, he decided to watch some late-night television and caught a depressing investigative programme on the rise of a shadowy far-right group that prided itself on stirring up extreme racial hatred. The name of the group was Fortress 35, a reference to the number of shire counties it deemed as being under its protection. Its leader was unknown, membership white and aged anything between eighteen and fifty, the only information gleaned from victims, in other words the lucky ones who'd got away. There was enough evidence to suggest that the group had been responsible for a number of murders, which had originally been passed off by the police as black-on-black killings when they'd been nothing of the sort. Based on witness statements, the group worked with slick and ruthless precision, targeting all who didn't conform to the organisation's brand of Englishness, which meant almost everyone, including the Welsh, Irish and Scottish. There was a lot of nationalistic ideology dressed up in the guise of defence of the realm, sovereign nation, unity, all the usual buzzwords, and a real, almost medieval belief in the spread of disease by foreigners coming into the country, citing the re-emergence of tuberculosis in the United Kingdom as evidence of an invasion. Although the group's beliefs were, in Tallis's opinion, frankly nutty, they were clearly a dangerous outfit that needed to be stopped. As soon as the programme finished, he went to bed, switched off the light and fell asleep. Just after two-thirty, the hotel phone started to ring. He picked up, instantly awake. It was Asim.

'How did you...?'

'I have an address. Hussain will be there.'

'When?'

'Within the hour.'

Tallis glanced at his watch. He hoped the location was near.

Tallis felt the night settle on him. He was standing in a modern Perspex bus shelter on the opposite side of a detached house in an unassuming street on the east of the city. Apart from the odd dog barking, the place was as quiet as thought.

He let out an involuntary shiver. In spite of it being high summer, the air temperature at that time in the morning was chill. Eyes straining, he missed not having a set of night-vision goggles on him. Although there was street lighting, it wasn't enough to illuminate the stake-out.

Unfurling his body and changing position, he wondered whether Hussain was actually inside, whether he was due at the address, or whether he was about to leave. Shit, he thought, if Hussain emerged, he'd have no choice but to bag him there and then, the call to Cavall and her thugs made afterwards. He winced at giving thought to the impossible. In his mind, he hadn't said im-migration officers but *thugs*. And what did that make Cavall?

A sudden noise captured his attention. He turned, looked, stepped out into the road. Next thing he was grabbed from behind, a hand in leather clamped over his mouth and nose, threat-ening to cut off his air supply. Whoever it was felt strong and unassailable. Hussain, Tallis thought, realising that Asim had laid the perfect trap. Thinking quickly, he let his body go limp, legs relax, acting the homeless drunk. It didn't work. Dragged backwards, he was manhandled onto a stretch of wasteland. Then he was let go and pushed away.

'Hey, man, take it easy,' Tallis said, slurring his words, taking several steps backwards and away from his assailant. Unfortunately, he hadn't fac-tored in that there were two of them. While trying to perfect his drunken dialogue, another shadowy figure started roughing him up, the guy who grabbed him asking the questions along the lines of who are you, and what are you doing here? Against every instinct, Tallis played dumb and defensive, grunting and groaning, fencing the blows, taking a strike to his jaw, his eye, biding his time, watching, listening. This was no mugging. Neither was it an ordinary assault. They weren't determined enough. Hearts weren't in it. Just knock-about stuff. And they were British.

'You're police,' one of the guys said accusingly.

'No...'

'Don't argue.'

'Whatever you say,' Tallis said. If that's what

they wanted to believe, he'd make it easy for them.

'Keep off our patch,' the man snarled, giving Tallis a final warning shove in the chest.

'Got it?' the other one said.

No point in argument, Tallis thought, dusting himself down, walking away.

In movies the hero took a beating that would kill most men, returned to wipe out the bad guys, and gets the girl. In real life, Tallis thought, feeling stiff and bruised after a relatively low-level bit of bother, he'd be lucky to get his own breakfast. It was one of those self-service operations: a teeny-weeny thimble of juice, a bowl of something that looked as though it had been swept out of a budgie's cage and some very strange-looking bits of cooked pig. The mushrooms were slimy, tomatoes raw, eggs overdone. The coffee, however, was excellent.

Tallis helped himself and sat down. Navigating his way through Manchester city centre in the early hours of the morning and trying to dodge the police – Excuse me, sir, been in a fight, have we? – had given him plenty of time to mull over the latest twist in events. Asim's intelligence, he had to admit, had been spot on, certainly explained the security service's interest. Even undercover police officers didn't operate like that, he thought, though he guessed SO15, or Counter Terrorism Command as it was known following a merger between Special Branch and the Anti-Terrorism Branch might be another possibility. Failing that, the highly secretive Serious and

215

Organised Crime Agency. Thing was, whoever they were, they'd marked his card. It meant he stood no chance – too many other agencies involved. And that was what truly bothered him. Cavall had stated categorically that none of the people on the list posed a terrorist threat, so why was Hussain being watched?

Once he'd finished his breakfast, Tallis decided to contact Cavall, explain his position and ask for clarification. He fully expected to be going home that morning.

Midway between lifting a piece of bacon and posting it into his mouth, he was brought up short by the sight of Asim walking into the dining room with a nimble stride, nodding and smiling at the other diners. After helping himself to coffee, he drew up a seat at Tallis's table. He sat down, full of apologies.

'This time I'll supply you with more cohesive information.'

'Cohesive?' Tallis said. 'This mean I don't get my lights punched out?'

Asim frowned. 'It was an unfortunate misunderstanding, I agree.'

Misunderstanding? Tallis thought. How much did Asim actually know? 'Doesn't matter,' Tallis said. 'If last night's warning was an appetiser, I'm not planning on sampling the main course.'

'The men you stumbled into last night have little or no interest in Hussain.'

'How do you know?'

Asim flashed an enigmatic smile. 'Their interest is in a man called Kahn.'

'Kahn?'

'He runs a military surplus store in Manchester.'

Tallis thought about the foreign man with the silver hair. 'Last time I checked, running a shop wasn't a criminal offence.'

'It's a front. Kahn's a gunrunner. The place you visited last night is his arms factory. He has suspected links to known terrorists abroad. That's why he was being watched.'

'And Hussain's under Kahn's protection?' God, this was getting murky.

'Not any more. Kahn was picked up last night.'

Christ, Tallis thought. The guys must have been from counter-terrorism. No wonder they were pissed off with him. 'And Hussain?' he said sharply.

'He wasn't there.'

'So, apart from putting me in the firing line, my trip was a wild-goose chase.'

'For which I apologise again.'

Tallis pushed his plate away. 'What makes you think I'd trust you this time?'

Asim leant forward, eyes twinkling. 'There's an Indian restaurant in Oxford Road.' Popular with the student quarter, Tallis recalled from his travels. 'The Spice Emporium. Hussain plans to be there tonight.'

'To eat tandoori?'

'To take the money. It's a very popular haunt.'

'Will he be armed?'

'Naturally.'

'Alone?' Of course, he wouldn't be.

'He and another. They work in pairs.'

'Like Jehovah's Witnesses,' Tallis said, without

217

smiling. 'What time's kick-off?'

'Half-past midnight, shortly after the restaurant closes.'

Tallis fell silent. Armed men, restaurant in a busy quarter populated by youngsters, height of summer. Not good. Not good at all.

'Need a gun? I can get you a very good one, if you want.'

From Mr Kahn's collection, Tallis thought, smiling coldly. 'I don't think so.'

CHAPTER EIGHTEEN

The Spice Emporium was on the apex of Oxford Road and Grosvenor Street, not far from Manchester University. Although students were officially on vacation, there were still plenty milling about, some working in the numerous bars to help pay their tuition fees.

Tallis spent the afternoon checking out the location, watching who walked past, how often, volume of customers. He wanted to obtain as much information as possible. Knowledge was power. It might also save his life.

Watching was relatively easy. The street was busy with punters and shoppers so he didn't stand out from the crowd and was able to make several trips up and down, identifying the entry points, the absence of CCTV cameras, gauge the general state of the building. By taking an avid interest in the menu outside, he had a good view through the large single window. There were probably forty or so covers at the front, twenty of them currently occupied by lunchtime diners. How many at the back was difficult to tell. Tallis pushed open the door and walked inside, and was immediately hit with the soft aromatic fragrance of coriander and cumin.

A short narrow corridor led to another door, through which there was a bar and reception area. Eyes adjusting to the change of light, Tallis asked a handsome-looking youth if it were necessary to book a table for that evening.

'No need, sir, but I will take your reservation if you wish.'

'Thanks,' Tallis said, eyes flicking to the back of the room, making a mental note of the number of potential covers, the fire exit, the sign for the toilets, the door to the kitchen, another door marked private.

'For one,' Tallis said, 'but I'd like to dine as late as possible.'

The young man reached for a book, turning the pages to the relevant day. Tallis registered two other waiters serving, wondered if any of them were in on the robbery. It wasn't so unusual. Often there was an inside man. A glance at the rota pinned up behind the bar suggested that four would be covering the evening.

'Last orders at eleven,' the young man said.

'Perfect,' Tallis said with a convincing smile.

'No problem. We look forward to seeing you this evening, sir.'

'Thanks,' Tallis said affably. 'Sorry, I don't know your name.'

219

'Kismet, sir.'

Tallis smiled, nodded and walked out. No evidence of CCTV inside. No sign of guard dogs. Had there been, even if locked in the private quarters, he'd have started sneezing by now. Unfortunately for Kismet, he'd be seeing him later.

Tallis glanced at his watch for a second time: ten minutes past midnight. He'd wolfed down chicken choyla, a Nepalese speciality, followed by lamb jalfrazi with a side dish of tarka dal and topped it off with a pudding of coconut and persimmon ice cream. Passing on the lager, he'd drunk mineral water. Catching Kismet's eye, Tallis ordered coffee.

Tallis had stationed himself halfway down the dining room with a clear view of the entrance. Most diners were paying their bills and drifting away, leaving five other tables occupied. Combined noise of conversation and cutlery had dipped enough for Tallis to hear the sublime strains of sitar music through the restaurant speakers.

'Busy night,' Tallis remarked as Kismet returned.

'And boisterous.' Kismet smiled.

At least the clientele were well behaved. He'd been in Indian restaurants in Birmingham where the customers were so rude he felt ashamed to be British. 'Business always this brisk?'

'Always,' Kismet said, glancing at the door.

'Profitable, then.'

Kismet nodded and, catching the eye of a diner

who wished to pay his bill, disappeared.

Tallis spooned sugar into his coffee-cup, slowly stirred the contents, watching as one table emptied, the other party on the other table engaging in a brief, amicable discussion as to who was going to pick up the tab. That left his and three other occupied tables. All situated towards the back of the restaurant, a party of ten celebrating a birthday, a starry-eyed young couple holding hands and three businessmen who showed no sign of going anywhere soon. Problem, Tallis thought. They'd consumed enough booze to attempt fight instead of flight.

Seventeen minutes past midnight. The young couple were making moves to leave. Kismet hurried over, keen to take their money and get them out, planting a single rose in the hand of the young woman and opening the door for them in a flurry of goodwill. Eighteen of us, Tallis counted, including the waiters, twenty when Hussain and his henchman arrived. Too many, he thought, for a clean job.

After rapid discussion, one of the waiters reached for his jacket and left, leaving the other three to clear up. Tallis watched them. One was older than the rest, probably early forties, his waistcoat buttons straining as he whipped off the tablecloths, the other, a hawk-faced man with a slight build and mild manner. Neither looked as though they'd put up a fight and although that was good, Tallis knew it was impossible to tell who became heroes in a crisis.

Kismet approached the birthday party and asked if they wanted anything else. Only the bill, one man said. Kismet smiled, went to the till, added up the items, printed off the chit and handed it back. All in less than forty-five seconds, Tallis noticed. As Kismet walked past his table, Tallis saw the young man's eyes flick in his direction. On his return, Tallis asked for a refill. Kismet nodded, an odd smile on his lips. His face was pale and his gaze was somewhere else.

More commotion as the birthday customers pushed back chairs, gathering up presents, reaching for jackets. Kismet raced to the door, flinging it open, throwing the flowers into the hands of the ladies, thanking all profusely for their custom.

'We have run out of fresh coffee, sir,' the mild-mannered waiter said to Tallis. 'I can put through some more, if you wish.'

'Why not?' Tallis smiled, catching Kismet's stony expression.

Twenty-seven minutes past and counting. One of the businessmen got up and lurched towards the toilets. Tallis fell in behind, watched as the bloke drunkenly bounced off the doorframe, farted loudly and let out a snort of laughter. Once inside, Tallis tapped him on the shoulder and as he lurched round hit him straight on the jaw. 'You'll thank me for it later,' Tallis said, catching the man and dragging him to the nearest cubicle, jamming the door shut after him. Next he returned to the door leading onto the main dining area, opening it a crack and seeing two men striding purposefully down the main aisle, one of them Hussain, his face paunchy either with drugs or booze. He'd beefed up considerably, his extra

weight added to his height giving him a formidable appearance. The other man, shorter and wiry
in build, brought up the rear. Slipping his
cellphone from his pocket, Tallis made the call to
Cavall, his eyes never leaving the two men.
Discretion was off the menu tonight. If Cavall
didn't like the idea of witnesses, it was too bad.

Kismet was nowhere to be seen. The older
waiter, obliviously washing glasses behind the
bar, moved like a sloth towards the front of the
restaurant, turned the open sign to closed and
bolted the door, effectively denying all means of
escape. This left the hawk-faced, mild-mannered
waiter in the firing line. As he approached the
two men, Hussain roughly ordered him into the
room marked private. No weapon, no gun. The
waiter appealed to his older colleague for help
but was met with blunt and hostile rejection.
Confusion engulfed the man's face followed
swiftly by alarm. In the seconds it took Tallis to
process what was going down, Kismet shot out of
the kitchen, and Tallis saw, to his horror, he was
wielding a meat cleaver and waving it frantically
at Hussain. Entirely misreading the situation,
one of the businessmen stood up and tried to
remonstrate with Kismet, the other falling silent
and transfixed. Hussain nodded silently at his accomplice who produced a knife.

The odds should have been in Kismet's favour
but youth, fear and uncertainty was no match for
a determined criminal. Stepping forward neatly,
he lashed out, slicing at Kismet's arm. The youth
let out a scream and dropped his weapon, blood
pouring through the white of his shirt onto the

carpet, dyeing the gold red. Like a beautifully crafted piece of choreography, the older waiter appeared, kitchen knife in hand, threatening the two remaining customers, insisting that he'd slit their throats if they didn't comply. Something about the coldness of his expression suggested that this was no bluff. Kismet gabbled something in Urdu to his former colleague, his expression pleading. The man merely flashed a contemptuous look and, dragging the man still seated to his feet, forced the two terrified customers through the swing doors of the kitchen, emerging minutes later with a wad of keys, tossing them onto a side table. Both waiters, mute with shock, were bundled into the room at the back. Nobody seemed to remember the two missing diners.

First, there was silence. Tallis tiptoed out and across the floor, ears keen. The air felt electric with violence and fear. Then he heard the low note of urgent voices, punctuated by a shout, a yell, the noise of shattering glass, furniture being overturned, rising to a crescendo and a terrible scream of pain. Picking up the redundant meat cleaver from the floor, he made his way noiselessly to the back of the room. Before he reached it, a door flew open, the treacherous waiter, pouring with blood, trying to claw his way out before being dragged back by Hussain's accomplice. Without breaking stride, Tallis burst in, eyes flicking as he took in the scene. One body down, blood on the floor, Kismet's beautiful face beaten to mush, the hawk-eyed waiter making a run for it, Hussain's henchman in pursuit. Hussain, his face cracked with menace, remained silent. Still no gun, just rank, brute fear. Planting himself firmly between the fleeing man and his aggressor, Tallis took a swing with the meat cleaver, catching Hussain's man full on the elbow, cleaving flesh from bone, almost severing the limb. The man's face contorted in agony as he collapsed and splayed on the floor, his jacket falling open. Tallis saw and reached for the gun just as Hussain pulled his, pointing it at Kismet's head. Tallis smiled. No guidelines, no restrictions, shoot to kill. His first shot hit Hussain between the eyes, felling him. The second, close up, dispatched him.

As Tallis ran to the terrified waiter, he heard a clamour, the sound of doors crashing, voices, clatter of footsteps, strangely familiar. The door to the office burst open. Three firearms officers piled in.

'Drop your weapon,' the lead firearms officer barked. 'You're under arrest.'

Tallis did as he was told, arms raised, letting them roughly push him to the floor, frisk and cuff him. Then he heard a voice that made his mouth dry. He lifted his head from the carpet. The stance was familiar as was the expression.

'Hello, Paul,' Dan Tallis said.

CHAPTER NINETEEN

They glared at each other. Histories of confrontation, accusation, lies and argument roared into the forefront of Tallis's brain. The room was so thick with mutual contempt it felt airless.

'This is completely out of order,' Tallis fumed. 'You're my brother, for Chrissakes. You're not allowed to interview me.'

They'd taken him to the nearest police station, read him his rights, put him in a holding cell for an hour before dragging him back out again. Dan, whom he hadn't clapped eyes on in over a year, gloated over every minute of it, just as he'd done when they'd been kids and Tallis had been taking a bollocking from their father. He looked well, Tallis thought, hair thick and shiny, eyes bright, and the pale grey jacket he was wearing fitted snugly and expensively across his broad shoulders. Power obviously suited him.

'So let's run through this again,' Dan said. 'You hit the guy with the meat cleaver, almost severing his arm, and then took his gun and killed his partner. Nice double tap, by the way.'

Tallis said nothing.

'The alternative scenario is that you were in on the robbery. Things got heavy and you decided to take the opportunity to eliminate your rivals and take the money for yourself.'

'Why would I do that?' Tallis said, cold.

'Because you're a washed-up nobody and need the loot.'

Tallis let out a laugh, the quickest way to antagonise his brother. 'What do the waiters say?'

'Haven't spoken to the witnesses yet.'

Too traumatised, Tallis thought, staring at Dan. Looking back through the history books, Tallis often considered how brother could fight against brother, father against son. The answer was usually found in the cause. In the case of the Balkans, nationalism led to ordinary decent people betraying their neighbours, often when they'd lived alongside them in harmony for many years. But this thing between him and Dan was not about a cause or a difference of religious belief or creed, not even about him taking his brother's wife. The seeds of hostility had been sown a long time before. When exactly, he couldn't put a finger on. 'I'm allowed a phone call.' One to Cavall, that's all he wanted. She wouldn't be able to spring him from this one, more likely to abandon him, but she might know a decent lawyer.

'But we're still having a chat.'

'I'm not bloody talking to you.'

'Think that's what you said the last time we met.' Dan smiled, his upper lip curling in contempt.

'Please, don't tell me that's what this is all about.' Tallis let out a derisive laugh.

'You flatter yourself.' Dan's eyes were like stone, reminding Tallis of their father.

'Moved on, have you? Repaired your wounded pride, or still playing victim? Just like you always do.'

Dan's jaw pulsed with hatred. 'Know what you are? You're a shag-and-run merchant.'

'Still clinging to convenient lies,' Tallis scoffed. 'Always have been. Always will be.'

'I'd rather be accused of that than a wife-beater,' Tallis said, leaning forward, eyes drilling into Dan. 'For the benefit of the tape,' Tallis repeated, 'Dan Tallis is a wife-beater.'

The tic in his brother's face throbbed a little faster. 'You have no evidence to support that allegation.'

'You deny it?'

'Not worth a response.' There was a shifty expression in his eye that only Tallis could detect. Tallis was determined to press home his advantage. He hoped the whole fucking station would hear about his lovely elder brother.

'So what are you saying, that Belle lied?'

Dan threw back his head and laughed. 'She constantly lied. About where she was, whom she was with, what she was doing. Why wouldn't she lie about that, too?'

'Because you've always had a vile temper,' Tallis said, pointing to the scar on his forehead.

'Not that old chestnut again,' Dan mocked. 'It was nothing more than a little high spirits. A simple childhood accident.'

'Wasn't high spirits with Belle, though, was it? The hospital reports tell a very different story.'

'What story?' Dan said with derision.

'The story that tells the truth.'

'The truth?' Dan exploded. 'Good, coming from you. Why didn't she press charges, then?'

Tallis sat back meditatively, folding his arms,

feeling the small of his back against the hard plastic of the chair. He suddenly felt totally and utterly in command. Reminded him of the day he'd confronted his father in the bus shelter, seen the fear in his eyes. 'You really don't know her, do you? And that was always your trouble, Danny boy. You neither took the time nor the trouble to find out.'

'Next you'll be telling me you were only interested in her mind,' Dan sneered.

Tallis felt his knuckles tense. If he hadn't been in a police station, he'd have punched his brother in the face. 'You're such an arrogant prat. You think she stayed quiet to protect you.'

'Nothing to protect me from. I didn't hit her. Never hit her. Wouldn't lay a finger on her.' He sounded confident but the sudden pallor of his skin told a different tale.

'I saw what you did to her,' Tallis hissed.

'All lies.'

But Tallis wasn't letting it go. Not this time. 'What kind of man hits a woman? Someone with problems, insecurities?' He thought of Demarku. 'Someone who can't get it up...'

Dan leapt from his chair, and launched himself across the table, grabbing Tallis round the throat.

'She wanted to protect Dad,' Tallis spat at him. 'She didn't want to break the heart of a dying man.'

Dan stared, frozen, his grip on Tallis tight then loosening. Seconds thudded by. For the very first time Tallis wondered how Dan would cope with their father's inevitable death. How badly it would hit him. Finally, Dan let him go. Dusting the shoulders of his jacket, Dan stood up and pressed the eject button on the tape recorder, slipping the tape out, holding it up. 'This one's faulty,' he said, spooling out the contents and scrumpling them up in his hand. 'Shame,' he said, walking out.

Instead of being questioned again, Tallis was taken back to his cell where he spent the next couple of hours asleep. Wasn't easy. His was the only cell not filled by the latest influx of overflow prisoners from Strangeways. Shortly before six in the morning, he heard footsteps outside, a woman's voice and the sound of jangling keys. As the lock sprang open, Cavall glided in, groomed and composed. There wasn't a hair out of place and her make-up was perfect. Tallis bet she was one of those women who regularly rose at four in the morning to work out.

'You're free to go.' She smiled.

'Power and influence,' he said, throwing her a quizzical look as he walked past. How the hell had she wheedled her way round this one? He thought it was supposed to be a black operation, that, in all likelihood, he would be disowned rather than rescued.

Together they collected his belongings, for which he signed. There was no sign of Dan. The only thing Tallis missed was not seeing the expression on his brother's face at the report of his release.

As he stepped outside he thought urban air had never smelt so good.

'Sorry I can't give you a lift,' Cavall said, indicating the car parked with its driver a hundred yards up the road.

'No problem. I'll walk you there.'

'Chivalrous to the last.' She smiled.

Tallis returned her smile and played escort. On reaching her car, he opened the back passenger door for her. 'Expect you're waiting for a vote of thanks for getting me out of another hole.'

She turned to him, agreed with her eyes, flashed another Kodak-moment smile.

'Well, I'm not going to,' he said, pushing her in and jumping in beside her. 'Tell him to drive,' he snarled.

Startled, Cavall told the driver there was a change of plan, instructing him to take a turn round the block.

'Can he hear?' Tallis said, his voice low.

'Not any more,' she said with a wintry smile, sliding the glass partition across. The driver looked into his rear-view mirror, concern on his face. Tallis beamed at him and nodded hello.

'Did you know my brother was going to descend?'

'Tallis, of course n–'

'You going to tell me what's going on?'

'For God's sake, Paul...'

'I've just killed a man.'

'What was the alternative?'

'Killing wasn't part of the deal.'

Cavall rounded on him. 'I never said it was going to be easy.'

'And you never said that people like Djorovic would die.'

'Oh, God, what is it with you and women?'

'She was a human being. She was supposed to be put on a flight home. She...' He stopped. Was

231

she? What was really supposed to happen to these people? Christ Almighty, what had he got into? 'Who are you?' he said, eyes drilling into hers. Then he suddenly remembered his very first impression of her. He'd had her down for a spook.

'I already explained,' Cavall said testily.

'Your explanation isn't convincing enough. I want out. Now. No argument.'

Cavall clicked her tongue. 'You're being tiresome. I don't like to point out the intricacies of your situation. I've done everything in my power to protect you, but...' She tailed off, let the full implication of what she was saying sink in.

'You're blackmailing me.'

'Please, don't be so dramatic.' She rested her hand on his arm. 'One more job and it will all be over. Money in the bank. You can sell up. Go abroad, if you want to. Clean slate. And we need never meet again.'

'What about Dan?'

'What about him?' Her brown eyes leveled with his. There was something in her manner that went way beyond the question. It seemed as if she was issuing him with an invitation to confess, but to what he couldn't fathom. They were almost back at the police station. She lifted a briefcase onto her lap, opened it, took out a file and handed it to him. It came with an ominous warning.

'Your patch,' she said.

CHAPTER TWENTY

Tallis returned to the hotel, picked up his belongings and checked out. He didn't want to shower, didn't want to eat. There were too many crazy ideas floating round his head. He was thinking of puppetmasters and puppets. He'd taken Cavall at her word, assumed she was working with the full backing of the Home Office and the Prime Minister. Finn had confirmed her credentials, but what if they were false? What if she had another agenda? What if someone else was pulling her strings?

The journey back was horrendous, tailback after tailback on the M6. He arrived home at half past twelve. After dumping his overnight bag in the hall, he walked round the minuscule perimeters of the bungalow, examining pot plants, furniture, and light fittings. Eventually, he found what he was looking for. An electronic listening device had been plated in the handset on his phone. How very antiquated, he thought, thinking of a number of more sophisticated devices and methods of eavesdropping currently in use. He wondered how long it had been there. Taking it out, he destroyed it. For good measure, he walked outside and tossed it into next-door's dustbin. Apart from the crudeness of the device, the easy deduction would be that security services were watching him. To what purpose exactly, he wasn't sure.

And, in any case, they were all supposed to be caught up and focused on the terrorist threat. He believed it. The intelligence service couldn't sustain another cock-up. But what if it was Cavall, operating quite independently, who was watching him?

Next, he checked his messages. There were four, two from Micky Crow: can you get in touch type message. The second was confrontational: 'We need to talk and soon.' One from Finn, the other from his mother. Finn's was short and to the point – call me. His mother's was loquacious. She sounded sad, Tallis thought, reminding himself of the oath he and Belle had taken. Never say anything. Never shatter his parents' dreams. Suddenly, he was transported back to that fateful night, almost two years ago now. Ironically, he had been visiting his brother's house on his mother's behalf; she'd wanted him to drop by with a gift for Dan's birthday. With his father falling ill, transport had become a problem; his dad had always insisted on doing most of the driving to the extent that his mother was no longer confident behind the wheel. Certainly, the thought of a trip to Birmingham had been out of the question for her. So Tallis had been acting as good Samaritan. It had been pouring with rain, he remembered.

Tallis rapped at the door for a second time. Rain was sheeting down, flattening his hair against his scalp, some of the moisture trickling down inside his collar. The house was in darkness save for one sickly light shining faint in the hallway. At first, deciding that they were both out, he began to return to his car when he heard a noise, a human voice, like something muffled, a sob maybe.

'Belle?' he said. 'Is that you?'

This time he heard the sound more clearly. Yes, it was definitely someone crying. 'Belle, it's me, Paul.'

'Sorry, I can't come to the door.' Her voice was so strained and quiet, he had to put his ear up right against the wood to hear her.

'Come on, it's pissing down out here.'

'Paul, just go away.'

Go away? What the hell was going on? 'I'm not going anywhere. Come on, let me in.'

'Can't,' she gulped, weeping again.

'Surely, whatever's wrong, it can't be so bad,' he said gently.

More tears. Goodness, he thought, has someone died? 'Is Dan there?'

The sobbing verged on the hysterical. Christ, Tallis thought, he's left her. It was the only conclusion that seemed to make sense. 'Is this about Dan?' he asked tentatively.

This time she broke down completely.

'Belle, honey, please, open the door.' He must have pleaded for at least another five minutes before she did. When he saw the half-closed eye, the swollen lip, the cuts and bruises, it was the most shocking sight he'd ever witnessed.

'How could I ever have been seduced by him?' she howled as he put his arms around her in a simple act of kindness. And that's how it had all begun.

He'd found it easy to lie to his father. He'd

235

never been believed by him even when he'd been telling the truth so what did it matter? His mother had been different. She knew him too well. To protect her, he'd become distant, secretive, falling into the role of guilty son, which he supposed he was if he were honest, letting her think the worst of him.

Taking his cellphone, he went outside and walked down the road to the little row of shops and found a bench to sit on, allowing the distorting clamour of city traffic to form a natural barrier to anyone trying to listen in. He phoned Crow.

'Ah, the elusive Mr Strong,' Crow said, her voice rasping. 'I've been trying to get hold of you.'

'Really?'

'Yes. Been avoiding me, by any chance?'

'Not at all. I've had a family emergency to deal with.' Always good for an excuse, he thought.

A brief pause indicated that Crow was not convinced. 'Our mutual friend,' she began, a sarcastic note in her voice. 'Agron Demarku.'

'What about him?' Tallis said, nerves stinging.

'He was found dead.'

'How?' Tallis said. He felt no shock. An ugly picture was snapping into view. Except, of course, to Crow's eyes, it looked as if he had been part of it – the only reason she was on the blower.

'Fell out of a bedroom window onto metal railings.'

Ouch. 'That was careless of him.'

'I assure you, Mr Strong, there was nothing careless about what happened to Mr Demarku. He was most definitely pushed.'

'Where?' Tallis said, feeling slightly numb.

'Place in Camden, on my patch. I'd have come through a little sooner but I've been on leave. As soon as I heard, I remembered our cosy conversation down the pub, remembered your interest in the man, remembered the brothel that never was and our two famous woman-hating Croats. Oh, did I tell you, the woman they abducted died?'

His heart sank. Say as little as possible, he thought. That way she'd be less likely to trip him up.

'As I'm now handling the investigation, I'd like to interview you.'

'In what capacity?'

'In any capacity I deem fit.'

He thought about appealing to the dark side of her nature. Crow was no more a fan of Demarku than he was. She knew exactly what the man had been capable of but, like him, she was a professional. They both recognised that even bad people had rights. Demarku, care for it or not, had been a victim.

'Look, like I said, I'm simply writing about the bloke. You surely can't think I had anything to do with his murder. It's a matter of simple coincidence.'

Crow's laugh was cold. 'Was it also coincidence that you were seen in the area near his flat on the morning he was pushed?'

'What?'

'We have CCTV footage that proves you were there.'

'Well, maybe I was.'

237

'You admit it?'

'There's nothing to admit. Yes, I was there. Yes, I saw him.'

'In his flat?'

'Yes, but it's a stretch to suggest I was responsible for giving him the grand heave-ho. I mean, why would I do something like that?'

'You tell me, but this time we're going to do it by the book.'

'Fine,' Tallis said, thinking, Shit. 'I'll come down to see you. Will I need a solicitor with me? I'm not under caution or anything, am I?'

'No.'

That sounded better. 'Thing is, might be tricky just at the moment.'

'With your family emergency.' There was an edge to Crow's voice that Tallis didn't care for.

'Yes.'

'We can send a car.'

'All the way from London? I'm sure that won't be necessary.'

'Think I'll decide what's necessary, Mr Strong, if you don't mind.'

Oh, God, he thought, how was he going to explain about the name change, that he wasn't really a journalist at all? 'Yes, of course. I didn't mean–'

'Tomorrow morning, ten o'clock. That all right?'

'Thing is...' Tallis swallowed.

'Yes?'

'The funeral's tomorrow.'

'Oh.'

Good, he thought, that should knock the wind

238

out of her sails. He decided to get even more creative. 'My brother was an alcoholic. Years of abuse finally caught up with him. Heavy smoker as well, you see. We've had a terrible time, as you can imagine.'

'Yes, of course. Sorry,' she burbled. 'Sorry for your loss.'

'So, if we could do this another time?'

'Day after tomorrow, then?' The edge had crept back into her voice.

Fuck, he thought. He'd hoped to buy himself more time than that. Without a choice, he politely agreed.

Tallis got straight on the phone to Cavall. He didn't quiz her about the bug in his sitting room. He didn't moan about the mishap with Djorovic, or the cock-up with Hussain, or the latest information on Demarku. He laid everything on the line for her.

'You want me to pull strings to prevent you meeting with Crow?'

'Can you do it?'

'This is becoming a little repetitive,' she said icily.

'Fine. I see Crow. She'll discover my real identity, know that I'm a liar, and have me arrested. I won't be much use to you if I'm stuck in some prison cell.'

'True.'

'We have a deal?'

'This is the last time I bail you out.'

Tallis smiled. He liked balance and right now the scales were even on both sides. She needed

239

him as much as he needed her. Next he contacted Finn.

'Nothing on Cavall yet,' Finn announced, 'but a guy, believed to be Agron Demarku, was found dead.'

Tallis didn't tell Finn that he already knew. He wanted to find out if Finn had different information or another angle on the murder.

'According to my source at the MET,' Finn continued, 'they think he was involved in a turf war with other dealers.' Interesting, Tallis thought. Crow hadn't mentioned that particular line of enquiry. She was clearly acting on information that only she was privy to. 'Apparently the guy tried to escape by hiding in the loo, but whoever was after him smashed down the door. Whether he was pushed, hurled or jumped is unclear. What was clear he was absolutely rat-arsed.'

'You mean drunk.' *Just like Djorovic*, Tallis thought.

'That's what that expression usually means.' Finn laughed lightly.

'Demarku was a Muslim. He didn't drink.'

'Come on, Paul. How many times have you heard about the celibate priest having a fling with his parishioner?'

Wasn't the same, he wanted to say. The plight of the Lithuanian girl flashed across his mind. What had they done to Elena, whoever *they* were? 'How do you view the investigation?'

'Quite honestly, and this is only my take on it, I'm not sure the cops are that focused.'

That's not the impression Crow gave, Tallis thought. Something that was clear, however, there was little communication between the police and the Home Office. Finn was still speaking. 'The bloke, as you said, was here illegally and was a complete bastard by all accounts. Think they view it as one drug dealer taking out another. Happens all the time.'

Trust Micky Crow to take over and get the bit between her teeth. Just my luck, Tallis thought. 'Thanks, Finn. I appreciate all that.'

'You all right?'

'Yes.'

'You don't sound it.'

'This thing with Felka,' he said vaguely.

'Max's au pair? Yeah, tough one.'

Neither of them spoke. Tallis broke first. 'Finn?'

'Yeah?'

'This whole thing with Cavall. Tread carefully, won't you?' Watch your back was what he meant.

Tallis made a pot of strong coffee and sat and drank and thought, trying to work out the schematic. All three foreign nationals were dead, two by parties unknown, one by his own hand. Like it or not, it looked as if a death squad was at work. Tallis frowned. A killing machine given the full backing of the British Government? Surely not, and, more to the point, why? Killing a few illegals wasn't exactly something you boasted about, which meant there had to be another motive, another game plan. Christ, if Cavall was working under orders, it left him with nowhere to turn. So what was the other scenario? That she was acting alone, a rogue agent? But her credentials were impeccable. No, Tallis thought, her *legend* was impeccable. It had happened before. There had always been traitors in the camp. And Cavall wouldn't be the only one. She was probably a cog in a very large machine. Trouble was, who was fronting it and where did that leave him?

Putting his own position to one side for a moment, he returned to what lay behind the operation. He'd often thought that halfway to cracking a crossword was working out how the architect of the crossword thought. Applying that kind of logic, and working it backwards, there were certain pointers – perfect choreography, manipulation, ruthlessness, above all, power. Conclusion? The people he was charged with tracing, without doubt evil in their own right, were victims. Was there a pattern there? Were there links? Apart from the obvious common denominators, he couldn't see any.

As for Cavall, his enquiry about Djorovic had been perfectly understandable, arising as it had from the newspaper report. If he called Cavall again, demanding to know what had gone wrong in the arrest of Demarku, she'd know he'd been digging and become alert to his suspicions. So, he concluded, if he were to find out what was really going on, he had to play along, act the willing partner in her plan, lull her into a false sense of security. Cavall was his only contact to someone much bigger and higher up the food chain so he would use her. The last case – except he now realised there would never be a last case, would always be one more job, one little operation – provided him with the perfect opportunity.

242

This time he wouldn't let the target out of his sight until he could guarantee full and utter security. If that meant taking on Bill and Ben, who he was now absolutely convinced were bogus immigration officers, Cavall and her paymasters, so be it. He had no choice. They'd kill him anyway once he'd reached the extent of his usefulness. He drained his cup. He imagined the scenarios – car accident, falling into a canal, taking his own life after cracking under the strain, too much booze in his bloodstream, a mugging that went disastrously wrong.

He got up, went into the kitchen, pulled out a bottle of Scotch from the cupboard under the sink, found it virtually empty. Cursing, he grabbed his keys, walked to the off-licence, the sun like a blowtorch upon his back. On his return, he thought how only weeks ago he'd taken his existence for granted. It hadn't been great. He'd felt unfulfilled personally and professionally, but he'd got by. And now...

There looked like some kind of scuffle up ahead, three white youths swinging punches at a foreign-looking lad, no more than fifteen or sixteen by the look of him. The lad had both hands up in a defensive gesture, trying to reason with them, his shoulders bowed with fear, but mindless violence was what the blunt-heads wanted. Everything about them, from the pale snarl on their faces, the erratic eye movement to the way they moved, jerking around the pavement, circling the boy, confirmed Tallis's worst suspicions: they were looking for prey.

Tallis called out, but his shout was lost in a

sudden clamour of fists and kicks. The lad went down heavily onto the pavement to whoops of delight by his tormentors. As the boots went in, Tallis dumped the Scotch in the hedge and ran, charging the biggest and most aggressive of the trio, sending him flying into a telegraph pole. For good measure, he picked him up by the collar of his shirt and threw his head back against the solid wood, knocking him unconscious, then turned and started on the others. As one lad came straight towards him, Tallis parried with his left hand and threw a right hook with his other, connecting with the youth's leaden jaw, pole-axing him. The third lout, a thin stick of a guy with greasy long hair and bent features, was continuing to scream abuse at the youngster on the pavement, calling him a Paki, vicious toecaps connecting with the victim's groin.

Tallis felt a red mist of anger descend. Grabbing hold of the youth by his hair, he forced him to his knees, and bumped him along the pavement. 'You're a fucking moron, know that?' Tallis yelled at him, dragging him back and forcing him close enough to see his victim without giving him the chance to hit him. 'Now say you're sorry.'

'Fuck off,' the youth spat.

Tallis changed position, grabbed the guy's arm, pushing it back, straight, making him howl. 'Say sorry.'

The lad gasped.

'*Say* it.' More bend, more snap.

'Sorry,' the lad screamed.

'Louder.'

'*Sorry.*'

'Better,' Tallis snarled, letting him go. Tallis wondered, as the stringy-looking youth took to his heels, hugging his injured arm, if it was mere coincidence that the number on the back of his shirt was 35, or whether it spoke of a secret allegiance to Fortress 35.

He went over to the lad on the ground, helped him to his feet. He was clearly in pain, looking shocked and shaken, but no lasting damage seemed to have been inflicted. 'Are you all right?'

'*Si, si. Gracias, signor.*'

Tallis smiled, responded to him in Spanish, asked his name.

'Jose.'

'And what are you doing here, Jose? Where are you staying?'

'I am on holiday with my family. My uncle has a house nearby. He lives there.'

'Come, I'll take you back,' Tallis said.

'It's no problem.'

But Tallis insisted. After retrieving his bottle of whisky, he saw the youth to his door. He left before he was invited in and treated like a conquering hero.

Back home again, he pulled out a pad and pen, considered pouring out a large tumbler of whisky, but settled for a pot of tea instead. It wouldn't have the same kick but it would keep him alert and on the straight and narrow. He began to read the latest file. It concerned one Rasu Barzani, an Iraqi Kurd who'd fled his homeland in the 1990s, at the same time as the

245

Balkans had been engulfed in one of the bloodiest conflicts in modern Europe. Tallis gave a self-deprecating smile. Serving in the British army with the Staffordshires at the time, and feeling a familial pull, he'd hoped to be posted there.

Instead, he'd been sent out to liberate Kuwait as part of Operation Desert Storm. The conditions had been horrendous – one hundred degrees, weighed down by webbing, weapons, Kevlar and ammo, respirator and biological suit at the ready. He instantly recalled the filth, the taste of dry sand in the mouth, the smell of burning oil, eyes stinging. He also remembered sweating with fear, terrified by the very real prospect of chemical or biological attack in addition to the more straightforward, if no less deadly, threat of being cut down by machine-gun fire. He'd been scared, if he was honest, not so much that he might be killed but that he would have to kill. How would it feel to take another man's life, to see the fear and desperation in his eyes? The older, experienced soldiers assured him that anxiety was part of the deal, a good thing, a safety valve. Those who professed not to give a fuck were madmen. Sadly, Matt, Finn's brother, had been one of them. Tallis sighed, took a swig of tea and returned to the file.

Via a main transit route for asylum-seekers, Barzani had apparently been smuggled out by Turks on a boat heading for France, from where he'd continued his journey into the United Kingdom by lorry via the Channel. Since Barzani spoke little English, how he'd fetched up in Birmingham was a mystery. Tallis made a note on

246

the pad and pulled out Barzani's mug shot. The last exile, Tallis thought, staring into the man's sad eyes. He had a wide forehead, high pointed cheekbones, bridge of his nose straight, unbroken, skin slightly pitted. Couldn't call him a handsome man, Tallis thought, yet there was something deeply compelling about him. His was a face you couldn't easily turn away from. The dark, liquid eyes seemed to hold histories of painful secrets. Tallis returned to the main file.

Barzani had found employment as a paint sprayer in the body shop of a garage and haulage firm in Smethwick owned by a Mr Len Jackson. Nasty occupation, Tallis thought, especially if Barzani didn't have all the right protective kit. Poor bastard must have thought he was back home and being gassed again by Saddam Hussein. According to the prosecution, when Barzani's boss found out that he was living in the UK illegally, he went round to Barzani's bedsit in Oldbury, some miles away, and threatened to turn him in to the authorities. Tallis wrote another note. *Surely the guy knew about his illegal status from the off?* He read on. A row ensued between employer and employee. Tallis checked the time noted in the report. It said nine-thirty in the evening. Jackson left ten minutes later to go back to the garage. Barzani panicked, followed his boss, planning to persuade him to change his mind with the help of an iron bar, a popular weapon used by Turkish and Kurdish criminals with Mafia-style connections. A fight broke out and Barzani smashed the guy's head in.

Taking another drink of tea and putting the

247

mug to one side, Tallis pulled out the crime-scene shots, which were horrific. Walls and ceiling were coated with blood spatter and viscera. From the mess of overlapping footwear impressions, it was clear that a ferocious struggle had taken place.

Interestingly, Tallis noted, returning to the file, at first Barzani was deemed too violent to interview. Taken to a police cell, he was left to cool off while a full risk assessment was carried out to see whether it was safe for a doctor to talk to him via an interpreter. Six hours were lost. Eventually, Barzani was seen and interviewed but was later sectioned under the Mental Health Act and sent to a secure unit. Tallis made a further note. *What was wrong with Barzani?* He knew that in instances like this embassies sometimes got involved. The Home Office had agreements with certain states regarding crimes committed by foreign nationals with mental health problems, but Tallis guessed that Barzani, probably because of his refugee status, had fallen through the net.

Whether Barzani was given any form of medication wasn't clear, but eighteen months later he was considered fit enough to stand trial at Birmingham Crown Court, where he was sentenced to twelve years, serving his time at Winson Green Prison. Tallis made a note to try and talk to someone in the welfare department. Throughout the trial Barzani maintained his innocence. He admitted that he'd argued with his boss but over his working conditions not his illegal status. Apparently, Barzani had been injured a couple of weeks before and had broken some ribs in an accident at work, for which he blamed Jackson.

Further, Barzani maintained that his boss had attacked him, cuffing him round the head, giving him a bloody nose, treating him like a dog, he said. Barzani agreed that he had defended himself but denied ever leaving the bedsit, maintaining he'd been nowhere near the garage when the killing had taken place. Unfortunately, he had no alibi.

Turning the pages, Tallis cut back to the interview notes. Even making allowances for the cold-blooded nature of a black-and-white transcript, the line of questioning came across as positively medieval. It appeared that even very basic procedure had been thrown out of a very high window. Recorded times of the interview beginning and ending looked as though they had been scrawled in as a hasty after-measure, and the fundamental rule of allowing a detainee continuous eight hours' rest during any twenty-four-hour period simply hadn't taken place. It pointed to a gross failure in duty of care. That it should happen to a man who spoke no English and had a history of mental problems was unforgivable.

It got worse. Barzani was linked in time and place to the murder scene and indeed had sustained a minor injury during the row, yet a conviction could not be secured simply because the suspect's blood had been found at the scene. Moreoever, there was no record of Barzani ever boarding a bus from Oldbury to Smethwick, or getting a taxi, and no weapon was ever found. And, Tallis thought, nobody seemed to have considered the fact that Barzani's overalls and clothing were clean when they should have been soaked in blood. *Forensics,* he scrawled, thinking of Belle, feeling that old, familiar tug on his heartstrings.

Tallis spooled back the pages, skimming over the text. A cleaner was first on the scene and made the grim discovery. Police were called, family informed. Jace Jackson, the son, identified the body of his father. Tallis sat back. Nobody at the Jackson household seemed to register that Len Jackson was missing. Why not? Did it point to sticky relations between husband and wife, or a simple oversight, misunderstanding? He went back to the file, his retinas almost detaching as he caught sight of a name buried in among the rest. Blinking in disbelief, he read it again, feeling the blood congeal in his veins. The first police officer on the scene of the killing was none other than a young constable: P.C. Daniel Tallis.

CHAPTER TWENTY-ONE

Tallis went for a run. He'd read the entire contents of the file twice. Could be coincidence, but he was starting to get a very queasy feeling about his elder brother. The more he thought about the fraternal connection, the worse it became until in the end he just gave himself up to pounding the pavement, anything to drum out the questions circling in his head. Sweat pouring off him, he ran back home and took a long shower, dressed and went through the motions of preparing something to eat, which wasn't easy when he hadn't visited a supermarket for a bit. Working on the premise that an army didn't march well on an empty stomach, he fell back on an old standby and knocked up a passable pasta sauce, adding some chopped bacon and half a tin of mushrooms, combining this with a pan of well-cooked Fusilli – he detested the fashion for eating pasta al dente.

A further rummage yielded a bottle of wine he'd bought for a party and somehow managed to leave behind. Wine wasn't the same as whisky, he told himself, and a little might do him some good, steady his nerves. One glass later, he realised that certain wines were for pleasure, others for getting hammered. At a blowsy fourteen and a half per cent, this one fell into the latter category. He put the cork back in, paced the sitting room, sat down, switched on the television, watched half of one soap, switched to another, considered the possible merit of an *X Factor* for stand-up comedians and caught the ten o'clock news. Two black guys had been beaten up and knifed in a Nottingham park by a gang of Asian thugs. More doom and gloom. Switching off the TV, he picked up his mobile and stared at it. He knew she'd be up, knew she'd be there, knew that she'd let voice mail take the call just like she always did, except this time he didn't want only to hear her voice. This time he needed her.

Taking a breath, he punched in Belle's landline number. It rang three times. He was waiting for the message service to kick in. It didn't. It kept on ringing. Puzzled, he hung up and called again. Same result. No matter, he thought, punching in her mobile number. This time it didn't even connect. Rattled, he picked up his car keys, walked outside. Breath caught in the fading light, he got into his car and drove to the house Belle had once shared with his brother.

He'd never liked Victorian properties, semi or detached. There was something too austere about them, he thought, drumming his fingers on the steering-wheel, wondering what sort of reception he'd get. He glanced at his watch for a second time. It was approaching eleven.

Lights were still on downstairs. He could hear the faint sound of classical music drifting through an upstairs window. Strange, he thought. Didn't know Belle was a classical music fan. So much he guessed he didn't really know about her. He looked at his watch again. Thirty seconds had passed. This was ridiculous, he thought. He felt more nervous now than he'd ever felt before attending a firearms incident.

He got out of the car, locked it, walked the short distance to the house and rapped on the door. His hands were sweating. The sound of heavy footsteps rang hollow in the hall. The door swung open and a middle-aged man with thick black spectacles stared at him with a quizzical expression.

'Belle in?' Tallis said, wondering who the hell he was.

'Belle?'

'Belle Tallis. She lives here.'

The man's face suddenly brightened. 'Oh, Mrs Tallis. Not any more. Moved two weeks ago.'

'Any idea where to?' Tallis said, feeling as though someone had punched him in the stomach.

'Well, I'm not sure whether...'

'Police,' Tallis smiled, taking his wallet from his jacket and flashing it, hoping to God the man didn't ask to examine his credentials.

'Right,' the man said, nodding his head slowly, digesting the latest piece of information with great seriousness. 'Hold on a second.' He disappeared, leaving Tallis nervously on the doorstep. The music dipped in volume, replaced by the sound of low male voices. Had a woman answered the door, Tallis doubted he could have pulled it off. Women were more suspicious than men. They thought in terms of stalker, ex-husband, serial killer. The man with the spectacles returned, followed by a younger guy dressed in a smart suit. 'There you go,' he said, handing Tallis a piece of paper with an address scrawled on it.

'Serious, is it?' the young man said shamelessly fishing. He was coarse-featured and his voice had a suggestive quality.

'Nah. Need her to help us with some enquiries,' Tallis smiled, pocketing the note, thanking them, moving quickly down the steps and away.

He drove towards the city centre with a hollow feeling in the pit of his stomach. Why hadn't Belle let him know? Why had she cut all ties? Christ, all the time he'd been thinking of her being there, she'd been somewhere else. All crap, he thought sternly. Why should she let him know?

Why wouldn't she cut all ties? That's what they'd agreed. He was behaving like a sentimental schoolboy.

He turned off Broad Street and into Gas Street, parking the car outside the Tap and Spile, an old pub with water-side views of the canal. Royal Mailbox, the note said, a B1 address. Certainly a step up in the world, Tallis considered, walking back up the street and into the wide entrance of a newly built development of apartments lit up like a Christmas tree. He'd always fancied a place like that – modern, with style, appliances new and fully functional. Worlds apart from his decrepit bungalow. Passing the gates to the underground car park, he drew the collar of his jacket up. The night was clear and it wasn't particularly cold, yet he felt a chill as though a light inside his heart had fused.

The apartments had a concierge service. A big black guy was sitting at a desk that stretched from one wall to another. He was reading a magazine and eating a sandwich. On seeing Tallis, he bundled both away, wiped his mouth with a paw of a hand and nodded. This was the provider of eyes and ears, Tallis thought, rather than security. Probably there to log people's comings and goings, take the odd delivery. Even so, he was worth getting onside.

'Come to visit 313.'

'She expecting you?' The man beamed, unaware that in one simple question he'd given away the sex of the occupant.

'Yes,' Tallis said. If he said no, he'd raise the man's suspicions. Just hoped to God Belle played along. Hell of a long shot.

The man waved him through. Tallis walked up the slight incline and came to a set of electronic gates. On the wall was an entry system not dissimilar to the one he'd advised Max to install. It had an infrared camera enabling the occupant to view all visitors. Underneath was a panel of numbers with a search name and call facility. Taking a deep breath, Tallis punched in the number and pressed the call button. There was a small pause then the sound of Belle's low voice.

'Hello?'

'Belle, it's me, Paul.'

'Paul?' she said, astounded.

'I need to see you.'

'But we had an agreement.'

Tallis felt his blood pressure rise. Please, he prayed, don't blow me out. 'I know. I'm not doing this lightly. I wouldn't have come but this is really important. I need your help, Belle.'

'But–'

'Please. I'm in trouble.' He waited for what seemed like minutes. A motorbike roared down a road nearby. The sound of summer evening revellers punctuated the warm night air.

'All right,' she said, buzzing him through. 'Second door to the left across the courtyard.'

Tallis let out a breath, thanked her and went inside, following her instructions. On his approach, the door clicked open, allowing him in. Impressive security, he thought, taking the lift. He wondered if Belle had deliberately chosen it, if she feared that one day Dan would come back and give her a hiding.

The apartment was directly opposite the lift. To his surprise, the door was open. It led into a small hall with a large chrome mirror on the back wall, the entry phone with visual display to his left. His was given the impression of complete white-out – white walls, white furnishings, pale, bleached wood.

There were two doors on each side, the one furthest away on the left revealing an extremely feminine bedroom, all crisp linen, Belle's red stilettos keeled over on carpet so thick he felt guilty for not removing his shoes. Opening the second door to his right, he entered a large open-plan living and dining area, ultra-modern kitchen, with glass-topped dining table and two chairs, Venetian in style. The sofas were squashy leather, caramel-coloured. Stairs led down to another level, which he presumed was a second bedroom or study. Like a man with a burning thirst, he took it all in – prints on the wall, low lights, everything in muted soothing shades.

Belle had her back to him. She was looking out of a window facing the courtyard. From the set of her shoulders, he could tell that her arms were tightly folded. He sensed her anger.

His shoes were noiseless as he crossed the floor. Belle didn't turn, made no motion. She was wearing a bright white shirt and pale denims brilliantly cut to accentuate her tightly formed rear. An image of her naked and him fucking her flashed through his mind. The closer he came, the more her perfume scented the air. The night felt electric. The sight of her dark hair cascading down her back made him shiver. Closer now, he thought, feeling a familiar thrust of desire, one more pace and he could touch her, put his arms around...

'What the hell are you doing here?' she snapped, whirling round, dark-chocolate eyes flashing. 'We had an agreement. We made promises.'

She looked angry and sounded desperate, yet she was still the most beautiful woman in the world to him. Her finely boned face was as exquisite as the day he'd met her over a decade before. Two years older than him, fine lines were just starting to appear at the corners of her eyes. Made her look sexier than ever, if that were possible.

'I know,' he said simply. 'I wouldn't have come but—'

'Paul,' she pleaded. 'There can't be any buts. Why do you think I left no forwarding address?' Her face suddenly fell into a deep frown. 'How did you track me down?'

'By stealth and deception.' He smiled.

'You shouldn't have done,' she said, her mouth a short straight line. 'You had no right. You—'

'For God's sake, Belle, calm down.'

'Don't tell me to calm down,' she railed. 'I'm trying to get my life together and then you come along and—'

'Spoil things?' His voice was shot through with anger. Christ, was it always this exhausting between them? He'd forgotten.

'Typical of you to put words into my mouth.'

'Fuck this. I haven't come to fight.'

'No, then what have you come for?'

'This,' he said, taking hold of her, his mouth

257

searching hers, feeling her lips resist then open, her tongue entwine with his, her body firm against his own. The rest was a blur of teeth, skin and lust. Only afterwards when they'd stumbled to the bedroom did he realise that they'd done it in full view of anyone looking across from the other side.

'You look tired, Paul,' Belle said, tenderly tracing his eyelids with her finger. He noticed, as if for the first time, she no longer wore her wedding ring.

''Course I'm tired.' He grinned. 'I haven't had sex in over a year.' Not that he hadn't tried. If he had an undeserved reputation, might as well have a bash at living up to it, he'd thought foolishly. Somehow he hadn't been able to work up the requisite amount of enthusiasm. Combined with the undesirability of the bungalow as a potential love-nest, it had left him shamefaced on more than one occasion. He couldn't quite admit that making love was more than just sex. That if it wasn't with Belle he wasn't interested. Sounded too much like angst.

'That all you wanted?' Her eyes were smiling.

'If I say yes, you'll be offended. If I say no, you won't believe me.'

She let out a laugh. Her eyes sparkled, lighting up her face. 'How like you to cover all the options.'

'How like you to ask all the questions.' He grinned again.

'I'm a scientist, remember.'

He let his hand rest comfortably on her slim waist.

'Ah,' she said shrewdly. 'You're after my professional services.'

'That obvious?'

'Yeah, but you didn't have to sleep with me.'

'You complaining?'

She brushed his lips with her own. 'No.'

He squeezed her flank. A look of concern flashed over her features. 'You said you were in trouble.'

'Remember when Dan first joined the police, did he ever discuss the case of an Iraqi guy called Barzani?'

'God, you're going back a long way.'

'Barzani worked for a bloke running a garage in Smethwick.'

Belle shook her head. 'Not that I remember.'

'One night, Barzani beat his boss's brains in with an iron bar.'

Belle frowned. 'Why the interest?'

'Curiosity.'

Belle poked his ribs with her elbow. 'You'll have to do better than that.'

He grinned. She always knew when he was lying. 'Seem to be a few anomalies with the case.'

'What sort of anomalies?' she said, jacking herself up onto the pillows, revealing her wonderful breasts. He tried not to get distracted.

'Lack of certain evidence, for starters.'

'Christ, Paul, what are you suggesting?'

'Not suggesting anything.'

'Dan's a lot of things but he's not bent.'

Tallis wasn't so sure. He'd always wondered how Dan and Belle had afforded the house they'd once shared in Moseley even on combined incomes. Park Hill wasn't exactly a housing estate.

You didn't get much for less than five hundred K. However, it had to be admitted that Dan, as a young PC at the time, wouldn't have had that much influence. Tallis said the same to Belle.

Belle's face revealed little. He wondered, however, whether he detected a gleam of relief in her eyes. 'So why the doubts?' she said.

Tallis told her. The intelligence in her expression made him feel as if every word he spoke was important. When he'd finished, she asked him again about the overalls.

'There wasn't a spot of Len Jackson's blood on them.'

'Impossible. You say he was hit with an iron bar.'

'That was never found.'

'Imagine the impact. You'd have blood and bits of brain and tissue everywhere.'

'Exactly.'

'Which leads me to draw a very simple conclusion.' She smiled impishly.

'Yeah?'

'Barzani did what a lot of killers do – he destroyed his clothes.'

'Maybe, but the more I think about the fight, the more uncertain I feel. Barzani claimed that Jackson was the aggressor. He gave him a bloody nose so, of course, his blood was on Jones's clothes.'

'Linking him in time and place.'

'But that's my next problem. Barzani's bedsit was in Oldbury. You telling me he travelled all the way to Smethwick on a bus, an iron bar in his hand, to duff his boss up? Barzani was apparently the last to see Jones alive, but what if Barzani was telling the truth? What if someone else went to the garage?'

'Is that likely?'

'Why not?'

'Motive? Anything stolen?'

'No.'

'Police would have covered all the angles.'

Tallis was silent for a few moments. 'DNA testing has improved over the years, right?'

'Lots. Coming out with new techniques all the time. Problem we have is that analysis doesn't always keep step with DNA detection methods. The latest breakthrough is in disseminating between mixed DNA samples from crime scenes. We can work with what was originally classed as too poor in quality or too small. We're looking at cold cases as far back as ten or twenty years ago. Should put the fear of God into those who think they've got away with murder.'

Yeah, Tallis thought. He hoped so.

CHAPTER TWENTY-TWO

He left the next morning against a breaking light. They made no plans to see each other – it was implicit they would. With his dad so ill they'd just have to take special measures to keep it a secret. Walking back to the car, he felt lightness in his step, warmth in his heart. Whatever else was going on around him, he could deal with it if he had Belle. A faint noise behind him broke his concentration. He kept on walking, conscious of footsteps shadowing his own. As he got to the car, he whipped round, peered into the morning shadow. Nothing. Nerves, he thought.

Once home, he checked the place for electronic bugs – found none – showered, dressed, nipped to the nearest Tesco Express and stocked up on basics then bought himself a new mobile phone to match any new identity he might want to assume. As before, he ensured that the number was untraceable by anyone wishing to return or check his call. Back home again, he phoned the prison. Answered by a recorded message offering a range of options, Tallis waited patiently for an operator. Next followed a short spell of Vivaldi's *Four Seasons* before an unusually bubbly tele-phonist with a Yorkshire accent greeted him with a 'Hiya'. Tallis cranked himself up into flirt mode and explained that he was writing a book and wanted to check some basic facts with someone in the prison service.

'Ooh, is it a thriller?'

''Fraid not.'

'Shame. I love that *Wire in the Blood*. Tony Hill, he's gorgeous.'

'You mean Robson Green,' Tallis said, referring to the actor playing the part in the TV pro-gramme.

'What? His name's Tony.'

'Yeah, 'course,' he said, thinking asylums and lunatics. 'Who'd be best to speak to, do you think?'

'Our governor. He's ever so nice. Comes from the north, like me. Hold on.' After a lot of clicking and whirring, the telephonist came back. 'Sorry, he's tied up in a meeting. How about you speak to the deputy? She's the youngest female deputy governor in the country. We had the BBC down last year doing an interview.'

'Good for her,' Tallis said, feeling himself carried away by the telephonist's rampant enthusiasm. Unfortunately, it wasn't shared higher up. Stonewalled by a humourless secretary, he was told to contact the press office in London. Thanks but, no, thanks, he thought. Press officers were paid to sell a line, not give out information. Deciding he needed a different approach, he had some breakfast and left it an hour before he rang again. Same opening rigmarole, different telephonist. This time he asked directly for the probation and welfare department, most specifically the individual in charge of lifers. More clicking and buzzing and a guy called Ron Farrow picked up the call. Sounded warm and friendly enough, Tallis thought. From the seasoned tenor of the man's voice, he estimated Farrow's age as around mid-fifties. Tallis explained that he was writing a book and wanted to include an account of the Barzani case.

'Rasu Barzani?'

'Yes.'

'May I ask why?' Slight edge.

Tallis took a deep breath. Impersonating a police officer was a serious offence punishable by a prison sentence. He'd already transgressed once when he'd waved his wallet instead of a warrant card in front of the new owner of Belle's house. In for a penny, he thought. 'I was the original officer

263

on the scene. My name's Tallis.'

'Right,' Farrow said. 'Writing your memoirs?'

'Such as they are.'

'You know Barzani was due for deportation?'

'I did, actually. He got away. Some sort of data-sharing cock-up, wasn't it?'

Farrow wisely resisted a comment. 'I'll have to run a background check.'

'Sure,' Tallis said.

'Give me a few minutes and I'll call back.'

No, he wouldn't, Tallis thought. People in institutions never did. He managed to cram in a *Thanks, really appreciate it* before the line went dead.

Tallis paced up and down, filled the kettle, spooned coffee and sugar into a mug, deliberated whether he really wanted a hot drink and decided he didn't then changed his mind. The cellphone rang as the kettle was boiling.

'Tallis,' he said confidently.

'Hi, Dan. Ron here. You related to Paul Tallis?'

'Brother.'

'Rotten business, all that.'

Damn right, Tallis thought.

'So what did you want to know?'

'Gather Barzani continued to protest his innocence throughout his sentence.'

'That's right.'

'What do *you* think?'

There was a moment's hesitation. 'That's a very unusual question, especially from someone who arrested him.'

'I've had years to consider it.'

'Well,' Farrow said, 'while we get a fair number

264

of lifers who show little or no remorse, some protest their innocence. Of that small percentage, I'd say, there's a tiny proportion that are either extremely good actors or, and this is strictly off the record, are telling the truth. You have to understand it's not my job to have an opinion or pass judgement. My role is simply to look after their welfare.'

'Barzani had some mental health problems, didn't he?'

'Considering what the guy had been through, he seemed remarkably well balanced.'

'Been through?'

'In Iraq. Saddam Hussein did his best to wipe out most of his tribe in 1983. Rasu managed to escape but all twenty-nine members of his immediate family were killed in the most appalling fashion. Then the village he fled to was caught up in the notorious Anfal campaign.'

'The gassing of the Kurds?'

'Frankly, no horror was unimaginable to this guy.'

If that wasn't bad enough, Tallis thought, remembering the history, when the Kurds and Shi'ites had rebelled after the 1991 Gulf War – fuelled by plenty of Western encouragement – the Allies had fucked off, leaving them to a terrible fate. No surprise Barzani had gone mental. Any brush with authority would evoke horrific memories of his past. 'And the brief, violent episode after his arrest?'

'The only one. As you know, his mental state deteriorated considerably after his initial interview, and he was sectioned for a period of twelve months during which he received medication. Once convicted and sent here, he was drug free.'

Explaining why there were no medical reports suggesting otherwise, Tallis thought. 'I remember he barely spoke a word of English. We had to get an interpreter for him.'

'Viva Constantine. We still use Miss Constantine periodically.'

'Any chance of getting her number?'

'Don't see why not. Hold on.'

Tallis started to relax. This was going much better than he'd dared hope.

'Yup. Got a pen?'

Tallis took the number down. 'One last thing. How did Barzani strike you as a person?'

Farrow took his time to answer. 'I liked him. He seemed a very genuine, a very dignified man. As you know, offenders who refuse to acknowledge their guilt receive a rougher time in prison. Privileges can be axed. Journalists who might want to dig into the case are discouraged from doing so, visits limited.'

'Did he have any?'

'Visitors? Miss Constantine kept in touch.'

Kind of her, Tallis thought.

'Over the years, Rasu became resigned to what had happened to him without ever losing sight of his unshakable belief in his innocence. If I had to sum him up, he was a man of stoic endurance.'

'You wouldn't say he deserved to be hunted down and kicked out of the country?'

'He's here illegally,' Farrow said, sounding as if he was sticking to the party line.

'Off the record, think I got the wrong guy.'

'The system got the wrong guy.' There was a moment's pause. Farrow let out a laugh. 'But, of course, I never said that.'

Len Jackson's garage on Cape Hill wasn't listed in telephone directories – probably went out of business after the murder, Tallis thought. Determined to find out, he drove to Smethwick.

It was a blazing summer day, sun high in a sky of powder blue. Nothing, however, lifted the pall of dirt and deprivation hovering like a dark noxious cloud as he drew towards the town. Faces, black and white, young and old, looked careworn. Row upon row of terraced houses lined depressing-looking streets strewn with litter, vomit and cigarette ends. Razor wire the most common accessory to factory and warehouse security. It hadn't occurred to him before but the entire area seemed to borrow names from other places – Londonderry, Soho, Waterloo. Something and nothing, he guessed.

Cape Hill was a reservoir of pubs, accountants and firms selling cash registers and stationery supplies. He saw two ambulances, one with lights blazing, siren blaring, heading for City Hospital. There was no sign of the garage, although plenty of possible sites were boarded up.

He pulled up outside the Dog and Gun pub and walked into a dark and dingy interior, lights on in spite of the odd blade of sunshine trying to force its way through windows coated with grime on the outside, decades of nicotine on the inside. Four men had their backs to him. Four heads turned, stared and returned to their mild and bitter. A surly-looking bloke with a thin body and shaved head was standing behind the bar. Looked like a skull on a stick, Tallis thought. He asked him about the garage.

'Gone,' he said, the upward inflection of his Black Country accent making it sound like a question.

'Gone or located somewhere else?'

'Ah.' Tallis did the translation. He was fluent in Black Country: yes.

'Know where?'

'Cor help you.' Can't help you.

'Remember the murder?'

Skullhead viewed him as if he'd just crawled out of a swamp. Tallis eyeballed him, took out his wallet and slapped two ten-pound notes on the bar. Both stuck to the surface. Four pairs of eyes swivelled to the counter then fastened on him. Skullhead peeled off the notes with a bony hand and slipped them into his pocket. 'Darkie battered the old man's head in.'

Old man? Tallis didn't think fifty-four was that ancient. Unless, he realised, Skullhead was differentiating between father and son. 'Follow the case much?'

'Hard not to. Cops all over the fuckin' road, pokin' their noses in. Dunno why. Clear who the murderer was.'

'Fuckin' blacks for you,' one of the drinkers muttered. Tallis smiled at him. Tosser, he thought. 'And the old site?'

Skullhead answered. 'Which way you come?'

Tallis told him.

'Driven past it. Between the newsagent's and

268

the bookie's.'

'Business just died, then?'

The bloke who'd made the racist remark chipped in. 'New garage, ay it?' New garage, isn't it? 'Moved to Harborne.'

'Gone up in the world,' Tallis said.

'Ay called Jackson's any more neither.' Not called Jackson's any more either. 'Poncy fuckin' name. Trans Logistics and Distribution.'

Tallis met the man's expectant gaze. Ordinarily he'd have bought him a drink for volunteering the information. Fuck him, he thought, walking out.

Boarded up and cordoned off, the old site was a wasteland of footings, broken bottles, syringes and fly tipping – home to nobody other than rats and junkies, Tallis thought, peering through a hole in the fence. Stepping back onto the pavement, something connected in his brain. He stopped, went back to the fence, looked again, thinking, wondering, the vague thought that had briefly penetrated his consciousness floating away.

The betting shop was awash with punters so he went to the newsagent's on the other side.

A small very dark West Indian was serving. He wore a Rasta hat even though it was hot as hell.

'Wonder if you can help me?' Tallis smiled. 'The site next door, know much about it?'

'Been talk of developing it for the past fourteen years,' he drawled.

'Who owns it?'

'Jace Jackson.'

269

'Jace as in Jason?'

'Jace as in Jace, man.'

Tallis guessed there was a whole generation of kids whose parents had decided to call them something weird in order to give them a direct in-road to celebrity. 'Any relation to the previous owner?' He knew but wanted to check anyway.

'Guy who had his head smashed in?'

'Len Jackson.'

'Son,' the West Indian said.

'He runs Trans Logistics and Distribution?'

'You got it.'

Tallis smiled, thanked him, went to the door then turned. 'You ever have any trouble with rats?'

The West Indian frowned. 'This is a food shop, man. We sell sweets and stuff.'

'It's cool.' Tallis grinned. 'I'm not from Environmental Health or anything. Just curious, what with the site being empty next door.'

'To tell the truth,' the black guy said, lowering his voice, 'we always had a problem, bats as well, but you can't do a damn thing about them, protected species and all.'

'The rats, where do they come from?'

'Canals, waterways.' The black guy shrugged.

'Much you can do about it?'

His eyes lit up. A broad smile stretched across his face. 'Kill them, man.'

An early memory of his dad cornering a rat in the garden shed flashed through Tallis's brain. His dad had hit it with a shovel, virtually decapitating the poor creature. Tallis had run away crying. Dan, waiting in the wings, had catcalled him, telling him he was a sissy. Tallis could still remember his old man's laughter ringing in his ears. 'How?'

'Rat poison. Kills them stone dead.'

CHAPTER TWENTY-THREE

Ravenous with hunger, Tallis stopped off at a pub in Harborne and, breaking all the rules, ordered a pint in a straight glass and a BLT sandwich with a side order of chips. The barmaid had as much vivacity as a dead slug. Fortunately, she wasn't on duty long enough for him to mind. Her replacement, a bright-eyed blonde with the most beguiling smile, more than made up for her. He made a point of sitting at the bar.

'All right if I eat here?'

'Darling, you can eat wherever you like.' She beamed. He watched as her pert little body busied about, picking up glasses, serving customers, everything done with a minimum of fuss and maximum of good humour – a joy to behold.

His food came and he ate slowly, waiting for business to slacken off.

'Haven't seen you before,' he said at last.

'Haven't seen *you* before.'

His eyes twinkled. Her eyes twinkled. He smiled. She smiled. Advantage Tallis, he thought. 'Know a bloke by the name of Jace Jackson?'

'Unfortunately.' This time the smile was less intense. 'Mr Big Mouth we call him. Fuck,' she said, looking suddenly worried. 'No relation, is he?'

271

'Best mate,' Tallis said, deadpan, watching the mortified expression on her face before he winked and flashed a grin.

'Bastard,' she said, giving his arm a playful slap, letting her hand linger longer than it should have done. 'Christ, you had me going there.'

'Couldn't resist. You usually so frank?'

''Fraid so.' She broke off to serve a customer. When she'd finished she wandered back to Tallis. 'I'm Fliss, by the way.'

'Dan,' Tallis said.

'Well, Dan, why do you want to know about Jace Jackson?'

'Thinking of doing some business with him.'

'Don't.' Her blue eyes darkened. She suddenly looked quite serious for a cute little blonde.

'Why not?'

'He's dodgy.'

'In what way?'

'In every way.'

'This based on female intuition, or something more concrete?'

'I had a friend who went out with him.'

'And?'

'He's not nice.'

'Like to elaborate?'

She glanced over her shoulder, looked back, leant towards him, put her lips close to his ear. 'He almost raped her.'

'Almost?'

'A bloke walking his dog disturbed them.'

'Sure it was rape? Sure it wasn't one of those situations where things got a bit steamed up and out of control?'

She drew back. 'You normally make love with a knife in your hand?'

'Really?' he said, astounded.

'Really.'

'Did she report it?'

Fliss gave him a sharp look. 'Got to be joking. She left and went back to Scotland. Another pint?' she said, hiking an ash-blonde eyebrow.

'Better not, I'm driving.'

'Soft drink?'

'Why not? Straight tonic, plenty of ice and lemon.'

Tallis watched as Fliss took out a fresh glass and did the honours. 'Get you one?' he said, pulling out his wallet.

'Thanks.' She smiled, helping herself to a fruit juice.

'I'm not defending the guy...'

'Should bloody hope not,' she said, taking his money.

'But doesn't necessarily mean he's bad in business.'

'I wouldn't trust him as far as I could spit. He's got lorries transporting stuff all over Europe. God knows what he's up to.'

'Think he's doing something illegal?'

'Put it this way,' she said, smoothing her hips with her fingers. 'If the cops arrested him tomorrow, I, for one, wouldn't be in the least bit surprised.'

Smart outfit, Tallis thought. CCTV everywhere, the yard neat and tidy, lorries clean, and of those he could see, tax discs were in order, tyres in

273

good nick. He watched as a trucker backed up a huge pantechnicon into a warehouse that resembled an aircraft hangar. The skill employed to reverse the beast of a machine into its bay was awesome.

Tallis entered a glass-fronted reception area. Apart from the usual office gadgetry, the walls were festooned with huge maps of Europe and the UK. No smell of diesel oil but rather the olfactory-jerking heavy citrus scent of cheap perfume. A bleached blonde with hair extensions and a formidable tan swayed in and beamed at him. 'Help you?'

'Like to talk to Jace Jackson.'

'Let's see if he's in.' She smiled, picking up a phone. He noticed her nails were very up to the minute, square cut, French manicured. 'You are?'

'Name's Craig Jones,' Tallis said, falling back on one of his invented names. 'He won't know me.'

'What shall I say it's in connection with?'

'Rasu Barzani.'

'That all one word?'

'Just say Mr Barzani.' Tallis smiled tactfully.

Two minutes later, he was sitting in Jace Jackson's office with the man himself. Jackson was a stocky five-ten, mid-thirties. He had black hair, wide features, Latino colouring and a passion for bling, judging by the gold earring, thick gold chain around his neck, gold wristband and heavy signet ring on his pinkie. He wore a black T-shirt and black tailored trousers, the waistband a little too high for his trim torso. His feet were clad with white top-of-the-range trainers, giving him a slightly bizarre appearance.

274

Jace, as he insisted Tallis call him, clearly loved himself. Mouth working around a wad of chewing gum, he invited Tallis to sit down. 'Coffee, tea, drink?' he said, affably.

'Coffee would be good.'

Jace winked at him, pressed a button on an intercom. 'Bab,' he said, in thick Birmingham dialect. 'Get us two coffees, will you?' He looked at Tallis. 'About all she's capable of. Now, what can I do you for, Mr Jones? Destiny said something about Barzani. Murdering fucker been caught yet?'

'Not to my knowledge.'

'Pity,' Jackson said, parking his feet up on the desk. 'Nike, Airmax,' he said, pointing at his trainers like they were a work of art.

'Sound,' Tallis said, doing his best to look appreciative. 'Me, I'm more of a K.Swiss man.'

'Nah, mate, they're shit.'

'You an expert?' Tallis grinned.

'*The* expert. Been collecting for years. Got a room at home just for my trainers.' Seeing Tallis's baffled expression, Jackson burst out laughing. 'Gotcha.' Slow to see the joke, Tallis was glad when Destiny interrupted with two mugs of coffee, which arrived on a tray with a paper doily. Bending over in Jackson's direction, Destiny exposed several acres of cleavage. 'Help yourself,' Jackson said to Tallis with a louche grin, pushing a sugar bowl in his direction so that Tallis wasn't entirely certain what was on offer. 'Watching my waistline,' Jackson added, smoothing his six-pack, flicking an appreciative glance at Destiny's departing rear. The door closed, Jackson leant back expansively in his leather office chair. 'So, Craig, not quite following the drift here.'

Tallis slowly helped himself to sugar, plopping one cube in and stirring it then the other. 'I've been asked to track down Barzani.'

'Going to deport him?'

Good, Tallis thought. He thinks I'm from Immigration, or some other body dealing with illegals. Might as well play along. 'Uh-huh.'

'Thank Christ for that. With a bit of luck he'll be shipped back to Iraq and blown to smithereens.'

Tallis worked a smile onto his mouth then moved on swiftly. 'First, I'd like to say how sorry I am about the dreadful way in which your father died, and I apologise in advance for any distress I might cause. Thing is, Jace, I need your help.'

Jackson looked doubtful. 'Not sure how. It was a long time ago. I was only a kid really.'

'How old were you, if you don't mind my asking?'

'Twenty.'

'Hard.'

'Fuckin' hard.'

Tallis waited a respectful beat. 'Remember where you were at the time?'

'Here. Well, not here, working for my dad at the garage in Smethwick. I mean not at the time of the actual murder. I was at home then.'

'You knew Barzani?'

'Oh, yeah,' Jackson said, rolling his eyes. 'Never liked him. Shifty-looking bastard. I warned Dad about him.'

'Warned him of what?'

'Not to trust him.'

'Why?'

'Something about him, I guess. The way he was always watching, snooping. You get an instinct with people.'

Certainly do, Tallis thought. 'I understand your dad had no idea that Barzani was an illegal immigrant.'

'That's right. Went mental about it. My dad was a real stickler for rules, obeying the law. He'd panic if he thought his library book was overdue, know what I mean?'

Tallis nodded with a smile. 'How did he find out?'

'Find out?' Jackson frowned.

'About Barzani being an illegal.'

'Bloody good question. You know,' Jackson said, thoughtfully stroking his chin, 'I never considered it. Perhaps Barzani gabbed to one of the employees.'

'Difficult as he didn't speak much English.'

'Well, there you go. No idea, mate.'

'Keep records of staff?'

'Do now. Didn't then.'

'Seems a bit out of character.' Tallis took a sip of coffee.

'Not sure I follow.'

'What with your dad being a stickler for rules.'

'Oh, right.' Jackson grinned. 'What I mean is we kept records but got rid of loads of stuff in the move.'

Tallis nodded, looked around the office with an expansive smile. 'Certainly got a pretty cool place here.'

'Think so?'

'I do. Didn't know haulage could be quite so glamorous. Must have invested a fair amount of money.'

'Got to these days if you want to get anywhere.'

'What about the night of the murder?'

The fast change of subject barely caused a blink of Jackson's eye. 'Yeah? What about it?'

Agile mind, Tallis thought. 'You said you were at home.'

Jackson flicked him a suspicious look. 'It's all in the police reports.'

'Ever read one of those things? Dull as shite. I was hoping to get a more personal account. See, Jace, I've really got very little to work with...'

'I was at home with my mother and my then girlfriend.'

'They ever meet Barzani?'

'Think Astrid did once. She didn't like him either.'

'You and Astrid still an item?'

'You with the same bird you were with fourteen years ago?' Jackson grinned. 'Me, I like the single life. Love 'em and leave 'em, that's my motto.'

Tallis flashed him an all-guys-together smile. 'Know where Astrid is now?'

'Not a clue, mate.'

'Got a surname for her?'

'What is this?' He was smiling but his eyes were hard.

'I'm following every available lead. I want Barzani off the streets and up and away as badly as you do.'

'Silly bitch won't remember.'

'You'd be surprised what women remember. Memories like elephants.'

'Right there, mate.' Jackson laughed.

'So?' Tallis smiled.

The laugh faded. Jackson, unless he wanted to look a complete prat, had no choice but to answer. 'Stoker,' he said. 'Probably married with kids.'

Tallis took a gulp of coffee. 'Any idea where Barzani would have gone?'

'Back with his own kind,' Jackson said darkly. 'Anywhere there are immigrants, which means half the sodding country.'

Tallis flicked a smile. 'I gather Barzani met with an accident when he was working for your father. Know much about it?'

'Tripped and hit a piece of machinery. Tried to make out it was my dad's fault.'

'Broke a couple of ribs, I understand.'

Jackson pulled a face. 'Not sure I remember. They don't do much about that nowadays. Don't even bother strapping you up.'

Tallis knew. He'd cracked some ribs several years before. He'd been amazed by how painful it was. 'So he didn't see a GP or go to hospital?'

'God, no. It was nothing, really.'

Tallis nodded thoughtfully. 'The murder weapon...'

'Iron bar,' Jackson said ruefully.

'Seems odd. You'd think he'd have used something from the garage, a jack, wrench or hammer, something close to hand.'

'Premeditated, wasn't it?' Jackson said, tapping the side of his head. 'Thought about it, thought what he was going to do, got it all worked out in that nasty little foreign head of his.'

'Still seems an odd choice. I mean, I've got all sorts of stuff at home I could use as a weapon if I had to, but iron bar, clean out.'

Jackson shrugged. 'Probably part of their culture. Bit like all them Eastern Europeans carrying knives. It's what they're used to.'

Tallis stood up. Jackson sprang to his feet.

'Thanks for your time,' Tallis said. 'Sorry to rake it all back up again.'

Jackson seemed philosophical. 'No worries. Get on and make the best of things, I say. No point whingeing.'

They both walked back out towards Reception.

'What type of goods do you transport?'

'Carry anything,' Jackson replied, flashing a warm smile in Destiny's direction.

'Bit like the old Martini ad,' she chimed in. 'Any time, any place, anywhere.'

CHAPTER TWENTY-FOUR

Tallis returned home and combed through the file again. He'd noticed it before on the second read-through, buried in the medical notes from the secure unit, which was why he'd made the connection, but hadn't put it into context until now. He contacted Belle. 'All right if I come over?'

'You eaten?'

'Not since lunchtime.'

'I'll fix something.'

'Bring a bottle?'

'Wine, make it red.'

The concierge beamed at him and waved. Tallis got the impression that the man approved of what he considered a fledgling romance.

His entrance went a lot smoother than the previous time. The door was open, as before. Tallis walked in. He could hear the sound of a fan, bathroom probably. 'You really should be more careful,' he called. 'I could be a serial killer.'

'That I doubt,' Belle said, popping her head round the door. She was wearing a slate-blue towelling robe with nothing underneath. Her hair was wet and swept back from a face still glistening with water. He felt an urgent stab of lust.

'Want some help?'

She sneaked a smile. 'Last time someone dressed me, I was in kindergarten.'

'Who said anything about dressing?' He took her hand and pulled her towards the bedroom.

'No.' She smiled lasciviously. 'This way.' She led him through the living area and down the five stairs that led to the other room, which was, as he'd rightly guessed, a second bedroom doubling as a study. There was a full-length mirror in the corner. To the right was a door.

'What's through there?' Tallis said, nuzzling her neck.

'Leads out onto another floor.'

'Sneaky. The perfect escape route for a lover.'

He let Belle set the pace, which meant obliterating. Neither of them had been much good at

281

slow, languorous sex. He guessed it was due to the clandestine circumstances in which their affair had been cradled. And she was visual. Unashamed to use her glorious body, she was happy for him to watch, to have the lights on, to try anything. She rolled back over, starting on him again, her appetite for sex mind-blowing.

'Christ, you're killing me, Belle,' he growled, watching her eyes as she took him in her mouth and glanced mischievously up at him.

Afterwards, they bathed, and went back to bed. Much later, Belle went to the fridge, pulling out smoked salmon, salami, cheese, olives and salads. Girl food, he thought, not really giving a toss. Excluding his mother, it had been a long time since he'd shared a meal with someone. He realised how much he'd missed it.

While he opened the wine, Belle piled everything onto trays and brought it back downstairs. The conversation took a predictable turn. 'Heard you were working at a warehouse,' Belle said.

'Security.' He broke off a piece of baguette. 'But not any more.'

'No.'

'So what *are* you doing?'

Tallis chewed slowly, buying time, thinking. 'Can't say.'

'You mean can't tell?'

Tallis let out a sigh. 'Not yet.'

She nodded pensively. He knew Belle well enough to know that she wouldn't let it go. 'Is that why you're in trouble?'

'Sort of,' he said evasively.

'And why you were asking about Dan and the

Barzani case?'

'Partly.'

'This isn't a vendetta, is it?'

'Vendetta?'

'Against Dan.'

'God, no.'

She suddenly looked sad, drew her knees up to her chin. 'What are we going to do?'

'About what?'

'About us?'

'We have to do anything?' Can't we just see each other, stay together, be together? he thought.

'People will know,' she said anxiously.

'Only if we tell them.'

'I don't like living a lie.'

'We've been doing that ever since we decided to cover Dan's sorry arse.'

She flashed him a sharp look. 'You sure this isn't about you and him?'

'Promise.'

She twitched a smile, leant over and kissed him. 'What was that for?' he asked.

'Nothing at all.'

'Nothing?' he said, reaching out and stroking the inside of her thigh.

'For coming back,' she whispered.

'Belle?' he said. It was three-thirty in the morning and he'd been awake for the past hour, his mind coruscating with questions.

'Uh-huh,' she said sleepily.

'What happens when you break your ribs?'

'They hurt,' she murmured.

'No, I mean, what's the treatment?'

283

'Nothing.'

'I had a friend in the army fractured his ribs. About two weeks later, he had a pulmonary embolism.'

'Did he die?'

'No.'

'Bloody lucky. It's fatal in one in three cases.' She was starting to sound more lucid, more awake.

'But when I did my ribs in, I was fine.'

'People generally are. It's only if you have a predisposition to clotting. Other factors are being on the Pill, long-haul flights and post-operative complications. Sometimes it can be the joker in the pack in the case of cancer, the embolism striking before the cancer gets to the final stages. Paul?' she said, looking at her watch. 'Do you know what the time is?'

'Sorry.'

'Why all the questions anyway?'

'Barzani was on warfarin. That's what they found in his DNA.'

'Which they found traces of on Jackson?'

'Yes.'

Belle turned over and snuggled down. 'So he did it, then.'

Viva Constantine lived in Saltley, a suburb to the east of Birmingham, roughly one and three quarter miles from the city centre. It felt more like a suburb of Islamabad, Tallis thought as he attempted to drive down the high street, the morning sun beating down on streets overflowing with colour. Everywhere he looked there were fruit and vegetables, market stalls and people. The shops were mostly Asian. Even the amusement arcade was run by Khan Bros of Kandor. Food shops advertised pure ghee sweets, clothes shops the finest saris.

The driving style was foreign, lots of horns blaring, lots of undercutting and gesticulating. Everyone seemed intent on putting a dent in his Rover, including two police officers in a patrol car racing down the road, siren blazing. Nobody as much as glanced up, let alone broke off from conversation. Tallis wound down his window, expecting an aroma of spices and curry. Instead, the air smelt of fried English breakfasts. Strange.

He was in a logjam. Undeterred by the traffic or the double yellow lines, a white Mercedes with blacked-out windows forced its way down the inside lane, half of the vehicle on the pavement. It pulled up outside a halal shop. The door flew open, almost hitting Tallis's wing. A heavy-looking Asian man with wraparound sunglasses got out, not the sort of bloke you engaged with, Tallis thought, instinctively looking away and catching sight of the Saltley and Nechells Law Centre. It was all metalled up, closed, lots of bags outside full of litter.

At last, he was on the move again. Indicating left, he pulled off into a side street of tiny terraced houses. Two blokes in full Islamic dress were walking side by side deep in conversation, their trainered feet their only concession to Western culture. Tallis followed the road to the end and turned right into another road solid with parked cars. He eventually found a space some distance away near a twenty-four-hour corner shop.

Walking back, he came to a house that looked different from the rest. The small garden was a tumult of colour. Hanging baskets in full bloom hung both sides of the Lincoln-green front door. Windows were clean, the frames freshly varnished. There was a small slate house sign fixed to the wall. It read THE HAVEN.

Viva Constantine was not what he'd expected. Her green eyes were so deep set you couldn't see the lids, features heavy, almost jowled, skin sallow. Her mouth was her best feature. Full, the top lip was a perfect Cupid's bow, giving her the appearance of a pre-Raphaelite. He guessed that when she smiled, her face shone. Big boned rather than overweight, she was dressed in a long green linen skirt. Her blouse was burnt orange. She wore fashion flip-flops, around one ankle a thin gold chain. Her toenails were painted silver. The overall impression was one of Bohemia. For some unfathomable reason, he'd thought she'd be academic looking, thin, in her fifties. Constantine was difficult to place, but she was probably only ten years older than him, maybe less.

She stood at the door with a hovering expression in her eye. 'Yes?' Softly spoken, he noticed.

'I understand you acted as interpreter for Rasu Barzani?'

'That's correct.'

'I wonder if it's possible to talk about the case?'

'You a journalist, police officer?'

'Neither.'

'Then who are you?'

'Someone who wants to protect him.'

Constantine's expression was cool. 'You're fourteen years too late.'

'I know,' Tallis said, 'but if I don't find him, someone else might.'

She cast him a hawkish look. 'Really? And what makes you think I can help?'

'I need to know where to find him.'

'Why would I know where he is?'

'Because you visited him every week he spent in prison.'

Her face revealed nothing. He expected her to close the door. 'How did you get my name?'

'Ron Farrow.'

She nodded, her eyes giving nothing away.

'Can I come in?' Tallis said, glancing behind him.

'You haven't told me your name.'

He hesitated. If she checked with Farrow and found he'd been lying, she'd never trust him. 'Tallis,' he said.

'Any relation to Thomas Tallis, the sixteenth-century composer and master of counterpoint?'

'Not a clue.' He smiled.

'All right,' she said slowly, 'but I have to go to work soon.'

'What do you do?' he asked, stepping into a narrow hall with two closed doors on either side. A flight of stairs went straight up to the first floor.

'I work at the library.'

A large hand-painted mirror hung on the wall, framing a slender side table on which sat a Buddha. The floor was stripped pine. Constantine led him towards a kitchen then apparently

287

changed her mind. 'Here,' she said, pushing open a door. Inside mirrored outside. The woman was clearly courageous with colour. Furnishings were in purple, red and gold, all colliding with each other. It was glorious and terrifying. Suddenly, his own home improvements looked drab and British and boring.

'Sorry about the mess,' she said, gathering up a pile of newspapers.

'It's fine,' he said, sitting down on a large squashy sofa festooned with cushions. Constantine shoved the papers into a magazine rack. It had an ornamental elephant design on it. In fact, there were elephant ornaments all over the place, giving him the impression of sitting in the middle of an Indian bazaar. Constantine sat down on the floor, tucked her legs gracefully underneath her.

'It's an unusual skill to speak Arabic,' Tallis said.

'Only certain dialects,' she said self-effacingly. 'Pity more people don't. They might understand a little better, criticise a little less,' Constantine said provocatively. 'My father was a diplomat. I spent most of my childhood in Tripoli.'

'We share common ground. I'm half-Croatian.'

'Speak the language?'

'Yes, and a few others. I'd like to get around to Chinese one day.'

'"All the world's a stage, and all the men and women merely players."'

'"They have their exits and their entrances,"' Tallis finished. Constantine's eyes sparkled with pleasure. He hardly knew the woman yet he felt as if he understood her. It felt as if a pact had been made. She fell silent. He had the idea that silence was something she prized.

'You've made it very nice here,' he said, trying to find another foothold.

Constantine wasn't buying the warm-up routine. She came straight out with it. 'I don't know where he is,' she said, eyes unblinking.

Tallis didn't say anything at first. Just let the weight of her words invade the room and glide in the air. 'He gave no indication of where he might go?'

'You obviously don't know Rasu.' She flashed an embarrassed smile. It was true. Her face really did shine, especially when she mentioned Barzani's name. 'I'd be the last person he'd tell.'

'But why?'

'What I don't know, I can't reveal. Rasu would never put me in a position where I might be hassled.'

'Or might betray him?'

Constantine said nothing, her face a mask.

'Anyone else come calling?' he said.

'No.'

But he was supposed to have been deported, Tallis thought. Police were supposed to have been on the case. Surely somebody had asked questions? Then he remembered Crow, the conversation about workload and targets.

'You certain?'

'Think I'd remember.' She flicked another smile. 'You said you'd come to protect him.'

'You know he's officially on the run?'

'You make him sound like a criminal.'

'Wasn't he?'

'No. Rasu's seen too much cruelty and blood-shed to inflict it on someone else.'

'You believe his story?'

'I do.' Her expression was unwavering.

'You sound confident.'

'It's the easiest thing in the world to pin a crime on a man who shouldn't be in the country, who barely speaks the language.'

'But he had the motivation. Len Jackson was going to turn him over to the authorities.'

'Wasn't what the quarrel was about,' she said simply.

'No?'

'Rasu was fed up with the conditions. He was paid a dirt wage for doing a dangerous job.'

'The paint spraying?'

'You're supposed to have protective equipment, a mask at the very least. He had nothing. It was making him sick. His lungs couldn't cope with it. Then he had the accident. Stupid, really and so avoidable,' Constantine said, her eyes sparking with anger.

'What happened?'

'Jackson's son had been working on a car for his own private use. He left a wrench on the floor, which was never too clean at the best of times. Rasu slipped, tried to steady himself but fell down a badly marked inspection pit.'

'Surprised he wasn't killed.'

'He knew something serious was wrong, but the Jacksons did everything to persuade him not to go to hospital.'

Not what Jace Jackson had said, Tallis recalled. It had been nothing, really, according to him. 'Why?'

'Fear.'

'Of being investigated?' Nowadays Health and Safety would have a field day, Tallis thought.

'Of being found out.'

Tallis met her eye. She was first to break contact. 'Like to explain?' he said.

She spoke slowly, carefully. 'Rasu came into the UK by lorry. It was no accident that he fetched up at Jackson's garage in Smethwick.'

'You mean Jackson smuggled him in?'

'That's what Rasu believed.'

'You mean he didn't know?' Tallis said, incredulous.

'You have to understand there are many people involved in trafficking, many links in the chain. The person you pay the money to, the one you see at the beginning, in the middle and at the end, is not necessarily the same. Rasu thought Jackson was doing him a huge favour at first, offering him gainful employment. As time passed and he realised what was expected of him, the more suspicious he became. There were other lorries coming back, other people moved in the middle of the night.'

'Why didn't he say something? Why didn't you say something?'

'Because Rasu had no hard evidence, couldn't communicate, and it was ages before he told me. You have to put it in the context of what he'd already suffered. Authority isn't something you tangle with. He thought he wouldn't be believed. And anyway he feared being sent back. By the time he told me, it was already too late – he'd been convicted.'

'You didn't think to appeal?'

'On what grounds? Didn't alter the material facts of the case.'

'All right,' Tallis said, wondering if jokey Jace was continuing the family tradition. 'Going back to the accident. Rasu ignored advice and went to hospital anyway?'

'Not until a week later. He was getting terrible chest pains. When he tried to walk up the flight of steps to his bedsit, he began to cough up blood. Alarmed, he went to the nearest A and E where he was examined and it was discovered he'd had an embolism.'

'They keep him in?'

'For a week. He was given heparin to start with, to break any other clots down, then prescribed a course of warfarin.'

'Which is what Forensics found in his DNA.'

'Except they couldn't have.'

Tallis smiled kindly. 'I know there's a current trend for discrediting DNA evidence as the be all and end all but...'

'Know how warfarin works?'

'It's a blood thinner.'

'An anticoagulant. It works by inhibiting the action of vitamin K but the dose has to be carefully monitored. Too much and you bleed too freely. Too little and it's not terribly effective. Mostly it's used in the short term. Only patients, say with a history of heart or blood problems, are on it for life.'

'But Rasu. That was only for a short period?'

The hesitation was fractional, almost imperceptible, but it was there. Tallis believed he saw her

292

decide to lie. 'Yes.'

'So what are you saying exactly?'

'Warfarin stays in the bloodstream for a certain period of time, which is why if patients require an operation, or even a tooth out, they have to come off the drug, or take a greatly reduced dose so that they don't bleed too profusely during surgery.'

Which explained why Barzani's nose had bled so freely when he'd only had a minor blow, Tallis realised. Sorry, Miss Constantine, he thought, you're definitely not telling the truth. 'How come you know so much about it?'

'My brother's a GP.'

Tallis nodded for her to continue.

'At the time of the murder, Rasu had finished his course of tablets. He was only on a low preventative dose of three milligrams in any case.'

'What was the time frame?'

'Forty-eight hours.'

'Cutting it fine, surely? Maybe the guy's got a slow metabolism.'

'He didn't do it,' she insisted.

Tallis returned to his car and called Belle at the Forensic Science Service where she worked. 'I need you to get hold of the SOCO notes on the Barzani case, forensic evidence as well, if poss.'

Belle's voice dropped to a whisper. 'Paul, I can't.'

'I wouldn't ask unless it was important.'

'My job's important. For God's sake, Paul, why are you still going on about that Iraqi?'

'I want to know whether he did it or not.' Not

293

that it would help in finding him. Not that it would make any difference. Well, a moral difference maybe. 'Something else.'

'Yeah?' She sounded weary.

'Warfarin – how long does it stay in the body after a patient stops taking it?'

'Don't know. I could maybe find out.'

'It's a rat poison, isn't it?'

'So?'

'Maybe the site had rats on it. Maybe someone put poison down to get rid of them and it got muddled up with the blood sample.'

'I have to go,' she said tersely. 'Talk to you later.' She hung up.

Tallis drove back to the bungalow via the newsagent's. Making himself coffee, he parked himself on the sofa and started to read a report about a corrupt immigration official helping failed asylum seekers to stay in the country by exploiting a loophole in the law in exchange for cash, but Tallis's eyes only skimmed the print. His mind was elsewhere. He was thinking of forensics, of Belle, of the familial connection. He was thinking of Jace Jones, of the illegal trade in people. Bigger picture or both unrelated threads? What if Belle was protecting Dan? he thought, stomach churning. What if–? His phone was ringing. He wandered through to the kitchen, picked up. It was Finn. He sounded worried.

'We need to talk.'

'Sounds urgent.'

'It is.'

'When?'

'Soon as.'

Tallis glanced at his watch. 'Be with you by one-thirty. Come to the house.'

'No, make it the pub.'

'Dog and Duck?'

'Too local. The Catherine Wheel.'

'All right.'

'No, second thoughts,' Finn said, agitated. 'I'll meet you at Cirencester.'

'You sure?'

'One-thirty at the Wagon and Horses.'

CHAPTER TWENTY-FIVE

The pub was quiet for a Friday in summer. Tallis had finished his pint of IPA and was wondering whether to order another. Finn, always so punctual, was late. Tallis told himself that it was roadworks, an accident, some last-minute hitch at home, but Finn hadn't phoned to say he'd be late, and he hadn't returned either of the two calls Tallis had made. It was just coming up for twenty-five minutes to three.

Tallis ordered a mineral water, took it back to his corner, nursing it, trying to work things out. The more he thought about it, the more choices he realised he had. Not great choices, admittedly, but as long as Barzani was on the run, he and Barzani were safe. The moment he tracked him down, another death would be added to the growing list, and afterwards quite possibly his own. So, at the moment, he had more control than he'd originally thought.

Half an hour later, Tallis emptied his glass. Still no sign of Finn. Leaving a message with a friendly-faced girl behind the bar, in case Finn should turn up, Tallis headed for the car park, slipped into the Rover, and drove it like he was in the Z8. If it didn't fall to bits after this, he thought, haring down the A road towards the M4, he'd be amazed.

Bartholomew House, a solidly built red-brick family house next to a garden nursery, lay in the middle of the farming community of North Wraxall, eight miles outside Bath. Tallis tore up the drive, sending bits of gravel flying and disturbing a family of geese who made their displeasure known by hissing and honking loudly, wings flapping. Finn's car, a Volvo, was nowhere to be seen, though deep ruts in the drive suggested that he'd left in a hurry. What disturbed Tallis most was the open front door. Finn and Carrie often boasted how safe they felt living where they did. Since a spate of burglaries, however, they'd started to take more security measures. They'd even had an alarm installed.

Tallis crossed the gravelled drive and rang the bell, keeping his finger full on for several seconds. Nothing. He pressed it again then stepped quietly inside, the silence as startling as the vision of chaos. One chair lay overturned, a vase of flowers upended on the floor, toys everywhere. Seized by a dark cold fear, he silently checked and cleared each room. He didn't know if anything, other than people, was missing. On wandering through to the utility room, he found the alarm on the wall and cringed. Inky marks on the keypad, evidence of constant use, showed exactly which digits formed the combination. A determined intruder could work out the code and disable it in minutes. Had Finn been seized? Where were Carrie and the kids?

Tallis sat down, trying to think, guilt obstructing any clarity of thought. He shouldn't have involved his friend. He'd been told to keep things secret and time and time again he'd blatantly disregarded the advice. He was a stupid, arrogant fool. Obviously, Finn had made a discovery, hence all the cloak and dagger about rendezvous, but what exactly had been discovered? Had to be something about Cavall, Tallis thought.

The sound of a car careering up the drive got his attention. He stood up, went to the window, not recognising the silver-grey Yaris parking outside. When Finn got out, Tallis was jubilant with relief.

'Christ, am I pleased to see you,' Tallis said, clapping his old friend on the back.

'Sorry, sorry, sorry,' Finn said, clearly agitated. He was smaller than Matt had been, although there were certain similarities so that sometimes Tallis felt as if it was the old days, and Matt was still alive. Both brothers had similar sandy-coloured hair, a complexion that burnt easily, ice-blue eyes. In character, they were quite different. Bit like him and Dan, he supposed, except Finn was a decent human being who didn't thump his wife.

'What happened? You look as if you've been up all night?'

'I have, actually. It's Maeve.'

'The baby?'

'She hasn't been well for a couple of days, snuffly nose, bit of a temperature, you know the sort of thing.' Tallis didn't but nodded sympathetically anyway. 'Carrie took her to the doctor's this morning after yet another dreadful night, but he couldn't find much wrong so I never gave it a moment's thought when I arranged to see you. Shortly after I put the phone down, Maeve had a febrile convulsion.'

'Christ. Is that serious?'

'Not as terrible as it sounds. Basically, Maeve's temperature soared and she overheated, making her fit. Frightened the shit out of Carrie and me. We literally dropped everything, bundled the kids into the car and drove to the hospital.'

'Poor Maeve. She all right now?'

'Seems to be. They packed her with ice to bring down her temperature, which she didn't like terribly much. They reckon our GP missed a brewing throat infection. I've left Carrie with Maeve at the hospital, and dropped the kids off with Carrie's mum. Even had to borrow her car as mine's run out of petrol. Sorry I didn't phone.'

'Don't worry about it. Look, you obviously need to get back to the hospital. We can do this another time.'

'No,' Finn said, fixing his ice-blue eyes on Tallis. 'There are things you should know.'

'That serious?'

'Depends. Give me five minutes to collect some stuff for Carrie and the babe. You can follow on in your car.'

They went to a pub called The Crown. It was quiet, only the odd tourist enjoying an afternoon pint and a couple of girls discussing boys. Finn suggested they sit out in the garden. Tallis got the drinks, single Scotch for Finn and yet another mineral water for himself.

'So,' he said, watching as Finn took a healthy gulp.

'Christ, that's better. All right,' Finn said, his blue eyes lasering Tallis. 'Sonia Cavall. I take it you've met her?'

'Several times.'

'What did she ask you to do?'

'I'd rather not say.'

'Fair enough.' Finn took another gulp. 'Did she tell you that she was born Sonia Carew?'

'No,' Tallis said, feeling his gut sharpen.

'Sonia Carew was the daughter of James and Josephine Carew. When Sonia was nine, her father was killed by a hit-and-run driver. Sonia, who was walking with him at the time, witnessed the entire event. Having been dragged several yards down the road, James died in her arms.' Finn picked up his glass, swilled the amber contents round the base. He was like a barrister setting the scene before working himself up to the final cross-examination, Tallis thought, remembering with anxiety his last time in court – the wigs and the robes, the rising and sitting, the drama, the deference, the pecking order. Intimidation masked as theatre. If he hadn't been giving evidence in the dock, he'd have found it enjoyable. Finn continued.

'The man who committed the crime was driving without a licence. In fact, he shouldn't have even been in the country. He also happened to be black, a fact that assumes later significance.'

Oh, God, Tallis thought.

'Sonia's mother suffered a nervous breakdown and Sonia went to live with relatives for two years. When her mother finally recovered, Sonia was taken to live in Germany. While there, Josephine met Ralph Cavall. They married and Sonia took his name.'

'How do you know all this?'

'Some of it care of the Freedom of Information Act. Some of it worked out from Public Records, the rest from a source who'd prefer not to be named.'

'Be wrong to draw conclusions.'

'I agree,' Finn said, disarmingly.

Tallis took a sip of water, wishing it was whisky and nodded for his friend to continue.

'Cavall didn't let her tragic past stand in the way of her education. You often find children who've lost a parent go on to excel in their chosen field,' Finn said, more as an aside. 'After glittering results, she went to Cambridge...'

'And studied political science.'

'Where she was tutored by a guy called John Darius.'

'Darius,' Tallis murmured. The name was strangely familiar to him. 'Hang about. Isn't he BFB?'

'Britain for the British,' Finn agreed. 'But actually he's better known in business circles for his chain of health spas and leisure centres. He also has a rare knack for buying up ailing companies and turning them around.'

'An entrepreneur with the Midas touch.'

'I'll say. He's reputed to have a personal fortune in the region of forty million. He's also rumoured to have links with a shadowy right wing organisation calling themselves Fortress 35.'

'A reference to the thirty-five shire counties, defence of the realm and all that stuff.'

'You've heard of them.'

'Only because I caught the tail end of a documentary on TV.'

'They make all the official outfits and even some of the heavy-duty splinter groups like Combat 18 look like Boy Scouts.'

Tallis resisted rubbing his hands over his face. 'Think Cavall was recruited to the cause?'

'You tell me. All I've given you is the facts.'

Tallis stared at him. Finn was smart. It wouldn't take him long to piece things together. 'What's Darius like?'

'I've never met him but people say he's a charmer. An educated man, he enjoys the good things in life. Lives in some bloody great pile in the Essex countryside.'

'Yet he appeals to uneducated people.'

Finn smiled. 'That's only your take.'

'You know what I mean.'

'I agree the supporters of the BFB aren't what one would call liberal thinkers.'

'This new group you spoke of. What are its aims exactly?'

'To destabilise society. They want to create

301

anarchy by stirring up hatred for anyone who doesn't fit their particular brand of Englishness, never mind Britishness. With the current debate about immigrants, Muslims and the terrorist threat, they've taken every opportunity to exploit the situation. They may have the Cross of St George as their symbol, but there's nothing terribly chivalrous about their methods. If you hear a black man's been found dead with an ice-pick in his head, don't be surprised if the perpe-trator hasn't had some link, however tenuous, with the group. They work in exactly the same way as al-Qaeda, tiny cells all over the country, motivating the faithful.'

'To kill?'

'Yes.' Finn downed his whisky and looked at his watch.

'Another?' Tallis said.

'I should say no, but, yes. I'll get them.'

Tallis sat quietly. This was one of those *oh, my God* moments when everything was supposed to snap into sharp focus. Except it didn't. He sud-denly realised that all the things that had attracted him to the mission, the fact that he'd been his own boss with no rules to be obeyed, no notebooks required for police evidence so that a smart-arse defence lawyer couldn't crucify him in court, had cruelly exposed his vulnerability. Finn returned with the drinks. 'Got you a Scotch. Look like you need it.' Tallis flashed a grateful smile, held Finn's eyes with his gaze. 'Want to know what this is all about?'

'You asking me, a journalist?' Finn grinned. 'I'm dying to know.'

302

'Swear to keep it secret? Swear not to investigate?'

Finn's face creased into a frown.

'Swear!'

'All right.'

Tallis let out a hesitant sigh. 'If I tell you, it may compromise your safety.'

'Think I already worked that one out.' Finn laughed.

'Cool with this?'

'Icy.'

Tallis began at the beginning, starting with Cavall's visit, her proposition, his instant refusal then change of heart following Felka's murder. He told Finn about each of the targets, the way he'd traced them, the handover, reminding Finn of the way in which Demarku and Djorovic had died, what had happened in Hussain's case.

'Not all of this may be linked. Some of this could be sheer bad luck,' Finn pointed out reasonably.

'Not something I believe in, especially with what you've told me about Cavall.'

Lastly, he told Finn about Barzani, his suspicions of a miscarriage of justice, the odd coincidence of Dan's involvement. He told Finn that he believed the Iraqi to be innocent.

'And in danger?'

'Yes.'

'Know where he is?'

'I've a shrewd idea how to find him.'

'Then you should warn him.'

'Easy enough.'

'But what about Cavall?'

303

Tallis felt a sudden, grim inevitability about the path he'd chosen. 'Can't fail to win.'

'But this is legalised murder,' Finn protested.

'And I'm an accomplice,' Tallis said with a wry smile. 'Who am I going to complain to?'

'She's not above the law.'

'She works for the British government, a government who had this great idea of tracking down the very people they released.'

'That's only what she told you. She could have been making it up.'

'She could, but how do you think the great British public would react if this got out?'

'Rioting and worse in the streets,' Finn said glumly.

'Exactly,' Tallis said. 'Out of the law-abiding, there's a large proportion of people who believe we should never have got into Iraq or Afghanistan, that we went to war on a lie. They think dossiers were sexed up, whistleblowers silenced, even that a weapons scientist was bumped off. I'm not saying it's true,' Tallis said, in answer to Finn's exasperated look, 'but nobody would believe the government line. It's a matter of trust and, rightly or wrongly, they lost that some time ago.'

'So, if you went to the top, they'd say thanks very much and bury it?'

'And Cavall would deny everything.' She'd made that perfectly clear from the outset. 'Probably have me killed.'

Finn gave an involuntary shudder. 'These people you talk about, Bill and Ben.'

'A bloke and a woman, actually.'

'Where do they fit in?'

304

'Obviously part of the conspiracy. If they're truly immigration officials then I'm the President of the United States.'

'So, let me get this straight. Cavall is using you to track these people down for her thugs–'

'Or Darius's thugs,' Tallis chipped in.

'To eliminate them.'

'Correct. But there has to be more to it, some greater political motive.'

'To discredit the government, maybe?'

'Maybe.' Tallis shrugged. He took a pull of his drink. 'The BFB. They hold rallies and meetings, don't they?'

'Yup. Next one's in Barking.'

'How appropriate,' Tallis said drily. 'Where?'

'A meeting room over a pub in Axe Street.'

'Gets better. When?'

'Sunday morning.'

Tallis pulled a face. 'Odd time for a meeting.'

'Imbues it with a religious flavour, I guess.' Finn's face was engulfed by sudden worry. 'You're not thinking of going?'

'Straight into enemy territory? Shouldn't think so.'

Finn threw him a disbelieving look. 'There must be someone you can turn to?'

'The police?' Tallis's laugh was bitter. 'Have to hand it to her, Cavall picked the right guy when she came to me. Remember all that stuff in the newspapers about being trigger happy, about us being racist pigs? I fit the profile brilliantly.'

Finn looked pained. 'Anything I can do?'

'Done enough already.' Tallis flicked a smile. 'Sure?'

Tallis let out a sigh. 'You could check out the whereabouts of a woman called Astrid Stoker. Fourteen years ago she used to go out with the garage owner's son, name of Jace Jackson.'

'Same garage owner who wound up with his head smashed in?'

'Yup. Astrid gave Jackson Junior an alibi for the night.'

'Gotcha. Could be tricky. Might have got married.'

'Thought you were good with names. You managed to trace Cavall.'

'I'll give it my best shot,' Finn said, draining his drink. 'What are you going to do?'

'Only one thing I can: stop it before they kill anyone else.'

CHAPTER TWENTY-SIX

He didn't return to Belle's that night. He should have done, wanted to, but something in his psyche made him hold back. Everyone he touched and came into contact with these days seemed to wind up dead.

On his way home, he popped into one of the charity shops and bought a navy and tan baseball cap. As soon as he reached the bungalow, he checked for signs of intruders: none. Checked for electronic listening devices: none. After a thrown-together supper of bacon and tinned tomatoes, he played CDs, early Oasis, attempting to loosen his thinking without the lubricant of alcohol. So what had he got? Cavall working in partnership with Darius, her old mentor, who had links to Fortress 35. Cavall must have gone to Darius and leaked the Home Office policy. Perhaps she'd even been instrumental in setting the policy in motion. Either way, it didn't matter. Somehow the real immigration officers had been intercepted and agents from Fortress 35, Bill and Ben as he so fondly thought of them, had infiltrated.

His mind returned to the night of the Djorovic handover. He remembered the popping sound of gunshot, the flash of fire and subsequent explosion. He remembered Bill and Ben's blank looks when he'd mentioned the baby. They hadn't known anything about it. He scratched his head. But surely Cavall would have told them about the child when she'd given them the order to pick up Djorovic? Unless, Tallis thought, there was no direct line between Cavall and the pick-up team. Maybe she communicated via Darius or, more likely, simply tipped Darius off once she'd made the call to the real immigration officers and then Darius tipped off whoever at Fortress 35. So, there was a two-way traffic system with Darius at the centre, Darius the educated man. But Tallis thought, coming full circle, feeling a chill crawl down his spine, what had happened to the real pick-up team, the real immigration officers? And who was the founder of Fortress 35? Was he or she, too, an educated individual, or a different animal altogether? Was the relationship between BFB and Fortress 35 the equivalent of the old relationship between Sinn Fein and the IRA, one the respectable political voice, the other lawless and violent?

Belle didn't call and he didn't call her. Turning in at midnight, he spent a restless night in bed and got up the next morning around five. Donning his new headgear, he drove a circuitous route to Saltley, checking in his rear-view mirror for signs of being followed. Around five-forty, he parked the car metres from Viva Constantine's house. Tipping the seat back, he waited and watched. At seven, heavy drapes from an upstairs room were drawn open. At nine, a Tesco delivery van turned up. Tallis counted the bags, a lot of home shopping for one person, he concluded. At nine-thirty, he watched as Constantine walked out of the house and down the road to wait at a bus stop with several other people. Abandoning his car, Tallis followed, at the last moment sneaking onto the same bus as Constantine, riding with her until she got off and covered the short distance to Birmingham City Library. While she was inside, he hung around outside, amusing himself by watching the rolling news on a big screen in Chamberlain Square. A temporary kiosk nearby, providing burgers and coffee, kept him fed until lunchtime when the sky darkened and it started to rain. Around a quarter to two, Constantine emerged and crossed the square, walking down the main steps, past the fountain and into a dispensary in New Street. She had an easy gait, unhurried, blissfully un-aware of being followed.

Tallis skulked in one of the aisles, ostensibly viewing the selection of shampoos and conditioner, and watched while Constantine handed in a prescription and took a seat alongside two other women. She didn't look nervous or in the least bit agitated. By the familiar way she was chatting to one of the shop assistants, he guessed she'd been there before.

Several minutes later, a male pharmacist appeared. 'Repeat script for Mr Smith,' he said, looking around the dispensary. Constantine stood up. 'Two lots of tablets,' the pharmacist explained, 'three mills in one, one in the other. Single payment as they're all one drug,' he instructed the shop assistant so she could charge the right amount. Constantine signed and paid and, collecting the package, walked back to the library. Tallis took up his old position again, hanging around, buying a copy of the *Big Issue* and making small talk with the vendor, both of them sheltering from the wet by standing on the steps of the City Museum and Art Gallery. An hour later, Constantine left the library and caught the return bus to Saltley, Tallis in pursuit. He waited until she had the key in the door and was already turning it before rushing her.

'No,' she cried out, half fear, half protest. He let his gaze rest on the package of drugs in her hand. 'It's not what you think,' she said, trying to push him back out, difficult with Tallis's tall frame filling the entrance.

'What do I think?' Tallis said pointedly.

She dropped her hands to her side. 'I can explain.'

'What is it, warfarin?' he said, snatching at the bag, reading the attached note. 'Thought you said he was on a short course, but he wasn't, was he?'

'Please, leave – now,' she said, eyes flashing to the phone in the hall. 'I didn't invite you in.'

'What are you going to do, call the police?'

She swallowed. 'If I have to, yes.' She didn't sound very confident.

'He's here, isn't he?'

'No.'

'You're lying again.'

'No, I–'

'Look, you've nothing to fear.'

'Are you crazy? You barge your way into my home, make demands and tell me I've nothing to be afraid of.' She was pale with rage.

'OK,' Tallis said, putting both hands up in a defensive gesture. She glared at him. 'Truly, I want to help.'

Constantine shook her head, chewed her lip.

'How long do you think you can live like this?' he said.

'Like what?'

'Sheltering him, providing sanctuary. Isn't that what your house sign says – The Haven?'

'I don't know what you're talking about.'

'You have no idea the danger he's in.' Or me, he thought grimly.

'You're lying.'

'No, *you* lied, and if you want me to help you, both of you,' he added with emphasis, 'you have to tell me the truth.'

'Nothing to tell.' She flicked a cold, belligerent smile.

The sound of footsteps made both of them

310

turn. A figure stood in the kitchen doorway, dark and lean, the crushed expression on the man's clean-shaven face one of acute suffering. He reminded Tallis of a tiger he'd once seen in a zoo. The poor thing looked as if it would rather die than live another hour in captivity. 'I will co-operate with you,' the man said in English, his sorrowful eyes fastening on Tallis. 'And if I have to go back, I'll go, but, please, Viva is innocent. She has done nothing wrong other than take pity on me.'

Slack-jawed, Constantine looked in desperation and pleaded with him in a language Tallis instantly recognised. 'This man is the one I spoke of, Rasu,' she said in Kurdish. 'He has come for you. He will take you away, put you in detention, have you deported and then they will kill you. Please, if you think anything of me, flee. You cannot go with him. You cannot trust him.'

'Yes, you can,' Tallis said, extending his hand to Barzani, speaking his language. 'I give you my word, Mr Barzani. Believe me, I need your help as much as you need mine.'

'They'll kill you,' Viva insisted, ignoring Tallis, eyes only for Barzani.

'They?' Tallis said looking from one to the other.

Barzani smiled. 'I am a Kurd. My life has been in danger since the day I was conceived.'

'When was the last time you were in Iraq, Mr Tallis?'

'Ninety-one.' A sudden desperate vision of a canvas-sided truck, peppered by machine-gun fire, flashed through his mind. The young Iraqi

311

occupants lay mutilated inside. They hadn't stood a chance. So many hadn't stood a chance.

'Then you know that you left my people to be crushed.'

'And they're still being crushed,' Constantine said hotly. 'When an Iraqi is kidnapped or abducted, nobody, apart from his family, gives him a thought. When an American or a British soldier goes missing, or an Israeli, you have drones flying over, cities closed down, checkpoints, and war.'

'I was a soldier,' Tallis said. 'I didn't make the policy.'

Barzani nodded gravely. 'Is that where you learnt my language?'

'A little.'

'You never said.' Constantine's voice was lacerating, full of injured pride and fury.

'Look,' Tallis said softly. 'I'm sorry for blasting into your home and your life like this, but I'm speaking the truth. I really have been asked to find Rasu.'

'Well, now you've found him,' she said, bitter tears in her eyes.

'Who has ordered this?' Barzani said.

'The British Government, or so I thought.'

'Don't you know?' Constantine said, flashing with anger.

'I've come to warn you,' Tallis said. 'You need to get out of here, go somewhere safe.'

'This was safe,' Constantine glared at him.

'Why would you want to help a convicted murderer?' Barzani said simply.

'I don't believe you killed Len Jackson, but that's really not the issue. If I hand you over, you'll be murdered before your foot hits Iraqi soil.'

Barzani narrowed his eyes and gave him a curious look. 'Your name is Tallis. Aren't you the officer who arrested me?'

'His brother.'

'Oh, I get it,' Constantine flared again.

'I'm afraid you don't,' Tallis said. 'Think we could sit down and I'll explain?'

When he'd finished, both of them stared at him. 'As long as I stay alive, you stay alive,' Barzani said slowly.

'Yes. I need time to eliminate the threat.' Christ, Tallis thought, he was reverting to firearms-speak. 'To find out who's behind it.' And what's really going on, he thought. 'Afterwards, I'll help clear your name.' If there was an afterwards.

'You do not see me as an illegal?' Barzani said.

'I see you as a refugee, my friend.'

'Friend.' Barzani's face drooped a little. 'So long since I had one of those.'

Tallis looked down, embarrassed.

'You say this man, Darius, is connected?' Constantine said.

'Would seem so.'

Constantine looked at Rasu who took and held her hand. She leant into him close. It was a perfect gesture of love between the two of them, Tallis thought. He found it immensely moving. Feisty and difficult, the woman had remained constant. Throughout fourteen years of Barzani's arrest, committal to trial and prison sentence, she'd never given up on him.

'Is there anywhere you can go?' Tallis said.

313

'I have an aunt in Kent,' Constantine replied. She was much calmer now, less threatened, he supposed. That, and the fact Barzani had that kind of effect on people.

'Too obvious. Think of somewhere with no connections.'

'Cornwall?'

'No offence, but Rasu will stand out like a sore thumb. Head for a city.'

'Somewhere multi-cultural,' Constantine said, irony in her voice. 'What about Glasgow?'

Tallis thought of Stu. If he was a typical example of the inhabitants, he wished them well. 'Why not?'

'When should we leave?'

'Tonight.'

'But—'

'I can't overstate the danger you're in. It's quite possible I'm being followed.'

'You said there were others,' Barzani said, looking at Tallis.

'Other foreign nationals,' Tallis said. 'Do you think there are any links?'

Barzani shook his head.

'You never met these people?'

'No.'

Damn, Tallis thought, he wanted a different angle to the one he'd come up with.

'Why do you believe I am innocent?' Barzani said.

'Two reasons. If you've committed a crime, like entering a country illegally, the last thing you do is draw attention to yourself by committing another.'

'People do,' Constantine pointed out reasonably.

'Yes, but it's not as common as we're led to believe,' Tallis said. 'Secondly, in every murder inquiry, you have to look at who stands to gain the most. The answer, in this case, is Jace Jackson.'

'Your brother's friend?' Barzani said.

Tallis felt as if someone had cauterised a wound on his skin without anaesthetic. 'They knew each other?'

'Why, yes.'

Tallis frowned. 'No, it's not possible. Anyway, how do you know?'

'I saw them together.'

'When?'

'Your brother often came to the garage.'

'In uniform?'

'Sometimes, sometimes not.'

'Perhaps he came to have his car fixed?'

'To talk. That's why I recognised him when he came to my home.'

'You're absolutely certain? I mean, by your own admission, you spoke little English back then. It would be hard for you to judge, surely?'

Barzani shrugged. 'I assumed they were friends. Perhaps I was wrong.'

'And the warfarin?' Tallis said to Constantine, endeavouring to break an ugly train of thought clattering through his brain. 'You lied about that, didn't you?'

She glanced down. 'I thought if I told you, admitted that Rasu has a problem with his blood, that you'd never believe me. Thing is, at the time of the murder, Rasu was off the medication.'

'It is the truth,' Rasu said. 'It wasn't until ten months later I went back onto it.'

'While you were at the secure unit?'

'Yes.'

So that's why the date wasn't mentioned in the medical reports from the prison. By the time of the court case and trial, Barzani had already been routinely prescribed the drug. Ron Farrow's assertion that Barzani had been drug free had simply been a reference to the fact he'd stopped taking medication for his mental health problems. 'Did you know there were rats on site?'

Rasu smiled. 'Everywhere. English people make a lot of fuss about them. Where I come from they are commonplace.'

'They used rat poison to get rid of them. Warfarin, of course,' Constantine gasped in realisation.

'Contaminating Rasu's blood sample at the crime scene. Well, that's the theory. Not sure about the science yet but I'm working on it.' At least, he hoped Belle was. He stood up. 'I'd better go.'

'Do we stay in touch?' Constantine said anxiously.

'Too risky.'

'How will we know if we can come back?'

There was optimism for you, Tallis thought. 'Watch out for the personal ads in the Friday edition of *The Scotsman*.'

CHAPTER TWENTY-SEVEN

Time to shake things up a little, Tallis thought, driving onto the forecourt of Trans Logistics and Distribution. He walked into Reception. Destiny was filing her nails. She looked up and beamed at him. 'Your lucky day.' He beamed back. 'You can go home early.'

Destiny glanced at the door leading to Jace Jackson's office. 'You sure?'

'Absolutely positive,' Tallis said, reaching for her jacket and popping it round her shoulders. 'I'm sure a pretty girl like you has got better things to do with her time – Saturday night and all that.'

'Well...' She grinned awkwardly. 'It is tempting.'

'There you go, then. Don't worry, I'll square it with the boss,' he said, breaking down any further resistance by guiding her firmly and purposefully towards the door.

When Jackson appeared twenty minutes later, Tallis had his feet up on the desk and was eating an apple Destiny had left in her drawer.

'Fuck you think you're doing?' Jackson said, shock swiftly superseded by anger.

'Thought that was obvious.'

'Where's Destiny?'

'Bit of a philosophical question for a Saturday afternoon.'

'Now, look here, if you don't get out–'

'You'll call the police,' Tallis finished, parking his size tens on the floor and standing up. Jackson really was a little squit, he thought, towering over him. 'You know, that's the second time someone's said that to me this afternoon. Gets a trifle dull after a while. Thing is, Jace, I am the police, or rather I'm bigger than the police. I don't have to do things by the book. I don't have to caution you, or observe PACE – Police and Criminal Evidence, for your information – or follow procedure. I really am a law unto myself.'

Jackson stared in confusion then broke into a nervous smile, a feral expression in his eyes. 'Hey, Craig, it's cool. I'm cool. You should chill. Why don't you and I have a drink? Got a lot going down at the moment, business and stuff, but I can take time out for a mate.'

Tallis batted back the smile with a withering version of his own. He was neither in the mood for being humoured nor given the brush-off. 'Talking of mates, you never said you knew Dan Tallis.'

'Dan who?' Jackson frowned, putting a hand to his forehead.

'The copper who arrested Barzani.'

'Fuck me, why would I? I told you, Craig, I wasn't there.'

'Of course,' Tallis said, a facetious note in his voice. 'You were with your mum and girlfriend, having a quiet night in.' A belt-and-braces alibi, Tallis thought. 'You deny ever meeting Dan? Used to pop in quite a bit, as I understand.'

'Well,' Jackson said, blowing out between his teeth, 'now you come to mention it, there was a

318

bloke by that name. The garage was on his beat. Like you said, he'd drop by, have a chat, proper community policing before they had all them cutbacks. Spoke to my dad more than me. Let us know if any cars had been stolen, plates nicked, that kind of thing.'

'Tipping you off,' Tallis said darkly.

'Not the way you mean,' Jackson said, clipped.

'And which way's that?'

Jackson said nothing.

Tallis let it lie. 'Why didn't you tell me about Barzani's accident?'

'Nothing to tell.'

'You said it wasn't serious.'

'It wasn't.'

'Is that why you told him not to go to hospital?'

'I did no such–'

'What were you trying to protect?'

'You're talking shit, know that?' Jackson said, an unlovely twist to his mouth.

'See, I've been doing some thinking.'

'Dangerous.'

'For you, yes,' Tallis fired back. 'Did you know you're in exactly the right business for smuggling in illegals?'

'That's bollocks,' Jackson burst out.

'Shit, bollocks – my, you're coming out with everything today, Jace.'

Jackson scowled. Tallis wasn't giving up. 'Is that how Barzani got here? Travelled in one of your trucks? Was your dad in on it, or did he find out and blow his stack?'

'You're mental,' Jackson sneered.

Tallis leant towards him. 'First thing you've

319

said today that's true. I'm not sure exactly what happened that night your father was killed but, educated guess, you were involved. In fact, I reckon you're in shit up to your eyes. Think about that. Nice trainers, by the way.' Tallis glanced down before heading for the door.

'Found Barzani yet?' Jackson screamed after him. 'Found the real fuckin' murderer?'

'Yes,' Tallis said, without looking back. 'Standing behind me.'

Jackson locked up the premises ten minutes later and climbed into his car, a silver Mitsubishi Evo VII, a shit off a shovel motor in Tallis's opinion. Tallis followed several cars behind, thanking God it was rush-hour, both vehicles similarly impeded by traffic.

Jackson drove south-east towards Selly Oak. In spite of the rain, the city was a river of colour – buildings, people, all shades of faces and dress. Still heading south, they passed through the leafy avenues of Bournville, home to the Cadbury chocolate family. At last, the traffic freed up, the Evo putting on a deliciously quick show of speed, wheels sticking like chewing gum to the hot tarmac, before finally slowing down as it approached King's Norton then speeding back up again. Tallis eased back. The Evo, with its rear spoiler, was easy enough to spot. Weaving its way surely down streets and across junctions, the Evo finally slowed and turned right into Grassmoor Road, which Tallis knew to be a cul-de-sac. Pulling over, he got out, locked up the Rover, and went the rest of the way on foot.

Tallis found Jackson's car on the drive of a large family-sized detached house with a white two-door garage fixed to the front. Divided from the next-door property by trees on one side and fencing on the other, the house backed onto natural woodland – probably explained why it had the rather unoriginal name of The Spinney, Tallis thought. At the end of the drive stood a large green wheelie-bin.

The flash of activity coming from upstairs was unmissable, Jackson moving from one bedroom to another with the same urgency as a man intending to flee the country. Tallis smiled with satisfaction. He'd probably put enough wind up Jackson to goad him to do something really stupid. He returned to his car and called Belle.

'Hi, stranger,' she said.

'Missed me?'

'Sound as if you're fishing for compliments.'

'Sorry I put you in a tricky position yesterday.'

'Apology accepted.'

'Find anything out?'

'You're incorrigible.'

'And insatiable.'

'Coming over?'

Tallis looked at his watch. 'Later?'

'How later?'

'Couple of hours, maybe more.'

'Could be less?'

'Why?'

'I fancy going out to eat.'

'OK. I'll do my best,' he said, cutting the call.

Heavy rain darkened the sky. Some summer it was turning out to be, Tallis thought, and all that stuff about global warming. He wondered idly where they'd eat out for dinner later. There were a number of places round The Mailbox: Thai, Indian, Italian, French. Be like old times but without the deception. Much against his will, his thoughts turned to Dan again. As much as he despised his brother, he found it hard to believe that Dan had malign connections with Jackson. When they'd been kids, Dan had always mixed with the right crowd, the good lads. He'd always been a bit of a swat, truth be told. He himself, on the other hand, had always been attracted to bad boys, to the thrill of breaking rules, of taking risks. Homework and learning had been for dullards.

Tallis looked at his watch. Unbelievably an hour had passed. Maybe he wouldn't get to eat at all. Maybe Jackson would stay in for the evening, phone a mate, rent a thug...

Suddenly the Evo blasted out of the driveway and sped off towards the main road. Tallis climbed out of his car and walked quickly back to The Spinney. Fortunately, the road was quiet. Most people were either inside or rescuing the remnants of washed-out barbeques. A smell of burning impregnated the air. Opening up the wheeliebin, he pulled out several black bin-liners, each tied neatly apart from one at the bottom, which he opened. Inside was another bag. It felt as if it contained a box – cardboard, judging by the feel. Tallis drew out the parcel and unwrapped it, lifting his elbow up so that his jacket formed a natural shield from the rain. Sliding off the lid, he looked inside and smiled. Nestled in the box like a baby in a crib was a single pair of old Adidas trainers.

'Present for you.'

'Rubbish?' Belle looked confused.

'Evidence.'

Confusion was swiftly replaced by disapproval. Didn't make any difference. She still looked gorgeous to him. She was wearing a dress the colour of crushed garnets, sleek-fitting, displaying her wonderfully lithe figure. Her legs were tanned and bare, heels high. If they weren't going out to eat, he could think of a much better way to spend the evening. 'Come on,' he said, putting the bag down and taking her hand. 'We can talk over dinner.'

They went outside and crossed over the bridge, Belle's heels clicking against the metal supports. 'Where do you fancy?' he said. He felt in an incredibly good mood. Things weren't exactly going his way but the small triumph of finding the trainers, which would, he was certain, implicate Jackson, made him feel a lot better.

'Not fussy. Somewhere simple. Cafe Rouge?'

'You sure? It's a bit ordinary.'

'I like ordinary.'

'Is that why you like me?' He gave her slender waist an affectionate squeeze.

'Nothing ordinary about you,' she said, squeezing him back.

They went inside and received the warmest greeting imaginable. A table was found, menus produced, drinks orders taken. Out of five staff, three were Polish, including the young woman running front of house. The service was charming and the waitresses, Tallis thought, were all easy on the eye. The Poles had probably done more to improve the service industry in the UK than any other nation, Tallis thought. If this was the Polish invasion, bring it on.

Their drinks arrived – lager for Tallis, white wine for Belle – the food order taken.

Belle leant across, took his hand. Her eyes looked tawny in the muted light. 'Where did you get to last night?'

'Home. Things to do.'

'You weren't cross with me?'

'No,' he said, taking a drink. 'You with me?'

'A little.' She smiled.

He smiled back. Belle blushed. All of a sudden she looked utterly vulnerable. He guessed that was what had first attracted him, long before Dan had married her, or laid a finger on her. Not that he'd ever acted on his attraction. Belle had been his brother's girlfriend and later his wife. To cross the divide would have been like breaking the biggest taboo imaginable.

'I spoke to one of the SOCOs involved in the original case,' she said.

'They remember that far back?'

'Memories like PowerMacs.' She took a sip of wine. 'I'll start with the easy stuff first. Warfarin is prescribed in varying doses, anything from three or four milligrams up to twenty. The dose is dependent on the clotting mechanism, which is measured by what's called an INR test, basically a blood test carried out on the patient.

324

Varying factors, which might influence this, are weight gain or weight loss and whether he or she has consumed alcohol. In Barzani's case, he was on a relatively low dose, didn't drink, weight low. The most it could stay in his bloodstream would be around thirty-six hours. As you suggested, in theory it's possible that the rat poison at the scene could have contaminated the sample.'

He nodded, motioned for her to continue. It wasn't a critical factor any more.

'No sign of break-in, which figures.'

'No, it doesn't. Len Jackson returned to the garage at around ten o'clock that evening. Chances are he'd have locked the door after him, meaning that if Barzani was the killer, he'd have forced his way in.'

'Surely, as an employee, he'd have a key?'

'Maybe,' Tallis conceded. 'But not necessarily.'

'Could easily have stolen one.'

'All right, point taken, but there was the small problem of how he got there. No record of him travelling by bus or cab?'

'Maybe he hitched.'

'Wouldn't someone remember?'

'Doesn't mean to say they'd come forward.'

Tallis flashed a smile. 'You seem to be shooting all my theories down in flames.'

'Not quite,' she said, eyes gleaming. 'Remember, this was the early nineties. DNA technology wasn't as advanced as now. According to my very observant source, there were lots of overlapping footwear impressions from victim and assailant, but there was also a fresh single print that didn't match the rest.'

'You mean it belonged to a guy with one leg?'

Belle burst out laughing. 'Hadn't thought of that. No crutch marks were mentioned.'

'A guy with no legs.' He grinned. 'They manage to isolate the prints?'

'The assailant wore trainers, universal brand so not much help.'

'Barzani known to wear trainers?'

'Yes, but there was no direct link.'

'You mean a trainer belonging to him wasn't found to have blood on it?'

'No.' She took a sip of wine, her eyes suddenly widening. 'That explains the trainers in the box.'

Tallis flashed a knowing grin.

'Where did you get them from?' she said, lowering her voice to a whisper.

'You tell me.'

She leant towards him. 'You want me to analyse them?'

'No, wear them. Of course I want you to analyse them,' he said with a sharp smile.

'We might not have the wearer's DNA on our database,' she protested.

'Odds on you will.'

She let out a long heartfelt sigh.

'Please, don't give me all that stuff about your job,' Tallis said. 'There's a bloke out there who's a murderer and a thief.'

'A thief?'

'He stole fourteen years from Rasu Barzani.'

The food arrived. He'd ordered a pancake stuffed with smoked haddock. Belle had ordered the mussels. After he'd taken the edge off his hunger, he reminded her about the single foot impression.

'Right,' she said, popping a mussel into her mouth and licking her fingers. 'It belonged to a heavy-duty shoe, size eleven.'

'Could have been someone from the emergency services?'

'All people who had a legitimate reason for being there were traced and excluded. In any case, blood had dried by then. This was a print in fresh blood.'

'Like someone taking a peek then legging it?'

'Maybe.'

Could be Barzani, Tallis thought, feeling less certain. 'So what happened to the mysterious foot impression?'

'Not a lot. Patterns on soles can identify brands and manufacturers but, although everyone wants to point to a smoking gun, it isn't always that easy. However,' she said with a smile, 'trace evidence confirmed that Jackson had been in contact with Barzani and Jackson Junior.'

'As you'd expect.'

'And Jackson senior's wife?'

'Uh-huh.'

'But there was something else.' She smiled.

'Yeah?'

'Hair fibre.'

'Belonging to?'

'Sadly, not known. Although analysed, no match was ever made, but we still have it.'

'Right,' Tallis said, feeling suddenly and unaccountably glum. What did any of this matter anyway? Whether Barzani was guilty or not, it wasn't really the issue. He glanced at his watch. He hoped the lovers had taken his advice. With luck, they'd be miles away by now.

'Hair, as you know, is extremely durable,' Belle continued brightly. 'By studying it under a microscope, it's possible to differentiate between races and, to some extent, age. This was a short dark hair, undyed, so points more to a male than female.'

'Doesn't happen to come with a name tag?'

'I don't perform miracles.' She laughed.

Their plates were cleared away. Belle was presented with a prawn and langoustine salad, Tallis a steak, rare. He fell upon it like a starving man. Eventually he asked Belle about Dan.

'Don't ever hear from him, thank God. Someone said he's splashed out on a new car.'

'Let me guess – Saab.'

'You've spoken to him?' she said, genuinely taken aback.

'Sort of,' Tallis bluffed. If you could call a fierce exchange in a police station a conversation. 'But I honestly didn't know about the car.'

'Then how did you know the make?'

'Same type of personality.'

'A car has a personality?' she smiled, shaking her head.

'Take one look at the dash. It's a show-off, designed to resemble a cockpit so the driver can pretend he's flying an airplane. Dan's big on pretence, isn't he? Then there's the whole creature-comfort thing, heated leather seats, etcetera. All extras come as standard. Doesn't have to pay more for them – appeals to his mean streak. As for

328

the performance...'

'Character assassination complete,' she quipped. 'Can we talk about something else?'

'Pudding?' he said with a hopeful smile.

CHAPTER TWENTY-EIGHT

Tallis left Belle a shade after five the next morning. He felt torn. A Sunday, they could have spent it together, acted like any normal couple, except to Tallis's ears that sounded too staid and boring a description. Theirs was never going to be a shopping-at-Tesco, visiting-a-garden-centre, seeing-the-in-laws type of relationship. It couldn't be. Already there were too many restrictions. With them the usual rules didn't apply, or was he guilty of falling into the trap of thinking that theirs was a unique kind of love affair never before experienced in the whole history of mankind or the universe?

After filling the Rover with petrol, he started out for London. The sun was already belting down.

For most of the journey, he found himself dredging through his last conversation with Finn. He thought about Cavall's difficult childhood, how it had shaped and defined her, how the violent and sudden death of her father had turned her into a woman bent on retribution. Yet it was inconceivable that the Home Office was blind to her background, unthinkable that

Cavall's link with John Darius was unknown and unreported.

He didn't arrive in Barking until midmorning. As Tallis parked the car and stretched his legs, he felt as if he'd wandered into the type of wasteland you found round an empty nuclear reactor. Street after street of flat-looking two-up-two-downs. Second- and third-hand Ford cars, alloys missing, lined roads that were grey and lifeless in spite of the climbing heat of a summer sun. Emptiness permeated the heart of the place. Empty factories, empty warehouses, empty lives. And there was fury and betrayal. The air seethed with it. Tallis could smell it.

The pub was off a set of traffic lights, easily identified by the number of cars in the car park. Tallis walked inside. He couldn't tell if he was in a lounge or public bar. It was all one dirty homogenised stew of colour, dark plum and aubergine, brown, the odd splash of orange. Oddly seventies, or how he imagined the seventies to have been. The air felt sticky with old cigarette tar. As for the people, they either looked up for a fight or recovering from the previous night's brawl. There were a lot of shaved heads, bad complexions, a lot of gnarled-looking faces, every one of them white. With his darker colouring, Tallis almost felt under threat.

'Meeting upstairs?' he murmured to a surly-looking barman. The guy was small, ferret-faced, with a large birthmark spreading from his neck to his cheek. The answering grunt was indecipherable. Not particularly fluent in Neanderthal, Tallis bought an overpriced soft drink and drifted among a group of likely looking supporters who were making for a rickety-looking staircase.

The meeting was already well under way. Tallis inched past a thickset minder with white-blonde hair and razorsharp cheekbones. Feet creaking noisily against the wooden floorboards, Tallis slipped into a place at the rear, standing room only. He was met with a sea of sturdy backs, men and women, young and old, their attention focused on the raised platform at the far end, on which was a microphone, table and two chairs. A woman with oppressively dyed blonde hair was sitting down, a tall corpulent-looking man with pale eyes standing and speaking.

'Up to five hundred foreign psychiatric patients with criminal records freed when they should have been deported. Rapists granted leave by the Home Office to remain for an indefinite period. Paedophiles and murderers released on bail when they should have been sent packing back to their own countries.

'We have immigration officers who are so poorly trained they wouldn't recognise a black man in broad daylight.' Faint titter of laughter from the back. 'And, incidentally, my friends, did you know that the default position in Immigration is to allow these people in?' The crowd groaned with censure. 'And what do our politicians say?' The speaker paused, rolling his pale blue eyes for effect. 'That they want to give all illegals an amnesty because they're afraid they'll be exploited.'

This time a bitter twist of laughter rippled right across the room.

'Not content with allowing these foreign

331

criminals to stalk our streets, they invite *more* foreigners into our country.'

'To take our jobs,' one bloke shouted out.

'Yes,' the speaker said, raising an index finger to emphasise the point. Tallis noticed that sweat was breaking out on the man's forehead. No surprise. It was roasting in the room and the man was wearing a suit and tie. 'And where you and I have to have a national insurance number to enable us to work, these people can do so without any such restriction.

'Brothers and sisters, I tell you that the wages of the British working man have halved since the latest flood of Eastern Europeans. Migrants have cost almost 100,000 British men and women their jobs. And you don't have to take my word for it. Experts, far more knowledgeable than I, are saying the same, as if you needed further proof,' the man added with a derisory smile.

A deep rumble of approval echoed off the walls.

'Look around you. See the rows of boarded-up shops, boarded-up lives. It breaks my heart,' he said, his deep voice cracked with emotion. 'And all because our country has been ruined by this foreign invasion. Oh, yes.' He flashed a cold smile. 'The politicians in government will tell you that we need these people. We need their skills, their willingness to work for dirt wages, that their culture is good for us. Well, they are wrong.

'Our very identity, our entire way of life is under threat. To continue to court the ethnic minorities, we risk race riots and civil war. *That* is the reality.' Another pause. Tallis glanced at his watch, wondered if the guy was working up to a grand finale, perhaps finish off with a round of audience participation. 'There are those in this country who say they want separateness. Well, *we* want separateness.'

'Hear! Hear!' a woman shouted out from the crowd. 'Send them back to where they came from.'

'They say we should be sensitive to their culture. Well, I say they should be sensitive to ours,' he said with a grotesque grin, to the clear delight of the assembled. 'And those not of our faith should respect our religion and our customs. They say they want freedom. Well, I say to you, I want freedom – freedom from unfair discrimination, freedom to say what I think, freedom to have my children grow up without fear of them being brainwashed into thinking their lifestyle is wrong, their beliefs ungodly, without fear of them being blown to bits or raped. I want to have open debate without being labelled a bigot or racist, or risk being thrown into prison or charged with harassment, unlike the Muslim clerics who can say the vilest things about us, stir up racial hatred, and nobody lifts a finger to prosecute them. Just another example of one law for them and another for us.'

More shouts of approval.

'But if love of country and the people who truly belong here means that I'm accused of being a racist, a member of the far right, then bring it on. I want our country back for our people. I want us to be great again. And I leave you with one final question. When the day of reckoning comes, as it will,' he said, his voice falling to a new darker pitch, 'when there are rivers of blood in our streets, who will you fight for?'

The applause was rapturous. People were on their feet, clapping, shouting and chanting like football hooligans, *'Dar-ree-us, Dar-ree-us,'* the man virtually mobbed by his supporters. The woman sitting at his side tipped up on her toes and kissed him. Wife, maybe, Tallis thought. He watched as Darius glad-handed, laughed, joked. He looked on as Darius put his arm around a weeping woman's shoulders, whispering words of comfort in her ear, observed as Darius switched to mood music and touched the tender heads of sleeping babies and children, Christ-like in his bearing. The image of a millstone slung round Darius's thick neck flitted through Tallis's mind. As a sea of people parted to allow Darius through, Tallis stepped forward, catching the great man's eye. John Darius smiled graciously. 'Not seen you here before.'

'Surprised you noticed. There must be at least a hundred people in this room.'

'I always perk up at the sight of a new face.'

Close up, Darius was bigger and broader than he looked on stage. Anywhere between mid to late forties, he wasn't fat exactly but he had one of those fleshy faces that made him seem so. He wore a beautifully cut dove-grey suit, blue shirt with a striped tie. His blue eyes were sharp and intelligent, his smile warm and friendly. Easy to be conned by him, Tallis thought. Darius's affable and appealing manner lent a lie to the vicious words that poured from his mouth.

'Did you know that Darius was a Persian king?'

Tallis said.

'Who subjugated Thrace and Macedonia, 500 BC, I believe.'

'Five-twelve BC.'

'An educated man.' Darius twitched a smile. 'But I'm sure you didn't come here today to tell me that.'

'I didn't. I was interested in your view of the government – the police, in particular.'

'May I ask why?'

'I used to be one of them.'

Darius rested a hand on Tallis's shoulder. It weighed heavy. 'What are you doing now?'

'Well, I work for–'

'Sorry, I apologise for not making myself clear. What are you doing next?'

Tallis shrugged. 'Having a drink, I suppose.'

'Why don't you join me and my family for lunch?'

'What now?'

'Yes.'

'Well, I–'

'Be my pleasure. It would provide the perfect opportunity for us to talk.'

Tallis was transported out of Barking and into the Essex countryside in a new Range Rover Sport. Red, with a big chunky design, thrusting square exhausts servicing a V8 engine, it was as aggressive looking as John Darius's philosophy. The ostentatious blonde was indeed Darius's wife. 'Liz,' she introduced herself, twisting round in the passenger seat. Her voice had a definite Southern twang.

335

'Craig,' Tallis said. 'Sure this is all right?'

'Of course. Sunday lunch is a big thing with our family. We often have friends join us. You won't be the only singleton, if that's what you're afraid of.'

It wasn't.

Tallis looked out of the window, noted the route, making small talk only when he was spoken to.

'Craig used to be a police officer,' Darius explained to his wife.

'Used to?'

'Got disillusioned and left,' Tallis said.

'Not surprised,' Darius chipped in. 'It's a terrible job for any right-thinking individual nowadays, what with all this politically correct nonsense.'

'And half the officers they recruit now are black,' Liz said with distaste. 'Where was your patch?'

'Birmingham.'

'In the thick of it.'

'Gun crime at an all-time high, I believe,' Darius said.

Actually, it had dropped a little. Nottingham was the new kid on the block. 'Uh-huh,' Tallis said, noncommittal.

'I hear if you get shot in the city nowadays, you have to wait an hour before armed response turn out,' Darius said.

'That a fact?' Liz said. 'Shocking. Is that your experience, Craig?'

'Heard something similar,' Tallis said, looking out of the window, his eyes almost popping as the Range Rover swept up an immense drive with views of what looked like a stately home. Like its owner, the nearer they got, the bigger the house seemed. Queen Anne, at a guess, Tallis thought, surveying the plain simple lines. 'This is fabulous,' Tallis enthused. 'How long have you lived here?'

'Been in my family for several decades,' Darius said with pride.

A nightmare to maintain, Tallis thought, wondering whether the health spas and leisure centres was his only source of funds. He commented on the lack of obvious security.

'We've just passed through a laser-activated alarm that sounds in the house,' Liz said proudly. 'Nobody can get inside without us knowing. And, of course, there's the dogs.'

A number of cars were already there. Several children were scooting about outside.

'It's such a fabulous day we're eating in the garden,' Liz said, climbing out. 'You two go on through. I'll check on the kids.'

'Are you married, Craig?' Darius said as they walked into a huge marble-floored hall with a regal-looking staircase ascending from two sides. Tallis noticed that Darius had a slight limp.

'No.'

'Should give it a try. Best sort of stability there is.' Again the false smile. 'Get you a drink – wine, spirits?'

'Glass of red would be good.'

'Why don't you go out onto the terrace, introduce yourself, make yourself at home?'

Tallis gravitated to where there was the most noise, passing through a separate living area with

337

huge baronial-style chairs, and into a dining room, which exuded grandeur. The table, he noticed, was laid for twenty-five. Huge French windows opened out onto a terrace and open-air swimming pool. To one side of a deep bed of roses lay a long trestle table laid for lunch.

There were three distinct groups of people, none of whom Tallis recognised from the meeting and none sporting two heads and a tail. The accents were British, Southern, a hint of cut glass mingling with estuary. They all turned to look at him, smiled, voices dipping, but Tallis had eyes for one face only: Sonia Cavall's.

CHAPTER TWENTY-NINE

Blood buzzed in his ears. Hot and sweaty, he felt nauseous. He hadn't factored in that Cavall would so openly consort with Darius – sneak information to him for sure, but not actually appear in public. A big part of him seriously wanted to turn tail and run. Instead, he forced himself to walk straight towards her on legs that felt like metal girders. She issued one of her coldest smiles.

Tallis dropped his voice. 'What the...?'

'Fabulous house, isn't it?' Cavall said loudly.

'Can we dispense with the games?'

'Games, Mr Tallis?' she said softly, her expression one of extreme menace. 'Seems you're something of an expert.'

'How long have you...?'

338

'Arrived about an hour ago,' Cavall said, looking over his shoulder and smiling at John Darius stalking towards them.

'There you go,' Darius said, planting a glass of wine in Tallis's hand. 'You two know each other?'

'No,' Tallis leapt in

'You all right, Sonia?' Darius said, concern on his face. 'Look a little peaky, if you don't mind my saying.'

'I'm not good in the heat.' She smiled, tipping her glass to her lips.

'Thank God Liz put the table in the shade. Can't have you keeling over on us,' Darius laughed. 'Oh, sorry,' he said, turning to Tallis. 'This is Sonia Cavall, one of my oldest friends. Used to be at uni together. Sonia, meet Craig.'

'Craig?' Cavall said, narrowing her eyes.

'Jones,' Tallis said, pointedly.

'Craig Jones,' Cavall repeated, as if trying the name out for size. She flashed Tallis a wicked smile.

Fuck this, Tallis thought. 'So, what do you do, Sonia?'

'She works for the Home Office,' Darius said with a smug grin.

'Nice one,' Tallis said, holding her gaze. 'Isn't this rather off your patch?'

'I see no contradiction,' she said, lofty. 'I'm off duty after all.'

'Wonder if the chaps at the Home Office would take the same view.'

'Whatever do you mean?'

Tallis shrugged. 'Just wondered what they'd say.'

'Say or do?' she said, unflinching, staring at Tallis as if he'd left his toenail clippings in her bath.

'Fact is, they don't know,' Darius said with emphasis. *And we want to keep it that way* was what he meant. Which was why Cavall hadn't been at the meeting, Tallis thought. MI5 had those kind of gatherings covered, which meant he, too, was under the spotlight. He looked around him, studying the faces, nobody under thirty, most over forty, all part of the deception, Tallis thought. He wondered how Darius bought their silence.

'Not that we have anything to be ashamed of or hide,' Darius added smoothly.

'Course not,' Tallis agreed. 'Don't get me wrong, I entirely support BFB philosophy, but don't people in the Home Office view you as a bunch of dangerous right-wing fascists? Present company excluded,' he said, skewering Cavall with another smile.

'Dangerous?' Darius said, his eyes suddenly narrow and hard.

'Politically.'

'Ah.' Darius smiled. 'That's the trouble when you have a weak opposition. Like you, Sonia is disillusioned with the way things are going in our country.'

'Why not effect change from within?' Tallis said, eye-balling Cavall, who threw back her head and laughed. 'Flattered you think I have such power. I'm only a humble adviser.'

'Humble?' Tallis arched an eyebrow.

She threw him a stony look. 'There are certain constraints.'

340

'I'm sure there are,' Tallis said.

'EU laws for one,' Darius cut in. 'Means we can't control our own borders.'

'And no political will to get things changed,' Tallis said.

'Hit the nail on the proverbial,' Cavall said, surprising Tallis by agreeing with him, but, of course, he thought, they were both acting a part.

'Problem is time,' Darius said.

Cavall agreed. 'We need a radical approach to a fast-escalating situation.'

'How radical?' Tallis said, meeting her eye.

He felt someone touch his elbow and turned. It was Liz. 'Come on, you three, lunch is ready. Everyone else is sitting down.'

Tallis was amazed by the number of children – five from the Darius clan, six assorted others. He wasn't very good at age when it came to kids, but he supposed they were between six months and eleven years old.

Liz sat one end, Darius at the other, Cavall on Darius's left, Tallis opposite Cavall and on Darius's right. He had little choice but to look at her, to meet her cold, treacherous eyes. Now he understood why she'd worked so hard to protect him, and cover his tracks when he'd strayed into trouble. All so that her vile plan could be carried out. The bitch, so utterly composed, was clearly enjoying her power of life and death over him. He was in no doubt that, with one word, she could betray his real identity to Darius, tell him that the man sitting at his table thought he was working on behalf of the British Government, that he considered his job to be a legitimate one. If he

341

was lucky, Darius might view him as an invaluable asset to the cause. He was, after all, hunting down the foreign scum about which Darius held such a low opinion, but after Darius had had time to think about it, to fully digest the implications, he'd start asking questions. Why had Tallis given a false name? Why was Tallis wasting time, instead of tracking Barzani? Where did Tallis's real allegiance lie? As for Cavall, she clearly considered him useful. Tallis wondered how long he'd got before she changed her mind.

Several staff served roast beef and Yorkshire pudding. He loved food but in such a climate of heat and political intrigue he had little appetite. Now that his worst suspicions had been confirmed, he felt light-headed with dread.

'What bothers you most, Craig?' Cavall said, brown eyes drilling into his.

Tallis swallowed, looked from Cavall to Darius and back to Cavall.

'Darius mentioned your disillusionment,' Cavall said shrewdly. 'With what in particular?'

'Illegal migrants,' he said, clearing his throat, conscious Darius was listening intently. 'Whole situation has got completely out of hand. And, of course, the Muslim threat, the way we have to treat them with kid gloves, give them special rights,' he said, stealing a theme directly from Darius's speech.

'Indeed, it's no surprise previously moderate Christian groups are getting uppity,' she said. 'For too long the government have banged on about multi-culturalism and tolerance, without extending the same open-mindedness to its own

342

people. No wonder universities and colleges are becoming flashpoints.'

'Craig used to work for the police,' Darius chipped in.

'Really? In what capacity – police officer, fire-arms?' Cavall said, a dangerous look in her eye.

'Police officer, wasn't it?' Darius said, piling beef and potatoes and Yorkshire pudding onto a fork and pushing it into his mouth.

'Yes,' Tallis said, swallowing some wine. He didn't know what he was drinking but it was very good.

'Plenty of opportunity to nail blacks?' Cavall said, hiking a provocative eyebrow.

Tallis met her eye, nodded. 'I was interested by the final part of your speech.' He turned to Darius. 'You really think there'll be blood on our streets?'

'Certain of it. The people we're up against are tribal by nature.'

'You endorse violence?'

Darius smiled. 'I think we have a right to defend what's ours, but I'm certainly not advocating violence, goodness me, no.'

'So you don't agree with more radical groups, like Combat 18?' Or Fortress 35, Tallis thought.

'One may disagree yet appreciate their aims.'

Appreciate not understand, Tallis thought, thinking it an interesting choice of verb. 'You condone what they do?'

'Not in a position to,' Darius said, with all the guile of a politician.

Tallis leant towards him, his eyes flicking challengingly to Cavall. 'If I knew of a group that

343

had armed struggle as part of its agenda, I'd join.'

Darius let out a laugh, stole a glance at Cavall. 'Bit of a firebrand, isn't he?'

'You said yourself we need to do something radical,' Tallis said.

'To change people's opinions,' Cavall insisted, unsmiling. 'You don't do it by fear or violence.'

'Surely nobody ever got anywhere by being nice,' Tallis said.

The rest of the afternoon passed in a haze of conversation. Controversial subjects less, wine more. The kids, most of them in waterwings, swam in the pool, splashing and sending up plumes of water. Cavall moved among the Darius family and guests as if she were part of their scene. Always had been. And that was the truth of it, Tallis thought sourly. At all times, Darius was never far from Cavall, or she from him, although neither spoke to the other alone. That would keep for later, Tallis suspected. Once, when gazing across lawns of such magnitude he felt as if he was at the Oval, he noticed, out of the corner of his eye, Darius studying him, his hand stroking his clean-shaven chin as if weighing something up in his mind. When Tallis glanced across, Darius turned away.

Finally, Tallis made noises about making moves to leave. He told his host that he'd get a cab.

'Wouldn't hear of it,' Darius said. 'One of my staff will drive you.'

'It's really not necessary. You've already been so kind.'

Darius was immovable. Tallis had no choice but

to agree. He wondered what was planned.

'Nice to meet you,' Cavall said, extending a cool hand. 'Hope we meet again.'

'I'm sure our paths will cross.'

'Sooner rather than later,' she murmured, walking away.

'I've really enjoyed our meeting, Craig,' Darius said, shaking his hand. 'You must come again. What are you finding to do with your time at the moment?'

'Bit of security work, nothing special.'

'We must do something about that. A person of your calibre would be an asset to an organisation like ours.'

Tallis forced the warmest smile imaginable. 'I'd like that, John. Thanks very much.'

'Here,' Darius said, giving Tallis his card. 'Give me a call. Soon as you like.'

To his surprise, Tallis was driven back to Barking without mishap. On full alert, he'd half expected the driver to pull over and put a gun to his head. Nothing happened. Maybe he'd pulled it off with Darius. Maybe Cavall would keep her counsel for the moment. Maybe he was considered a better ally than enemy.

Maybe.

Much later, John Darius walked out into the night and, torch in hand, dogs at his side, headed for the far reaches of his grounds, which were considerable. He moved with some pain, even though the warmer summer weather seemed to have a less devastating effect on his injured kneecap, the residue of an old injury. As the dogs bounded on ahead, all muscle and slavering jaws, he was thinking over the day's events, his meeting with Mr Jones one of particular interest to him. The truth was that, right from the very beginning of the operation, he had been worried about putting this particular individual's name forward, about placing him in the mix, using him. Darius had argued vociferously against the choice, but was eventually persuaded. 'He'll provide the perfect smokescreen,' he was told.

Now that he'd actually met the man, he wasn't quite sure what to make of him. He certainly didn't compute with the description he'd been given. He was more educated, for a start, more intelligent, and clearly skilled in the art of detection. Darius thought it quite possible that he could be sidelined with regard to furthering his own political ends. He recognised the resentment flickering in the younger man's eyes. Yes, the tenor of the conversation had generally pleased him, although he was too old to take everything he heard from the lips of a stranger as gospel. After all, Jones had already lied about his identity. It was also entirely possible that Mr Jones was too smart for his own good, in which case he would have to be dealt with. And that would be a great waste and a pity.

He was nearing the old clock tower. Square, with inscriptions from the early nineteenth century, it stood guard over the land of his father and, now, his land. In generations to come, he wanted his home to be viewed as the seat of patriotism, of allegiance to king and country, as a symbol of pride in Britain and her people – the real people, not the imposters.

The dogs were on the scent of something. He could tell from the way their docked tails, like shortened metronomes, twitched in the moonlight. Rabbits probably. There were hundreds of them scooting around at that time of night, a Rottweiller's dream come true. Both dogs moved with a nimble stride that belied their weight and size. A little like himself, he thought with a smile. He may be slightly over the hill but he liked to think he still retained a certain charm. It came down to being open, to being flexible, about being clear about what you wanted and obtaining all goals by whatever means possible. He thought this was as important in his personal and private life as in the public and political field.

Abhorring sloppy thinking, his mind didn't so much as drift as home in on Sonia Cavall. He recalled when she'd first come to him. He had been impressed by her sincerity, he remembered, the passion of her views, her eloquence, their similarity in attitude and thinking. To be honest, when she'd agreed to join him and, as a sign of good faith, leak the details of the Home Office Operation, he had been delighted. Naturally, he'd been smart enough to treat her newfound loyalty with a dose of suspicion – one could never be too careful even with old acquaintances – which was why he'd kept her at arm's length from the sharp end of the organisation. Apart from having the unpleasant task of having to eliminate a couple of real immigration officers involved in the Djorovic case, something that Cavall was not entirely happy with, thus far it had been mutually agreed that the operation had gone according to plan, but he felt a shadow of concern that the least controllable aspect of the venture had turned up on his doorstep. Moreover, Cavall's initial response to the man's arrival had been off the mark. Why hadn't she, at once, openly admitted that she knew him? Why had she colluded with him – some would say protect – instead of exposing him? Or was he being too hard on her? Darius wondered. He knew as well as anyone that roles had to be maintained, that secrecy was of paramount importance. And, of course, there was the embarrassment factor. Cavall had not been at all happy that her charge had turned up unannounced. She'd said as much after the man who'd called himself Jones had left. Yes, the man's arrival made him look at the situation anew, question facts previously taken for granted, and challenge certain loyalties. Like all shrewd businessmen, he'd met the challenge obliquely rather than head on. The old adage – keep your friends close but your enemies closer – had always had a certain resonance for him.

He looked up at the moss-encrusted tower. The clock said half past midnight. Liz would be asleep. She wasn't a particularly clever woman but she was compliant, by far the most important characteristic in a spouse. He pulled out his cellphone and called a number.

'John here,' he said. 'I think we have a problem.'

CHAPTER THIRTY

Tallis drove back to Belle's. She wasn't happy.

'Where've you been?'

'Had something to do.'

'The sort of something where you drink vast quantities of alcohol?' She had a hand on her hip. Her face was tight with anger. 'You're almost combustible. And you've been driving.'

'I can explain,' he said, contrite. Had he really had that much to drink?

'It's Sunday, in case you've forgotten. I thought we were going to spend the day together.'

'Sorry,' he said.

'And you switched your phone off.'

'I know.'

'Well?'

Tallis let out a sigh. 'It wasn't pleasure.'

'Don't tell me.' She let out a cool laugh. 'Someone forced your mouth open and poured booze down your throat.'

He stared at her.

'What are you looking at me like that for?'

'It's nothing. Just something you said, the way you said it.'

'Said what?' She stamped her foot. She only did that when she was really mad, he thought.

'It doesn't matter.'

'Yes, it does.'

'Look, I'm knackered and I certainly don't

want to fight. Things are tricky at the moment, but I swear, once I've got them sorted, we'll spend more time together.'

'That's what you always used to say.'

Was it? he thought. He supposed he must have done.

'You don't remember, do you?'

He put a hand to his temple. Christ, he was tired. 'Remember what?'

'Doesn't matter.'

He shot her an angry look. Why was it that when a woman said it didn't matter, it did – more than ever?

'Is this connected to the trainers?' she said at last. That was better, he thought. She looked less loopy. He actually had time to notice what she was wearing: a low-cut white shirt over a gypsy-style skirt. Her feet, he noticed were bare, nails blood red.

'Kind of.' He took a step towards her.

'Are you all right, Paul?' she said softly, moving towards him, her anger dissipating then gone.

He nodded. In his imagination, he saw himself sliding his hand under her skirt, running two fingers along the inside of her thigh, feeling them disappear inside her. He put his arms around her, drew her close, felt himself harden under her touch.

This time Belle left him. 'Be here when I get home?' she said, dropping a kiss on his forehead.

'Not sure. I'll phone.'

'All right.' She smiled. 'Try and stay out of trouble.'

He turned over, buried his face in her pillow, inhaling Belle's perfume, her skin, trying to block out the events of the day before. Finn would suggest he turned himself in, spill his guts to the Home Office, but what he had to tell them would seem so preposterous to the grey men in suits, either they wouldn't take him seriously or they'd arrest him for murder. Whatever he did, he bet Cavall had her tracks concealed. Barzani was his only bargaining chip. He couldn't deliver him, would never deliver him.

Glumly, stepping out of bed, he wondered when Cavall's dispatch team would come calling, how long he had to spend looking over his shoulder.

He took a shower, dressed, foraged for something to eat in Belle's refrigerator, finding the healthy options contained in it too damned healthy. He couldn't remember the last time he'd seen a pot of yogurt masquerading as a breakfast choice. He was just pouring out some juice, orange with mango, when his mobile phone rang. It was Finn.

'Astrid Stoker,' Finn announced.

'You've found her?'

'Yup, but you won't like it.'

'Try me.'

'She was badly beaten up on Saturday night by an unknown attacker. She's currently in Heartlands Hospital.'

Tallis closed his eyes. This was his fault. That little shit, Jackson, he flared inside. 'Hello, Paul. You still there?'

'Yes. Is it serious?'

351

'Broken arm, smashed-in face.'

Tallis groaned inside.

'Any other developments?' Finn said.

He hesitated. 'No.'

'Everything OK?'

'Yes.'

'I've been thinking.'

'Uh-huh?' Tallis said cautiously.

'Isn't this a matter for the security service? Defence of the realm and all that?'

'Probably.'

'Can't you go to someone there?'

'I don't know.' For once, he was speaking the truth.

Tallis had often seen women with their faces mashed, Belle no exception, he thought with a shiver, but Astrid Stoker's still managed to shock. With her grotesquely swollen features, the crisscross of stitches in her cheek and chin, it was impossible to tell whether the woman had been pretty before her facial injuries or not. Her right arm, encased in a cast, lay like a dead elephant's leg on the bed. Passing himself off as a friend, he was warned by a harassed-looking nurse, who seemed far too young to be running a ward, that Miss Stoker was still a little woozy from the painkillers.

Tallis drew up a chair next to the bed. 'Astrid,' he said softly.

The woman inclined her head. 'I know you?' she croaked.

'No.'

The woman's entire face and body visibly froze.

'It's all right. I'm not here to hurt you. I've come to talk about what happened.'

'Police again,' she hissed. 'Already told you I fell down the stairs.'

'No, not that,' he said. 'About what happened fourteen years ago.'

Blood drained from her cheeks. Cursing, she started to fumble for the switch to ring for a nurse, but was too incapacitated to reach it.

'I'm not here to make trouble for you,' Tallis insisted.

'Sure,' she said, caustic.

'I mean it.'

'You don't understand.'

'I do. Did Jace do this to you?'

'No, I told you,' she said, a mutinous look in her eye. 'I fell.'

Feeling a pair of eyes bore into his back, Tallis turned, caught the eye of an old man watching them, a suspicious expression on his lined face. Tallis smiled and turned back to Astrid. 'You sure?'

'Yes,' she snapped.

'Fair enough,' he said, stretching his long legs out in front of him as if he was making a morning of it.

She looked at him again. 'That it?'

'Guess so,' Tallis said, without moving a muscle.

'Then fuck off.'

Tallis broke into a smile. 'How old are you, Astrid?'

'What's it to you?'

'I'd say you're about thirty-three.'

'Thirty-one,' she countered.

'Know anything about alibis?' He didn't wait for an answer. 'An alibi is when someone vouches for you being in one place at a certain time. If that person says you're in one place at a certain time when, in fact, that person is somewhere else, that's not an alibi. It's a lie. And you can be sent to prison for it.

'Now, having met Mr Jackson, I understand your reluctance to tell the truth, particularly as you were only an impressionable seventeen-year-old at the time. But Jackson was no more with you and his mother that night than I'm a finalist in *Strictly Come Dancing*.

'On Saturday I rattled Jackson junior's cage. He responded by throwing out the only piece of evidence linking him to the scene – his trainers – which I now have in my possession. Once they've been analysed, I have absolute confidence that we'll nail him for the murder of his dear old dad. So, you see, Astrid, whether you continue to lie to me or not doesn't make much difference. We'll still get our man.'

'Wasn't him,' she muttered.

'Whatever you say.'

'No, really wasn't him.' She was murmuring so low Tallis had to strain to hear. He leant towards her, looked into her bloodshot eyes. She wasn't lying any more.

'One of his goons?'

'Dunno.'

'You get a look?'

'He was wearing a mask.'

Then how do you know it wasn't Jace? Tallis thought. 'All right, you're doing well,' he said, gently patting her hand. 'How tall was he?'

'Same height as you, maybe a little taller, bigger build.'

'Voice?'

'Sorry, not much good at voices.'

'Sound like you?'

'No.'

Not a Midlander, then. 'From the north?'

'Maybe, more north than south, I suppose.'

Narrows it down a treat, Tallis thought. 'Nothing else distinctive about him?'

'Sorry.'

'Never mind,' Tallis said, standing up.

'Wait,' she said. 'This won't go any further, will it?'

'Not if you don't want it to.'

'I won't have to make a statement or nothing?'

'Couldn't be further from my mind.' Tallis smiled.

The call from Cavall came as he was leaving the hospital. 'Why am I not surprised to hear from you?'

'I don't have time for sarcasm,' Cavall sniped back.

'And I don't have time for you.'

'We need to talk.'

'Do we? I thought we did enough talking yesterday.'

'Things have changed since yesterday.'

'What things?'

'I'll tell you when I see you.'

'Tell me now.'

'Thought we could meet somewhere discreet,'

355

she said, ignoring him.

'I'm not stupid,' he burst out.

'I don't doubt that,' she said, cool.

Silence. He could feel a nerve spasm in his face. Calm down, he told himself. 'If I meet you, it has to be somewhere public.' Less chance of being shot, or having my throat cut, he thought.

More silence. 'All right,' she said at last. 'The bandstand, Calthorpe Park, three o'clock this afternoon.'

Tallis looked at his watch: eighteen minutes past eleven. She must be joking – give her far too much time to have the place staked out. 'I've got a better idea. In fact, it's the perfect place, somewhere you'll feel right at home.'

'Where?' she said tetchily.

He smiled. More used to calling the shots, aren't you, darling? he thought. 'The cosmetic department of the House of Fraser. Meet me by the Lancome concession.' Belle liked the cosmetics and it was the only place he could think of.

'That's ridiculous.'

'Take it, or leave it,' he said, hanging up.

It had been many years since Tallis had seen Terry Hyam. A former firearms instructor, Hyam had fallen foul of the law and spent several years in prison on a corruption charge. Since his release, it was well known that Hyam had set up his own little business in the basement of a former factory in Wolverhampton, renting it out to those who wanted to test out their firing skills, no questions asked. It was also reputed that if

356

you wanted a gun, Hyam could source one.

'Mr Tallis.' Hyam smiled, opening the door to his neat backstreet semi. Having driven through a collection of housing estates more akin to shanty-towns, Tallis thought Hyam's home positively wholesome by comparison. There remained, however, the lingering stench of hops from Banks, the local brewery, percolating under the heat of a ferocious sun. 'Heard on the grapevine you'd left the force,' Hyam said, inviting Tallis inside. A thin, wiry guy with a salt-and-pepper moustache and big, spaniel-like eyes, which lent him a benign appearance that was misleading, Hyam didn't look too bad after his spell in prison. Older certainly, but he hadn't lost any of his spark. Tallis put it down to the fact that, underneath the soft exterior, Hyam was as hard as rock. 'Denise,' Hyam shouted up the stairs. 'Give us a moment, would you, love? Got a mate wants to do a bit of business.'

'You going to be long?' Denise called back.

'About the same time it takes you to slap on your make-up.' Hyam winked at Tallis. 'Just bought us a couple of hours.'

Tallis was shown into a freshly decorated kitchen. Spotlessly clean and tidy, the cupboards and drawers were hand-painted in cream and blue, the flooring expensive. 'Nice, isn't it?' Hyam said proudly. 'Did it all myself. Drawers are brilliant,' he said, opening one and letting it slide gently shut. 'See, no noise.' He gave Tallis a shrewd smile. 'Don't suppose you came to appreciate my DIY skills. What can I do for you?'

Tallis cleared his throat. Never in a million years

had he thought he'd be looking up an old associate – an old *disgraced* associate, he reminded himself – to make such a grave request. 'I need a gun.'

Hyam pinched one end of his moustache. 'What for?'

Tallis smiled. 'You usually ask your clients that question?'

'You're not your average client.'

'I'm not planning a bank raid, if that's what you mean.'

'Protection?'

'Let's put it like this. If I'm pushed into a corner, I want to be able to look after myself.' Who was he kidding? Tallis thought. The best he could hope for if things cut up rough was to bag a companion to take with him en route to the pearly gates.

'Got anything in particular in mind?' Hyam said.

'Something light, portable that won't leave shell casings all over the place. Maybe a .38? Depends what you can get hold of.'

'What about a Colt, Detective Special?'

A powerful revolver designed specifically for the police in the States. 'You can get hold of one?' Tallis said, amazed.

Hyam smiled, reached for his keys, signalling to Tallis to follow him. 'Just popping out for an hour,' Hyam called up the stairs.

'Well, don't be long. I want to go shopping later,' came back the prickly reply.

They went in Hyam's car.

'When was the last time you fired a gun?' Hyam

said, thin fingers pulling on the chunky steering-wheel, the car nipping through side streets with agile speed.

'Over a year ago,' he lied. He wasn't going to admit that in the past few weeks he'd killed a man, even if it had been in self-defence.

'You'll no doubt want some practice.'

Tallis nodded. The thought had already occurred to him. He glanced at his watch: plenty of time to hone his skills.

Hyam drove to an even less attractive part of town and pulled up outside a red-brick building with large, ugly windows. A vent at the side belched out steam. A sign on the wall said LAWSONS, PRINTERS. Hyam beckoned for Tallis to follow. As they stepped inside, the noise of Heidleberg presses going at full belt was deafening.

'Going downstairs,' Hyam bellowed to a large bloke with small silver-rimmed spectacles and hair that stuck out at angles like that of a mad scientist. The guy nodded with a thumbs-up gesture.

'This way,' Hyam shouted in Tallis's ear, pointing towards a door. Hyam unlocked it and led the way, switching on the lights as they descended via a wooden flight of steps into the basement.

'Used to belong to a local radio station,' Hyam explained, the noise from above magically disappearing as the door swung shut. 'Then it got taken over by a freelance sound engineer who turned it into a recording studio. Perfect sound-proofing, which comes in real handy. When he moved to London, I made him an offer he couldn't refuse,' Hyam said with a wry grin, pushing open another door, clicking on a light.

Apart from the paper targets and bulletholes in the walls, it was like one of those rooms used by churches for youth clubs or crèches. 'Hang about,' Hyam said, disappearing into another room, reappearing minutes later, gasping and grunting, as he manhandled a crate into the centre. He opened it up, lifted out a number of silver alloy cans. Tallis noticed Hyam had put on a pair of leather gloves.

'Printing ink.' Hyam winked, reaching down to the next layer and prising off the lids, drawing out a single gun, wrapped in thick wadding, from each can. Tallis studied the arsenal: Webleys and Rugers, Smith and Wessons and Colts, and a couple of Spanish weapons that he immediately discounted. 'Got other stuff in the back,' Hyam said, 'including a nice little Mac 10.' The type of weapon that had killed two girls at a New Year's Eve party in Birmingham some years before, Tallis remembered. The firearms team had been criticised by several members of the public for not turning up sooner.

Tallis eyed the guns with awe. 'How do you know this isn't a sting, that you can trust me?' he said, looking up at Hyam.

Hyam let out a laugh. 'Easy, son. I'm too important to too many people. You shop me and you're a dead man.'

Tallis flashed a nervous grin. 'Nice balance of power.'

'I'll say.'

'What about ammo?'

'Depends what you choose.'

Tallis picked up and handled the Special, pulling back the thumb catch as if he was unloading it. Didn't feel right. Next he tried a Smith and Wesson model 60. That didn't feel right either. 'Changed my mind, Terry. Screw the casings. Got a Glock or Beretta?'

Hyam grinned, nodded, methodically put the guns back in the cans, returned to the next-door room and reemerged with another case, dragging it across the floor.

Tallis tried the Beretta, standing in front of the target, feet apart, lining it up with his best eye, taking aim, flicking off the safety and squeezing the trigger. 'Not bad,' Tallis said, giving it back to Hyam, who handed him a Glock. Tallis went through the same routine again, except with the Glock there was no manual safety device. Much better, he thought, felt as if he'd never left the firearms unit. 'Much more your style, if you don't mind my saying,' Hyam said, as if he were a tailor complimenting a customer on the cut of his jacket.

'Ammo?' Tallis said.

'No prob.'

Tallis wasn't surprised. Nine-millimetres were as common as paper clips. Hyam scurried off again. The old guy appeared to be getting quite excited. 'Here,' he said, handing Tallis a magazine. 'Have a crack.'

Tallis did, emptying three shots into each of the paper targets, two in the torso, one in the head.

'Like riding a bike,' Hyam said admiringly.

361

'Would you like to try our new fragrance, sir?'

Tallis smiled into the pretty blonde's feline-green eyes. He'd already had two other hits of headache-inducing cologne splashed onto him. He thought what the hell and stretched out his hand.

'Only twenty-seven ninety-nine,' she said, looking up at him from under her lowered lashes.

'I'll think about it,' he said, throwing her a lingering smile before starting another circuit of the ground floor of the department store. The lighting was bright and it wasn't particularly busy, not surprising at these prices, he thought, yet amidst so much good-looking totty, Cavall wouldn't be that easy to spot. He was beginning to think that make-up departments were better places than pubs and clubs to check out the local talent. Not that he was on the lookout any more. Belle had taken care of that.

Gone three, and still no sign of Cavall.

Bored, he wandered into the adjacent shoe department, eyes skimming stilettos in all shades and sizes, crocodile and fake snake, sandals and next season's boots, not a brogue, Oxford or loafer in sight. He beat a hasty retreat and washed up in a stationery concession. Shit, he thought, he'd completely forgotten his godson's birthday.

Tallis glanced at his watch again: three-fifteen. He checked his phone for the third time. Yes, it was switched on and, no, there were no missed calls or messages. Knowing how uncomfortable he'd feel in such an alien environment, keeping him waiting was probably Cavall's idea of payback. Or, he thought, sliding a hand into the

362

pocket of his jacket and feeling the comforting weight of the gun, a means to draw him out into the open and into a trap.

He decided for a less obvious way out, avoiding Corporation Street completely and heading for Temple Row and the crescent of parked cars congregated on the perimeter of the financial sector of the city. About to cross the square, something glancing across his peripheral vision made him turn. Sure enough, parked outside one of the building societies was Cavall's car, engine running, though he couldn't see the driver.

Tallis backtracked the way he'd come, crossed over the road and onto the pavement, checking the street for a possible sniper or someone walking towards him with a newspaper strategically placed in front of their shooting hand. Apart from a couple of middle-aged-looking mothers with pushchairs and a number of smartly dressed city types, too old or fat to make convincing assassins, the street looked clear.

Cavall was sitting in the back, as usual, briefcase on her lap. Bait or blarney, Tallis thought, his right hand closing snugly round the stock, ready to draw it out, before wrenching the door open with his left hand and sticking his head inside the interior.

'You're late.'

Cavall said nothing.

'This had better be good,' he said, climbing in next to her, drawing out the gun.

Silence.

He twisted round to face her, saw the blank-looking eyes, her lips slightly parted as if in a kiss.

There was a trickle of blood in the corner of her mouth. It had dripped and stained the white of her collar. Then he spotted the not-so-immaculate hair, the hole behind her ear where the bullet had made its entry, the distinctive rim burn mark around the opening suggesting that the weapon had been held directly against the skin. Hand reaching for the door, he snatched it open, slid out onto the pavement and, closing the door softly behind him, walked swiftly in the opposite direction.

CHAPTER THIRTY-ONE

The gun was like a burning coal in the pocket of his jacket. As two female special police constables sauntered towards him, he willed himself to smile, nodded a warm hello, kept straight on walking. He felt as if every man, woman, child and stray dog were staring at his retreating form.

For some reason, he couldn't remember why, he'd caught the bus into town, fearing, he supposed, now that his brain was starting to engage properly, that a car would be too much of an encumbrance.

Cutting into Corporation Street, he suddenly realised his mobile was still on him. Shit, he thought, might as well be bugged. All they, whoever they were, needed to do was triangulate his calls and work out the location. Spying a rubbish bin nearby, he pulled his phone out and dropped it discreetly inside.

The streets were filling up, making it difficult for Tallis to move with any speed. On the plus side, the crowd provided perfect cover. A vision of Cavall's dead features flashed across his mind. He wondered how long it would be before someone made the grisly discovery, how long before police ordered roadblocks and a lockdown of the city. He hadn't spent long enough with Cavall's corpse to know, but instinct told him that she hadn't been dead that long. Maybe he'd been meant to discover her. Maybe it was a message for him.

Luck, for once, was on his side. A bus destined for Quinton was making slow progress down the street. He hopped on, paid his fare, sat down near the front so that he could make a quick exit if necessary. Everything and everyone seemed to burble around him. He had the strange sensation of being in darkness underwater, drowning.

Progress was painfully slow. Streets were packed, the numerous pedestrian crossings changing from green to red with a speed that made his stomach burn and chafe with frustration and anger. As the bus started to chug away, a volley of police sirens could be heard screaming through the city. Tallis stared straight ahead, willing his pulse rate to settle, trying to think out his next move, feeling the most crushing form of claustrophobia. By the time the bus reached the lights at the turning for the Wolverhampton Road, he was already off and making his way on foot. He needed air even if it was filthy. He had to be out in the open, anywhere away from people.

With each step he tried to work out the schematics. He'd thought Cavall had been Darius's mole. Everything Finn had told him fitted the profile. For God's sake, he'd witnessed her betrayal with his own eyes, yet if someone inside the Home Office suspected Cavall of treachery, discovered her in the act, would they really react with such open violence? Sure, get rid of her. There were plenty of exits they could have chosen, but to have her slotted in the middle of the day in broad daylight, with all its concomitant risks, was insane.

Unless it was another means to frame him. *His prints and DNA were at the crime scene.*

Tallis continued to pound the pavement. Darius was in danger, he realised. Should he be warned? Whatever Tallis thought about the man, his ideals, everything he represented, he should be offered at least the chance to protect himself. The fact that he might actually need Darius did not escape him and, though abhorrent and peculiar, Tallis felt he had no choice.

He was almost at the corner of the avenue before the climb up the short hill to home when the most surreal thought crossed his mind. What if Darius had been behind the hit? But why? Tallis asked himself. What would Darius gain by eliminating Cavall? The more he grappled with the possible answers the more confused he felt. Nothing made sense. As far as Darius was concerned, Cavall was in the middle of handling a daring operation. If Darius had dispatched Cavall, how would he trigger the rest of the killing machine? Then another creepy thought flashed into his head. What if his arrival at Darius's meeting yesterday had somehow jeopardised Cavall's position? He'd no idea what had transpired after he'd left, what had been said. Had he, unwittingly, signed Cavall's death warrant? If he had then it gave added credence to the plain fact that Cavall was not who she said she was.

With the utmost caution, Tallis approached the bungalow, checking and clearing each room, gun at the ready. There was no noise. No sign of another. Nothing looked disturbed. Next, he examined the undercarriage of the Rover. Satisfied that it hadn't either been tampered with or had a device fitted, he climbed in and, without a second glance, drove away in the direction of Max's house. If he was going to reach London by nightfall, he'd need the Z8.

As anticipated, dogs, the huge slavering type that tore you limb from limb, greeted his arrival, barking and snapping, yowling like banshees. Tallis stayed in the car, doors locked, and put his hand on the horn. Mistake. Both dogs went crazy. One roared up to the car and hurled itself at the door, dashing itself against the steel in a psychotic frenzy. Fuck, Tallis thought, eyes watering at the thought of the cost to the paintwork. Eventually the front door swung open. Recognising the heavy with the white-blonde hair and razor-sharp cheekbones, Tallis took his hand off the horn and flashed his lights twice. The guy walked towards the car, cool as you like, the dogs bounding and howling, neither making any attempt to harm their boss. Tallis slid the window

367

down half an inch. The mutts might be fine with Razor-Bones, but he no more trusted those animals not to take a lump out of the car and then start on him as he trusted in the tooth fairy.

'I've come to see John.'

'He's not expecting anyone.'

'It's urgent.'

The man blinked, told the dogs to sit, which they both did.

'Tell him Craig's here to see him.'

'Tell him yourself. I'm not your errand boy.' The voice was big on disdain.

Great, Tallis thought, a heavy with a chip on his shoulder. 'Those your dogs?'

'They belong to Mr Darius.'

'Judging by the way they're behaving, I'd say they only had eyes for you. All right if I get out?'

The man nodded slowly. Tallis opened the door. The more aggressive of the two beasts, the one who'd launched himself at the car, got down on its belly, threw back its head and let out a long heartfelt yowl. The other cast Razor-Bones a pleading look. *Go on, let me have him,* his expression seemed to say. Tallis smiled nervously, felt his knees jackhammering. There was a horrible tingling sensation in his nose, an allergic reaction to the dogs. He pinched his nostrils together with a thumb and forefinger, desperate not to sneeze and frighten the mutts into a violent response. 'What was that saying about don't shoot the messenger?' He'd hoped for a laugh, for something to break the tension. The man looked at him as if he was speaking Latin.

It was the longest walk imaginable. The dogs

padded along behind him, one at each side, sniffing at his clothes, tongues flicking with frustration, stinking breath hot against his trouser legs. With every step, Tallis felt as if he was a centimetre away from jaws and teeth and tearing skin, a nanosecond nearer to certain and agonising death. Too frightened to speak, he controlled his fear by humming an old Chris Rea number in his head, 'Road to Hell'. By the time they reached the steps of the great house, he was wet through with perspiration. Razor-Bones frisked him. Tallis was expecting it, which was why against every instinct he'd left the gun in the glove compartment. Pity, he thought, the walk would have been so much more agreeable knowing he could have blown the psycho-mutts to pieces in the time it took to say Pedigree Chum.

'Go on through,' the man said. 'Mr Darius is in the drawing room.'

Which one? Tallis thought, crossing the marble floor. In the lower light, the interior seemed more impressive, if that was possible. The chandeliers alone were probably worth as much as his bungalow.

'In here, Craig.' Tallis followed the voice and entered a room of extraordinary grandeur. It felt as if he'd walked into the court of the Sun King. Darius was standing by a vast white marble fireplace flecked with what looked like gold onyx. 'Hadn't expected to see you so soon,' Darius said. 'Not that I'm complaining,' he added with a brisk smile. 'Drink?'

'Scotch, thanks.'

'That was quite some show of courage,' Darius

said, crossing the thickly carpeted floor. So he'd watched, Tallis thought, considering what Darius's response might have been had the animals turned on and toyed with him for their amusement. Darius was more casually dressed than the day before. Oxford weave dark green shirt, fudge-coloured chinos. 'Not many people trust themselves to my dogs.'

'I didn't. I trusted myself to your manservant.'

Darius cracked a smile. 'I'm sure Heller would be amused by the phrase. Do sit down, by the way.'

Tallis preferred to stand but did as he was told. As Darius walked towards the drinks cabinet, his limp seemed more pronounced than before. Tallis commented on it.

'Riding accident many years ago. Kneecap's virtually wasted away. Keep meaning to have the operation but it's finding the time.'

'Is it painful?'

'Agony. Find this stuff helps.' Darius grinned, lifting a bottle of Chivas Regal and pouring out two generous measures. 'That's better,' Darius said, taking a sip, hobbling over to Tallis, handing him a tumbler. Darius took up a position by the fireplace. Classic ploy, Tallis thought. By inviting him to sit, Darius assumed an authoritarian stance, he himself the role of supplicant.

'I'll come straight to the point,' Tallis said.

'Please, do.' The smile was kindly. The eyes were devious.

'Sonia Cavall was found dead this afternoon.' Tallis took a drink, watched the reaction. He had to admit, Darius, if he knew anything, covered it well. His jaw dropped open, eyes went wide.

'My God, I don't know what to say. I'm absolutely astonished, no, staggered,' he said, sitting down heavily. 'What on earth went wrong?' Not how did she die, Tallis thought, suspicions aroused. He remembered Darius's Oscar-winning performance in the pub, the theatre and heavy reliance on drama. Was this just another example of the same?

'She was shot.'

'Murdered? Oh, dear. Oh, Lord. And her poor mother. She'll be absolutely devastated. Sonia was an only child, you see. How on earth did you find this out?'

Tallis glanced at the floor. He'd known he'd be asked the question. 'We arranged to meet in Birmingham today. Didn't she tell you?'

'Good God, no. I'd no idea. Were you two...?' he broke off. 'No, that's not possible. Sonia preferred women.'

Christ, Tallis thought. He'd never have guessed. Bang went his cover story. 'It was terrible,' Tallis said. 'Imagine the shock.'

'You found her?'

'She was in her car, sitting on the back seat, driver nowhere to be seen. To be honest, it looked like a professional hit.'

'Really? My Christ. But who would do such a thing?'

'That's what I was hoping you might be able to tell me.' Tallis's voice was neutral but his eyes were anything but.

'Me?' Darius said, a curl to his lip. 'Whatever gave you that idea?'

'You had no inkling of her aspirations?' A much nicer way of putting it than murderous ambitions, Tallis thought.

'Depends what you mean, but...'

'And I'm afraid I did something really stupid.'

'Oh?' Darius said, eyeing him over the rim of his glass.

'I panicked and ran.'

'You poor fellow.'

'Sounds ridiculous, what with me being an ex-copper, but, you see, I know how these things pan out. You know, wrong place, wrong time. And my prints all over the damn place.'

'Yes, I see,' Darius said slowly, gravely. 'Probably best to lie low. See what transpires.' There was a shifty expression in his eyes, suggesting that he was most definitely not in the market for offering help should it be asked for. Darius took another pull of his drink. 'I'm extremely sad, of course, and I'm grateful for you letting me know, but I'm still not quite clear what you think this has to do with me.'

'I thought you might be next.'

Darius let out a hearty laugh. 'This some sort of warning?'

'More a tip-off.'

'I'm touched. I really am. To think you've driven all this way, but there was absolutely no need.'

'No?' Tallis threw him a penetrating look. Because you ordered the hit, he thought, or knew the identity of the person who ordered it? He was starting to think he wouldn't get anywhere with Darius by playing softball.

Darius took another thoughtful sip. When he spoke there was more grain to his voice. 'You never said why you were meeting her.'

'It rather followed on from our conversation over lunch. Sonia led me to believe my skills could be more fully utilised.'

'Still not sure I follow,' Darius said – making a good attempt to look confused, Tallis thought.

'Remember I told you I favoured armed struggle?'

'And both of us pointed out the disadvantages, as I seem to recall.'

'So you knew nothing of her plan to remove illegal immigrants?'

'Remove?'

'Kill.'

Darius's jaw dropped open. 'I most certainly didn't.'

'You weren't sponsoring the programme?'

'Do you realise what you're saying?' Darius snorted. 'You're accusing me of plotting to murder.'

Oh, I'm doing a lot more than that, Tallis thought. He had to hand it to Darius. He was very, very good at playing the innocent. 'Only words.' Tallis gave a playful shrug. 'You said yourself you wanted the freedom to say what you thought.'

Darius's response was to smile broadly. He leant towards Tallis in a paternal way. Something snagged inside Tallis. He realised that his dad had never looked at him with that kind of fond regard, never engaged him in argument without allowing his fists to fly. No wonder his brother had beaten Belle. He'd learnt it from their dad. 'You don't start a revolution by knocking off a few illegals,' Darius said. 'All that happens is a tit-for-tat response.'

'Leading to full-blown civil unrest.'

'Not a very appetising prospect' Darius said. 'If what you say is true, I'm not surprised Sonia wound up with a bullet in her head. She always did play fast and loose. But tell me, Craig, I find it a little hard to believe that you found out so much about Sonia's venture on such short acquaintance. Am I right in thinking that you'd met before?'

'Yes,' Tallis said. What else could he say?

'Thought as much.'

'But neither of us expected to run into each other here.'

'I see,' Darius said, his eyes suggesting that Tallis was not believed. 'I have to say, Craig, I'm surprised and yes, a little disappointed in you.' That too sounded like his dad, except, strangely, with more threat to it.

'You understood our need for discretion, surely?'

'Perfectly, but I'm sorry you didn't feel able to trust me. Perhaps if Sonia had confided in me, she'd be alive today.'

Tallis nodded gravely.

'Still we can all be clever with the aid of twenty-twenty vision,' Darius said, as if that was the end of the matter.

'Thing is, John, can I trust you now? You must know that what I've told you, if it reached the wrong ears...'

374

Darius smiled, touched Tallis's arm in an affectionate gesture. 'But nothing's happened, has it? Simply a crazy idea that never saw the light of day, thank God.

'We're not so very different, you and I. We have the same passion. I spotted that the moment I met you. But the manner in which we get things done couldn't be further apart.'

'Yet you speak of revolution,' Tallis said. Maybe Darius was telling the truth. Perhaps Cavall really was acting alone, which meant he'd been suckered. The thought that he was little more than a hired hand, no different to Bill and Ben, suddenly hit him with the full force of a freight train. And yet...

'Indeed,' Darius said, a chill note in his voice. 'It will come and when it does I will be ready.'

For what, Tallis thought, to be the voice of British nationalism, to seize power? Tallis had a terrible vision of what might happen in the country he loved based on what had already happened in the Balkans – persecution, ethnic cleansing, minorities being driven to extinction. 'Is it possible Sonia had connections elsewhere?'

Darius gave a slow shrug. 'I suppose so. There are other groups, as you yourself alluded to, but she never discussed anything with me.'

Tallis studied the older man's face. He and Cavall had discussed everything. Darius had been her tutor, for God's sake, her mentor. He had to be lying. 'Fortress 35, know much about it?'

Darius looked vague. 'Fortress what?'

'Thirty-five. A far-right group dedicated to stirring up racial hatred.'

375

'Like I said, I steer clear of anything that's likely to land me in trouble or get me killed,' Darius snapped a smile. 'I'm tempted to ask you about the mechanics of what exactly Sonia had in mind, but I think the less I know, the better it would be for everyone. I'm sorry to say, Craig, that if anyone should be looking over their shoulder, it's you, my young friend.'

CHAPTER THIRTY-TWO

Darius invited him to stay. There was no pressure. Tallis didn't feel that by either staying or leaving, his life was in danger. Darius wouldn't be so stupid to sully his own doorstep. Tallis was offered another drink, which he declined. Nothing more was said about Tallis's possible recruitment to Darius's workforce. He guessed the older man felt it better to put some distance between them. And who could blame him? But it still left many unanswered questions. If Tallis thought that Cavall's death brought an end to his involvement, he might sleep easier in his bed. Sadly, he thought Darius had a better handle on the situation. And that was the problem. With Cavall, to a point Tallis knew what he was dealing with. Now that she was dead, he no longer recognised his enemy. It didn't even have a face or personality.

Tallis reached Max's house around four in the morning. The light was breaking, songbirds singing, crows sitting in a line on a nearby telegraph pole, sharing a raucous conversation. Sounded to Tallis's ears as if they were discussing last night's events.

Letting himself into the house, he went straight to the guest room he always used when he stayed over at his friend's, pulled back the sheets, concealed the gun under a pillow and lay down. Dog tired, he slept for a full twelve hours.

Rising around five in the afternoon, he showered, found some clean clothes in Max's wardrobe and dressed. He'd lost weight, he realised, patting his flat stomach, adrenalin and fear the best dietary aids there were.

There was one single news report on the radio detailing a suspicious death in the centre of the city. After that: nothing. It was as if a clean-up squad had moved in and Cavall had never existed.

He considered calling Belle but was afraid of being drawn into a conversation that would reveal his whereabouts, not that he was under any illusion. If whoever had killed Cavall was determined to get him, they'd find him soon enough. There had been a time when he'd have thought that it didn't matter any more, but that had been before he'd got back with Belle. Later, after dark, he decided to go down to the village and make a call from the only phone box.

There was no fresh food but plenty of eatables in the freezer. Penny had all her groceries delivered from the high-class end of the supermarket business. No shortage of choice if you fancied exotica, but he had a strong yen for home cooking, something simple. In the end he settled for a venison and red wine pie. While it was cooking, he wandered into a room Max called the library, and for good reason. All four walls were lined with bookshelves of limited editions, hardbacks and reference material. Tallis's hand hovered over the collected works of Shakespeare. Scanning the spines, he found *Richard II* and *Richard III*. For some unremembered reason, they were his mother's favourite plays. She'd been able to recite whole chunks from both and she'd often raved on about the marvellous film version of *Richard III* with the lead played by Sir Laurence Olivier. Something scratching at the back of his mind, he took out both copies and flicked through them for a clue that might or might not be there. Coming up empty, he returned to the kitchen, made a pot of fresh coffee and sat and considered his options. They looked distinctly limited.

Any revelation of a plot to any authority, be it the police or security service, would have serious implications. With his kind of track record, why would anyone believe that he was an innocent pawn? Further, he'd shot one man and had connections to two separate crime scenes: Demarku's and now Cavall's. He no longer had the protection, such as it was, that Cavall had afforded him. He'd probably been spotted at the BFB meeting and, for all Darius's assurances, Tallis had no doubt that he would throw him to the wolves, or the dogs in this instance, if it was a question of saving his own credibility and skin. For all Darius's denials and convincing patter,

Tallis suspected he knew a great deal more than he was letting on – he wasn't taken in by Darius's eye-rolling display of shock concerning Cavall's death. What remained inescapable was the fact that he was caught up in a conspiracy from which there was no escape. And he was no nearer the truth now than he had been a few days ago. And that was dangerous.

He ate his meal in silence. Much later, he stole out of the house and, gun in pocket, found the call box and phoned Belle on her mobile. There was no reply, which he found faintly worrying. He left a brief message, saying that he was fine, that he'd be in touch soon. Next he called Finn and explained that Cavall was dead.

'Jesus Christ.'

'Might be advisable for you to go away for a while,' Tallis said.

'You're not serious?'

'I wouldn't ask otherwise.'

'But what will I tell Carrie?'

The least of your worries, Tallis thought. For a journalist Finn could be incredibly lacking in judgement. 'I'm sure you'll think of something. Kids are still off school. Can't you take a holiday?'

'What about you?'

'I'm OK.'

'Where are you?'

'Sorry, Finn, have to go.' He cut the call.

He went back to the house, checked everywhere was secured, and retired to bed at midnight. He lay flat on his back, looking at the ceiling. He knew he was missing something. All the conversations

379

he'd ever had with Cavall, from the moment she'd stepped into his life to her final words, raced through his head. She'd known everything about him, from the public to the deeply personal. He assumed she'd used her extensive contacts in the Home Office to gather the information yet, if she'd been working alone, she'd have wanted all enquiries to remain secret. No point in arousing unnecessary suspicions that might later jeopardise the mission. Unless Darius was involved, Tallis thought, mind racing, and had conducted his own market research. A man of considerable means, he could afford it.

He rolled over, reached for a glass of water, took a drink. The situation still pointed to someone talking. He thought of friends and colleagues, everyone he'd ever known, everyone a potential traitor, everyone with something to win or lose. Not so unusual in uncertain times, he thought, tossing and turning, sensing he was losing his mind. He went back to the Barzani case, the happenstance of his brother's involvement. Bad guys and good guys, people not being as they seemed... Shit, he thought, throwing the covers back. What if *Cavall* hadn't been what she'd seemed, but one of the genuine good guys? So far, he'd assumed she'd been part of the conspiracy, but what if he was wrong? What if she'd been a mole in Darius's camp rather than the other way round? What if she'd exploited her relationship with Darius to try to find out about Fortress 35? Jesus, what if she'd been working for MI5?

He got up, went downstairs, found a bottle of fine malt whisky in Max's extensive booze

380

cabinet, poured himself a mind-bracing dose, stared at it for several seconds and threw it down the sink, opting instead for a glass of plain, unmucked-about tap water. If he was going to think this thing out and stay alive, he needed to be absolutely sober. Taking the glass back upstairs, he lay down on the bed again.

So this is how it played, he thought. Cavall had really been part of the security services, working in the Home Office but undercover. That would explain the degree of power she'd wielded, the knowledge at her disposal, the way she'd been able to track him at a moment's notice, clean up after him. There was a popular belief that people who were spooks rushed about defending the realm unsupervised. It was a myth. There was structure, certainly someone in charge. There were rules. That was the reality. And that meant that his name hadn't popped into the mix by accident. But what had made her come to him, of all people? Why had he, in particular, been selected? Why not a security service officer, someone who could be trusted? And how much exactly was Darius being played, or was it more a case of one playing off another? He must have fallen asleep because the next he knew the sound of a visitor at the gates was echoing through the house. He got up, grabbed his gun, reflex action. If it was someone with malign intent, they'd hardly announce their arrival by pressing the security key-pad. The noise persisted. Dull and desperate. For a horrible moment he wondered whether Max had arranged for friends to come and stay in his absence. It would be a typically generous act. Stupid, Tallis reminded himself. If that was the case, they'd have a key.

Senses on full alert, he moved downstairs, his feet noiseless against the plush carpet. The entryphone was in the kitchen, just inside the door. He looked at the image on the screen, his mouth dropping open. He couldn't believe his eyes. How on earth had she got here? How had she known where to come? Then he realised. He'd told a lie to protect his identity and she'd believed it. He spoke into the panel. 'Elena?'

'Max,' she cried.

'You alone?'

'Yes. Please, Max, let me in.'

'All right' Tallis said. 'I'm coming down.'

CHAPTER THIRTY-THREE

She was cold, hungry and dirty. Exhaustion had rendered her speechless. When Tallis put a supportive arm around her, she stumbled and would have fallen had he not swept her up and carried her through the grounds back to the house. She weighed nothing. He could feel her ribcage through her clothes. How long had it been since she'd gone missing? he wondered. Three, four weeks? What had happened in that period? Had he really invested so much time in a murderous cause?

He took her into one of the children's rooms, stripping back the covers, gently putting her into bed. Within minutes she was asleep. As he stared at her matted hair, the shadows under her eyes, the pale, pale skin, he was grateful that at least something good had come out of the nightmare.

Apart from leaving her to use the bathroom or make more coffee, he stayed by her side through the night and into the following day. When eventually she stirred, he fed her *caj sa limunom*, tea with lemon, like his grandmother had taught him to make, found some of Penny's clothes and ran a bath for her. Elena watched him with big eyes. While she bathed and dressed, he defrosted bread and butter from the freezer and opened a tin of cock-a-leekie soup. He laid a place for her at the kitchen table and drew the chair back for her as she came into the room. He treated her as if she were a princess.

'Pretty,' she said shyly, touching her shirt.

'Jeans are a little big,' he said with a smile.

She nodded, frowned, tugged at the waistband.

'Never mind, you'll soon be all right again.' Prostitution, beating, starvation – who was he kidding?

'Where is your wife, your family?' she said, looking around the large kitchen as if they might suddenly pop out of a cupboard.

'Oh, they're away, staying with my wife's parents. School holidays.' He twitched a lying smile.

He watched her eat. It was the second time since their worlds had collided, he remembered. On this occasion, however, she didn't offer to share. She ate greedily, not caring whether the soup dribbled down her chin. When she'd finished he poured the rest of the soup into her bowl. She ate again, more sedately, silently spooning each mouthful, using the bread to mop up the dregs. After he'd cleared away he asked if she wanted anything else.

'To go home,' she murmured.

He let out a sigh, pushed a straggling strand of hair back behind her ear, making her flinch. How many times had she shuddered at being touched by a man? In truth, he'd already foreseen the complication. Without a passport, Elena wouldn't be going anywhere.

'And where is home?'

She broke into a smile. 'A little place called Sakiai not so far from the big town of Kaunas.'

'You must be on the borders of Kaliningrad?' A Baltic naval base in Western Russia.

She nodded.

'You have brothers, sisters?'

Her face clouded with worry. 'A sister, a year younger.'

Tallis lightly touched her arm. 'She'll be fine. I'm sure.'

He gently asked how she had wound up in England. It was a depressingly familiar story. A family friend had told her of lucrative work abroad as a waitress. The rest was a medley of trickery and betrayal. He asked what had happened to her at the brothel after their final meeting.

She spoke quietly of two men who'd come for her. 'Duka argued with them,' she said, with animated eyes. Tallis smiled. He could handle most things, most people, but Duka was not a woman to be crossed by any sane or sensible individual.

'What about?'

'Me. They said they want to – how you say?' she

384

said, frowning. 'Have me together, spit-roast, I think they say.'

Demarku and Iva, Tallis thought. 'You sure? They used that expression?'

'Yes. They say they will pay more money, but Duka says no.'

'You recognised these men?'

'No.'

'Describe them?'

She wrinkled her nose. 'One is bit smaller than you, brown hair.'

'Eyes?'

She shrugged. 'Maybe blue. I did not see.'

'Build?'

'Thin, I think.'

'Age?'

'Maybe like you, or younger.'

'No distinguishing features?'

'I do not understand.' She frowned.

'Sorry,' he said. 'Did he have marks on his skin? Scars,' he said, pointing to the fine white line that ran along his forehead.

She shook her head vigorously. 'He is not a man to remember.'

Ben, the bogus immigration official, Tallis thought, stomach snatching. 'And the other guy?'

'Old,' she shivered with disgust. 'Big.'

'Fat?'

'No.' She gestured with her hand, pointed it up in the air.

'Tall?'

'Yes,' she said. 'He had white eyes.'

'White?' Tallis laughed. 'You mean pale?'

'Yes.' She laughed, too.

'Anything else?'

'He had...' she floundered, stood up, walked around the kitchen, dragging one of her feet behind her.

Fuck, Tallis thought, Darius.

'So what happened again?'

It was two hours later. They were drinking a bottle of fine burgundy from Max's cellar. Elena was getting tipsier by the second. He, on the other hand, felt stone cold sober, mainly because he'd hardly touched a drop.

'I tell you, the other man, he starts smashing the place up. Duka gets very angry. She screams.'

'Screams?' He imagined it would sound like something between a wounded rhino and bison.

'Yes,' Elena said, big-eyed. 'Then she pulls a knife. It is long with thin blade, and I run,' she said, making a skittering motion with her hands.

'Then what?'

'I keep running. First night, I spend in shed.'

'In someone's garden?'

She nodded enthusiastically. 'I eat bread for the birds from the grass. I walk and hitch to London. There I find place.'

'A hostel?'

'Yes. Two nights I stay. I eat and sleep. But,' she said, wrinkling her nose again, 'I have no money. I have no papers. I am afraid people will send me to the police and I will be in trouble. So I leave. I walk the streets. I...' Her voice cracked and faltered. She looked up at him and smiled awkwardly. 'I make money. Sometimes I sleep, how you say, roof?'

'Rough,' he corrected her.

'Yes, rough. Is not so bad when weather is good.'

Between the days of sunshine, Tallis remembered, it had been appallingly wet. It was a wonder she hadn't developed pneumonia.

'By day, I find a café with Internet. I find where Belbroughton is. I come and, presto,' she said with zest, 'I find you.'

'You mean you walked?' Tallis said, astounded.

'Some time by bus. Never lorry. Bad men in lorries.'

Bad men everywhere, Tallis thought.

Later, when Elena was asleep, he stole out and phoned Belle again.

'Where the hell are you?' She sounded tense and tired and overwrought.

'Did you get my message?'

'Fine, be in touch,' she repeated facetiously.

He opened his mouth to speak but Belle got in first. 'And don't tell me that there are dark things happening in your life.'

You have no idea, he thought, imagining he heard her snort or sigh or something. 'Those trainers?' she said at last.

'Yes?' he said, sharpening.

'I have a result that may surprise you.'

'Go on.'

'Come and see me.'

'Belle, I can't. It's difficult.'

'Never mind,' she said maddeningly dismissive. 'It will keep.'

'Belle, for God's sake, tell me now.'

'Tell you next time I see you.' There was a

playful note in her voice.

'This is ridiculous. It's blackmail.'

'Sorry, Paul,' she said with a small laugh. 'If it's the only way I can get you to come home, then that's the way it has to be.'

Then no dice, he thought, cutting the call.

He was back in the library. This time he took a short cut and pulled out the *Oxford Dictionary of Quotations*. Going to the index, he looked up the word *fortress*. There was one reference under Shakespeare. He looked it up. *Richard II* (1595) act 2, sc 1, line 40:

This fortress built by Nature for herself
Against infection and the hand of war,
This happy breed of men, this little world,
This precious stone set in the silver sea.

Was that how the name of the group had come about? Did its members regard themselves as the happy breed of men, England their little world, their precious stone to be protected at all costs from disease and foreigners? Was Fortress 35 the real goal for Cavall? Was that what she'd been trying to unlock? And had he been her key to opening it? Now what?

He went back to bed and lay awake considering Darius's next move, his mind spinning back to their conversation over lunch. Darius had been scathing about any outlandish plan to remove a few illegals from the earth. Not worth it, abhorrent idea, or some such words that boiled down to the same thing. But the more Tallis thought of the political capital to be gained by Darius, the more reasonable it seemed. Men like John Darius existed to create tension, to destabilise society, to fan the flames of fundamentalism. Tallis imagined the newspaper headlines: BRITISH GOVERNMENT SANCTIONING DEATH SQUAD.

The outcry and backlash would be phenomenal. It would result in a free-for-all. After suffering slow genocide in the Balkans, the Iraq War, Abbu Graib, Afghanistan, Muslims could turn round and finally say *I told you so*. There'd be rioting in the street and worse. With fears of reprisals, non-Muslims would turn in droves towards something and someone they could trust, and that didn't mean a soft opposition or a party that had voted to go to war, but someone who was a real, identifiable, knowable figurehead, who had deeply held beliefs about country, the alleged good society, who, however right wing and outspoken they appeared, would never stoop to killing off his enemies in the way the British Government had done. From John Darius's point of view, the day Cavall had come knocking on his door, looking up an old mentor, talking about the deplorable state of the nation, he must have felt all his Christmases had come at once. Except, Tallis thought, from the security service's point of view, they were taking one hell of a chance, a risk that seemed to him way too high.

As for Darius, either he would do nothing or he'd eliminate him, as Cavall had been eliminated. What was utterly inescapable: Tallis knew too much and his life was in danger from both sides of the divide. His best hope was to do what he'd clearly been set up to do: find out the identity behind Fortress 35, its workings, and pass on the information to the security services.

By morning, he had no more answers. He got up. The irresistible smell of bacon cooking was wafting up the stairs. He found Elena in the kitchen. She was wearing one of Max's blue and white striped aprons, far too big for her, and was poking the contents of a frying pan.

'Where did you get the bacon?'

'I went out. I found money in your jacket. You're not cross I take it?' she said suddenly looking anxious. Thank God he'd taken the gun out, he thought.

'But how did you get back in?'

'I left the gate open.'

'Fucking hell, Elena,' he said, grabbing her by the shoulders. 'Please, promise me you won't do anything like that again.'

Her face drooped. A tear appeared at the corner of her eye. 'I am sorry,' she said. 'I do not think. You are angry.'

'No, I'm not angry. It's just that we have the gates for security. There's no point having them if they're left open. I'd better go and check,' he said, making for the door.

'What about breakfast?'

'Keep it warm.'

He walked the entire grounds. He checked the fences, the summerhouse, the shed where Max kept his lawnmowing equipment and tools. He went into the swimming-pool area and sat down on the lounger, remembering the last time he'd been there, with Felka. 'You are sad,' she'd said. 'I can tell.' Then he remembered the rest of the conversation and wondered why it was that something so obvious, so blatant hadn't struck him before. Suddenly there was a horrible kind of logic to everything that had happened to him. He likened it to the wedding car: everyone looking at the chauffeur driven Rolls-Royce or the vintage Bentley, admiring the sleek lines and the ribbons and bows, but paying little or no attention to the occupants. For the first time in many years, Tallis put his head in his hands and wept.

'Tell me about the men who came to the brothel,' Tallis said. He didn't like asking the question but he had one last, faltering hope.

Elena averted her eyes. 'I do not remember.'

'You have regulars?'

'Regulars?'

'Men who visited more than once?'

She nodded.

'And they asked for you?'

'Sometimes.'

'The fat man – had he been before?'

'No.'

'What about the man he was with?'

'Yes.'

'For you?'

'No.'

Tallis stroked his chin, felt several days' worth of stubble. 'Remember, when I was coming to visit you and you weren't there? You'd been booked by another man.'

'Yes, I remember.'

'What was he like?'

She looked at him with injured eyes. 'Rough.'

'Did he hurt you?'

She nodded, unconsciously touching her bottom lip with a finger.

'Can you describe him?'

She nodded again, and looked at him with such clarity it broke his heart. 'He has dark hair, brown eyes. He is taller than you, broader across here,' she said, touching her shoulders. 'He says he is a police officer.'

'And you believed him?'

'Why, yes.'

'And his name?'

'I do not think he told me.'

'You sure?'

'Ah,' she said, pointing a hand to her head. 'I remember. He had strange name, like he was Russian.'

Tallis felt his spirits soar, hopes lift and rise. Being wrong had never felt so good.

'Yes, I remember now,' Elena said, her face sparkling with animation. 'He says his name is Kredge.'

CHAPTER THIRTY-FOUR

'My name is Paul Tallis. I used to be a firearms officer for the West Midlands Police. I was approached and recruited by a woman called Sonia Cavall who up until her recent sudden death worked for the Home Office, but whom I suspect was working for MI5. I was instructed to track down foreign nationals who should have been deported from Britain after serving prison sentences, but were mistakenly released into the community. They are Agron Demarku, Ana Djorovic, Mohammed Hussain, Rasu Barzani. All, apart from Rasu Barzani, are dead. They were victims of Fortress 35, a far-right organisation, which exists to create racial hatred and anarchy. The founder of that organisation is my brother, Detective Chief Inspector Dan Tallis of Greater Manchester Police. He has links with John Darius of the BFB.

'During his early career as a police officer, Dan Tallis was involved in the Len Jackson case, and possibly colluded with and covered for Jace Jackson in the murder of his father at a garage in Smethwick. I suspect, but have no evidence, that Tallis turned a blind eye to Jace Jackson's people-smuggling operation in return for bribes. Belle Tallis, former wife of Dan Tallis, and a scientist at the Forensic Science Service, based in Birmingham, has Jace Jackson's trainers in her possession. It's suspected but not yet proven that trace evidence will confirm that he was at the crime scene on the night his father was killed. I also believe that hair found at the scene, together with a single foot impression belong to DCI Tallis.

'One other death you should investigate: the murder of Sonia Cavall. I believe Dan Tallis was directly implicated in, if not directly responsible for, her death.

'Should anything happen to me, I want Elena Landsbergis flown back to her home country of Lithuania. I want Rasu Barzani to be pardoned and granted asylum, and I want guaranteed protection for Belle Tallis and Finn Cronin and his family.'

Tallis turned off the CCTV camera, ejected the tape and locked it in Max's safe. He'd already phoned Belle at the FSS and told her not to go home.

'This had better be good, Paul,' she said.

'Your life's in danger.'

'What?'

'Can you go to your mum's?' Even Dan wouldn't try anything there, and Belle wasn't his target – he was.

'What's it all about? This to do with Jackson?' She didn't sound so cocky any more.

'Kind of.'

Silence. Please, don't ask me to spell it out, Tallis thought. Please, don't make me say it on the phone. If he mentioned Dan's involvement, he knew that she'd react with disbelief and, quite probably, fury.

'What about work?'

'Throw a sickie.'

More silence.

'Paul, I'm sorry. I should have told you.'

'Told me what?' He thought his heart had stopped beating.

'You knew it was him, didn't you?'

Tallis blinked. Him? Which him? 'Belle, I...'

'I found Len Jackson's blood on the trainers,' Belle burst out. 'Jace Jackson had to have been at the crime scene on the night of the murder.'

He felt light-headed with relief. If he thought that Belle had inside knowledge of the operation, known about Dan, he would have died inside. With Dan, it was different. Dan had been twisted from the time he'd been conceived.

'When will I see you again?' she said, plaintive.

'Soon, sweetheart. I just need you to lie low for a while.'

'You'll call?'

'Yes.'

'You promise?'

'I promise.'

'And, Belle,' he said, 'I love you.'

There is nothing like betrayal. Friends come and go, desert and hurt. Colleagues shop, inform and stick the proverbial knife in the back. It's called politics. But when it's your own flesh and blood...

Tallis remembered when Dan had been a lad, how he'd track his every move, spy on him, everywhere he went and whom he went with. And always it had been to report his findings back to Daddy. Something sharp twisted inside. Till the day he died, Tallis would never understand the man who, from the time he'd uttered his first word, taken his first step, had seemed to hate him. Tallis had never fathered a child. He didn't really think consciously about the possibility of having children, but of one thing he was certain. He would never, ever treat a son the way his father had treated him. Never favour one child more than another. Never create such a poisonous and destructive relationship between brothers.

No wonder Dan made a good copper, Tallis thought bitterly. He suspected that his brother, rather than Cavall, was responsible for the listening device he'd found in the bungalow. Mind flashing back to the brothel, Tallis also realised that Dan must have tailed him. To be honest, so drunk had he been at the time, he wouldn't have noticed his brother, of all people, following his movements. Tallis raised a sour smile. In his twisted way Dan had, no doubt, fucked poor Elena as payback for Belle.

In torment, Tallis found himself returning to the past, his rotten childhood. Dan never needed an excuse to spend time with Dad. It was their father, not their mother, who occupied a special place in his heart. You could see it in his eyes when their father walked into a room. Dan, who deferred to nobody, would capitulate with one word from him. Father was always right, always knew best, always, always. And over time Dan had listened to and absorbed their father's more extreme, right-wing views, regurgitating them as if they were his own.

His brother's strong attraction to the police at a time when the force had been both sexist and racist had come as no surprise to Tallis. Dan had fitted into the system as snugly as a key inside a lock. He'd flourished in the macho male environment. To outsiders, Dan looked strong and powerful and determined. Only Tallis saw the corruption in his brother's heart, a vice denied by others, particularly their father. In his eyes, Dan could do no wrong. When father looked at the one son he loved, he saw a more vibrant vision of his younger self. It gave him strength. He fed off it. They fed off each other.

But times changed. His father's health was failing. More women were entering the force, more ethnic minorities represented. When both brothers had been speaking to one another, before Belle, before the affair, Dan had once complained bitterly to Tallis about the shifting climate of correctness, the weakening of moral and political will, of the disaster that would ensue if *things weren't put right*. In the darkness of his heart, Tallis wondered if the events of the last weeks were his fault, if, as a result of taking his brother's wife when he had, he'd tipped him over the edge and into a cycle of revenge and chaos.

Before he left Max's house, Tallis told Elena that if he didn't return by the following day, she was to call a friend of his. He wrote the number down on a piece of paper for her.

Elena took it, looked at him, mystified. 'It says Max.'

'Yes.'

'But you are Max.'

He really didn't have time for this. 'I'm sorry. I

397

lied to protect my identity.'

'You are not as you say,' she said, fear in her eyes. 'You have done something bad?'

'Perhaps.' It was true. He'd been the final corrupting nail in his own brother's coffin.

'And this is not your house?'

'Wish it was.' He smiled.

She nodded, her expression grave. 'So who are you?'

'I'm one of the good guys.' At least, he wanted to be.

Taking the Z8, he drove straight to the bungalow. The sky was veined with light from a persistent sun, clouds jinking in the blue. Cruising slowly past, he could make out a figure stalking the sitting room. No, not any figure, a woman. For a confusing moment he wondered whether it was Belle. Who else would be in his home? But it wasn't Belle. Of that he was sure. This was someone older, bulkier. He drove to the end of the road, turned the car round and parked metres short of the driveway. As he got out, he slipped his hand into his pocket, felt for the comforting shape of the gun, took it out, held it at his side, the barrel pointed at the ground.

Jimmy next door was in full flight, a hot medley of power chords and licks, the guitar swooping and yawing at ear-bleeding volume. Grateful for the ground cover, Tallis slipped down the side and round the back. To his surprise, the door was ajar and there was no sign of forced entry. He crept in, sniffed the air, catching the distinctive smell of cigarettes. Baffled, he moved silently forward through the kitchen, hugging the wall, pausing by the arch.

'Well, well, well, the plot thickens,' Crow said, a scabrous smile on her thick-set face. She was standing with her back to the living-room window, a cigarette poised between her fingers, the evidence of plenty more shoved unceremoniously into the fruit bowl on the table. By the look of it, she'd spent most of the morning there. 'Paul Tallis, alias Mark Strong, alias fuck knows who. And, for Christ's sake, Mr Tallis, put that sodding gun away.'

'How did you get in?' Tallis said, keeping the gun right where it was.

'Through the door.'

'It was open?'

'No, I'm a ghost.'

'How did you get here?'

'I walked,' she said, blowing out a large plume of smoke. He had to hand it to her. She was a very cool character under pressure.

'Where's your car?'

'Would you drive with a drink habit like mine? And of course I didn't fucking walk. I got a train and caught a cab. Now, are you going to put that gun away, or not? I won't ask where you got it from, or am I to assume,' she said, her voice drenched in sarcasm, 'it was special issue?'

He lowered his weapon, placed it on the coffee-table in front of him and sat down.

'You look terrible,' she said.

'Don't look so good yourself.'

She issued one of her dreadful smiles. 'You didn't seriously think I could be warned off by some officious tart from the Home Office, did you?'

'The dead officious tart who also happens to work for the security services?'

'Dead?' Crow flinched.

'Shot.'

For the first time Crow looked at the gun, looked seriously worried.

'It's all right. Wasn't me.' Even though there are bits of my genetic imprint all over the sodding place, he thought. Hopefully, if Cavall was who he thought she was, a team had already moved into place to eliminate all trace of her in the same way Cavall had arranged to clean up after Kelly Simmons, the girl in Devon.

'If I'd had a quid for every time I'd heard that one, I'd be a millionaire.'

'What did Cavall say?'

'That you were working for the government on some highly important mission, and that I was to leave you out of the loop. All the usual classified claptrap, need to know, for-your-eyes-only bollocks.'

'You ever do as you're told?' Tallis said with a tired smile.

'Not unless there's a major inducement. Going to tell me what this is all about?' Crow said, lighting one cigarette off the other.

'Do you have to do that?' Tallis said.

'Do what?'

'Puff fumes everywhere.'

'Don't think you're in much of a position to argue. So far, you've lied to me, pretended to be someone else, and your name's cropped up in a murder inquiry. What should I call you, by the way, apart from Houdini?'

Normally he'd have said Tallis, but he wanted to make a clear distinction between himself and his brother. 'Paul's fine.'

She eyed him darkly. 'That your car outside on the road?' So she'd spotted it.

'Borrowed.'

'Really?' she said, elevating a suspicious eyebrow. 'Friends in high places. Paint looks a bit scuffed.'

Yes, it was. Christ knew what Max would say. 'The murder?' Tallis said, bringing her back on track.

'Agron Demarku.'

'You can't seriously think—'

'I can think what I like.'

Tallis let out a long low sigh. 'You alleging I did it?'

'I'm saying that, as far as I'm concerned, you were the last person to see him alive...'

'Not exactly...'

'And you're no writer, hack, whatever you want to call yourself,' she said with a glare. 'Which brings me to a question. Who do you work for?'

'The honest answer is I don't know.'

Crow stared at him with incredulity. 'I think you'd better start talking.'

Tallis glanced at his watch. He hadn't worked out Dan's next move. Did he have time to confide in Crow? What difference would it make? And yet he felt strangely drawn to the curmurgeonly heap of humanity that was taking up so much space in his living room. He felt as if he needed to talk to someone who would maybe understand.

'All right,' he said. 'Could take some time.' Not something he had.

'Fine by me,' Crow said, pulling out two packs of twenty cigarettes and putting them on the coffee-table. 'Fire away,' she said, lighting up.

CHAPTER THIRTY-FIVE

He left nothing out. Every conversation, every detail, each nuance was described and explained and put into context. Crow said little, endlessly chain-smoking, her face expressionless, apart from the eyes. They danced like wet sparks in a wood fire. When he'd finished, she said nothing at first, making an endless ritual of stubbing out her final cigarette, laying it beside its numerous brothers and sisters.

'*Cherchez la femme.*'

'I admit Cavall played a pivotal role,' Tallis began.

'What about Belle?'

'Belle?' he said, astonished. 'Belle's got fuck all to do with it.'

'You sure?'

'Absolutely.' The idea was preposterous. He glowered at her.

'She was married to your brother for a long time,' Crow said reasonably. 'Maybe she belonged to the organisation, was part of the set-up. Maybe she was the trap.'

402

Tallis shook his head, adamant. He wasn't even going to allow himself to feel rattled by Crow's ridiculous assertion. He knew Belle, had the measure of her. He loved her, for Chrissakes.

'One thing you're quite wrong about,' Crow said. 'Neither Dan nor these flowerpot characters are coming to get you.'

'Bill and Ben?' Tallis smiled. 'How come?'

'No need. You've crossed enough lines and dished out enough rope to hang without them. All your brother has to do is drop a few words in the right ear and you could be spending the rest of your days banged up in a secret prison in an orange jumpsuit on some tropical island.'

'Thanks for the optimistic appraisal.'

She issued another of her hideous smiles. 'In the meantime, your brother can get on with his plans for world domination.'

'Hardly,' Tallis said. 'Whatever I think of Dan, he falls a shade short of Hitler.'

'Never underestimate the ambition or designs of evil men.'

'Which is why he has to be stopped.'

'I agree,' Crow stood up, knees creaking with the sudden movement. 'Your best chance is to go to the security services and come clean. If Cavall was working for them, they'll be aware of the situation and be sympathetic to your cause.'

He was right. This was out of Crow's league. 'For such a cynic, I'm astonished at your naivety. With my track record, I'm not going to be believed. Christ, they might even view it as brothers working in tandem against the state.'

'Interesting idea, but you have to leave this to

us now.'

'No,' Tallis said. 'This is between him and me.'

Crow laughed. 'You're not in some bloody spaghetti Western.'

'Pity, makes life so much simpler.' He snatched the gun off the table and pointed it at Crow.

Her eyes briefly widened in shock. 'Don't be stupid.'

'Sorry, can't afford to let you screw things up.'

'*Me* screw things up?'

'Phone,' he said, gesturing with his free hand.

'You'll regret this,' she said grumpily, taking her phone out and throwing it across the table.

'Quite possibly. Now cloakroom.'

'I don't want the cloakroom.'

'Trust me, you could be here for some time,' he said, motioning for her to move.

'I'm the only friend you've got,' she snapped.

'Sorry to disappoint,' he said, pushing her into what used to be a hidey-hole-cum-broom cupboard before its conversion. He hadn't yet got round to taking off the bolt that his gran had fixed to the outside.

'You can't do this,' she shrieked, making a half-hearted effort to resist. Not easy with a gun pointed at your abdomen.

'Just did,' he said, giving her an almighty shove. 'Now, be a good girl and I might come back for you later.'

'What about my fags?' she yelled, hammering a fist against the wood.

'Cold turkey,' he called over his shoulder, running out of the house and heading for the car. There wasn't a moment to lose.

CHAPTER THIRTY-SIX

He drove at speed in the direction of The Mail-box, parked in the street near Belle's flat and ran up the drive to where the concierge was stationed. The black guy with the wide smile was finishing his lunch. When he saw Tallis he looked startled.

Tallis didn't mess about. 'She in?'

The black guy nodded.

'Alone?'

He shook his head and looked down.

'There a problem?'

'I don't know. She said she was all right, but she didn't look happy. She–'

'How many?'

'Just one guy.'

'Know who he is?'

The concierge looked down again. 'He said he was her husband.'

Fuck. 'Can you get me in?'

'Well, I d–'

'He's not her husband any more. He has a history of violence towards her. Think how you'll look if she gets beaten up, or worse.'

The black man flinched. 'All right. I'll get you in.' He swiped a bunch of keys from a rack behind him and they both moved towards the gates. The concierge punched in a code, releasing the lock, then crossed the courtyard to another door where he punched in another.

Tallis followed him inside. 'This is the key,' the concierge said, pointing it out to Tallis. 'I'll call the police.'

'He is the police,' Tallis said, making for the stairs.

The corridors were empty, the door to the apartment closed. He silently drove the key into the lock, turning it, the thickly carpeted floor masking the sound of his feet as he crept inside. He could hear voices: Belle and Dan's.

'You tricked me,' she said hotly.

'Easy, wasn't it?' he sneered. 'I only have to mention his name and you come running.'

'Where is he?'

'All in good time. Must say you've got a nice place here. Cleaning me out obviously came in handy.'

'Clean you out?' she raged. 'You're bent, Dan. You've got more money than you know what to do with.'

'And you didn't know?' he sneered. 'Come on, sweetheart, didn't hear you complain about the nice house, the smart cars, foreign holidays. How else do you think I could have afforded that kind of lifestyle?'

'You covered up for a murderer,' she yelled. 'Your hair was found at the scene, your footprint.'

'So what? Got another of those foreign spongers off our streets. Result, I'd say. You really shouldn't go poking your nose in where it's not wanted. Is the head of the science unit aware you've been trawling through an old case without permission, interfering in the natural laws of justice?'

406

'What would you know about justice?'

'You're not going to go all moral on me? That would be rich, coming from you, a lying little tart.'

'I didn't kill anyone.'

'No,' he said thoughtfully, painfully. Made Tallis wonder about the emotional damage they'd inflicted on him. Dan was talking again. 'There's an old Mafia maxim. Avoid killing if you can. If you can't, be discreet. Well, we were discreet. Unfortunately for my lunatic brother, he's been quite the opposite of discreet – reckless, I'd say. Did you know he was working for us?'

Tallis swallowed.

'My, I can tell by the look on your face you'd no idea. You don't know my brother very well, do you? He was a sleeper for our group. He tracked *people*.' Sounded like *vermin*. 'Then he handed them over for disposal.'

'You're lying.'

'Ask him.'

'He wouldn't do that.' Her voice cracked.

'Ask him about the murder of a pregnant young girl who got in his way. Ask him about the shooting of a Home Office official. His prints were found at both scenes. Add it all together, he could go down for years and years.'

'And you'll be coming with me,' Tallis said, stepping inside. Belle was standing over by the window, arms rigidly crossed in front of her. Dan was sitting on the sofa. Dressed all in black, wearing an expensive set of sunglasses, he cut a threatening figure.

'There, what did I tell you?' Dan said, looking

at Belle. 'The man with the gun.'

Belle's jaw went slack. Fear and confusion flashed across her eyes. And something else: despair.

'What are you going to do now, Paul?' Dan said, goading. 'Shoot me?'

'Don't tempt me.'

'Paul,' Belle cried. 'Whatever you've done, it doesn't matter. This isn't the way out.'

'As it's truth time,' Tallis said, staring at his brother, 'did he tell you about his shady relationship with John Darius, leader of the BFB?'

'What?' Belle cried in horror.

'Did he tell you about his nasty little team of people, the kind of scum who take pleasure in bumping off foreign nationals? *Immigration officers*,' Tallis scoffed, 'Where did you recruit them – prison?'

Dan leant back expansively, smiled. Something in his expression reminded Tallis of their father, a man that could disembowel a son with just one look.

'Thing is, they weren't the only ones pretending. The Home Office official,' Tallis said with a penetrating expression, 'that's where you really cocked up.'

'Me, cock-up?' his brother sneered.

'Big mistake to bump her off, Dan.'

'Fancied her, did you?'

Tallis said nothing.

'Bet you did. She was a great shag, by the way. Just your type.'

'My type? Don't think so. She was gay.'

Dan's face froze for a second. Nobody other

than a brother would notice. Tallis decided to go for the jugular. 'And that wasn't your only mistake, Danny boy. You read it all wrong. Patience was never your strong suit. You thought she was on your side. You thought you could manipulate her, just like you manipulate everyone else in your life. You used John Darius as your go-between, letting him feed misinformation about me to Cavall so that she would think that I was part of the plot, *your* plot. Except you're not quite as smart as you think. Cavall was with MI5.'

'That's bollocks,' Dan jeered. 'She was nothing more than a bored government tart who tried to play fast and loose with the big boys.'

'Sent to ingratiate herself with Darius,' Tallis persisted, 'infiltrate the BFB, and find out who was running Fortress 35 and break it.'

Dan, hatred in his eyes, tipped back his head and laughed so loudly Tallis almost missed the shouts from outside. 'Get down! Get down!' At once a shot rang out, shattering the window, followed by the sound of two more shots, different from the original. Tallis instinctively ducked but it was too late for Belle who was in the line of fire and already falling. Tallis crashed to the floor, elbowed his way across the room, belly down, gun at the ready.

He looked down at Belle in horror. Blood was oozing from her mouth. She was pale, sweaty, eyes flickering. He slid his arm underneath her, making her moan with pain. As he cradled her in his arms he could feel the gaping hole in her back, her blood warm on his shirt. He looked around him desperately, blinded in anguish, torn between trying to get help that he knew would arrive too late and staying with and holding the dying woman he loved. All the precious times they'd spent together flashed before his eyes. In disbelief, he wondered how it was that in a matter of seconds life could be so suddenly and with such cruelty snatched away.

'Don't leave me,' he cried, his eyes misting with tears. Images of Rinelle Van Sleigh, Matt Cronin, his best friend, floated before his eyes. He'd heard their last dying breaths, too, witnessed the fear in their faces, but nothing could have prepared him for this. Nothing.

'I'll always love you,' she said softly. 'Find Dan. Don't let him get away.'

A shadow fell across them both. As Tallis glanced over his shoulder, he saw that his brother had gone. In his place stood Asim, the man who'd been so keen to offer his assistance in Manchester. He had a gun in his hand.

CHAPTER THIRTY-SEVEN

'Leave her, Paul. She's gone,' Asim said.

How can I ever leave her? Tallis thought, holding Belle tight, rocking her back and forth, feeling the warmth go out of her, his eyes blinded by tears. He didn't care about anything any more. Asim could shoot him.

'Paul,' Asim said gently, the pity in his voice like an electrode to Tallis's brain. Blind hatred consumed him. 'You killed her,' Tallis raged, raising his weapon.

'No. I'm an intelligence officer with MI5. I was working with Cavall.'

Tallis blinked, mystified.

'It's the truth.'

Truth? What the hell was that? Tallis thought. 'You're covering for my brother,' Tallis said slowly, deliberately, rising to his feet. 'You let him get away.'

'I came up the stairs. He took the lift.'

'I don't believe you.'

'Then believe what you can see,' Asim said, dark eyes flashing. 'Look,' he said, pointing out of the window.

Tallis let out a cold mirthless laugh. 'Classic trick. I don't think so.'

Asim put down his gun, kicked it away. 'Now look.'

Bewildered, Tallis scooped up the weapon, glanced out of the window, saw the bodies of a man and a woman lying in the courtyard, Bill and Ben, gunshot wounds to their heads. Residents were already running to the scene, mobile phones in their hands, the concierge trying to herd them away. Tallis looked back at Asim.

'I'm sorry I didn't get to them soon enough. Sorry about Belle,' Asim said gravely, positioning his body in the entrance to the flat, blocking Tallis's exit. 'But, truly, I'm on your side.'

'I don't know whose side you're on, but it's definitely not mine.' Tallis turned, darting down the stairs to the study and second bedroom, heading for the secret unmarked door. Wrenching it open, he scooted through, finding himself in a corridor on the second level. Dropping the catch after him, he ran. Revenge was in his heart and on his mind.

He had been taught in the army that a mission must never be jeopardised by casualties. A man down was just that. You didn't stop, loiter or go back. You remained focused on the job. You kept on moving. If ever he'd needed to draw on that training, it was now.

Dan wouldn't have got far, Tallis thought, but which way? And how had he got there – by car, by train? Insanity to take the car in the middle of rush-hour traffic so, he concluded, however Dan had travelled, he must have escaped on foot, which meant there was a fifty-fifty chance of him heading for the station at New Street. Bigger and heavier, Dan had always been a lousy runner. It was the only advantage Tallis had over him. That and the fact he was armed.

He raced along the side of the canal, the water sparkling in the glare of a beaten sun. Feet clattering over the bridge, he passed the restaurant in which he'd so recently eaten with Belle. One of the Polish girls was standing outside, ready to welcome the next diner. Their eyes met briefly. She smiled then saw the blood on his shirt, her expression changing to one of horror. Tallis stared back with a heart that felt numb and cold, the misery inside him suddenly welling over, all-consuming.

Up the steps and into the entrance to The Mailbox, he pounded through the cloistered confines of the empty lower floor, his footsteps eerie and hollow in the relative silence then out the other side, feet flying down the steps and dodging through a stream of heavy traffic, car horns blaring as he wove in and out. Eyes scanning the horizon for sight of his treacherous, lying, murderous brother, he saw nothing other than a wall of people. In desperation, he speeded up, hoping for some underdeveloped sense of fraternal direction to kick in, knowing that Dan could have taken off in the other direction, that he could be anywhere by now.

Stubbornly, Tallis continued at a calf-burning pace, his gun concealed, though, from the startled and terrified expressions of strangers, there could be no mistake about the intent in his eyes. Kids leapt out of the way. Dealers stared after him with grudging respect. It never occurred to Tallis to give up. Doing anything other than continuing the pursuit would signal defeat and allow the heavy surge of mixed emotions room to come flooding in.

The sun was lower now, less cocky as it bounced off walls of brick and concrete and steel. Automatically, Tallis narrowed his perfect twenty-twenty vision, scanning the crowds of commuters and city dwellers, buses slow with lassitude, the ever-changing lights. That's when he spotted a figure in black up ahead. As if by instinct, the figure turned. No longer wearing sunglasses, Dan's eyes locked with his. In that moment, it was as if the city was empty of people. It was just him and his brother and the deep-set hatred between them.

Both men took off, Tallis kicking hard on the

back foot. Although Dan was moving more quickly, dodging in and out of the crowd, the gap was lessening with every passing second. To Tallis's amazement, they were no longer taking a direct route to the station. Dan appeared to be aiming for the Bull Ring, formerly the centre of old Birmingham, the original market dating back to the twelfth century. Currently, it was a vast, modern, glass-fronted shopping mall and throbbing retail heart of the city.

Tallis felt his mouth dry as he shot down the main drag, memories of another time flashing through his head, the not-yet-developed Rotunda looming over him like a prophet of doom.

A *Big Issue* seller, foolish enough to try and collar Dan, was rewarded with a swift punch in the gut, felling him and causing a small riot of disturbance. Two young police officers ran to the aid of the victim, one of them talking into his radio. Tallis sidestepped the lot of them, ran on, the ground between him and his brother swiftly diminishing.

They were in sight of the bronze statue of the bull, the symbol of the shopping centre. Dan had a choice, Tallis saw, whether to disappear inside, or flee, or give himself up. He did none of those things. He pivoted on one foot, turned, a slow, satisfied smile on a face cracked with decades of bitterness and resentment. Tallis stared at the gun. Diving to the pavement, he saw the flash, heard the shot, the screams of shoppers ringing in his ears. Then there was another: aimed, guaranteed to maim, not kill. Tallis saw Dan fall, the weapon spinning from his hand. He ran forward and knelt at his brother's side, instinctively tearing off his shirt to bind the wound in Dan's shoulder.

'Finish the job, you fucker,' Dan snarled, his face contorted by pain.

It would be easy, Tallis thought, payback for all the death and destruction, for Belle. What use would life be without her? he thought. What would it matter if he spent the remainder of it in prison?

'Come on, what are you waiting for?' Dan goaded.

Tallis raised his weapon, looked into his brother's eyes, saw the darkness reflected inside, and realised that he didn't want to be like him. He didn't want to give Dan the satisfaction of winning. Dan had taken the heart and best of his life, but he didn't have to hand him the rest. He put the gun down on the ground quickly before he could change his mind.

'You stupid? It's an order,' Dan screamed.

'Stop. Armed police.'

Tallis looked round, saw eight police officers armed with Heckler and Kochs. He knew the drill and got down on the ground, spread-eagling himself. 'My brother needs an ambulance,' he said as he was frisked and searched.

'Fucker tried to kill me,' Dan cried out. 'I'm a police officer, Detective Chief Inspector with Greater Manchester.'

'Not for much longer,' a voice said. Tallis glanced up.

'Think it's about time you and I talked,' Asim told him.

CHAPTER THIRTY-EIGHT

It took Asim less than an hour to extricate Tallis from the clutches of West Midlands Police. Shades of Cavall, Tallis thought as he was escorted out of Lloyd House. But Asim, he explained, would have to wait.

'I have to go back to the apartment.'

'I'll take you there,' Asim said.

'No.' He didn't want this man near him. He didn't want anyone.

'They won't let you in unless I'm with you.'

Tallis glared belligerently at Asim, saw the sharp intelligence in the man's eyes, saw something else – kindness, he thought. With great reluctance, Tallis agreed.

As expected, the place was crawling with SOCOs and police officers and medical bods. Tallis looked on as a guy in a white suit efficiently examined Belle's body and gave the signal for her to be zipped into a body bag and moved. Part of him wanted to help, to be close to her one last time, to arrange her limbs carefully, make sure her hair was placed just so, but already he could see that death had settled on her beautiful features, that Belle wasn't Belle any more.

Afterwards, they found a quiet corner of the lounge of the Burlington Hotel, a genteel, old-style establishment that incorporated Burlington arcade. It was the kind of place where you took tea. They ordered whisky. Tallis listened while Asim did the talking.

'So there really was a Home Office operation,' Tallis murmured at last.

'Yes.'

'Christ.'

'But there was never any intention of state murder,' Asim said.

Tallis hiked a disbelieving eyebrow.

'Cavall met John Darius while at Cambridge. He was her tutor, but she had no sympathy for his beliefs and had nothing to do with him afterwards. As you're aware, many young men hold idealistic, sometimes anarchic views, but lose them or see them as largely irrelevant as they grow older.'

'Except he didn't.'

'The BFB has a respectable and legitimate front, even if you don't agree with the philosophy.'

'But Fortress 35...'

'We knew of its existence. We knew very little about the organisation. Like many terrorist groups, they work on a cell network.'

'There are others?' Tallis said in alarm.

'Quite possibly.'

Fuck, Tallis thought. 'So, as I thought, Cavall used her old contact with Darius in a bid to unearth Fortress 35 and nail the elusive and shadowy Mr X.'

'Who turned out to be your brother,' Asim said. As if he needed reminding, Tallis thought, frowning. 'You have to remember Darius is looking after his own interests,' Asim continued. 'In many

417

respects he resembled the double agent, supplying info from Dan to Cavall and vice versa.'

'Which was how Darius put me in the frame.'

'In the beginning, we thought you were part of the conspiracy.'

No surprises there, then, Tallis thought. Except...

'Cavall noted your seeming reluctance to get involved in the operation,' Asim said, as if reading his mind. 'But you wouldn't be the first to engage in a little pretence.'

'She also knew of my doubts about the shooting of Rinelle Van Sleigh,' Tallis said pointedly.

'Which was why we reckoned you now had the motive,' Asim continued. 'Resentful and bitter after your career was brought to a crashing end, you decided to take the law into your own hands. Either you were working for Darius, or provided us with the opportunity to find out about the armed wing of the group.'

'You used me.'

'We used each other,' Asim said with a pragmatic smile.

'And you never suspected my brother?'

'Why would we? A serving police officer, clean record, cleared from the very top.'

'But Cavall and Dan at the police station.'

'Think about it. For quite separate reasons, it was in both their interests for you to continue. For Cavall, to see where the trail led. For Dan, to pull you deeper into the shit.'

'Going back to Barzani...'

'Sheer fluke that your brother was involved in the case,' Asim smiled. 'Your brother had no idea that we'd singled out Barzani as one of our most wanted.'

Fluke or hunch, Tallis thought, not at all sure he believed Asim. 'And the others were singled out at random?'

'Pretty much. The idea was to whet Darius's appetite.'

'You used those people as bait,' Tallis said, tight with sudden anger. 'Every time you made a move, you let Darius know about it. Why the hell didn't you put Darius, or those two henchman of his, under twenty-four-hour surveillance and find out where the trail led?'

'We tried,' Asim said, a dark glint in his eye.

No, Tallis thought. You'd rather use someone like me to do your dirty work. This was never about due process, about evidence or court trials. This was about eliminating the enemy. He wondered what on earth would happen to Dan. 'And what happens to Darius now?'

'Nothing.'

'Nothing?' Tallis said, mystified.

'He's more use to us where he is. If we arrest him, someone will take his place.'

Tallis opened his mouth to protest.

'In circumstances such as these, it's more fruitful for us to leave a player in situ. It's what intelligence officers are trained to do.' So that's why Cavall was also left in place, despite the obvious risks, Tallis thought. Asim was still talking. 'And now that we have your brother safely tucked away, Darius is going to think twice before he does anything to undermine his own position.'

Tallis frowned. How many dictators were

propped up because they were considered more malleable than someone with more scruples? 'Going back to the real immigration officers, what happened in the case of Demarku?'

'Unfortunately, they went to the wrong address and by the time they found the right one, Demarku was already dead.'

'Turning what should have been a PR coup into something of a disaster.'

'It got worse. We put in our own officers for Djorovik, but they never arrived at all.'

Of course, Tallis thought, the road accident, the fireball. 'Intercepted en route, shot and their car set on fire.'

Asim smiled in admiration. 'Seems to me you were one step ahead of the game.'

Not quite. If he had been, Belle would still be alive. 'So that explains why there was little mention of it in the press.'

'Same reason there was no mention of the girl in Totnes,' Asim said matter-of-factly, 'or the brothel in Hounslow.'

'Or Cavall?'

Asim nodded.

'You cleaned up?' He found it very, very hard to understand this entirely alien world. Having always been a bit of a conspiracy rather than a cock-up theorist, he was beginning to think they were indivisible: cock-up preceded a cover-up followed by conspiracy.

'With Hounslow, it revolved around split-second timing,' Asim said.

It would have done, Tallis thought. As soon as he'd left Elena, Darius had turned up and confronted Duka, fleeing minutes before the clean-up team had moved in, followed by the hapless Crow. He screwed up his eyes, suspicious. 'What about Kelly's mother?'

Asim said nothing. Tallis pressed the point.

'She was told her daughter died in a road accident,' Asim said, meeting his eye.

So that's how things are done, Tallis thought, depressed. 'And the guys who roughed me up, what was that all about?' he asked Asim.

'Cock-up on my part.'

'Let me guess, crossed wires with another branch of Intelligence?'

Asim smiled warmly. 'You're getting the hang of it.'

Tallis blinked. What was this, some kind of protracted job interview? 'Why not call the whole thing off? Innocent people were dying. You could have had me tailed...'

'You need to let people run before you can reel them in. Thankfully, I managed to track you to Belle's apartment.'

Tallis flinched. How was he going to spend a lifetime forgetting her? He flashed Asim another sharp look. He was beginning to feel like a fish in an angling contest – drag him out, check him out, chuck him back in. 'It was an extremely audacious plan. You were taking a hell of a risk.'

'We always had Darius as a firm target,' Asim said. 'The rest was down to you.'

'I still don't understand why it was allowed to go this far. Why didn't you send more of your people, instead of letting Dan's henchmen move in?'

'As I explained, we tried.'

Tallis said nothing, shook his head in disbelief.

Asim sighed and spread his hands in front of him. 'Because it was too late. Once the killing started, we lost the moral imperative.'

Because you had nothing to lose, Tallis thought, seeing Asim in a new, unattractive light. Because what were a few men and a woman, all of them bad people, when matters of state were at risk? They were all so expendable. And so was he. Asim was still talking.

'We needed enough evidence to lead the trail positively back to Dan and nail him.'

'How much, for Chrissakes? You let seven innocent people die, and there were God knows how many other casualties.'

'Seven?'

'Belle Tallis.'

'Regrettable, I agree.'

Regrettable? That was the kind of catch-all word politicians used when civilians, mistaken for soldiers or terrorists, were killed. And they weren't even going to arrest Darius. 'And Cavall,' Tallis spat out.

'Ah, Cavall,' Asim agreed.

Something in his eyes suggested to Tallis that she had been a victim of her own lack of judgement. What would they call it – a miscalculation? And then it hit him: when he'd turned up at Darius's house, Cavall had been trying to protect him. 'And two others from your own side,' he pointed out.

'Agreed, but the others,' Asim said, lip curling, 'innocent?'

'Yes, innocent.'

'In matters of state one always has to look to the greater good.'

Asim's words had a strangely echoing effect. Someone had once told Tallis the same thing after the shooting of Rinelle Van Sleigh. He hadn't believed it then and he didn't now. He was so consumed with thought he almost missed what Asim was saying. 'We'd like you to join our team.'

Tallis stared in astonishment.

'Think about it.'

'To do what? To chase people who never mattered anyway? Bloody foreigners, aren't they?'

'Paul, it's n–'

'You touched on something earlier. Made me think about the Balkans, the Middle East, the continual neglect of swathes of people in Africa. Know why all that came about?'

Asim frowned. 'I sense a lecture on Western politics.'

'No, I'll make it really simple for you. It's because we don't care. We allow it to happen and then we watch it happen. If there was more political will, massacres on a colossal scale could be averted, wars prevented before they began. Just so we're really clear,' he said, angry now, 'there are too many places where blind eyes are turned. What's happened here,' Tallis said, voice brittle with anger, 'is no different. It doesn't matter what the colour of your skin is, or the faith you believe in – violence is violence. Those people never stood a chance, were never meant to stand a chance. They were simply pawns in the political machine's game. And you expect me to become a part of it,' he jeered. 'No, thanks.'

Asim leant towards him. 'What would it take to make you change your mind?'

Tallis got up, crossed the floor. He was almost out of the door. 'Pardon Rasu Barzani,' he called over his shoulder. 'Make him a British citizen.'

'We need you,' Asim's voice rang after him.

Tallis didn't look back. A woman locked in his cloakroom needed him more.

CHAPTER THIRTY-NINE

While Jace Jackson was being arrested for the murder of his father based on new evidence, and Astrid Stoker and Jackson's mother were receiving a visit from the police, Tallis was sitting in a hospital room, flanked by armed officers. Dan sat bolt upright, eyes cold as if the fire had gone out in them a long time ago. If Tallis expected remorse, he wasn't shown any. But that wasn't what he'd come for.

'You talked to Mum, didn't you?'

'Sons usually talk to their mothers, Paul.' Insolence in the tone.

'Not you. You don't really like women, do you?' That's why you find it easy to hit them, to kill them, Tallis thought. A match had already been found between the gun Dan had been carrying and Forensic evidence found at the scene of Cavall's murder.

Dan looked at him, boredom in his expression.

'I'll bet you pretended to be a reasonable kind of guy, forgiving maybe, but really you were pumping Mum for information about me, how I was faring after I left the police, my state of mind.'

Dan said nothing, but the accompanying smile was devious. 'It was necessary, yes. For the cause. Have to say that little Polish friend of yours getting herself killed like that was a godsend. I knew then you'd change your mind.'

'I understand. But why?'

Dan flashed him an exasperated look. 'I just told you.'

'You told me the reason but didn't explain the hatred.'

'Hatred?' Dan sneered. 'You're way off the mark. I did all of this because I love my country and my country, in case you hadn't noticed, is falling apart. Look at the crime statistics, the spinning and cover-ups. Violence is at an all-time high and we stand more chance of being blown to bits by our so-called fellow countrymen, wolves in sheep's clothing...'

'Spare me the ideology, Dan. I mean why did *you* do it?'

A sly smile crept across his brother's face. 'You want absolution.'

Tallis remained impassive.

Dan leant towards him, making the sheets on the bed rustle. 'You think this is about you and Belle, that your sordid little affair drove me over the edge. I founded Fortress 35 five years ago. That good enough for you?'

It was. Tallis stood up and walked out of the room.

CHAPTER FORTY

The woman was running. Running for joy.

They were in western Scotland on the waterfront at Helensburgh in Strathclyde. The wind was lifting the waves off the slate-grey water and dancing.

'Let me see it again,' Viva said to Rasu, snatching the newspaper off him. She read it for a second time.

Come home, last exile. All is forgiven. Bring V with you. Regards, your sixteenth-century counterpoint friend.

Rasu Barzani put his arm around his love and smiled. His joy was not for himself but for the woman who'd breathed life back into him.

'We can go back,' she laughed, kissing him. 'We can have a life.'

'Yes,' he said simply. He had long ago taught himself to expect nothing, to ask for nothing. It was the way of the exile. This man, Tallis, had not only given him his freedom. He'd restored his hope, his faith and identity, immeasurable gifts.

'No more on the run, no more hiding, no more subterfuge or looking over our shoulders,' Viva said, clapping her hands, dizzy with delight. 'Not that we have to go back. We can go anywhere we choose.'

The last exile smiled, kissed his love, and drew her close.

Tallis guided Elena through the check-in at Heathrow and waited with her until her flight was called. She was like a small girl waiting for Christmas, excited and emotional. She couldn't stop thanking him. He couldn't stop telling her thanks were unnecessary. Both of them knew that the chances of them ever meeting again were remote.

'You take good care,' he said when at last it was time to say goodbye. 'And watch out for that little sister of yours.' He smiled, giving her a final hug, watching her walk away with tears in her eyes.

Afterwards, he drove west, through the spires of Oxford, skirting leafy Gloucestershire and on to Hereford. He wanted to see his mum and dad, to try and explain and, if possible, mend fences. Well, that's what he fondly imagined. After the revelations about Dan, his father's health had taken a nosedive. Discharging himself from hospital, the old man insisted he wanted to die at home.

Neither of Tallis's parents knew about his impending arrival. He didn't know how or if he'd be welcomed, but something inside told him that he had to make an attempt, to break the impasse. He guessed he'd inherited his father's stubborn streak.

Familiar landmarks snapped into view – the river Wye, the cathedral with its chained library, streets where he'd walked as a small boy. As the urban landscape evolved and became more rural, he recognised places he'd visited and played in as a lad, the farm where he'd worked for a summer, the ratty old pub where he'd washed dirty dishes, the school he'd attended with his brother, all of them triggering memories more bad than good. His feelings towards Dan remained raw and confused. To say he hated him was almost too simple because when he looked at Dan, he remembered Belle. When he looked into his brother's eyes, Tallis saw his father staring back.

The ringing of his mobile phone cut into his thoughts. Glancing in the rear-view mirror, he pulled over. It was Asim.

'How are you doing?'

Not great. 'As well as you'd expect,' Tallis said evasively.

'Wondered if you'd had time to reconsider my offer?'

Christ, this bloke didn't hang around. Sod the tea and sympathy. 'No.'

'No as in no, or no you haven't had time to think about it?'

Tallis looked out of the window. Two crows were fighting on the side of the road over a piece of stolen bread. 'Haven't thought much about anything.' That, at least, was an honest answer.

Asim continued to talk. 'The best cure, Paul, is work.'

'That right? I'd rather thought a holiday.'

'Perfect,' Asim said, a laugh in his voice. 'How does Turkey sound, all expenses paid?'

'Turkey? SIS territory, I'd have thought.'

'Precisely,' Asim said mischievously.

'And the catch?'

'Does there have to be one?'

'There's always a catch.' Tallis smiled. A

sparrow had joined the fray. While the crows continued to fight, it was helping itself to lunch.

'Just want someone out there to soak up the atmosphere, keep their ear to the ground.'

Tallis grimaced. Asim would have to do a lot better than that. 'Look, Asim. I don't want to join your club, or any club.'

'But–'

'And actually I'd be far more use to you on a freelance basis.'

'Not the way we do things.'

Then what had the last few weeks been about? 'Well, there you go,' Tallis said, starting to enjoy himself, mainly because he didn't care. Either they played by his rules or not at all.

'That's your final word?'

'It is.'

There was a moment's considered silence. 'I'll be in touch,' Asim said in a way that left Tallis in no doubt.

Tallis closed the phone and pulled back onto the road. Almost within sight of his parents' home, he could already imagine the gate, the stony path, the cared-for garden, the wheelbarrow full of flowers outside, the bright red front door and the plain curtains at the window. Home, he thought, that strange seat of happiness and sadness, of warmth and hostility, of conflict and passion. And then he remembered the streak of suppressed violence simmering just below the surface in thought, in word, in deed.

Seeing an open gateway, Tallis stopped, reversed the car into it, turned around and drove away.

The publishers hope that this book has given you enjoyable reading. Large Print Books are especially designed to be as easy to see and hold as possible. If you wish a complete list of our books please ask at your local library or write directly to:

Magna Large Print Books
Magna House, Long Preston,
Skipton, North Yorkshire.
BD23 4ND

This Large Print Book for the partially sighted, who cannot read normal print, is published under the auspices of

THE ULVERSCROFT FOUNDATION